Assembly Kentucky. General

Biographical Sketch of the Hon. Lazarus W. Powell, (of Henderson,

Ky.)

Governor of the State of Kentucky from 1851-1855

Assembly Kentucky. General

Biographical Sketch of the Hon. Lazarus W. Powell, (of Henderson, Ky.)
Governor of the State of Kentucky from 1851-1855

ISBN/EAN: 9783337016319

Printed in Europe, USA, Canada, Australia, Japan

Cover: Foto ©Raphael Reischuk / pixelio.de

More available books at **www.hansebooks.com**

BIOGRAPHICAL SKETCH

OF THE

HON. LAZARUS W. POWELL,

(OF HENDERSON, KY.),

GOVERNOR OF THE STATE OF KENTUCKY

FROM 1851 TO 1855,

AND A

SENATOR IN CONGRESS

FROM 1859 TO 1865.

PUBLISHED BY DIRECTION OF THE GENERAL ASSEMBLY OF KENTUCKY.

FRANKFORT, KY.:
PRINTED AT THE KENTUCKY YEOMAN OFFICE.
S. I. M. MAJOR, PUBLIC PRINTER.
1868.

IN THE HOUSE OF REPRESENTATIVES OF KENTUCKY,

MARCH 5, 1868.

Mr. McKenzie moved the following resolution, viz:

Resolved, That a Committee of three be appointed by the Chair to prepare a Biographical Sketch of the Hon. L. W. Powell, and that the Public Printer be directed to print five thousand copies of said Biography for the use of this House, together with the speeches delivered on the occasion of the announcement of his death, in pamphlet form, accompanied with a lithographic portrait of the deceased.

Which was adopted, and the following named gentlemen were appointed to perform the duty indicated by the resolution, viz: Messrs. J. A. McKenzie, of Christian county; S. I. M. Major, of Franklin county; and R. M. Spalding, of Marion county.

IN THE SENATE OF KENTUCKY,

MARCH 6, 1868.

Mr. Alexander moved the following resolution, viz:

Resolved, That a Committee of two of the Senate be appointed by the Chair, to act in conjunction with a similar Committee of the House, to prepare Biographical Sketches of the Hon. L. W. Powell and the Hon. John L. Helm, and that the Public Printer be directed to print three thousand eight hundred copies of each Biography for the use of the Senate, together with the speeches delivered on the passage of the resolutions in regard to their death in the Senate and the House, the same to be published in pamphlet form, accompanied with lithographic portraits of the deceased, and that they be mailed to the members of both Houses, postage paid.

Which was twice read and adopted. Senators Joseph M. Alexander, of the county of Fleming, and Ben. J. Webb, of the City of Louisville, were appointed, in pursuance of the resolution, to perform the duty assigned thereunder.

INTRODUCTION.

It is to be feared that the effort we have made to depict the character and public services of the Hon. Lazarus W. Powell will be regarded, by many of our readers, more as a eulogy than a biography. Every written memoir of a truly good man must necessarily partake of this character. Had there been anything in his private life or in his public career worthy of general condemnation, or even of severe censure, we cannot suppose that the duty we have endeavored to perform would ever have been imposed upon us by the General Assembly. The maxim, *de mortuis nil nisi bonum*, is always applicable where there are living representatives of one's blood and name to be affected by the condemnation of the dead. The fact, therefore, that the representatives of his own people, so soon after his death, have directed his biography to be written, is evidence of the purity of his record—of the high estimation in which he was held by their entire constituencies.

It is a singular circumstance, in connection with our search after details concerning the private life of Governor Powell, that our inquiries, with rare exceptions, have met with only general answers. "He was a most genial gentleman," is the usual reply that we have received from men of all parties and all creeds, at home and abroad. One writes: "He was always true to his principles and to his friends, and he was ever ready to forgive those who had done him injury." Another writes: "He was the soul of honor, as he was of candor; conscientiousness and urbanity had in him their consistent representatives at all times and under all circumstances; he was sympathetic in the presence of human misery and bereavement, and to the poor he was always a liberal benefactor."

One who knew him well writes:

" There was a geniality about POWELL in social life that was not only the delight of his friends, but which had often the effect to make his bitterest political foes forget for the time that he was not of themselves. In mixed companies, it was a habit with him to introduce topics for conversation that were unlikely to provoke contention. When he found it impossible to prevent this, he was always uneasy until he or others had turned the discourse into other channels. His influence in the United States Senate was greatly in excess of his importance as a party politician. He was known to be a man of sound discretion and of incorruptible integrity, and his advocacy of measures in which no political policy was involved seldom failed to bring to his aid a certain number of votes from the opposition benches."

The Hon. THOS. C. MCCREERY, his life-long friend, who now fills the position he so greatly distinguished in the Senate of the United States, thus writes to one of the Committee:

" I should find it difficult to write a lengthy biography of Governor POWELL, from the fact that those traits of character which endeared him to all may be stated in a few sentences. Everywhere, at all times, and under all circumstances, *he was the same.* In social and private life, he was a kind, genial, hospitable gentleman. When you approached his door, no cloud shaded his brow; but the gushing warmth of his welcome made you feel that you were entering the portals of a friend. In public life, he never failed to come up to the full measure of his duty. He was possessed of a high order of talents, which he industriously employed in supporting measures the jus-

tice of which, in his mind, amounted to positive convictions."

So far as we are able to discover, his patriotism was
never the subject of suspicion in any quarter, except at
the beginning of the late civil war, when he boldly took
his stand against the rightful assumption of power, on
the part of the Federal Government, to make war upon
the seceded Commonwealths of the South, for the purpose
of coercing them back into the Union. Not even then
were his motives impugned by any large number of those
who were clamorous for the war. The result of the
attempt which was made in 1862 to expel him from his
seat in the United States Senate is clearly indicative of
the high estimation in which he was held by many among
the leading members of the Republican party. That attempt failed by a vote of *twenty-eight* to *eleven*, a majority
of his political opponents voting against expulsion.

To sum up the result of our investigations as to the
character of Governor POWELL, both as a man and as the
trusted agent of his State, we find that he was beloved
by his own people, and everywhere respected; that he
was true to his political principles, and ardent in their
dissemination; that he was courageous in defending what
he conceived to be the truth, and was never discourteous
in debate—not even toward his bitterest antagonists;
finally, that he was exact in the performance of his
official duties, and was governed by prudence in his
recommendations of measures of public utility. It were
impossible to fulfill properly the duty that has been laid
upon us, in the face of a record so indicative of Govern-
or POWELL's wise statesmanship, of his official integrity,
and of his exalted character as a man, without giving to
our memoir the appearance of a panegyric.

We desire to acknowledge our indebtedness to a number of individuals, in different parts of the State, who
have most kindly furnished us with information of one

kind or another in relation to the late Governor's private and public life. Without such aid, it would have been impossible for us to have performed our task with any degree of exactness, or to have given to our picture even the faint outlines of resemblance to the original, which we have been thereby enabled to secure. Our acknowledgments are especially due to R. T. GLASS, Esq., and Gov. ARCHIBALD DIXON, of Henderson; to the Rev. J. B. HUTCHINS, of Marion county; to Col. S. B. CHURCHILL, Judge GEO. ROBERTSON, GRANT GREEN, Esq., and W. P. D. BUSH, Esq., of Frankfort; to the Hon. THOS. C. McCREERY, of Washington City; to the Hon. I. A. SPALDING, of Union county, and to the Hon. HENRY J. STITES, Col. PHIL. LEE, Governor BRAMLETTE, and others, of Louisville.

JOS. M. ALEXANDER,

BEN. J. WEBB,

Senate Committee.

J. A. McKENZIE,

S. I. M. MAJOR,

R. M. SPALDING,

House Committee.

HIS PRIVATE LIFE.

Every photographic artist knows that sun-pictures depend much for their truthfulness to nature upon the *marked* features of the object sought to be portrayed. Smooth faces and regular lines of landscapes are seldom caught in their full reality. This is because there are certain accessories to truthful delineation always wanting in such cases. It is impossible to secure, from the living face, the aspect of *unrest*, which frequently gives to it its greatest charm, its most distinguishable feature. It is the same with a certain class of inanimate objects. A regularly laid-out garden, or a smooth wall of bricks or granite, never makes a pleasing picture. In the case of the garden, the accessories are wanting of sunshine and cloud, fragrance, and the constantly changing lights and shadows produced by more or less commotion in the atmosphere. In the other case, however grand and noble may be the structure exposed to the eye, there are lacking the surroundings which are necessary to fix in the mind the ideas of fitness, comparison, propriety, and the like. The nearest approaches to exactness that have resulted from the photographer's art are to be found in the pictures it has given of old faces, old ruins, and other strongly marked aspects in the domain of nature.

In treating of the private life of Governor POWELL, one must feel that the difficulties he has to encounter are equally great with those of the photographer when he attempts to reproduce on his prepared paper the exact features of a landscape that presents no aspect of a marked character. This beautiful life, like a grand, but quiet stream, flowed on its peaceful course, blessed of all, and bearing blessings to all.

Although Governor POWELL was undoubtedly possessed of an ambitious mind, his whole life showed clearly that his ambition was worthily directed toward worthy objects. He desired to earn an honorable name through the practice of those civic virtues which, while they adorn their possessor, are the strongest supports of both society and government. Laudable ambition is but the directing of the forces and powers that fill the soul in the channel of the highest usefulness. To possess talents, and not to use them, is to bury one's treasures in the ground. To possess them, and to use them improperly, is to act as does the madman, who exerts his physical strength to the injury of every one he meets. The object of all laudable ambition is to deserve the plaudits of men for acts beneficial to mankind; and the highest encomium that one man can pay to another is to be able to say of him : He refused the powers that he could not exercise without injury to others. In its incipiency, laudable ambition is but the wail of the soul after those objects in the possible future which will bring it nearer to Truth—nearer to the summit where sits—*sedet æternumque sedebit*—the Spirit of Wisdom and Knowledge. There is no taint of sin in such ambition. It is but the putting to profitable use of the talents given into the keeping of certain of His creatures by Him to whom all service is due.

Every human nature, among the almost endless diversities of rational existencies, has its own capability for a specific work. It is inglorious to shirk the responsibilities of one's position in life—the obligations, the cares, the labors that are incidental to the possession, and the putting to proper use, of special mental endowments. The color taken by ambition is derived from the motives to which it owes its existence. If these be pure, if they be unselfish—that is, if they be directed to no good that will not also prove a good unto others—then is one's ambition no emanation from the abyss of depraved nature; but a spark from that Living Intelligence from Whom it originally descended; and toward Whom it must ever tend by the law of its nature.

LAZARUS W. POWELL was born in Henderson county, Kentucky, on the 6th day of October, 1812. His father, Capt. LAZARUS POWELL,* only a few years previous to the birth of the subject of our memoir, had settled on a tract of land lying twelve miles south of the village of Henderson, on the Morganfield road. Here he still resides, at the advanced age of ninety years. His mother was the daughter of Capt. JAMES McMAHON, of Henderson county. This gentleman had served in the ranks of the Kentucky volunteers in the war of 1812. He was a man of strong native intellect, but exceedingly eccentric in manner and habits. Though both of the late Governor's parents were possessed of average natural talents, neither had ever enjoyed the benefits of intellectual culture beyond its simplest rudiments. LAZARUS was their third son. Three of his brothers still survive, and one sister, the estimable wife of the Rev. D. H. DEACON, Rector of St. Paul's Episcopal Church, Henderson, Kentucky.

The boy, LAZARUS W. POWELL, at a very early age, began to exhibit those traits of character which, in their fuller development, caused him to be loved and respected wherever he was known. When he had arrived at an age to be able to appreciate the advantages of education, he used diligently the very inadequate means that were

---

* In the prime of his life, Capt. POWELL was recognized as a man of vigorous mind, and was noted for his energy of character. He accumulated a large estate, the greater part of which has been distributed among his children. He retained the old homestead, where he still resides. At the date of the Emancipation Proclamation, he was the owner of a large number of valuable slaves.

within his reach to acquire knowledge. The school he
first attended was a primary one kept by a Mr. Ewell
Wilson, in the village of Henderson. Here he learned to
read and write. Later, he became a pupil of the late
George Gayle, Esq., a gentleman of rare talents and attainments, under whose tuition he acquired a fair academical education.*

Young Powell was a manly youth, ingenuous and
truthful, and not a little ambitious. He had scarcely
reached the age of eighteen before he had marked out for
himself a pathway in life and chosen the profession in
which he hoped to acquire a moderate competency, and,
possibly, the other results of a reasonable ambition. He
did not say—for his aspirations were all civic—

"——— The world's mine oyster,
Which I with sword will open—"

but with a like spirit that breathes through this immortal
sentiment of the world's greatest poet, he pursued his
course, and allowed no obstacle to interpose between his
will *to do* and the accomplishment of the act he so willed.

Few farmers in Kentucky, at the time to which we refer (1830), were possessed of any great abundance of
ready means; and thus it turned out, when young Powell
was preparing to carry out his design of entering upon
the study of the Law, that his father was only enabled to
furnish him with a sum of money that was quite insufficient
to cover the expenses incident to the position he expected
to occupy. Early in the month of June, 1830, the young

---

* Mr. Gayle was a firm believer in the efficacy of the rod as an aid to the
impartment of knowledge. He was quick-tempered, but was seldom unjust,
whether in the bestowal of praise or punishment. He was eminently successful as an instructor of youth, and his memory is warmly cherished to
this day by a large number of his former pupils. After he had accumulated
a fortune ample enough for all his wants, he still continued to teach for several years, on account, as it is believed, of his love for the profession. In
October, 1862, his grand-daughter, Miss Mary A. Alves, was united in marriage with Henry Powell, Esq., the eldest son of the late Governor.

man rode over to the town of Owensboro, the county seat of the adjoining county of Daviess, for the purpose of consulting with an old legal friend of his father's, the late Ilon. Philip Thompson.* This gentleman was then engaged in a large practice in the circuit presided over by the Hon. Alney McLean.† Mr. Thompson readily assented to Powell's wish to enter his office as a student. He soon discovered, however, that the insufficiency of his young friend's educational attainments would be a great drawback to his hoped-for success in the undertaking upon which he had entered, and he urged upon him the necessity of suspending his legal studies until he could avail himself of the advantages of a classical education.

This was a great blow to Powell's hopes. He had the good sense, however, to see that the advice that had been given him was the result of a kindly interest in his affairs. Returning home, he set about revolving in his mind the unlooked-for difficulty and the means at his disposal for overcoming it. The result of his self-communing was a determination to visit Bardstown, then the seat of one of the best literary institutions in the State. Having obtained from Mr. Thompson a letter of introduction to the Hon. John Rowan,§ an old friend of the writer, he

---

*The Hon. Philip Thompson was a lawyer of great ability. He was a member of Congress from his district from 1823 to 1825. He was killed by one Jeffries in a street fight in Owensboro, in 1836.

†The Hon. Alney McLean resided in Greenville, Muhlenburg county, where he died in 1842. He commanded a company of Kentucky Volunteers at the battle of New Orleans; also a company in Gen. Hopkins' campaign against the Indians. He served his district in the Congress of the United States from 1815 to 1817, and from 1819 to 1821. He was for many years a circuit judge, a position that he occupied at the date of his death. He was a man of superior ability, of great popularity, and of high moral character.

§Judge Rowan was born in Pennsylvania, in 1773; emigrated to Kentucky when quite young; was a member of the State Constitutional Convention of 1799, and Secretary of State in 1804. He was a member of Congress from 1807 to 1809; Judge of the Court of Appeals in 1819, and a Senator in Congress from 1825 to 1831. He died in Louisville, Ky., July 13th, 1843. Judge Rowan was a Democrat of the Jeffersonian school. That he should

set out for Bardstown, at which place he arrived in the first week of September, 1830. His entire riches consisted of the horse he rode and less than one hundred dollars in money.

He took early occasion to present his friend's letter to Judge ROWAN, and was by that true gentleman treated with a degree of kindness and interest which he ever afterwards remembered and spoke of in terms of the deepest gratitude. Judge ROWAN was, perhaps, the most learned man of his profession in the State. In order to test the qualifications of the young man for the profession which he had chosen, he introduced into their conversation certain literary, scientific, and historical questions, which he deemed it important that every one should be acquainted with who had any thought of entering upon the study of the Law. The result was as unsatisfactory, in regard to young POWELL's scholastic attainments, as had been his former trial before Mr. THOMPSON. His natural good sense, however, and his evident candor, made a most favorable impression on the erudite statesman, and again he was strongly advised to apply himself to the acquisition of a thorough collegiate education.

With becoming modesty the young man acknowledged to JUDGE ROWAN that he had not sufficient means to defray

---

have been strongly inimical to the Whig policy, of which Mr. CLAY was the chief exponent and champion in Kentucky, was but natural. But he gave to Mr. CLAY little credit for exalted mental gifts, and less for statesmanship. He was often heard to express the opinion that DANIEL WEBSTER was much the superior man. He could not understand why it was that the Massachusetts statesman was so much in the habit, as he expressed it, of "playing second fiddle" to one so greatly his inferior. Speaking, on a certain occasion, of the distinguishing characteristics of these eminent men, he illustrated his idea by the following supposed case: "If," said he, "the two should happen to go duck-shooting together, Mr. CLAY would expect Mr. WEBSTER to assume the office of *spaniel* to bring out the birds, and the latter would not be able to perceive that there was any degradation in his assumption of such an office."

the necessary expenses of a college course of studies. Having arrived at the details of his present means and future prospects, Judge Rowan gave him hopes that the particular difficulty might be overcome. He told him that he was well acquainted with the Faculty and Professors of St. Joseph's College, and that, having some influence with them, he thought it highly probable that he would be able to arrange with them for his immediate matriculation and subsequent tuition.

Early the following morning Judge Rowan accompanied the young man to the college, where he was formally introduced to the President, the late Rev. George A. M. Elder.* Mr. Elder was a man of the kindest impulses. He was also an excellent judge of character. The manly appearance of young Powell, his candor. in stating his wishes and the inadequate means he possessed toward their realization, together with his evident disinclination to accept of unusual terms, or such as would compromise his own independence, all deeply interested the good ecclesiastic. Other members of the Faculty were called to the consultation, and, before they separated, the name of Lazarus W.

---

* Mr. Elder was a thoroughly loveable man. Though he occupied, for nearly twenty years, the post of President of a college in which were domiciled from one hundred and fifty to three hundred young men and boys—a large proportion of whom were natives of Louisiana and Mississippi, and, consequently, if there be any truth in the generally accepted saying, "a hot sun breeds a hot temper," may be supposed to have been difficult of control—he was never known to have had an enemy in the college. He had evidently studied human nature to some purpose. He won the hearts of all by making it clear to the perception of all that he possessed himself the most loving of hearts. He died at Bardstown, in the year 1838. The writer of this was seated, on the evening of his death, in the parlor of a friend, since deceased, and was conversing with several members of his family, when suddenly the tolling of the Cathedral bell hushed our voices into awe. Not a word was spoken until the iron clang had again thrilled through our ears, when, with a choking sob, one of the ladies present exclaimed, "O God, he is dead!" Few were the homes, indeed, wherein was heard that tolling bell, that tears and sighs and prayers were not its fitting accompaniment.

Powell was duly entered on the college register. It is scarcely necessary to state that every obligation entered into by Mr. Powell with the Faculty of St. Joseph's College was afterwards fully redeemed.

To say that young Powell was what is termed *popular* with both his Professors and his fellow-students, would inadequately express the general sentiment with which he was regarded in college. By the former he was beloved to a degree that can only be fully understood when reference is made to the bond that exists between parent and child. He was the pride of the latter, admired and looked up to as something to be made much of and copied after. There was no waywardness in their feelings toward their idol, because there was no blot on his escutcheon. He was listened to, and his advice followed, because of their respect for his character and their confidence in his judgment. Who can measure the restraining influence of such a mind over the weaknesses and latent propensities to evil of less steadfast associates? His young companions learned to respect virtue, principle, assiduity, and goodness, because of all these their friend was ever the consistent exponent.

Boys from fourteen to twenty are very frequently more zealous political partisans than are their elders. This was certainly the case with the students at St. Joseph's in 1830–3. Powell had been nurtured, as it were, in the principles of the Democratic party. The great majority of his fellow-students, on the contrary, had imbibed other notions—those that had for their chief exponent at the time the great Whig leader, Henry Clay. Controversies often arose between the students on the merits of the political questions which were then dividing public sentiment, and in these there was, no doubt, exhibited as much bitterness as usually accompanies disputes on any deeply interesting topic. Had the subject of our memoir been anything else than the man he was—sincere,

but calmly demonstrative—able to distinguish between
political heresies and the motives which incline men to
their adoption—he would scarcely have been accorded, as
he was, the championship of the entire school in everything in which a general interest was excited outside
of politics. No matter what were the partisan views
of any one of his fellow-students, it was impossible that
he should not respect the party that had an advocate so
entirely candid, and yet so cautious about giving offense
to others. Throughout his whole political career, in
after years, there was no wavering on the part of his
old fellow-students, when it was question of saying a
kind word or of doing a kind thing, for one who had
so much endeared himself to their hearts.

"It may be stated," writes one of his fellow-students
to the Committee, "with entire truth, that the standard
of Governor POWELL's scholarship would have been improved, had he passed though college at a less rapid
pace." He adds: "Poverty and ambition stimulated him
to great exertion, and he graduated in the class of 1833,
which numbered some of the sprightliest and ablest minds
in the South and Southwest.* "

* The class of graduates at St. Joseph's College for 1833 numbered eight
individuals, viz: LAZARUS W. POWELL, of Kentucky; R. F. ALPOINTE, of
Louisiana; G. W. RHODES, of Kentucky; J. B. MADDOX, of Louisiana; A.
LE BLANC, of Louisiana; R. C. BRASHEAR, of Kentucky; THOS. H. DUVAL,
of Kentucky, and WM. HOWARD, of Kentucky. Of these, R. C. BRASHEAR
fell at the Alamo, in the war for the independence of Texas. THOS. H.
DUVAL studied law, and removed to Texas, where he became a circuit judge,
and was afterwards Secretary of State. F. R. ALPOINTE studied medicine,
and became, and is now, an eminent physician in New Orleans. In regard
to the other members of the class of 1833, with the exception of Governor
POWELL, we have no knowledge concerning their after career.

Others of Governor POWELL's fellow-students at St. Joseph's were: The
late Hon. GEORGE ALFRED CALDWELL, of Louisville, a gallant officer in the
war with Mexico, and a Representative in Congress from Kentucky from
1843 to 1845, and from 1849 to 1851; the Hon. ROBT. WICKLIFFE, late Governor of Louisiana; Judge RICHARD A. BUCKNER, of Lexington, Ky.; the

2

Among the college friendships formed by POWELL while pursuing his studies at St. Joseph's was one which we cannot forbear mentioning. CLEMENT C. SPALDING, a younger brother of the present Archbishop of Baltimore and of R. M. SPALDING, Esq., the member from Marion county of the present House of Representatives of Kentucky, was pursuing his studies in the same institution during the entire term of Mr. POWELL's college course. His was regarded as the brightest intellect there. Though his graduation took place a year later—in the class of 1834—his scholastic attainments were, even then, in some respects, of a higher order than those of POWELL. Between the two, from the date of the latter's introduction to the school, there sprung up a friendship so warm that it was the subject of general observation among the students. They were the recognized leaders of the various debating clubs that had been organized in the institution, and it was in these clubs that they first essayed their powers of logic as well as of oratorical display.*

Early in August of the year 1833, only a few days after his graduation, Mr. POWELL entered the law office of the Hon. JOHN ROWAN, of Bardstown, Kentucky, for the purpose of resuming his legal studies, which had been inter-

---

Hon. THOMAS C. McCREERY, Senator in Congress from Kentucky; Col. S. B. CHURCHILL, Secretary of State of Kentucky; SAMUEL GLOVER, Esq., one of the most prominent lawyers of Missouri, now residing in St. Louis; JOSHUA F. and JOHN J. SPEED, Esqs., of Louisville, and the Hon. OTHO R. SINGLETON, a Representative in Congress from Mississippi from 1853 to 1859.

* Having finished his college course, C. C. SPALDING studied law, and, in 1836, entered upon the practice in Alexandria, La. His great ability, together with his strict probity and attention to business, soon enabled him to take a high rank in his profession. In 1837, while on his way to Kentucky to visit his relations, he was taken sick, and only reached Bardstown to die in that place on the 23d of July, 1837. Those who had frequent opportunities to see and converse with Governor POWELL will remember how fond he was of speaking of his deceased friend. Never, to the end of his life, did he cease to remember and to mourn over the great loss sustained by himself and the country in the early death of one so worthy to be loved, and of such brilliant promise.

rupted by his college course. The studious habits which ·
so remarkably distinguished him while passing through
college, equally characterized him in his new position.
He brought all the powers of his mind to bear upon the
acquirement, within the least possible period of time, of
that sum of knowledge of his profession which would
enable him to look forward to an honorable career in life.
He was happy in having for his legal preceptor one of
the master-minds of his day and the country. Judge
Rowan was not only a well-read lawyer, but he was also
a profound scholar and a man of the rarest natural intelligence. His diction was always elegant, and he spoke
without seeming effort.

Never have two men of acknowledged genius presented
so marked a contrast in almost every .particular as did
Judge Rowan and his celebrated rival at the bar, the late
Hon. Ben. Hardin. In every thing, except genius, they
were each the antithesis of the other. Rowan had a commanding presence; he was tall and robust in person; in
speaking, his voice was sonorous and his action graceful;
his speeches were filled with classical allusions; his sentences were never faulty, whether in rythm or grammati-
cal construction; he always dressed with care, but never
with ostentation. He was himself the soul of integrity,
and nothing ever so moved him to a display of indignation
as the lapses of his colleagues from a correct estimate of
the honorable character of the profession into the domain
of artifice.* He was immeasurably the superior of his

---

* The writer was himself a witness, on a certain occasion, of a scene in
the Circuit Court room of Nelson county, Ky., which strongly exemplifies
the statement in the text. An old citizen of the town had recently died, and
he had left his widow, with a large family of children, in straightened circumstances. A wealthy creditor of the estate had determined, by the
advice of an attorney whose general character was that of a legal trickster,
to institute a suit for the avowed object of recovering his debt, but which,
if successful, would have the effect to deprive the widow of her homestead—
a right to which the law then gave to her during life. At the moment when
the motion was being laid before the Court by the plaintiff's attorney, Judge

rival in his ability to touch the hearts of his hearers by
sympathetic appeals. He was his inferior in repartee,
and in the use of strong invectives. He was his inferior,
also, in that quickness of perception which enabled Mr.
HARDIN to take advantage of every legal quibble, every
blunder of opposing counsel, and every circumstance referred to in the witness-box, that could possibly benefit
his case.

The Hon. BEN. HARDIN, or "Old Kitchen Knife"—by
which soubriquet he was afterwards known in the Congress of the United States—was undoubtedly one of the
shrewdest advocates that was ever entrusted with a client's
interests in any court of the Commonwealth. He affected
a simplicity in dress that approached slovenliness. He
was lank in person, slightly stooping from middle age, and
exceedingly restless in manner. During the progress of
any important cause in which he had been retained, he
might be seen pacing the body of the court-house—without the bar, but within hearing of the proceedings—his
hands clasped behind his back, and muttering to himself
all the while—and thus were prepared many of his most
elaborate arguments. His voice was sharp and piercing,
and he was strongly energetic, both in action and delivery.
Wit—drollery—sarcasm—invective—these were his chief
forensic weapons, and terrible weapons they generally
proved in his hands. His many political canvasses are to
this day frequently talked about by the older citizens of
Nelson and the adjoining counties. He possessed, in an
eminent degree, the faculty of adapting himself to all

ROWAN happened to be sitting before a table within the bar, apparently engaged in arranging a number of papers that lay before him. The name of
his deceased friend struck upon his ear while the motion was being read,
and he was seen to assume a listening attitude. As the reading proceeded,
the old man rose to his feet, and scarcely had the tricky lawyer concluded,
when he found himself and his client the subjects of the most scathing rebuke
that was ever uttered by mortal lips in that little old court-house. The attorney sneaked away, crestfallen, and, thanks to her unfeed advocate, the
widow was permitted to retain possession of her homestead.

classes of men. At one time he would appear to be as deeply interested in the result of a foot-race, or a wrestling match, as the most ignorant boor on the ground ; and at other times he would discuss agriculture with the farmers, domestic matters with their wives, science with the learned, and politics with everybody. With talents so diversified, it is not to be wondered at that he should have acquired, in the course of time, a reputation for sincerity that was not particularly enviable.*

In addition to the two distinguished personages named, the bar of Bardstown, in 1833, was enriched by the practice of several scarcely inferior minds. The most noted among these were the HON. CHAS. A. WICKLIFFE,† afte -

---

* At home it was a common occurrence with Mr. HARDIN to address the court or jury in his shirt-sleeves. When engaged in legal work outside of his own district, especially in places where he was little known, he was observant of the proprieties of his position until he happened to become heated in argument, and then, first his cravat would be snatched off and cast aside; next, the collar and wristbands of his shirt would be unbuttoned and thrown back; and, finally, long before he came to the peroration of his discourse, especially if the weather was at all sultry, off would come his coat and waistcoat, and then, as nearly *in puris naturalibus* as it was possible for him in decency to go, he would thunder out invectives against some unfortunate litigant, or some still more unfortunate criminal, in a style that was not unfrequently fully in keeping with the tastes of his rough auditory. The death of Mr. HARDIN took place at Bardstown, in February, 1854. He was at the time a State Senator from the Nineteenth Senatorial District.

† The Hon. CHAS. A. WICKLIFFE is a native of Bardstown, Kentucky, where he was born in 1788. He served in the war of 1812, and was present at the battle of the Thames. Having served in the State Legislature for several terms, he was elected a Representative in Congress from his district in 1823, in which position he remained for ten years. In 1836 he was elected Lieutenant Governor of Kentucky, and on the death of Gov. CLARK, in 1839, he became Acting Governor. In 1841 he was appointed Post-Master General by President Tyler. In 1861—having previously been a member of the State Constitutional Convention in 1849—he again became a Representative in Congress from the Bardstown district. He was a member of the Peace Convention held in the same year. In 1862 he was a candidate for Governor, but was defeated through the instrumentality of the military that then occupied the State. He still resides on his place in the vicinity of Bardstown, but for several months has been suffering from a disease of the nerves of the eye, which has entirely deprived him of sight.

wards Governor of the State and Representative in Congress, who still survives, and the late BENJ. CHAPEZE, Esq., a lawyer of profound legal attainments, and a gentleman widely known and esteemed for his moral worth.

The advantages which intercourse with such minds afforded an ardent student like young POWELL, undoubtedly proved of great value to him in after life. He learned to contrast their powers, to subject their arguments to the test of his own reason, and thus to distinguish between logic and sophistry. He learned, too, under the inspiration of their impassioned eloquence, how to touch the hearts of the people, how to win their confidence and respect.

At the time of which we are speaking, the entire government of the country, both State and Federal, was in the hands of members of the legal profession. There were few other than lawyers to be found in any department of either government. In consequence of this state of things, the profession of the Law was almost the only avenue that led to political distinction. The gentlemen already named were all politicians, as was also, with rare exceptions, the entire legal body of the country. In choosing the Law for his profession, there is room to doubt if young POWELL was actuated by any other motive than the usual one with persons starting out in life—that of acquiring a competency in the manner most suited to his tastes. It is reasonable to suppose, however, that the circumstances surrounding him at Bardstown—the deep interest manifested by his preceptor and those with whom he was associated in the political issues of the day—should have bred in him a taste for political controversy, and eventually the desire to take part in the business of legislation.

Mr. POWELL remained in the office of Judge ROWAN until the winter of 1834-5, when he repaired to Lexington, with the view of attending a course of Law Lectures at Transylvania University. The Law Professors of the term were the Hon. GEORGE ROBERTSON* and the Hon. DANIEL MAYES. The former of these, even then, was regarded as the most profound legal theorist in the State. His present reputation is as wide as the country—his pupils filling exalted positions in almost every State of the Union and in the National Legislature. The rank accorded to Judge MAYES in his profession was but a little lower than that held by his gifted associate. He held for several years the position of Circuit Court Judge in the counties which then formed the Frankfort Judicial District. He was remarkably distinguished for the conciseness of his decisions. In these, the law, in its relations to the entire cause and the evidence adduced, was clearly stated, in language that was always clear and pointed.†

---

* Judge ROBERTSON is certainly one of the most remarkable men of his day and country. Though nearly eighty years old, he is now actively engaged in performing the duties of a Judge of the Supreme Court of the State, with mental powers apparently as bright as at any previous day of his long and useful career. In the year 1817, at the age of twenty-six, he was elected to the United States Congress from the Garrard district; since when, he has filled the offices of Representative in the State Legislature, in which he was Speaker of the House for four sessions, Secretary of State, Judge of the Appellate Court, and Chief Justice. He has repeatedly declined important offices, including missions to Columbia and Peru. The ability uniformly displayed by Judge ROBERTSON in the discharge of the duties of these various offices is acknowledged on every hand, not only by his political friends and associates, but by those who were at times bitterly opposed to his course. For more than twenty years he filled the position of Law Professor at Transylvania University. It is said that he has instructed in their profession no fewer than three thousand lawyers, over two thousand of whom graduated under his personal instruction. Notwithstanding the fact that Judge ROBERTSON and Gov. POWELL entertained diametrically opposite views of politics, they were warm personal friends to the end of the latter's life. Judge R. visited Washington during Gov. POWELL's Senatorial term, and he was often afterwards heard to express his high sense of the latter's courteous attentions to him on that occasion. It was, at one time, the earnest desire of POWELL to place his two elder sons under the control and tuition of his old preceptor, but circumstances prevented the consummation of his wishes in this respect.

† The late ISHAM HENDERSON, Esq., then a leading practitioner on the Shelby circuit, was once heard to remark: "Since Judge MAYES has been on the

Not only was POWELL assiduous in study during his stay in Lexington, and prompt in his attendance at the University Lectures, but he let no occasion pass in which it was possible for him to acquire a knowledge of the practical part of his profession, by making himself familiar with the proceedings of the Courts of Law, when these happened to be in session. The bar of Lexington had one advantage over that of Bardstown : the number of its prominent members was much greater. Among the resident practicing attorneys then in Lexington could be named such men as the Hon. HENRY CLAY, the Hon. ROBERT WICKLIFFE, Judge THOS. M. HICKEY, A. K. WOOLLEY, Esq., CHARLTON HUNT, Esq., JAMES COWAN, Esq., and MADISON C. JOHNSON, Esq., the latter being then a young man, but giving promise of the high reputation in his profession which he has since acquired.

The law session at Transylvania over, Mr. POWELL returned to Henderson in the spring of 1835, where he opened an office and sought for business in the line of his profession. His success equaled his expectations from the first; but, a few months later, having formed a partnership with the leading practitioner at the Henderson bar, ARCHIBALD DIXON, Esq.,* he was at once placed on

---

bench he has saved me a great deal of trouble. I have only to state my positions, without being under the necessity of *instructing* the Court, in long arguments, upon the law of the case." Judge MAYES removed to Mississippi many years ago, and died at Jackson, in that State, some time before the breaking out of the late civil war.

*The Hon. ARCHIBALD DIXON was born in North Carolina on the 2d of April, 1802. His father removed to Kentucky in 1804, and settled in Henderson county, where his son was reared and educated, and where he has since resided. He had no advantages of early education beyond those afforded in the "old field" school-houses of the neighborhood. His own energy and industry supplied the deficiency, and he soon took high rank in the profession which he adopted. He began the practice of the law in Henderson in the year 1825, and was eminently successful from that period until his final retirement from the active duties of the profession in 1860. He was elected to the Legislature of Kentucky in 1830, over HUGH McELROY, Esq., the Democratic candidate. In 1836 he was elected to the Kentucky

the high road to that eminence as a lawyer which he afterwards attained, as well as to the substantial remunerative benefits of an extended practice. His business connection with Mr. Dixon continued till the year 1839.

State Senate, his unsuccessful competitor being Dr. John Roberts, of Daviess county. At the close of his Senatorial term he was returned, without opposition, as the member from Henderson county, to the Lower House of the Legislature for the session of 1841-2.

In 1844 he was the candidate of the Whig party for the office of Lieutenant Governor of the State, and was elected over his opponent, W. S. Pilcher, Esq., of Louisville, by a handsome majority. He filled this position for four years with distinguished ability. In 1849 his name was presented by his friends for the position of Delegate to the Convention that had been called to form a new Constitution for Kentucky. He was elected to this office, and was the Whig candidate for the position of President of the Convention, but was beaten, on a party vote, by the Hon. James Guthrie. He took a leading part in the debates upon nearly every important question that was brought before the Convention, and was recognized as one of the ablest members of that body.

In 1850 he was the Whig candidate for Governor of the State. The Hon. L. W. Powell, the Democratic nominee, and the Hon. Cassius M. Clay, the representative of the small abolition faction—then for the first time in the history of Southern politics openly coming before the people for their suffrages—were Mr. Dixon's opponents. He was beaten in this race by Mr. Powell by a small majority; and, for the first time in many years, the control of the State Government was transferred from the long dominant Whig party to that which had been so ably and successfully championed by his Democratic competitor.

In 1851 he was elected to the United States Senate, to fill the unexpired term of the Hon. Henry Clay, whose failing health demanded his release from public service. In this new field, though suffering for most of the time from an annoying chronic complaint, he greatly distinguished himself by his able advocacy of the various measures of public policy which were from time to time brought forward by his party. He will long be remembered in the history of his country as the author of the famous Kansas-Nebraska bill—as accepted by Mr. Douglas—repealing the Missouri Compromise measure of a former Congress. While many persons, in the light of the consequences which have flowed from it, may reasonably doubt of the *policy* of this measure, no Southern man will likely question its entire *justice*. In 1862, Governor Dixon was elected to the Border State Convention, which assembled at Frankfort, and, together with the Hon. John J. Crittenden and other distinguished men, endeavored to prevent the disasters of war by the recommendation of measures of conciliation and compromise. This was his last public service.

Governor POWELL's reputation as a lawyer was not built upon any peculiar talent possessed by him for forensic display. In his addresses, to be sure, whether to the court or to the jury, he was always forcible, and often eloquent. But he depended more for his legal triumphs upon the careful analysis of his causes. It was his invariable custom to come into court fully prepared to meet the objections of opposing counsel, with his authorities before him, whether as to the law bearing upon the case, or to previous judicial decisions. Owing to this custom, he was always a formidable antagonist in the courts in which he practiced. What he lacked in readiness of suggestion, had its full compensation in the preliminary care which he never failed to bestow upon each particular cause as it came into his hands. His wonderful success in his profession is more to be attributed to this fact than to any other.

On the 8th day of November, 1837, LAZARUS W. POWELL was united in marriage with Miss HARRIET ANN JENNINGS, the orphan daughter of Capt. CHARLES JENNINGS, deceased, who had been an esteemed and prosperous citizen of Henderson county. During her brief life, Mrs. POWELL bore to her husband three sons, all of whom are still living, and are highly respected citizens of the community that had so long delighted to honor their father. The death of Mrs. POWELL took place on the 30th day of July, 1846; and, to use the expression of one of the late Governor's eulogists " for her sake he ever afterwards devoted to the children she had left to his care all the wealth of his manly and magnanimous heart."

When not occupied by official duties during the progress of the civil war, Governor POWELL spent most of his time at his home in Henderson, and in overlooking the farming operations upon his plantations in the county. This was for him, as it was for thousands of others in the State, a period of great anxiety. Suspected by the

government military officials, who had, for the greater
portion of the time, complete control in the river towns,
on account of his well-known antipathy to the bloody
method that had been adopted to preserve the integrity
of the Union; saddened at the sight of the utter ruin
which the war had brought upon many of his neighbors,
and which was threatening others; disgusted with the
cruelties of the vengeful military despots who were then
ruling Kentucky, and whose so-called retaliatory measures were continually involving the lives and liberties
of innocent men; indignant at the shameful venality
of some among these same despots and their pliant
subordinates, and at their contemptuous disregard of
even the forms of State laws, in taking upon themselves
all control over the elective franchise—Governor Powell,
no doubt, felt these years of the war to be the saddest
of his life.

Always circumspect in his conduct, and, for one of
his known views, in a certain degree trusted in by the
authorities at Washington, he was enabled to serve many
who had become involved in the troubles of the times,
not only in his own section, but throughout the South,
and never was his influence asked for in vain by a
worthy object. His means, too, were dispensed with a
lavish hand to those who found themselves reduced to
poverty by the military raids which were of common
occurrence in his own and the neighboring counties of
Southern Kentucky. Whether the sufferer happened to
be attached to one cause or the other, it was all the same
with him. Human misery was a plea that never failed
to awaken in him active sympathy, and with this plea
he never permitted consideration of party affinity, nor
even of policy, to interfere.

When the war finally closed, Governor Powell entered
upon the practice of his profession with more energy
than had ever before distinguished him, save during the

first years of his professional career. This was most
probably done with the view of introducing his eldest
son, who had then become associated with him in the
practice of the law, into the routine of his profession.
Up to the time of his mission to Utah, in 1858, he had
been a great sufferer from a rheumatic affection; and
though he had since been apparently entirely relieved
from the disorder, his nervous system, in consequence of
its ravages, as he thought himself, had remained afterwards in an exceedingly delicate condition. Seeing
him immersed in business, and, to all appearance, as
anxious in its prosecution as he had been when starting
out in life, thirty years before, there were those among
his friends who doubted if his physical strength was
equal to the labor he was imposing on himself. On
Wednesday of the last week in June, 1867, he appeared
for the last time in the streets of Henderson a living
man.

After a day of some fatigue, induced, possibly, more
from the shattered condition of his nerves than from any
great amount of physical or mental labor, he returned to
his house and immediately retired to his room. Nothing
was thought of this circumstance until the following
morning, when he was found to be seriously ill. The
family physician, Dr. PINKNEY THOMPSON, was at once
called in. The report made by this gentleman was sufficiently alarming; but neither did he nor the members
of the Governor's family at first apprehend a fatal ter-
mination of his sickness. It was at first supposed that
his disease was a slight attack of congestion of the brain.
A subsequent examination proved that a blood-vessel at
the base of the brain had become ruptured, and that this
had induced apoplexy, followed by a partial paralysis
of the right side, and, eventually, of the whole body.
During Thursday and Friday he was enabled to distinguish his friends as they approached his bedside. His

physician called to his assistance Dr. JOHN T. BERRY, of Henderson, and Dr. M. G. BRAY, of Evansville, Indiana. Their consultation took place on Saturday, and the result was a sorrowful acknowledgment that the case was hopeless.

When this opinion was made known among the Governor's neighbors and fellow-citizens, the effect was as if an impending calamity were threatening their own hearth-stones. Business appeared to be forgotten, and men and women gathered together in knots, brooding sadly, and speaking in whispers of the one absorbing topic which filled their thoughts. In the meanwhile the Governor lay in a comatose state, from which it was difficult to arouse him, at intervals, in order to administer such alleviatives as had been prescribed by his physicians. On Sunday, the last day of the month, his friend and neighbor, GRANT GREEN, Esq., made a persistent attempt to arouse him from the stupor by which he was overcome, and with such success, that faint hopes were induced of his ultimate recovery. On the following morning, however, he again relapsed into unconsciousness, and thus continued till death intervened, about three o'clock in the evening of July 3d, 1867.* Greater sympathy was never manifested by a community for one of its number when stricken, ill, and dying, nor were ever sincerer tears shed than when it was announced among

---

* A warm personal friend of Governor POWELL, who was frequently with him during his last illness, thus writes concerning his death to one of the Committee:

"All the aids of skill and experience, and all that devoted and unremitting attention on the part of family and sympathetic friends could accomplish, were employed to snatch from the embrace of death this son, dear to his State and the nation, this father beloved of his children, this friend enshrined in the hearts of all who knew him; but in vain. The fiat had gone forth—he had filled the measure of his fame, and now the silent land of the sleepers awaited him. His family and a few friends were present when he died. Among these were Mr. WM. S. HOLLOWAY, Mr. ROBT. G. BEVERLY, Mr. BEN. M. WINSTON, Mr. S. JOHNSTON ALVES, and the Rev. D. H. DEACON.

his friends and neighbors that his "spirit had gone to the
God who gave it."

The funeral took place on Thursday, the 4th day of
July, 1867. Among the pall-bearers were the Hon. AR-
CHIBALD DIXON, the Hon. JOHN LAW, of Indiana, GRANT
GREEN, Esq., and W. S. HOLLOWAY, Esq. The body was
borne to St. Paul's Episcopal Church, of which his
brother-in-law, the Rev. D. H. DEACON, was Rector.
Every business house and office in the town was closed,
and almost all were draped in emblems of mourning.
The Rev. Rector of the church was too much overcome
to trust himself to speak on the occasion, and his place
in the pulpit was supplied by the Rev. JAHLEEL WOOD-
BRIDGE, Pastor of the Presbyterian Church of Henderson.
The text of the discourse preached by the reverend gentleman was taken from the 46th chapter of Psalms—*Be
still, and know that I* AM *God.* On the announcement of
the text, a solemn silence seemed to wrap the entire
auditory, and this, till the close of the discourse, was
only broken at intervals by the stifled sobs and smothered
sighs of stricken hearts, as the eloquent divine glowingly
pictured the exalted character of him whose cold remains
lay coffined before them.

The Masonic body of Henderson, although Governor
Powell had never belonged to the Order, formed in procession and accompanied his remains to the grave. The
procession of citizens, on the occasion, was the largest
ever seen in Henderson. In it walked the rich and the
poor, women and men, and even little children. One
division of the mourners deserves to be specially noticed.
This was composed of the newly-created freedmen—his
own former slaves and those of his neighbors, who had
known him, many of them, all their lives. They had
come, some of them, from points ten and fifteen miles
distant, trudging on foot, in order to pay their tribute
of respect and gratitude over the grave of one who had

never ceased to be their best friend and counselor. No more genuine sorrow was exhibited on that mournful day than was evinced by the blacks of whom he had once been the master, and who, up to the day of his death, had been in the habit of addressing him by that title.

Governor Powell was especially distinguished as a promoter of innocent hilarity. In his own family circle there was little of that hushed *propriety* which, in many American households, is held for gentility. He loved to witness the mirthful gambols of his children and their young companions, and to hear their voices rising in gladful shouts. while at their play. Often, indeed, he was in the habit of taking part in their diversions, and then his own deep bass, in unison with their treble voices, formed a concert that was as pleasing to an intelligent ear as any that ever gained the plaudits of admiring listeners in the world of fashion and of cultivated tastes.

No more hospitable mansion than that of Governor Powell ever opened its doors to the personal friend or to the wayfarer. He appeared to delight in the providential blessings of fortune which he enjoyed, for the sole reason that they enabled him to gratify his hospitable tastes. He was especially fond of gathering about him of an evening a coterie of personal friends for social enjoyment. These gatherings were as far removed from orgies of dissipation as they were from conclaves met together for serious discussion. Governor Powell's habits in regard to eating and drinking were sufficiently abstemious to please an anchorite.* The enjoyment he derived from exhibitions of the truly humorous in discourse was with him a marked characteristic. When surrounded by gentlemen of like tastes in this particular, he always appeared, even when suffering from the

---

* Governor Powell was an inveterate *tobacco-chewer.* This was the only species of dissipation he ever indulged in.

twinges of his chronic enemy, rheumatism, as if he had
been immersed in an element that had the property
to remove all painful sensations. It was only when
humor degenerated into something akin to vulgarity,
that its exhibitions palled upon his taste. His laughter
was contagious. It seemed to well up from a soul overflowing with pleasantness and with kindly human sympathies. "Never," writes an esteemed correspondent,
"have I listened to a more hearty laugh than that with
which Powell was wont to greet the perpetrator of a
successful joke or witticism."

During the latter years of his life, the Governor seldom
spent his evenings away from his own home. When he
had no visitors, he was in the habit of retiring to his own
room for study, or in order to prepare the causes in which
he had been retained. When wearied with these occu-
pations, he would repair to the apartments of his daugh-
ter-in-law, and there amuse himself with the prattle of his
little grand-children. His family mansion was surrounded by ornamental grounds and a large garden. To the
embellishment of these grounds he devoted many of his
leisure hours, and found in such employment both health
and enjoyment.

One great source of care to Governor Powell, after the
Proclamation of Emancipation of President Lincoln, was a
number of helpless blacks—formerly his slaves—who had
no one else to look to for support and protection. Had
the Government, when it deprived him of his rights of
property in those of his slaves who were capable of performing manual labor, taken upon itself, at the same time,
the support of those who were incompetent to earn their
own living, there would have been little hardship in his
individual case, as there would have been little in thousands of other cases still more onerous. He might, to be
sure, had he been a brute, and no man, have *evicted* the
aged and infants among his former slaves from his planta-

tions, and have suffered them to die of hunger and exposure on the highway. Had the war bereft him of all his property, as it did hundreds of slave-owners in the South, even his well-known humanity could not have stood between these poor creatures and destruction. As it was, he never thought of them otherwise than as dependents on his bounty, whom it was his duty to serve and protect. Up to the day of his death, they were fed and clothed at his expense, and they are still cared for at the expense of his heirs. Had the unmistakable tokens of profound sorrow that characterized that portion of the mourners at Governor POWELL's funeral which was composed of his former slaves been witnessed by those whose fanaticism brought on the late war and all its horrors, they might well have stood in astonishment at a sight so foreign to all their notions of the relations that often existed between master and slave.

Governor POWELL, though he never professed any particular form of Christian faith, was unquestionably a firm believer in the truths of Divine Revelation. Many expressions are to be found in his speeches which show that he was familiar with the Bible, and had for that Sacred Book the most profound reverence. There was no one in the community in which he lived that was more liberal of his means for objects connected with religion. He appeared to have no preference for one denomination over another, but gave to all with a large-hearted liberality that was at once the evidence of his regard for religion in general, and of his esteem for those whose vocation it was to preach the gospel. His house was as free to all ministers of religion, without exception as to creed, who happened to be temporarily sojourning in the town, as it was to himself. On one occasion, which has come to our knowledge, he spoke seriously

3

of religion, and of his regret that he had not identified
himself in profession with the followers of Christ. Conversing with a Christian neighbor, he remarked that he
had long desired to make himself better acquainted than
he was with the peculiar doctrines of the various Christian Churches, and that it was his intention to enter upon
this study with the view to the profession of that form of
faith which should commend itself to his more enlightened
judgment.

It is said by some that Governor POWELL never exhibited any evidence of extraordinary genius. This may be
true, though there are abundant reasons to doubt it. The
placidity of his mind was such as to foil observers in their
attempts to detect the riches concealed in its depths. Of
the *erratic* in genius he was certainly totally void. But
even admitting that he gave to the world no extraordinary exhibitions of genius, it must be allowed that he
gave to it what are ordinarily of much more value—exhibitions of determination in the assertion and defense
of principles that were directly conservative of the best
interests of society and government—exhibitions of moderation and prudence in the performance of duty when
called to the discharge of high functions in the State;
and, in the hour of defeat or of failure, of unshaken confidence in the ultimate triumph of his own and his party's
patriotic purposes for the welfare of the nation. He was
no coward, and he never mistook present failure for final
defeat. In the darkest hours of the Republic he never
lost hope—never relinquished his right to appeal to the
reason of those who were permitting their passions and
their prejudices to sway their judgments and to control
their policy. He gave utterance to the convictions of his
mind, temperately yet firmly, and never in language calculated to alienate the respect of his opponents. However they may have doubted, or pretended to doubt, the

correctness of his views, they were convinced of his candor, and did homage to his manhood.

Gov. Powell well understood, what few public men have seemed to learn, that every truly beneficial measure—every wholesome reform in government—is to be secured and permanently retained only through efforts that have for their animus the *general* good, and not that of a section of the country or a party among the people. He may be said to have been a partisan in so far as he had definite notions in regard to the structure of the government and the proper policy to be pursued in order to promote the prosperity of the country and the happiness of the people; but he was no partisan in the general acceptation of the term. He never deferred principle to party, or the good of the masses to party success. Above all, he could and did distinguish between the individual and his party predilections, and never alienated the respect of the former by bitter denunciations of the latter.

Courtesy, whether in speaking to or about his political opponents, was a habit of his mind, and this habit, except under the provocation of unmistakable insult, he carried with him through life. A distinguished gentleman, occupying a high position at Washington, thus writes to a member of the Committee:

"In Washington City, Democrats and Radicals speak of him as a friend whose loss they deplore. No man was ever able to hate Powell long. Several undertook it; but he outlived their resentment, and at the date of his death he probably had not an enemy on earth."

What a noble eulogy is this! It tells us, by implication, that he had a just perception of what was due to others and what was due to himself. It tells us, also, that he possessed a mind that was capable of rising above those paltry passions which are, with the majority of men, so difficult of restraint in the hearing of false representations of facts and motives, of coarse invectives or tantalizing inuendoes, coming from one's political or personal foes. It tells us, further, that he possessed a heart that was all alive to those humane amenities that are resistless to propitiate good will and to curb dissension.

HIS PUBLIC LIFE.

"What constitutes a State?
  Not high-raised battlement or labored mound,
Thick wall or moated gate;
  Not cities proud, with spires and turrets crowned;
Not bays or broad-armed ports,
  Where, laughing at the storm, rich navies ride;
Not starred and spangled courts,
  Where low-browed baseness wafts perfume to pride.
No: men, high-minded men,
  With powers as far above dull brutes endued,
In forest, brake, or den,
  As brutes excel cold rocks and brambles rude;
Men who their duties know,
  But know their rights, and knowing, dare maintain,
Prevent the long-aimed blow,
  And crush the tyrant while they rend the chain—
These constitute a State."   [*Trans. by Sir William Jones.*

We can nowhere find a more appropriate introduction to our chapter on the Public Life of Gov. POWELL
than the above short poem from the Greek of Alcæus.
LAZARUS W. POWELL was emphatically a man of the
people. He never distrusted them—never doubted their
will to preserve free government, nor their ability to
do so. He knew—none better—that mere listlessness
on the part of a well-disposed people will occasionally
subject them to the domination of unworthy rulers. He
knew, too, that men under our form of government are
often led to support dangerous measures by reason of
their too great reliance upon those who advocate them.
Notwithstanding his knowledge on these points, he never
could be brought to doubt of the ultimate conservatism
of the people. He always appeared to feel, even when

the country seemed to be on the verge of ruin, in consequence of the evil legislation and the maladministration
of its chosen agents, that there was a sure and all-sufficient remedy for every ill under which it was suffering
in the hands of the people, which was certain to be
applied in time to prevent the overthrow of the governmental structure that had been reared by the fathers of
the Republic.

In July, 1836, at the earnest solicitation of a number
of his political friends, Mr. POWELL announced himself as
the Democratic candidate for the office of Representative
of the county in the Lower House of the Kentucky Legislature. The Whig party was largely in the ascendency
in Henderson at the time, and it was more for the object
of keeping up their organization than with any expectation of success, that the party in the minority proposed to
place a candidate in the field. Mr. POWELL's Whig competitor for the place was JOHN G. HOLLOWAY, Esq., a very
estimable and popular citizen of Henderson. While
the former industriously canvassed every precinct and
neighborhood of the county, making friends and securing
votes everywhere, the latter, relying on the party bias of
his proposed constituency, made little or no exertion to
win their confidence ; and thus he lost his election. The
result was as unlooked for by both parties as it was highly
honorable to the industry and address of the successful
candidate.

During the sessions of the General Assembly which
followed his election, Mr. POWELL proved himself a careful legislator. He was especially attentive to his duties
as a member of the various committees upon which he
had been placed, and was always alive to the interests
of his constituency and those of the entire State. At
the next general election he was again a candidate for
the office which he had so creditably filled for two years.
Whether it was that, by this time, party lines had become

more closely drawn, or that his old competitor had learned from his former experience to depend more for success upon his personal exertions in the canvass than upon the party predilections of the people of the county, certain it is, that Mr. Holloway beat him in the race by a considerable majority.

In the Presidential canvass of 1844, Mr. Powell accepted from his party the position of District Elector, and canvassed his own and the neighboring districts for James K. Polk. In this canvass he was brought prominently before the people of Western Kentucky, and, thus far, he laid the foundations of that personal popularity which afterwards enabled him to serve his party in more important positions. Mr. Polk was elected over his competitor, the Hon. Henry Clay; but the Democrats were defeated in Kentucky.

In the spring of 1848, the State Democratic Convention met at Frankfort, for the purpose of nominating candidates for the Executive offices of the Commonwealth, to be voted for at the coming August election. The choice of the Convention fell upon the Hon. Linn Boyd,* of McCracken county, for Governor, and the Hon. John P. Martin, of Floyd county, for Lieutenant Governor. Before the dissolution of the Convention, authority was given to the Democratic Central Committee of the State to fill all vacancies, if any, that should occur on the ticket proposed, by declination or otherwise. Upon being informed as to the action of the Convention, Mr. Boyd, in a letter addressed to the Chairman of the State

---

* The Hon Linn Boyd, at the time referred to in the text, was the most noted of all the Democratic politicians of the State. His influence in Western Kentucky was paramount. He represented, for many years, the First Congressional District in the National Congress, and was universally regarded as the leader of his political associates in all their struggles for mastery against the dominant Whig party. He was a man of acknowledged patriotism and of exalted private character. He died in Paducah, Kentucky, December 16th, 1859, in the 59th year of his age.

Central Committee—the Hon. JAMES GUTHRIE—formally declined the candidateship which his party friends had proposed; and it thus became necessary to put forward some one in his stead. A meeting of the committee was held, a few days subsequently, and the name of LAZARUS W. POWELL was placed at the head of the ticket. This result, it is said, was mainly due to the influence of Mr. GUTHRIE,* whose sound practical views of the situation,

---

* The Hon. JAMES GUTHRIE was born in Nelson county, Kentucky, in 1793. His father, Gen. ADAM GUTHRIE, much distinguished himself in the Indian wars of the West, and afterwards served in the Legislature of the State during several sessions. His son received a good academical education at McAlister's Academy, Bardstown. After leaving school, he commenced trading in the various products of the country, shipping the same on flatboats to the New Orleans market. He studied law under the late Judge ROWAN, of Bardstown, and practiced for several years in the courts of Nelson county. In 1820 he removed to Louisville, having received from the Governor the appointment of Commonwealth's Attorney. He opened an office, and being both studious and attentive to business, he became soon possessed of a lucrative practice. Mr. GUTHRIE has been the leading spirit in every enterprise undertaken for the commercial advancement of Louisville. It was mainly through his influence that the splendid court-house, which now adorns the city, was erected. The Louisville and Frankfort Railroad, the Jeffersonville and Indianapolis Railroad, and, finally, the Louisville and Nashville Railroad and its branches, were all enterprises which had in him their most unflagging supporter. His wise directory counsels were equal to the task of pushing them to completion, and of rendering them all paying investments. Until latterly, Mr. GUTHRIE occupied the positions of President of the Louisville and Nashville Railroad Company, President of the Louisville and Portland Canal Company, and President of the University of Louisville.

In politics, Mr. GUTHRIE has been a life-long Democrat, and, for the past twenty years, the recognized leader of that party in Kentucky. He has served, time and again, in the Legislature of the State, and in 1849 was a delegate from the city to the Constitutional State Convention, of which body he was elected President. He received in 1853, from President PIERCE, the appointment of Secretary of the Treasury, which office he held during the term of that Chief Magistrate's administration. His management of that office is regarded, on all hands, as having been masterly. His name was presented at the Charleston Convention of 1860 for the office of President of the United States; but, unhappily, the wise counsels of his numerous friends in that body were overruled. He was a member of the Peace Convention that met at Washington at the beginning of the war, as he was, also, of the Border State Convention that met at Frankfort. In 1865 he was elected to

and whose clear perception of the character and qualifications of the gentlemen whose names had been mentioned in connection with the candidateship, were never
more forcibly illustrated than on this occasion.

The Whig party in Kentucky had nominated as its candidate for Governor the Hon. John J. Crittenden,* who
was then a member of the United States Senate from
Kentucky, and undoubtedly one of the most deservedly
popular men in the State. At the outset of the canvass,
Mr. Powell was encountered by a feud in his own party.
The Hon. Richard M. Johnson,† of Scott county, had an-

---

the United States Senate for six years, which position he held till the 10th
of February, 1868, when his resignation of the office was placed in the hands
of the Governor.

Always industrious, and always governed by prudence in the investment
of his accumulated means, Mr. Guthrie has acquired a very large fortune,
the greater part of which consists of real estate. For more than a year past,
his health has been failing, and he is now closely confined to his room.

* John J. Crittenden was born in Woodford county, Ky., in September,
1786. He served as a Major under General Hopkins in the war of 1812, and
was Aid-de-Camp to Gov. Shelby at the battle of the Thames. He adopted
the profession of the Law, and was a most successful practitioner. He served
in the Legislature of the State for several terms, and entered the National
Congress as a Senator from Kentucky in 1817. He was again elected to the
U. S. Senate in 1835, in which he served until his appointment to the office
of Attorney General by President Harrison. After his resignation of this
office he returned to Kentucky and served in the State Legislature until he
was for the third time elected to the U. S. Senate. He resigned his seat in
this body in 1848, for the purpose of making the canvass for Governor
referred to in the text. He was successful in this race; but he held the office
for a brief period only, having accepted the appointment of Attorney General under Mr. Fillmore's administration. In 1855 he was again sent to the
United States Senate, and served till the end of the term in 1861, when he
retired, the oldest member of that body. In 1860 he was elected a Representative in the Thirty-seventh Congress. He died at Louisville, Ky., July
25th, 1863. The long public services of Mr. Crittenden were worthily
ended by his almost superhuman efforts to compromise the difficulties between the Government and the Southern States which culminated in the late
civil war. Had his famous "Compromise Measure" been adopted by Congress, the country would have undoubtedly escaped the war and all its dis-
astrous consequences.

† Colonel Richard M. Johnson was born in Kentucky in 1780. He represented his district in the Lower House of Congress from 1807 to 1813. In

nounced himself an independent Democratic candidate for the office of Governor, and had already entered upon the canvass. Perceiving that success would be out of the question with two Democratic candidates in the field, Mr. POWELL hastened to the home of his old friend, with whom he sought and obtained an interview, the result of which was entirely satisfactory to both parties. Col. JOHNSON not only declined to prosecute the race any further, but expressed his readiness to canvass his own district in behalf of the nominee of the Convention.

The energy with which the Gubernatorial canvass of 1848 was prosecuted in Kentucky by both Whigs and Democrats, was strongly indicative of the fears of the party in the majority, on account of the personal popularity of the opposition candidate, and of the hopes raised in the minds of the Democratic minority, by having for its standard-bearer one who was known never to have addressed his fellow-citizens without having made additions to the number of his friends. The beginning of the decadence of the Whig party in Kentucky may be referred to this memorable canvass. Everywhere the zeal of its advocates abated, and defections from its ranks were numerous. Mr. POWELL threw himself into the arena of political controversy with an energy that was resistless. Every part of the State was thoroughly canvassed, and every effort of

---

the latter year he raised a regiment to fight the British and Indians on the Lakes, and served during the campaign under Gen. HARRISON. He greatly distinguished himself at the head of his regiment at the battle of the Thames, the Indian Chief, TECUMSEH, as it is said, having fallen by his hand. He was Indian Commissioner, in 1814, under President MADISON'S administration. He was returned to Congress in 1815. In 1819 he was elected to the United States Senate, where he remained till 1829. On the expiration of his term he was elected to the U. S. House of Representatives, where he remained until 1837, when he became Vice President of the United States. Col. JOHNSON was a man of strong intellect and unflinching courage. He was also held in high esteem on account of his kindly disposition. He died at Frankfort, Ky., on the 19th of November, 1850.

the opposition was encountered and resisted. The Democratic political creed was defined and made known, by men who had been taught their principles in schools of statesmanship that had for their masters the greatest minds of the nation—the fathers of the Republic themselves, and those who immediately succeeded them in administering the government and in framing its laws.

The people were taught the true nature of the attempts that, even then, were being made to warp legislation from its rightful course, and make it subservient to sectional interests, and promotive of party purposes. They were made to feel that all stability in government is dependent upon the fairness of the law toward each and every citizen of the State; that the moment the law-making powers lose sight of the principle of *exact justice to all*, that moment the door is opened to dissension, and the whole structure of government endangered. The CONSTITUTION—the great charter of the people's liberties—was the text upon which POWELL and his associates in this canvass based both their right to a hearing and their appeals to the reason of those whom they addressed. They were strict constructionists of this instrument, since, alas, so shamefully abused and set at naught by its triumphant enemies. The canvass was a substantial triumph, though it ended in the defeat of the Constitutional party. The seed had been sown which was to spring forth richly laden with fruit for the coming harvest.*

---

* In connection with this canvass the following amusing anecdote is related: Having addressed a meeting of his fellow-citizens in one of the mountain counties, Governor POWELL was induced to accept the invitation of an old gentleman, residing in the neighborhood, to pass the night at his house. To do honor to her guest, the mistress of the establishment, an old lady of primitive tastes and habits, had spread her supper-table with all the luxuries at her command, prominent among which were a number of fruit and other pies. It is to be supposed that Mr. POWELL was not only hungry, but that his digestive faculties were in excellent condition. He helped and rehelped himself to portions of a pie that was convenient to his hand, and

In 1852 the claims of Mr. POWELL were fully recognized by the nominating Convention of the Democracy of the State. He was again put foward by that Convention as its candidate for the office of Governor of the Commonwealth. There were peculiar circumstances connected with the canvass of this year that rendered it in the highest degree extraordinary. Mr. POWELL's Whig competitor in the race was the Hon. ARCHIBALD DIXON,* a resi-

---

it was not until he had nearly cleared the plate of its contents that he bethought himself of inquiring as to the character of the fruit of which it was composed. "Madam," said he, addressing his hostess, "this is certainly a pie of most appetising qualities. I have never tasted anything better. Pray, tell me of what is it composed?" The old lady opened her eyes in astonishment, and exclaimed: "*Up for Governor, and not know huckleberry pie!*" It is scarcely necessary to state that the huckleberry, or whortleberry shrub, is indigenous to hilly regions, and that Mr. POWELL had never before seen or tasted of its fruit.

* For many years previous to his nomination as the candidate of the Whig party of the State for the office of Governor, ARCHIBALD DIXON had stood at the head of the bar in Southern Kentucky. He was then a most able, industrious, and cultivated lawyer. His management of all causes confided to him was marked by ability, but he made his greatest reputation as a *jury lawyer*. The fiery energy of his manner, his impassioned eloquence, the vehemence with which he hurled facts and arguments at the vulnerable points of his adversary's cause, the richness of his fancy, the beauty of his rhetoric, the crushing weight of his denunciatory power, and the sting of his satire, gave him an influence over a jury which few men wielded. As a criminal lawyer, *for the defense*—for he always refused to prosecute—he was for many years employed in nearly all the important trials in the district. He acquired a large fortune by his practice. As a political speaker, he was equally distinguished, and several of his efforts have rarely been surpassed for power and eloquence, and the influence they carried with them. He still lives, and no man is more generally respected in the community, or more warmly beloved by his intimates. Never were men more intimately associated, for years, than he and POWELL. Their legal and political encounters never engendered ill feeling in either, or caused the slightest estrangement between them. In business matters, they indorsed for each other, reciprocally, and for none others outside of their own families, without the consent of the other. Each held from the other a power of attorney to sign both names to any desired document, when either happened to be absent from the county. No more sincere or grief-stricken mourner bowed his head in sorrow over the grave of the dead patriot and statesman, LAZARUS W. POWELL, than did his life-long political antagonist and his life-long personal friend, Governor DIXON.

dent of the same town, his life-long personal friend, and, at one time, his partner in the practice of the law. For not one moment, whether before, during, or after the canvass, were the intimate personal relations between the two interrupted. They traveled together, spoke together, put up at the same houses, and had their meals at the same tables, and, except when brought into contact in the exposition of their dissimilar political dogmas, they exhibited toward each other, and before the public, a cordiality of demeanor that is as rarely witnessed between political antagonists as it was pleasant to contemplate.

It was in this canvass, most likely, that Governor Powell learned that perfection of self-control by which he was afterwards so greatly distinguished in the Senate of the United States. Both candidates had an all-sufficient motive in their personal friendship to shun displays of temper. Courtesy thus became a habit of their minds, and its influence lived long beyond the occasion that called it into activity. Mr. Powell secured his election by a small majority, while Robert N. Wickliffe, Esq., the candidate on the same ticket for the office of Lieutenant Governor, was beaten several thousand votes by his opponent, the Hon. John B. Thompson.*

Lazarus W. Powell was inaugurated Governor of the Commonwealth of Kentucky on the morning of September 5th, 1851. Accompanied by an escort, comprised of three military companies of the city, and a large number of prominent citizens, he left Louisville early on the morning of the day named, and reached Frankfort before ten o'clock. At the Frankfort depot he was met by a large concourse of citizens and strangers, and entering a carriage in waiting, with the Lieutenant Governor

---

* The Hon. John B. Thompson was born in Kentucky. He represented the Harrodsburg District in the United States House of Representatives from 1841 to 1843, and again from 1847 to 1851. In 1853 he was elected to the United States Senate for the long term.

elect, the Hon. JOHN B. THOMPSON, he was driven to the State House building, when he was formally welcomed to the seat of his future magisterial labors in a congratulatory address by the Hon. JUDGE HEWITT. The Governor elect, having been introduced to the assembled multitude by the retiring Governor, the Hon. JOHN L. HELM, replied briefly and appropriately to the address of JUDGE HEWITT, and returned his thanks for the confidence that had been reposed in him by the people. He expressed his distrust of his ability to discharge properly the duties of the office to which he had been elevated; but declared his determination to use such powers as he possessed for the maintenance of good government. He would administer the government, to the best of his ability, in accordance with the Constitution and laws, and in the interests of the whole people of the State. The oath of office was administered by Judge SHANNON.

The General Assembly of the Commonwealth met on the 3d day of November, 1851, and, on the following day, the first message of Governor POWELL was presented to, and read before, that body. The local issues and interests discussed in that document need not be here referred to; but the annexed extract from the message will be found, in view of the events that have since occurred in the country, deeply interesting:

"The dark and lowering clouds that recently threatened the existence of the Union of the States of this glorious Confederacy are happily passing away. Kentucky is the firm and devoted friend of the Union; and is for maintaining inviolate, and carrying out in strictness and in truth, in letter and in spirit, the compromise measures passed by the last Congress of the United States. She acknowledges the high and inestimable blessings which the Union, under the National Constitution, confers on each and all the States, and holds that all the provisions and guaranties of that sacred instrument are binding upon each and all. She invites no aggression, and places the cause of the Union on the binding obligations of the Federal Constitution; and declares to the citizens of all the States that good faith, in strictly and justly carrying out the provisions of the Constitution, is essential to its preservation. The General Government is one of limited powers, and it was never designed that it should interfere with the domestic institutions of the States, and every attempt on the part of the National Government to interfere with the right of property, or abridge the free exercise or control of property in the States, is a violation of the national compact, and an encroachment upon the sovereignty of the States; nor has Congress the right to interfere with the question of slavery in the Territories. It is a matter of domestic concernment, and its settlement should be left exclusively to the people of the Territories.

" It is deeply to be regretted that a portion of the citizens of some of the Northern States of the Confederacy have resisted, and attempted to resist, the execution of the fugitive slave law. All forcible acts of resistance to the execution of the laws are treason against the United States, and those who advise, aid, or abet such resistance, are traitors to the Constitution and enemies to the best interests of the Republic. It is to be hoped that a rigorous prosecution and punishment of such offenders will cause the Constitution and laws to be respected, and that their execution will no longer be resisted from any quarter. Kentucky expects from her sister States a faithful and impartial execution of the laws, and whilst she most cheerfully acknowledges and accords to the Northern States all the guaranties of the Constitution, she demands that none of the guaranties of that sacred instrument be withheld from the South."

In his second message to the General Assembly of the Commonwealth, presented January 3d, 1854, Governor

POWELL congratulates the people's representatives "on the general prosperity of the State, and the happy condition of their constituents." "Since the adjournment of the last Legislature," he continues, "the people of our beloved Commonwealth have enjoyed unusually good health; our fields have produced abundant crops, and all industrial pursuits have been attended with great prosperity. The public credit has been preserved, and the public peace maintained." He calls attention to the wants of the "Public School System," and recommends the appointment of a commission to make a thorough "Geological Survey of the State." The annexed paragraphs from the message will be read with interest:

"Since the adjournment of the last Legislature, the State and the nation have been called to mourn the death of HENRY CLAY, distinguished alike for his lofty patriotism and commanding eloquence. His fame is inseparably connected with the history of the Republic; and his eminent virtues live embalmed in the memories of the people of Kentucky, whom he so long and brilliantly served in the national councils. We have more recently been called to mingle our grief with Massachusetts for the loss of DANIEL WEBSTER, her most illustrious citizen. I herewith transmit a communication from the Governor of South Carolina, and the resolves of the Legislature of that State, offering fraternal condolence to the States of Kentucky and Massachusetts, upon the death of Mr. CLAY and Mr. WEBSTER.

"South Carolina, too, has mourned the loss of her most distinguished statesman. Thus, within a short space of time, CALHOUN, CLAY, and WEBSTER, three of the most distinguished orators and statesmen of the Republic, have gone from us forever. That trio of illustrious orators and statesmen, who for near half a century adorned our history, swayed the Cabinet, and enchained the Senate by their matchless eloquence, have passed from our

midst; but their names and virtues will live with un-
diminished luster upon the pages of our country's history.

"Alabama, as well as South Carolina, Massachusetts,
and Kentucky, laments the loss of a favorite son. The
death of WM. R. KING, Vice President of the United
States, a citizen beloved and respected for the purity of
his character, eminent for his talents, and distinguished
for his long and faithful services to his country in the
many high and responsible stations to which he had been
called by his State and nation, occurred soon after that
of his illustrious compeers. The general sorrow produced by this national calamity exhibits the esteem with
which a free people always regard the faithful public
servant and benefactor of his country.

"I place at your disposal a medal, presented by the
citizens of New York, through me, to the State of Kentucky, designed by them 'to commemorate the public
services of Mr. CLAY, and to transmit to distant posterity
a perfect resemblance of his features.' The letter of the
committee of the citizens of New York which accompanied the medal, and a copy of my response accepting
it, on behalf of the State of Kentucky, are transmitted
herewith. I recommend that you direct that it be placed
in the Public Library."

During the entire term of Governor POWELL's Chief
Magistracy, his official duties were discharged with the
most commendable fidelity and exactness. For the greater part of his term of office the General Assembly of the
State had in it a majority of Whigs; yet at no time
did his relations with that body assume a partisan character. The most exacting among his political opponents
were obliged to acknowledge that his entire policy was
conceived and carried out with due reference to his re-

4

sponsibilities to the whole body of the people and the best interests of the State.*

In 1857, ALFRED CUMMING, Esq., who had previously held the post of Indian Agent in the Northwest Territories, was appointed by President BUCHANAN, Governor of the Territory of Utah. At the same time, Judge ECKELS, of Indiana, received the appointment of Chief Justice of the same dependency. There being at the time strong apprehensions of difficulties between the government

---

* The following characteristic anecdote of Governor POWELL is worthy of mention. Shortly after his inauguration, a distinguished lawyer from one of the upper counties of the State, and a personal friend of the Governor, called upon him for the purpose of presenting certain petitions for the pardon of a convict then in the penitentiary. The call was made at an early hour; and, on the door being opened, the servant in attendance asked for the visitor's card. "Card, the d—ll" exclaimed the excited Attorney; "does the Governor expect every man that calls on him from the backwoods to have his pocket filled with cards! Go tell the Governor that Joe A——, of F——g, is at the door, and wishes to see him." The Governor had overheard the conversation, and hobbling to the door on crutches (he was suffering at the time from rheumatism), relieved his visitor from further trouble on the score of etiquette. The petitions were presented, and it appearing evident to the Governor's mind that the young man to whom they referred had first been induced to drink to excess, and then seduced into the commission of an act of theft of which he had reaped none of the advantages, a messenger was dispatched to the keeper of the penitentiary, requesting that functionary's attendance with the prisoner at the Governor's mansion. When brought into his presence the Governor thus addressed the convict: "Young man, your friends think that you were led to the commission of an unlawful act by an accomplished rascal in whom you too confidingly trusted, who used you as a tool for his own wicked purposes. I am inclined to think that this was the case; and, on this impression, I have pardoned you. Your character must be reclaimed where you lost it. Now I wish you to go at once to the man you have injured, and to tell him exactly how you came to act as you did. Get him to employ you on his farm; and if he can't give you wages, work for him without pay, until such time as he shall become convinced that you were the victim of circumstances, and not deliberately criminal. As I suppose you have no money to pay your way back, here are seven dollars for that object. Mind, young man, that I shall expect to hear a good account of you."

It was but a short time before the Governor did hear a good account of the youth. The Governor's injunctions were obeyed to the letter, and the quondam convict is now a well-to-do and respected citizen in the very neighborhood where his crime was committed.

and the Utah authorities, three regiments of· United
States soldiers, properly officered, were dispatched to the
Territory, in company with whom traveled the newly-
appointed civil officials. The winter set in before the
expedition reached Salt Lake City, and Col. ALBERT
SIDNEY JOHNSTON,* into whose hands its command had
fallen, was compelled to go into winter quarters several
days' march from the capital of the new Territory. In
the meantime, the growing hostile sentiment against the
government indulged in by the inhabitants of Utah culminated in open rebellion. This state of things was
made known by a proclamation of the Colonel in command of the army.

In the spring of 1858, through the intervention of·THOS.
L. KANE, Esq., of Pennsylvania, President BUCHANAN was
induced to dispatch a commission to Utah, with the hope
of arresting the rebellion that had broken out in that
Territory. The Commissioners named were Gov. POWELL,

---

*The name of ALBERT SIDNEY JOHNSTON is too well known to the general
reader to require more from us than a simple record of the leading facts
connected with his career. He was born in Kentucky, and educated at
West Point. When yet under twenty-five years of age, he was married to
Miss HENRIETTA PRESTON, a sister of General WM. PRESTON, of Louisville.
Shortly after his marriage, he resigned his position in the regular army—
he then being a Lieutenant—and removed to Texas. When the war with
Mexico was decided on, he again entered the army as a volunteer. He was
soon advanced to the position of Paymaster in the army, and eventually to
that of Colonel of the Second cavalry regiment. This was his rank at the
time referred to in the text. His reputation as a military man stood very
high with his superiors. and in order to prevent ill-feeling on the part of
his elders of the same rank in the service on account of his promotion to
the entire command of the expedition, he was commissioned by the War
Department Brigadier General by Brevet. When the late civil war broke
out, he resigned his place in the United States army, and promptly offered
his services to the Confederate States Government. He soon arose to the
command of the Southern Division of the army of the new government,
and fell at Shiloh, at the moment, as has been generally conceded, when
that great disaster to the cause of the South alone prevented the entire
destruction of General GRANT's army. Of all those who lost their lives in
the late conflict, no name stands higher for courage, ability, and patriotism,
than does that of ALBERT SIDNEY JOHNSTON.

of Kentucky, and Maj. BEN. McCULLOCH,* of Texas. On the arrival of these gentlemen at the camp of the military expedition, they immediately issued the proclamation of the President, offering pardon to all Mormons who should submit to the Federal authority. This offer was accepted by the heads of the Mormon Church, and all trouble was arrested.

Governor POWELL was wont to speak enthusiastically of his trip across the plains to Utah, and of the richness and variety of scenery presented to his eyes in that far-off Territory. He had long been a sufferer from rheumatism, and he always attributed his complete recovery to the beneficial effects of the climate of Utah upon his health. The wild, free life of the plains suited him; and, long before he had reached the end of his journey, he felt, as he expressed it, as if he had gotten a new lease of life. He often spoke of the wonderful beauty and sublimity of the country surrounding Salt Lake City—of its towering mountains and rich valleys—of the immense

---

*Since the war for the independence of Texas, and up to the battle of Pea Ridge, in Northern Arkansas, in 1862, few names in the annals of the times have been more familiar to the ears of Southerners than that of the celebrated Texan Ranger, Maj. BEN. McCULLOCH. He proved himself, in the three wars in which he was engaged, not only the brave soldier, but the prudent agent, also, of his superiors, whenever his services were demanded for the carrying out their strategic designs. It was to his daring address while attached in the capacity of *scout* to the army of invasion in Mexico that was principally due the salvation of General TAYLOR's army, a few days previous to the battle of Buena Vista. With two others, he penetrated the enemy's camp, and ascertained that he was not only in overwhelming force, but that SANTA ANNA—who had, up to that time, been supposed to be an exile from his country—was in command of the Mexican forces, and was preparing a formidable trap for his too confiding adversary. The information gained by McCULLOCH enabled General TAYLOR to retrace his steps from Agua Nueva to Buena Vista, where the fiercest battle of the war was fought and won by the American General a few days afterwards. McCULLOCH volunteered in the Confederate States army in the late civil war, in which he commanded a regiment of Texan Rangers. He fell on the bloody field of Pea Ridge in the second year of the war, having reached the rank of Brigadier General.

saline deposits on the shores of the Lake, and of the
delight he experienced in bathing in waters, the buoyancy of which enabled him to float upon their surface
without exertion, as on a bed of down. His intercourse
with BRIGHAM YOUNG and the saints of Salt Lake was
agreeable and instructive. He had no faith in the sincerity of the Mormon apostles; but he always gave to
the masses under them credit for integrity. He described
YOUNG as a shrewd, plausible, and well-informed man,
of indomitable energy and of iron will, but of vast ambition, who dreamed of building up a great nation wedded
to the faith of which he had been for years the apostle,
independent of the United States Government, and rivaling it in power; and who would have scornfully refused
the demands of the government, had he believed he could
have successfully resisted, either by force of arms or by
cunning.

At the session of the General Assembly which took
place in 1859, Governor POWELL was elected to the Senate of the United States for the full term of six years.
Without extending this sketch to too great length, we
find it impracticable to give the reader more than a general outline of Governor POWELL's course while a member
of the Senate. His speeches to that body would of themselves fill a large volume, and these are all to be found
in the published reports of the congressional proceedings
of the period. He entered the Senate at a time of great
political excitement. A party had arisen in the country,
and was daily growing stronger, which had for its main
idea the extinction of slavery as a national institution, or
as one recognized in the fundamental law of the land.
By the governments of several of the Northern States the
fugitive slave law had been openly proclaimed a measure
which required from them no obedience. The Southern
States, disgusted at what they conceived to be want of
faith on the part of their Northern associates, and seeing,

from the complexion of the legislation of the country,
that they would soon be powerless to protect their constitutional rights against the requirements of a constantly
increasing majority in the National Legislature, already
were contemplating secession. In both Houses of Congress fanaticism ruled one part of the people's representatives, and, with but few exceptions, passion the
remainder. With these mutually opposing forces rancor begot rancor, and denunciation begot denunciation;
until, by both, reason was thrown to the winds, and the
seeds of suspicion and hatred were sown broadcast over
the whole land, to spring up, after a few short months,
into cohorts of armed men, striving for the mastery on a
thousand battle-fields.

The conservative ideas of the fathers of the Republic,
in accordance with which they were alone enabled to
construct a system of government in which opposing interests should meet and become reconciled, were lost sight
of in the reign of fanaticism and passion that preceded
the late war; and influential men of both sections, filled
with ambition and the desire to secure personal advantages, shut their eyes to the signs of the times, which por-
tended trouble, as they did to the teachings of history and
the counsels of the wisest among the nation's departed
statesmen. The people of the country, outside of the
small bands of fanatics in either section, and the great
army of corrupt politicians scattered all over the country,
had no notion whatever of the dangers that were threatening the very existence of the nation. They had been
educated, however, by the real instigators of the troubles
to the point of adherence to certain political dogmas, in
reference to the institution of slavery particularly, which
were enunciated by the leaders in whom they had placed
unreserved, but mistaken, confidence; and the result ensued, which had been contemplated from the first by the

fanatics and political tricksters—civil war between the sections North and South.

Few of our public men possessed a clearer understanding of the causes that led to the late conflict than Gov. POWELL. In a speech on the " Bill giving freedom to the families of negro soldiers," delivered in the Senate on the 9th January, 1863, Mr. POWELL remarked:

"Some call this a war for the negro; but, in my opinion, those who look upon African slavery as the cause of the war are greatly mistaken. This war was not designed by the large slaveholders of the South; they did not want the war. It is not a war of the negro; it is not a war of tariffs; it is not a war of any particular line of policy; but it is a war of politicians who were faithless to their constitutional obligations, and there the responsibility will be placed by the philosophical historian in all after time. If I were to describe it in a sentence, I should say that it was a war of the politicians, both North and South—a war of ambitious fanatical zealots, and they existed North as well as South. I speak of a class of politicians who are faithless to the law, faithless to their oaths of office, and who claim to be governed by a law higher than and above the Constitution. This war was not brought about by a majority of the American people in either section. There were higher-law fanatical Abolitionists in the North, who disregarded their constitutional obligations, which wise, honest, and just men were bound by; and there was a class called " Fire-eaters," in the South, who were fanatics too. Both parties were ready to take up any bone about which they could make the fiercest quarrel. They had the tariff bone at one time, and they came near wrecking the Union on that. If the bone of contention had been the spinning-jennies of New England, and they had thought that issue would have more aggravated the people than any other, they would have seized on that bone. The slavery question was caught hold of by these designing men as the one best calculated to excite the people. What the fanatics of the North said, the fire-eaters of the South re-echoed to their people, and the hard things said by themselves were taken up at the North for a like purpose."

It is well known that Governor POWELL was sincerely and consistently opposed to the war of coercion that was inaugurated by Mr. LINCOLN's administration in 1860, against the seceded Commonwealths of the South. With many of the wisest men of the country, he belived that war was "eternal separation." He loved the Union too well to endanger it by urging the government to go to war for its own nominal preservation. A Union "pinned together by bayonets," he regarded as unsuited to the genius of our institutions; and he therefore looked upon the action of the coercionists as subversive of every principle that underlays our structure of government. He revered the Constitution, and believed that, under its ægis, the people had ample protection against persistent wrong. He implored his Southern co-members in Congress to remain in their places and fight the battle of the Constitution on that civic field. Had they listened to his voice, war would have been impossible. He was equally earnest in his efforts to lull the excited passions of the majority, both before and after the Representatives of the seceded States had vacated their posts, and even after blood had flowed in streams on the first battle-fields of the new revolution. He advocated with zeal and energy every measure of compromise that was introduced in Congress, and only ceased to raise his voice in deprecation and warning, when, to have done so, would have but added to the exasperation of a conclave that appeared to be bent on revolutionizing the whole structure of government.

He heartily approved of the neutral position taken by his native State at the beginning of the war, though h e evidently feared that that position could not be, as it was not, maintained. In the session of 1860, when interrogated by the Senator from New Jersey (Mr. Ten Eyck): " How can the State of Kentucky, consistently with her duty to the Constitution, refuse to obey the President's call for troops?" he thus made answer:

" I will state to the Senator and to the country the view that Kentucky took of that question, as far as I am advised. Kentucky believed that this call for seventy-five thousand men was not necessary for the defense of the capital or of the public property. She believed that the calling forth of such an immense armament was for the purpose of making a war of subjugation on the Southern States, and upon that ground she refused to furnish the regiments called for. The Senator seems to be a little offended at the neutrality of Kentucky. Sir, Kentucky has assumed a position of neutrality, and I only hope that she may be able to maintain it. She has assumed that position because there is no impulse of her patriotic heart that desires her to imbrue her hands in a brother's blood, whether he be from the North or the South. Kentucky looks upon this war as wicked, unrighteous, and unnecessary. Kentucky believes that this war, if carried out, can result in nothing else than a final disruption of this confederacy. She hopes, she wishes, she prays that this Union may be maintained. She believes that cannot be done by force of arms; that it must be done by compromise and conciliation, if it can be done at all; and hence, being devoted truly to the Union, she desires to stay this war, and desires measures of peace to be presented for the adjustment of our difficulties.

" That is the neutrality of Kentucky, and that I understand to be the reason why she assumes to be neutral. It is the first time in the history of that proud Commonwealth that she ever failed to respond to the call upon

the country for volunteers; she never was called upon
to fight a public and foreign enemy that her true and
gallant sons did not rush to the standard of the country
in numbers so great that many had to be turned back.
In other wars, in the war of 1812, and the war with
Mexico, twenty times more men than could be taken
were presented; and she would be ready to do it again,
if it were a war against a foreign enemy; but she has
no desire to shed the blood of a brother, whether of the
North or South. I think her position is one that should
be admired and esteemed by all patriotic men, by all
Christian men, by all men who love their country and
love the Union.

"She stands in an attitude, if possible, of a peace-
maker, between the belligerents North and South, and
I hope she may be permitted to maintain that attitude.
It was one *not taken out of any hostility to the Government;*
she took it because she believed it was the only means
possible by which those difficulties could be averted,
our country saved, the Union restored, and our people
once more made prosperous, contented, and happy.

"I am aware that the position of my State is not pala-
table to gentlemen who rush fiercely on to this war. I
am aware also that persons in the extreme South, perhaps, are not satisfied with the condition of Kentucky.
They think we ought to unsheath our sword at once,
and make common quarrel with them. We have chosen
to act differently, and we will, with the blessing of God,
maintain our position of neutrality. This immense armament called out by the President looked to us as if this
were to be a war of subjugation, and not one in defense
of the public property. For that, in addition to the other
reasons I have stated, we wished to present, if possible,
a barrier between the fierce conflicting elements North
and South, and restore peace to this country."

In July, 1861, during the extraordinary session of Congress, convened by Mr. LINCOLN, a joint resolution was

introduced which was intended to legalize certain unlawful acts of the President—among others, his calliug
for troops, blockading the Southern ports, and authorizing the suspension of the writ of *habeas corpus.* Governor
Powell took part in the discussion which ensued, and, on
the 11th of July, he made a speech, from which we extract
what follows :

" Mr. President, we have fallen upon strange times.
The Congress of the nation has been assembled in extraordinary session for the purpose of considering matters
of the gravest importance. We are in the midst of
a revolution which has dismembered the Confederacy.
We are now called upon to vote for a resolution approving the acts of the President of the United States
that are specifically set forth in the resolution. Sir, I
consider that the President, in many of these enumerated
acts, has violated the Constitution of the land. The
powers and duties of the President are prescribed in
that instrument. That distinguished gentleman has no
more power to infract the Constitution or the laws than
the humblest citizen of the land. He has sworn to be
true and faithful to the Constitution. Each Senator and
each official of this government, upon entering upon the
discharge of the functions of his office, takes an oath
to support the Constitution ; and I should consider that I
was recreant to my duty as a Senator, if I did not oppose
the act of every officer of the government who, as I
conceived, had violated the Constitution of the country.

" I readily admit, that if the call for seventy-five thousand men was made solely for the purpose of protecting
this capital, and for the purpose designated in this resolution, it was constitutional and valid. If, however, the
purpose of the call for seventy-five thousand men was
for the purpose of making war on the sovereign States
of this Union, I hold the act to be invalid, because I hold
that we have no power to make war upon a State of this

Union. There is no such warrant in the Constitution.
Our illustrious fathers, when framing that instrument,
declined to give any such power. It was expressly proposed to clothe the government with power to coerce a
State; and, after a most elaborate debate, in which such
men as Madison, Hamilton, Ellsworth, and others par-
ticipated, it was unanimously rejected. However, sir, so
far as that is concerned, I shall say no more. The con-
stitutionality of the act calling out the seventy-five thousand men, in my judgment, depends altogether on the
uses the President intended to make of the army which
he organized. I confess that the creation of such a vast
army looked to me very much like desiring a war of subjugation.

"Is there a Senator here who believes that the President of the United States has warrant of the law and the
Constitution for suspending this act of *habeas corpus?* If
there is, he holds the Constitution in a very different light
than did the Supreme Court of the United States, Judge
Story in his Commentaries, and all other commentators
on the Constitution. I have, to some extent, examined
the decisions, and I find they all hold the very same doctrine.

"But some gentleman, as did the Senator from Massachusetts [Mr. WILSON] the other day, seem to think there
was some necessity for it. Where? There could be no
necessity that would authorize this violation of the Constitution. Several persons, I have heard, have been imprisoned under it—among them, a man by the name of
Merryman, in the city of Baltimore, and the police commissioners of that city, who are now at Fort McHenry,
and denied the privilege of this writ. I think there
could have been no necessity for it, because this writ, in
my judgment, should never be suspended, not even in the
cases prescribed in the Constitution, unless the judges of
the country are considered too corrupt to administer the

law. When the judges become too corrupt, in the opinion of the legislative department, to administer the law,
then I think that Congress might lawfully and properly
exercise the power to suspend this writ in the instances
prescribed in the Constitution, but not until then.

"The Chief Justice of the United States issued his writ
to have Mr. Merryman brought before him. It was refused. He then, I believe, issued an attachment for contempt against the commanding officer at Fort McHenry,
General Cadwalader, and the officer of the court was not
permitted to execute that last process. What harm could
there have been in having this man, John Merryman,
brought before the Chief Justice of the United States, if
he were lawfully imprisoned? It would have been the
duty of the Chief Justice to investigate the case, and if
he found that Merryman was improperly and unlawfully
deprived of his liberty, to discharge him. If he had been
of the opinion that he was guilty, and properly imprisoned, and the case was not a bailable one, he would
have to remand him to the prison; or if, in his judgment,
it were a bailable case, and the man probably guilty,
then to discharge him on bail. What harm, if the man
were really guilty, would there have been in bringing
him before the Chief Justice, and allowing the judgment
to be rendered? Why, sir, if you allow the Executive,
or any other officer, to suspend this great writ, who is it
that is secure in his person or his liberty? If the President can extend this power to all subalterns in the army,
notwithstanding the laws and the Constitution, which
allow freedom of speech, and to a Senator the privilege
to utter his sentiments here without being questioned,
you might be arrested and put into prison before you
reached your lodgings. I tell you, Senators, you should
pause before you approve the acts of your President,
thus ruthlessly violating the Constitution of your country
and suspending its laws.

"It is our duty, then, so far from approving what the President has done by our votes, to give that distinguished magistrate a stern rebuke for the power that he has assumed; for the violence he has done to the Constitution of his country. We should tell him that we consider that our liberties are held by virtue of the supremacy of the laws, and in no other way; and that we will allow no magistrate, with impunity, to violate the Constitution and the laws of the land without giving him a stern rebuke.

"I believe it was the custom in the free commonwealth of Athens to decree all her magistrates who did not administer her government, or execute the functions of the government according to law, to be tyrants; and it was well done, for that people knew that liberty dwelt only under the shelter of the supremacy of law. One of the most alarming symptoms, to my mind, of these troubled times, is, that although such bold, palpable, and unmistakable violations of the Constitution of the country have been committed, with the Legislatures of sixteen or seventeen States of this Union in session, I have not seen a single legislative resolve censuring the Chief Magistrate for his conduct. It appears as if the spirit of liberty that animated our ancient sires had departed, when we behold men ready to see the Constitution of their country overturned, and throw up their hats and shout praises to him who does the deed. To my mind it is a most fearful indication of the degeneracy of the times in which we are."

The unlawful arrests, which were so frequent during the continuance of the late civil war, were among the most trying incidents of that trying period. Many of Gov. POWELL's most masterly efforts in the Senate were made with the view to bring about a change in the policy of the Administration in respect to these arrests. On the 9th of January, 1862, he spoke thus on the Resolution of Inquiry, introduced by Mr. SAULSBURY, in regard to the arrest and detention of certain citizens of Delaware:

" I hold that there is no authority vested by the Constitution of the United States in the President, or any of his Cabinet Ministers, to make these arrests. The Constitution defines what are the duties of the various departments of this Government. The duties of the Executive, and of the Legislative and Judicial powers, are each plainly marked out in the instrument. With each the powers are separate and distinct, and when either goes beyond the powers prescribed in the Constitution, that department usurps an authority not given to it, and deserves, and should receive, the censure of every man that is loyal to the Constitution. I ask Senators to point me to the clause in the Constitution that authorizes the President and his Cabinet Ministers to make these arrests. * * * * * The suspension of the writ of *habeas corpus* and making arrests are separate and distinct acts. One may be done without affecting the other. Arrests can only be made in the mode pointed out in the Constitution. It is plain and explicit on that subject. No citizen can be properly arrested and held except upon probable cause. He is entitled to a speedy trial in the district where the offense was committed ; and the Constitution says that no citizen shall be deprived of his life, liberty, or property without due process of law. If you arrest a citizen without charge, lock him up in one of your prisons for seventeen months, and then discharge him without trial, as has been done in many instances since this civil war commenced, do you not deprive him of his liberty without process of law, and violate the plain provisions of the Constitution ? * * *

" One of the wisest men of Greece once said that that was the best government where an insult offered to the meanest and poorest citizen was an insult to the State. It was a wise maxim. But, sir, these insults and injuries are offered not only to the poor and helpless, but they have been offered to some of the most respectable and loyal citizens of the United States—men who are the peers of the President and Cabinet, and the peers of Senators. Such men have for months been confined in prison, where they have been cruelly languishing, for no assigned cause, with no charges made against them. In many cases their prison doors have been opened at length, and they have been discharged without trial. Senators call this mercy! Mercy! to drag a man from his family without charge, in violation of the Constitution; to put him in one of your Bastiles, and to keep him there on bread and water, and on a pallet of straw, for months, and then to turn him out without giving him a trial, when he has all the time protested his innocence and demanded a trial! Sir, if that is mercy, I want none of it!

"I believe, from first to last, that five thousand of my constituents have been imprisoned—not all of them without the State—some in military camps within the State—many of them only for a short time. The wives, the children, the fathers and mothers of them, have written to me on the subject; many of the persons imprisoned have written to me; and in every instance they have stated that they did not know the cause of their arrest. They were, consequently, I suppose, arrested on suspicion, for the larger portion of them have been released without trial. * * * I can tell you, Senators, that the people of this country have determined that these arrests shall cease. They have decreed it at the ballot-box, and the voice of the people, like leaping thunder, has demanded that the Constitution shall be respected and maintained."

In a speech delivered in the Senate of the United States, on the 19th of January, 1863, on a bill of the House of Representatives concerning "State prisoners and the suspension of the writ of *habeas corpus*." Mr. POWELL being interrupted by Senator WRIGHT, with the declaration: "War is declared; it is the law of the land; and it is the duty of all loyal men to sustain the Government and carry on the war by taxes, by money, and in every other way"—thus answered:

"Mr. President, I by no means concur with the Senator. That would depend altogether on the kind of war. If I thought the war was one to overthrow the Constitution of my country and the liberties of the people, I would neither give men nor money to carry it on. I BELIEVE THE WAR IN WHICH WE ARE ENGAGED IS ONE OF THAT CHARACTER. CONSEQUENTLY, I HAVE NEITHER GIVEN MEN NOR MONEY TO CARRY IT ON, AND SO HELP ME GOD I NEVER WILL. I believed from the beginning that this war was brought on for the purpose of overthrowing the institutions of the Southern States, to get rid of the institution of African slavery, and, if you could not do it by war, then to dissolve the Union. That has been my opinion from the beginning, and when there was a resolution offered here by Mr. JOHNSON, similar to the one offered by Mr. CRITTENDEN, I voted against it; and I said in my place that I did not believe that it contained the truth. The facts developed from that day to this have confirmed me, and shown me that I was right in the opinion I then formed. I love the Constitution of my country. I am devoted to the Union of the States. I believed that this war would forever tear the Union asunder, and bring on the people untold evils, onerous taxes, heavy debt, and do no good. I believed we could never hold the people together by arms. Hence, I opposed the war, and believing, as I did, and do, I have not supported, and will not support, such a war.   *   †   *   *   *   *   *   *   *

"The Senator (WRIGHT, of Indiana) advocates the use of the fagot and the sword, death and destruction, in putting down the rebellion, and, at the same time, he throws into his speech the most Christian sentiments about Abraham and Lot parting in peace. It seems to me that this is strikingly inconsistent. I hope that my friend may be animated by those Christian feelings, and that he will dismiss that ferocious spirit in which he talks

5

about the use of the fagot and the fire and the sword. Sir, I think it is unbecoming a Christian age and a Christian country. It is not in accordance with the sublime teachings of Christianity. I know it is unbecoming the Christian character of the honorable Senator. I trust he used those expressions in hot haste, and that he has already repented of them. Make war against those who have arms in their hands; but for God's sake do not go with fire and fagot and sword, and destroy all that they have, and leave the poor women and children to starve. Do not do this, sir, unless you would be a by-word and a reproach to all the nations of the earth."

The discussion of the bill referred to was carried to great length. On the 23d of February, Mr. WILSON, of Massachusetts, delivered a speech in the Senate, in which he made a fierce attack upon the position of the majority in Kentucky, and upon their representative in the Senate. Governor POWELL replied to the remarks of his Massachusetts associate on the same day, and from his speech on the occasion we quote a few passages:

"I can tell the Senator that the Democracy of Kentucky, whom he so fiercely denounces, will not be offended by his assault upon them. Had the Senator praised them, I have no doubt that each and every one of them would have instituted a self-inquiry, and exclaimed with the Psalmist, " Lord, Lord, what evil hath thy servant done, that wicked men do praise him?" Nothing that can fall from the Senator's lips can damage them, save and except his praise. But, sir, the Senator calls them traitors! Allow me to say that there is not a man among them who could not most favorably contrast his loyalty with that of the Senator from Massachusetts. They have been true, loyal men- to the Constitution of the country and to the Union of their fathers, while the Senator and his Abolition associates have been constantly assailing both. The Senator arraigns the Senators who left here, and the Cabinet of Mr. Buchanan, and he says they hatched treason. Where was the Senator's loyalty then, that he did not rise here to teach those men a lesson by denouncing what he calls their treason? The Senator, while in their presence, was as quiet as a sucking dove. He waits till they have been a long time absent, and are a great way off, and then he makes his assault. He says the Cabinet of Mr. Buchanan stole everything they could get. Yes, sir, he charged that Cabinet with plunder and theft. Why did not the Senator make the charge when they were here to meet it? I am not here to defend the Senators who have left their seats. I thought they did wrong when they left. But I will tell the Senator one thing: where the Cabinet of Mr. Buchanan stole one cent, those in power under this administration have stolen thousands upon thousands of dollars. If you look into the reports made by your own party friends on our tables, I will aver that, since the foundation of the world, there never was such robbery as those reports exhibit. I suppose the Senator is more anxious for the ascendency of the rogues among his own partisans, than for the purity, honesty, and perpetuity of the constitutional government of our fathers; otherwise we should have heard him denouncing his own party friends, who have plundered the government of millions of money."

We come now to an interesting event in the Senatorial career of Governor Powell. In February, 1862, one of the members from Minnesota presented to the Senate the famous resolution of expulsion against the Kentucky Senator. This resolution, with its accompanying preamble, had been drawn up by Mr. Powell's own colleague, the Hon. Garrett Davis.* In the latter were

* The Hon. Garrett Davis was born in Mount Sterling, Kentucky, September 10th, 1801. He studied law and came to the bar in 1823. He was elected to the Legislature in 1833, and was twice re-elected. He was a member of the last Constitutional Convention of Kentucky, and a Repre-

embodied certain specific charges touching the loyalty of his colleague, which were deemed of sufficient importance to be referred to the Committee on the Judiciary for investigation. Although the committee reported adversely to the resolution, Mr. DAVIS made a lengthy argument before the Senate in favor of its adoption. Governor POWELL defended himself on the floor of the Senate in a masterly speech, delivered on the 14th of March, 1862. We append a few extracts from this speech, in order that the reader may be able to judge for himself of the means used to effect the Senator's expulsion, and of the character of the defense made:

"My colleague," said Mr. POWELL, "was kind enough in the very lengthy, and, I must say, somewhat bitter speech, that he delivered, to speak kindly of me personally. For that I thank him. I shall not, I trust, be governed by that impetuosity of temper, if not bitterness of feeling, that characterized my colleague. He stated to the Senate that this was a very unpleasant duty he had to perform. I hope that it was unpleasant, but, notwithstanding my colleague's disclaimer, his bearing, his manner, his temper, indicated to my mind that he was engaged in what to him was a work of love.

---

sentative in Congress from his district from 1839 to 1847. In 1861 he was elected to the United States Senate, and re-elected in 1867. He was a dis guished leader of the American or Know Nothing party, on the breaking up of the Whig organization in 1854. He was strongly opposed to the secession movement in 1860, and, up to third year of the war, was regarded as the most prominent of the Kentucky politicians who were advocates of the war policy of the administration. In 1863, becoming convinced that the war was not being prosecuted in the interests of peace, and for the object of "restoring the Union with the rights of the States preserved," Mr. DAVIS ceased to act with the Republican party. From that time to the present, he has faithfully served his State in the United States Senate, not only with commendable zeal, but with distinguished ability. With his knowledge of the designs of the Republican party, came to him the sense of the injury he had done his colleague. He promptly retracted the charges that had been made against Gov. POWELL in the preamble referred to above, and the two remained warm personal friends to the end of the latter's life.

"My colleague is the author of the resolution. It is before me now in his own handwriting. It was presented, however, by another Senator. I have no complaint against the honorable Senator who presented it, because my colleague is presumed to know all the facts connected with this matter better than any other Senator, or at least the action of the State of Kentucky; and, as he makes the charges, I do not attach the least blame to any Senator for presenting the resolution. I think, however, my colleage acted a little ungenerously in this, that while he was laboriously engaged in drawing up his bill of indictment, he did not notify me of the fact. The first intimation I had of it was when the resolution was presented by the honorable Senator from Minnesota; and, I must confess, that when I looked at it at the Clerk's desk, and found it to be in my colleague's handwriting, I was somewhat amazed. I thought courtesy, at least, to a colleague, would have induced the Senator to notify me of what he proposed to do. He did not do it. The case went to the Committee on the Judiciary; and, as the honorable Senator from Illinois, the chairman of that committee, announced, I did promptly, and I trust delicately, ask the committee to give it the earliest possible attention. Before that committee, however, had time to conclude their investigation, such was the hot haste and zeal of my colleague, that he publicly, in the Senate Chamber, demanded of the committee to know why they had not reported, or at least urged them to report as speedily as possible. They did report that the resolution ought not to pass; and the very day that they made the report, my colleague notified the Senate that he would move on the next-day to take it up. It did strike me that if my colleage had been governed by that courtesy which I am sure I would have extended to him, he would have come to me and consulted with me as to whether it would

be convenient for me to have it taken up the next day or
not; but he said not a word to me about it. * * * *

"My colleague stated to the Senate that the neutrality
which I and others advocated was not the neutrality of
the Union men of Kentucky. I will show hereafter from
the resolutions of their mass meetings, their speeches,
and from their votes in the Legislature, that they were
for the very neutrality I was for. My colleague said that
they had assumed neutrality to divert the attention of the
people—that is, that they were not sincere in it, if I understood him. So far as that neutrality is concerned, I
shall show presently by incontestable records that it was
inaugurated by the Union party of Kentucky. After it
was inaugurated, I and many others who had no hand in
inaugurating it, assumed it for the purpose of keeping
peace within the borders of Kentucky. If my colleague
was correct in the announcement he made, that that
policy was adopted with a view to divert the attention
of the people, I assure him that I had no hand in that.
Whether those who first proclaimed it and who supported
it during two or three canvasses in Kentucky were in
earnest about it, I do not mean to say. I know that
when I co-operated with them for neutrality I was honest, I was in earnest, I meant it; and I was really as-
tounded when my colleague proclaimed to the country,
from his place in the American Senate, that they assumed
that position for the purpose of diverting the public attention; in other words, in order to cheat the people.

"My colleague announced, too, that if I had gone with
the Union party, they would have received me with open
arms. He was kind enough to tell the Senate that I had
very great personal popularity in Kentucky, and to say
that he had never heard a person speak otherwise than
kindly of me personally. For that I thank him. I fear
that he does me over-justice in that. But I will say to
my colleague, that if I have the great popularity of which

he spoke, I obtained it by acting with strict integrity in all my transactions, both public and private. As a politician, I never avowed before the people anything that I did not honestly believe. I never assumed a political tenet for the purpose of cheating and deceiving the people in any way whatever, and I trust and believe that the honest, the noble, the chivalrous people of Kentucky, if they esteem me at all, do so because of my direction, my sincerity, my truth, my devotion to their interests and to the interests of my country. They are a brave, honest, and generous people, and if they know that one of their public servants errs, but errs honestly, they are ready to cover his defects with the broad mantle of their charity."

It will be seen that the gravamen of the indictment made against Governor POWELL was his adherence to the *neutrality* policy which had been inaugurated by the citizens of the State when the war broke out. He proved incontestibly that Mr. DAVIS himself, and numerous other well known Union men of the State, had given their past support to this same policy. He was accused of inviting the Confederates into the State, of associating with rebels, and of other like offenses. The resolution failed by so decided a majority that no further attempt was made toward his expulsion.

On the 5th day of December, 1862, Mr. STEVENS (of Pennsylvania) introduced into the House of Representatives of the United States a bill, entitled "A bill to indemnify the President and other persons for suspending the writ of *habeas corpus*, and acts done in pursuance thereof." The bill was passed. On the 22d of the same month, the Hon. GEORGE H. PENDLETON (of Ohio) presented a lengthy protest against the passage of the bill, which was signed by thirty-six members of the House. The bill came up for discussion in the Senate on the 28th of January, 1863, when Governor POWELL thus spoke against its passage :

"The scope and object of this bill is to prevent those who have been injured in their persons and their property from having redress in the courts. Alfred the Great has received more approval and won more distinction for having brought justice to the doors of every Englishman than for having fought a hundred pitched battles. But here, sir, we find the Senate of the United States engaged in offering impediments to the cause of justice, by closing the ordinary courts against all causes coming from those who have been injured by the minions of power. You would transfer all such causes to the Federal courts. I do not believe that, under the Constitution, you can confer on the Federal courts any such jurisdiction as is contemplated by this bill. Senators, allow me to tell you that the public will visit this act, if it should pass, with the harshest condemnation. A free, virtuous, and upright people cannot but do so. To limit the bringing of these actions to two years, and to drive out of the State courts the hundreds, and perhaps thousands, of poor men who are hardly able to fee a lawyer in the counties where they have been wronged, and to compel them to go to the United States Courts, is an utter denial of justice in many cases."

During the discussion, the positions taken by the Senator from Kentucky were attacked by Senator DOOLITTLE (of Wisconsin) who said: "I have probably heard the Senator make a hundred speeches on this floor, and the whole burden of them for the last two years has been denunciation of the Administration; but I have never heard him utter one word in condemnation of the men—his late associates—who are dripping all over with the blood of our fellow-citizens." To this, Gov. POWELL made answer:

"Mr. President, the Senator from Wisconsin seems to be terribly shocked that I should in my place utter a word of denunciation of those who have, in my opinion, attempted to overthrow the Constitution of my country;

and he enters the usual complaint against me, that I have not denounced the rebels. Allow me to tell that Senator that I expressly disapproved, on this floor, of what those rebels had done, and that when they were present. I said in my place that I thought they did wrong. It is not my habit to denounce men that are absent. I am dealing now with the Executive of the United States."

A SENATOR—"Is he present?"

Mr. POWELL.—"He is present in the capital; he is here in the city, and he has friends in this Chamber. I am not, therefore, like some Senators, who vindictively denounce gentlemen who are now in the rebellion, which they never dared do when those gentlemen were present as Senators and occupied seats on this floor. * * * * * I think I have the right to arraign the President and all others in authority who violate the Constitution of my country. I have the right to do so, as a Senator of a free and sovereign State. I am under oath. I am to sustain the Constitution, and it is my duty to assail all who infract that Constitution."

On the 5th day of January, 1863, Governor POWELL introduced a resolution in the United States Senate, in reference to Gen. GRANT's extraordinary manifesto, issued on the 17th of the previous month, by which the Jews, "as a class," were expelled from the department of the Tennessee. The resolution came up for discussion on the 9th of January, when Governor POWELL made a speech favoring its passage, from which we extract the annexed paragraphs:

"I have in my possession documents that go to establish the fact beyond the possibility of a doubt that the Jews, residents of the city of Paducah, Kentucky, some thirty gentlemen in number, were driven from their homes and their business by virtue of this order of Gen. GRANT, only having the short notice of four and twenty hours; that the Jewish women and children of that city

were expelled under that order; that there was not a
Jew left, man, woman, or child, except two women who
were prostrate on beds of sickness. I have the evidence
before me, set forth in a petition, and attested by some
twelve or fourteen of the most respectable Union citizens
of the city of Paducah, among others the Surveyor of the
Port, that those Jews of Paducah had at no time been
engaged in trade within the active lines of General
GRANT; that they had all the while been engaged in
legitimate business at their homes, and that there was
but one Jew, a resident of Paducah, who had gone out
of the State into the cotton region, and that one was
not at home, and consequently was not expelled from
his residence by this ruthless order.

"Mr. President, if we tamely submit to allow the
military power thus to encroach on the rights of the
citizen, we shall be setting a bad and most pernicious
example to those in command of our army. We should
administer to those in command of our armies the
sternest rebuke for such flagrant outrages upon the
rights of the citizen. These people are represented by
the most respectable citizens of Paducah to be loyal
men. Many of them are men who were not engaged
in commerce. They were mechanics, attending to their
daily avocations at their homes. In my judgment, it is
incumbent on this Senate, as the matter is before them,
to pass the resolution, and let Gen. GRANT and all the
other military commanders know that they are not to
encroach upon the rights and privileges of the peaceful
loyal citizens of this country. Pass the resolution, and
the example will be of the greatest importance, particularly at this time, when the constitutional rights of the
citizens are being stricken down and trodden under foot
throughout the entire country by the executive and military powers. We have submitted already too long and
tamely to the encroachments of the military upon the

civil rights of the citizen. Many of these Jews who were expelled from Paducah were known to me for many years as highly honorable and loyal citizens. This order expels them as a class from the entire department, and prevents them having a pass to approach his person to ask a redress of grievances. General GRANT might just as well expel the Baptists, or the Methodists, or the Episcopalians, or the Catholics, as a class, as to expel the Jews. All are alike protected in the enjoyment of their religion by the Constitution of our country. They are inoffensive citizens; and it is set forth in papers that I have before me, that two of the Jews who were expelled had served three months in the army of the United States in defense of the Union cause.

"There is no excuse for General GRANT for issuing the order. It may be said that some Jews in his department had been guilty of illegal traffic. If so, expel them. I do not wish to shield a Jew or a Gentile from just punishment for the infraction of the law. He should have directed his order to the offenders, and should have punished them; but, sir, so far from doing that, he punishes a whole people as a class; without specific charge, hearing, or trial, he drives out inoffensive, loyal people, men, women, and children, from a city far distant from his headquarters, without giving them the least opportunity to meet and repel charges that might be brought against them. Such conduct is utterly indefensible. I regret that Gen. GRANT issued such an order. Gen. GRANT's conduct heretofore as a soldier has been that of a brave and a gallant officer; he has fought well on many fields; for that I commend him. But while I commend him for his gallant conduct, I must censure him for this most atrocious and illegal order. It is inhuman and monstrous. It would be unworthy of the most despotic government in the most despotic period of the world's history. Sir, we should rebuke such conduct. I regret that some other less meri-

torious officer of the army had not issued this order. I
regret that Gen. GRANT has issued it; but, sir, we owe it
to ourselves, we owe it to the civil and religious liberty
of the citizen, to put our condemnation upon it."   .

It is a well known fact that the freedom of elections
in Kentucky, Missouri, Maryland, and other States, was
imperiously contemned by the executive and his military
subordinates, from the moment the Federal power obtained control over the populations of these Commonwealths, through its stationary garrisons of armed troops.
In Kentucky, as early as 1863, the State Democratic
Convention that assembled at Frankfort, was dispersed
by the military, and its members threatened with arrest,
should they attempt to reassemble. With a Democratic
majority in the State of fully forty thousand votes, the
candidate of the party for the office of Governor—the
Hon. CHARLES A. WICKLIFFE—was defeated in the election
of that year, through the action of the military, who took
forcible possession of the polls in many places, closed
them altogether in others, and allowed none to vote who
were unwilling to do so in accordance with the views
of the party in power. In February, 1864, a bill was
introduced into the United States Senate " to prevent
officers of the army and navy, and other persons engaged
in the military and naval service of the United States,
from interfering in elections in the States." The bill
provided that all such officers, on conviction of having
interfered to prevent free elections in the States, should
be punished by fine and imprisonment, and should be
forever debarred from holding office under the Government of the United States. On the 3d and 4th of March
following the introduction of the bill, Governor POWELL
addresssed the Senate at great length in support of the
measure. The following paragraphs from this speech
will be read with interest:

  " It cannot be doubted that upon the keeping of the
elective franchise absolutely free depends the very exist-

ence of our form of government and our republican institutions. Free States, in all ages, have regarded the purity of the elective franchise as of the greatest and most vital importance, and have enacted severe penal laws for the punishment of those who interfered, by force or fraud, to prevent free elections. I believe there is no Government on the face of the earth in which elections have been carried on for the purpose of appointing any of the officers of the Government, save and except the United States of America, that has not had laws to punish, and severely punish, those who should interfere with the freedom of the elective franchise. All the Republics of antiquity had the severest laws punishing those who interfered with the freedom of their elections.

" By the spirit of the Constitution of the United States, and by the Constitution of every State in the Union, the military is to be kept in strict subordination to the civil power; and I suppose that those who went before us never thought we should have rulers so wicked and corrupt as to use the machinery of the Federal Government for the purpose of prostrating the freedom of elections in the States; otherwise, I am sure that such laws as the one before us would have been enacted long before this. I find, upon examination, that seven of the States of the Union have enacted statutes to prevent soldiers making their appearance on election day at the places where the elections are held.

" With us, Mr. President, sovereignty resides in the people, and the people, by the exercise of free suffrage, declare their will and appoint their agencies to carry on the Government. He who attempts to interfere with this most inestimable right, whether he be President, Major General, or citizen, is an enemy to the Republic, and deserves the harshest punishment. In order to have free elections, there must be free speech and a free press; the sovereign people must have an opportunity of forming an enlightened public opinion upon the questions at issue, which can only be done after full and free discussion. Free speech and a free press in a Government like ours are the soul of republican institutions; free suffrage is the very heart-strings of civil liberty. To be free, the elections must be conducted in accordance with laws so framed as to prevent fraud, force, intimidation, corruption, and venality, superintended by election judges and officers independent of the Executive or any other power of the Government.

"The Committee on Military Affairs, who made a very elaborate report, which I have before me, and which I shall presently review, justify the military in all they have done in controlling elections. The sole object and design of the committee, in their report, seems to be the justification and vindication of the military authorities for their atrocious assault on the rights of the States and the liberties of the people, and their wicked and illegal interference in elections; and they assault every person who says or does anything tending to prove that the military have usurped powers that belong to the civil officers of the States and to the people. The committee justify the President and the military authorities for this interference in elections upon the ground that it was right and proper that the military arm should have been so used to protect the voters—" the loyal voters," as they are called in the report. The Constitution prescribes the duty of the Chief Magistrate on this subject, and the President of the United States has no auhority or power to send his military into one of the adhering States for the purpose of preventing domestic violence at the polls, unless he had been invited to do so by the State authorities; for the Constitution plainly and distinctly provides that he shall do it on application of the Legislature, if in session, and if that cannot be, then on the application of the Executive.

"There never was a time, it does not exist now, and has not existed since this unfortunate civil war commenced, in which it was necessary for the President to overthrow the Constitution and elevate the military above the civil power. There is power enough in the Constitution to furnish the President every dollar and every man needed for this war. Congress can give him the sword and the purse. What more can you confer? Nothing. Where, then, the necessity and the excuse for these wanton violations of the Constitution, this reckless overthrow of the liberties of the people, this setting at naught the laws and the Constitutions of the States, the regulating of elections by the sword? None!—none! The genius of our Government is founded upon the principle that the military shall be kept in strict subordination to the civil power."

We have no room, either for the detailed evidence given by Governor Powell of the fact that the President and his subordinates had wrongfully interfered in the State elections, or for the authorities quoted by him in proof of his position that the Constitution gave no such power to interfere, whether to him or them. In the latter part of his speech, Gov. Powell thus pays his respects to Secretary Stanton and Gen. B. F. Butler, with reference to the extraordinary order of the former of November 30, 1863, by which he undertook to transfer certain Southern churches from the ownership and occupancy of their legitimate pastors and proprietors to parties whose loyalty he was not so much disposed to question:

"The Secretary of War, by virtue of what authority I do not know, has undertaken to administer the churches. Yes, sir, Edwin M. Stanton and General Butler are making themselves a kind of chief pontiffs, and are 'running the churches,' the one in the valley of the Mississippi and the other in Norfolk and Portsmouth. If the President had decided to appoint persons to regulate and supervise the churches, and to take the religion of the people under his ·control, I would have supposed he would have selected gentlemen distinguished for their charity, kindness, and benevolence; men of high moral tone, meek and gentle in their manners; men eminent for their piety and theological learning, whose lives were adorned with every Christian virtue, to have discharged this most responsible and delicate trust. The two persons who have unlawfully assumed the control of the churches have none of the qualifications that I have indicated. If the President had searched the entire country, I do not believe he could have found two persons upon whom to confer this delicate trust more unsavory than EDWIN M. STANTON and BENJAMIN F. BUTLER. In their manners and intercourse they are both heartless ruffians; they are strangers to kindness, gentleness, benevolence, and those elevated manly virtues that gracefully adorn the life of a Christian gentleman. But, sir, they have usurped the power to control the churches in the localities I have mentioned, in violation of the Constitution and the rights of the people who own those houses of public worship.

"There is a little curious history about this subject. I have here the order of the Secretary of War placing under the control of Bishop AMES all the churches of the departments of the Missouri, the Tennessee, and the Gulf, belonging to the Methodist Episcopal Church, South. This is one of the most startling usurpations of the military power that has fallen under my notice. The Constitution secures religious freedom to the citizen explicitly. Where did the Secretary of War get the power to transfer all these churches to the control of Bishop AMES?

"Sir, the first article in the Amendments of the Constitution says:

"'Congress shall make no law respecting an establishment of religion, or prohibiting the free exercise thereof.'

"The Secretary of War violated that provision of the Constitution when he assumed jurisdiction over these

churches. By what authority does he assume to appoint
indirectly, through Bishop AMES, ministers to all the
churches in the three departments mentioned belonging
to the people called the Methodist Episcopal Church,
South? Bishop AMES does not belong to that Church
himself. He belongs to the Methodist Episcopal Church,
North. The Methodist Episcopal Church, North, and the
Methodist Episcopal Church, South, are two separate and
distinct institutions. They divided, I believe, in May,
1845. Since then they have been separate and distinct
ecclesiastical bodies. Mr. STANTON, by this unauthorized
and unconstitutional order, has clothed Bishop AMES with
the power to take possession of all those churches. The
minister may be loyal, but if he happens to have been
appointed by a disloyal Bishop, he must be kicked out."

On the 19th of December, 1864, Governor POWELL
presented in the Senate a resolution of inquiry in reference to the arrest of "two prominent citizens of Kentucky, Colonel R. T. JACOB, Lieutenant Governor of
Kentucky, and Colonel FRANK WOLFORD, one of the
Presidential Electors of the State." During the discussion which followed the presentation of the resolution,
Governor POWELL thus gave expression to his views:

"The Senator from Missouri (Mr. HENDERSON) and the
Senator from Iowa (Mr. GRIMES), and others, have said
that they believe that, when the facts shall be made
known to us by his Excellency, the President, the military authorities will be vindicated for these arrests.
That may be, but I do not think it will be so. I believe
that these gentlemen have been arrested wrongfully.
They were certainly arrested without warrant as prescribed in the Constitution and laws of their country,
and I know them well enough to know that if they are
charged with any crime or offense, all they want is to
be brought before a legally constituted tribunal and
tried. As a personal and political friend of Lieutenant

6

Governor JACOB and Colonel WOLFORD, I court the investigation. They are Christian gentlemen; they are men of ability; they are men of honor; they are brave men, and they have attested their bravery on many a well-fought battle-field. Such men cannot be guilty of crime; and I will say here for them, as their friend and their representative, that all they ask is to meet their accusers face to face. One of them we know to be in close confinement; we know not where the other is; he was ordered through the lines, and it was said in the newspapers that the Confederate authorities refused to receive him, and he was brought back again. He is the second civil officer in the Government of Kentucky, and he ought to be there to attend to his official duties. These gentlemen, when they were arrested, were both citizens, though they had both been in the army and rendered distinguished service. I did not expect that any opposition would be made to this resolution. I had supposed that here at least there was still left some lingering love for the constitutional and civil liberties of the citizen. I had supposed that there was still some regard felt here for those who, during this rebellion, had periled their lives in the Union cause in a hundred battles."

On the 18th of January, Governor POWELL called up the resolution, some time before offered by him, by which the Secretary of War was directed to transmit to the Senate the report made by a commission appointed to investigate the conduct of General PAINE while in command at Paducah. A lengthy discussion followed, in which many Senators took part, the majority striving to stifle all inquiry into the doings of one of the most cruel, barbarous, and dishonest of all the bad men that were placed in authority during the war over the destinies of a suffering people. Governor POWELL supported his resolution in a speech of some length, in which he said that the report, of which he had read a newspaper account, "disclosed a degree of barbarity, cruelty, and pillage" which, he dared say, "had not been equaled in the annals of any Christian people. I have reason to believe, that when the facts shall be known, that in all the dark and bloody annals of tyrants, there never has been, in any Christian age, such acts of cruelty and plunder as have been afflicted on the people of Paducah and the surrounding country by this man PAINE and his confederates. I wish them brought to trial, and, if found guilty, to be punished with death; for if one tittle of the statements in these papers be true, that is the lightest punishment they deserve."

Mr. CONNESS, of California—"Mr. President, if it were not an ordinary circumstance for the honorable Senator from Kentucky to launch his denunciations against the officers of the Government in this Chamber, I would feel, for one, more inclined to vote with him on such occasions as the present. I confess that I am tired of listening to his *ex parte* statements; and I wish to put my protest here, and to invite the honorable Senator from Kentucky occasionally to divide his vengeance with the cruel and barbarous wretches who have persecuted, starved, and murdered our brave men in the field who have been taken prisoners."

Mr. POWELL—"Mr. President, one word to the Senator from California. He seems to think he is a kind of *censor morum* of the Senate, and says he is tired—tired of hearing my denunciation of Union officers. I dare say the Senator will grow much more tired than he is already. I am not responsible for the Senator's being wearied when he hears criminals, robbers, and thieves denounced. If it wearies the Senator to hear such men denounced, I care not if he should faint under the exhaustion. I have never denounced a soldier who did his duty. I honor the brave Christian gentleman and soldier who carries the flag of his country amid the storm of battle. All honor to the brave soldiers who fight and do not steal. Disgrace and infamy eternal to all pillagers and plunderers. Upon what battle-field did Gen. PAINE win honors? And of all the men who have been charged with peculation, and have been denounced by me, let the Senator point to a single battle-field where they carried the stars and stripes to victory. Men who go about punishing women and children, and plundering the people, are miscreants and cowards; they disgrace your arms when you intrust them with commands. I have denounced none except those who I believed were guilty of crime, of peculation, and robbery; and all I desire in regard to such is, that they shall be tried, and, if found guilty, punished. The Senator thinks I should denounce other people. I denounce all cruelty to prisoners, whether it be by rebel or Union men. No true-hearted and brave soldier will do anything of the kind. I think I know something about my duties here, and how I ought to present questions to the Senate; and I think it is not becoming in that Senator to tell me what character of speeches I shall make. Neither does it become him, when I am talking about the misconduct of an officer of my own Government, to demand of me that I go outside and abuse rebels and rebeldom."

When in 1864 the party in power threw aside the pretense that the war was being conducted for the object of restoring the Union, with the rights of the States preserved, and brought forward its joint resolution proposing amendments to the Constitution, one of which was to the effect that involuntary servitude, except for crime, should no longer be permitted to exist in any State of the Union, he denounced the action of the majority with great force and power. He "did not believe that it was ever designed by the founders of the government that the Constitution should be so amended as to destroy property." He continued:

"I do not believe it is the province of the Federal Government to say what is or what is not property. Its province is to guard, protect, and secure, rather than to destroy. If you admit the principle contended for by the gentlemen who urge this amendment, logic would lead them to the conclusion that the General Government could, by an amendment to its Constitution, regulate every domestic matter in the States. If it, by constitutional amendment, can regulate the relation of master and servant, it certainly can, on the same principle, make regulations concerning the relation of parent and child, husband and wife, and guardian and ward. If it has the right to strike down property in slaves, it certainly would have a right to strike down property in horses, to make a partition of the land, and to say that none shall hold land in any State in the Union in fee simple. It is not my purpose, however, to discuss the question in that light, for it has been elaborately discussed before.

"I do not think, Mr. President, that those who are now urging this constitutional amendment have acted in good faith toward the adhering slave States. If you will trace their history from the very beginning in connection with this whole subject of slavery in the States, I think you will find that they have not acted with that directness and candor that should characterize bold, honest, and fearless men. Why, sir, do you suppose that such propositions would have been proposed heretofore? Not at all. We were told by the Government, in every form in which it could speak, at the beginning of this revolution, that whatever might be the result, the institutions of the States would remain as they were. The President, in his inaugural address, announced that he had no constitutional power to interfere with the institution of slavery in the States. The Secretary of State announced it in a communication which he sent abroad. Congress, by a resolution, announced virtually the same thing when they declared that the object of the war was to restore the Union as it was and to maintain the Constitution as it is.

"All these measures and promises have been utterly repudiated by the party in power. It seems as if their sole object was to deceive in order to obtain power, and the moment they obtain power they exercise it. We are surrounded by circumstances that cause these valiant knights to think they can do this with impunity, and at once they go to work. Heretofore they have said that not only they had not the power, but whatever might be the result of the present contest, the status of this institution would remain as it was. I do not mean to say that they said they had no power to pass a constitutional amendment; but this portion of my remarks is directed to other policies that have been advocated and other laws that have been passed or are now proposed in this Chamber. I think it must be admitted by all candid men that the border States have been dealt with in bad faith. The Government has not kept faith with them. All candid, all truthful, all honest men must know it and must admit it."

The extracts which we have given from speeches made by Governor POWELL in the United States Senate will not only suffice to give the reader a competent idea of his style and the force of his language, but will enable him to see also how entirely consistent he was in the enunciation of his views. With all the master-minds of the era that preceded that in which wide-spread fanaticism involved the country in civil war, his idea of our form of government was, that it was a compact between sovereign States, binding upon each of its members so long and in so far as its reserved rights were acknowledged and protected thereunder. He did not believe that the Federal Government had any rightful power, under the Constitution, to make war upon the Southern States in order to keep them in the Union;

and believing so, he voted boldly and consistently against every measure brought forward in the National Congress looking to coercion as a means of restoring the Union. His sympathies were, doubtless, with the people of his own section, not because he thought their representatives had acted wisely or well, but because of the fact—which none knew better than he—that they had been goaded into a false position by a thoroughly fanatical and a thoroughly selfish majority, whose fixed determination it was, from the beginning, either to destroy the institution of slavery, or themselves to form a government from which should be excluded the entire slave territory.

As to slavery, abstractly speaking, he would doubtless have been well pleased if no such institution existed in the country. But the slaves were here. They had been recognized as property for ages. They could not live as equals of the whites in the same territory, and there was no possibility of colonizing them in other lands without bankrupting the country. As a general thing, they were treated humanely, and were contented and happy. Their situation was a thousand times better than was that of any of their race on the face of the globe. The humanizing and elevating influence of the Christian religion was being felt among them, and daily the acknowledged evils of the system were being diminished. These evils would have gradually disappeared altogether had it not been for the constant agitation that had been kept up for twenty years or more in the North against the system. Their own safety from violence at the hands of an ignorant and infuriated race obliged the people of the South to keep out of their territory the propagators of revolutionary ideas, and the dissemination in the South of books and papers in which these ideas were upheld naturally prevented Southern men from attempting to educate their slaves. For these reasons, and many others—the principal of which were the unfitness of the slaves for the responsibilities of a higher social position in the State, and their well known incapacity to take care of themselves—Governor POWELL, and thousands of other good and philanthropic men, were utterly opposed to any action on the part of the Federal Government looking to the immediate and enforced emancipation of the blacks.*

He felt keenly the great wrong which would be done to thousands of innocent parties all over the South by the enforced emancipation of their slaves. He could not see why the widows and orphans who were slave-owners in that section, and the many other persons who had taken no part in the rebellion, should be compelled to give up their property for an object that was deemed necessary for the welfare of the whole country, while the entire population of the North—though no more loyal— were to be exempted from any of its costs. He often referred in his speeches to the bad faith of the Government toward Kentucky and the other border States in regard to the enforced emancipation of their slaves, and the consequent destruction of the property of their citi-

---

* Emancipation, though now an accomplished fact, is still only an experiment; and, so far as the blacks are concerned, is thought by many to be one of extremely problematical value. No one now believes that the white and black races can live together on a footing of complete social and political equality. One or the other race will certainly have to take the inferior position, and that it will not be the whites that will do this, is sufficiently evidenced by the known characteristics of the two races. That the negroes, taken as a body, are as well cared for, as well fed, and as well clothed, or that they are less disposed to be vicious, or less subject to disease, since their emancipation, no one that knows anything about the subject will pretend to say. Wholly unprepared for the responsibilities of the position which they have been made to occupy, and prone by nature and habit to improvidence and carelessness in regard to the future, there can be but little hope that sudden emancipation will prove a benefit to them or to the country. That the whites of the South, if permitted, will labor to improve their condition, both social and moral, there can be no question. The character which Southerners have heretofore borne for humanity is a sufficient assurance of this. But whatever may be the solution of the experiment of negro emancipation, social and political equality with the whites will never be one of its permanent results.

zens. Kentucky had never seceded, and she had never been out of the Union. In the opinion of many persons, in the North as well as in the South, it was to this fact that was to be attributed the success of the Union armies. She had furnished her quota of men to the armies of the government, and her sons had laid down their lives fighting for the integrity of the Union, on almost every battlefield of the war. Her territory had been overrun by the armies of both sections, her substance eaten up, her fields laid waste, and her citizens plundered; and now, because, it would seem, of the very miseries she had endured, she was to be made to pay a heavier price for the removal of what was considered the great obstacle in the way of national unity and peace than all her sister Commonwealths of the North put together. Governor POWELL was in the habit of commenting with becoming freedom and with just severity upon this whole scheme of the administration, which he looked upon not only as highly dishonorable, but as cruelly unjust.

In the winter of 1866-7, the name of Governor POWELL was again presented to the Legislature, then in session, for the position of United States Senator. Many of the members of both Houses of the General Assembly for the session named had secured their seats through the influence and intervention of the military authorities which had been scattered over the State at the date of their election. None of these were Democrats, and few, if any, truly represented the views of their constituencies. Although constituting a minority in the body of which they were members, these Radicals and *quasi* Radicals found themselves numerous enough to prevent the election of one who had made himself especially obnoxious to them on account of his denunciation in the United States Senate of the means that had secured to them their seats. The balloting was carried on for weeks, without any result. At length, it becoming apparent to Governor POWELL that the object of the Radical element in the Legislature was to prevent, if possible, any election at all of a Senator in Congress during the session, and thus to leave Kentucky so far unrepresented in the councils of the nation, he wrote to his friends in that body a patriotic letter, in which he begged them to withdraw his name, and to make a nomination that would insure a number of votes sufficient to counteract the machinations of their Radical and anti-Democratic fellow-members. His advice was followed, and the result was the election of the Hon. GARRETT DAVIS.

In looking over the record of Governor POWELL's public life, we are struck with its singular unity and consistency. His political integrity was without blemish. Never did he assume a position that was not in perfect keeping with his political faith. He opposed secession, not only because he believed it to be no proper remedy for the evils it was designed to cure, but because, with his whole heart and soul, he was attached to the Union of the States. He opposed the war of coercion, not only because he believed that the Federal Government had no rightful authority to carry on a war against sovereign States, but because he felt that such a course would endanger the Constitution and tend to the formation of a consolidated and despotic government. He believed, with many of the wisest men of the country, that peaceful secession was better than war. He believed that the sober second thought of the people would soon discover a way to recover their abandoned unity, without expense, without bloodshed, and without that bitterness of feeling which is a concomitant of all civil wars. Who shall say that he, and the thousands of his countrymen that thought as he did, were wrong? Not, assuredly, any great number of his fellow-citizens of Kentucky. Not, certainly, they who, in their own names and in the names of the representatives of the people by whose authority they act, lay this tribute of their respect upon his honored grave.

APPENDIX.

At a meeting of the bar of Henderson, held on the 5th day of July, 1867, of which the Hon. ARCHIBALD DIXON was called to the Chair, and MALCOLM YEAMAN, Esq., appointed Secretary, the following expression, *in memoriam* of the Hon. L. W. POWELL, was adopted :

" The Great Creator having stricken in death the Hon. L. W. POWELL, we, his associates in the legal profession, deem it fit to add our tribute of respect to his memory. Some of us have known him from early life—all of us for many years. To know him was to love him, and those who knew him best loved him most. As a public man, his name and reputation are national, and inseparably interwoven with these are those rarest of jewels, seldom possessed by politicians—honesty and consistency. His highest aim was to serve his country—his greatest desire its peace, prosperity, and liberty.

" As a citizen, he was kind and gentle to all, ever ready to extend the hand of welcome to the stranger, and of help to the needy. As a lawyer, he was faithful to his trust, vigilant, and industrious—at all times bringing to bear his great powers of intellect to the interest of his client, and ever courteous and generous to his adversary. As a man, he was honest and true, bearing malice to none, and doing to others as he would have them do unto him. Always a lover of peace, and possessing a heart overflowing with kindly impulses, his loss will be great to the whole country, but none will lament it more than we who knew him best.

"It is our request that this testimonial to the memory of our departed friend be spread on the records of our several courts, and that our city papers publish the same.

"We tender to the bereaved family of the deceased our heartfelt sympathy and condolence.

"(Signed,)

"ARCH'LD DIXON, *Ch'n*,   S. B. VANCE,
"JOHN W. CROCKETT,   HENRY DIXON,
"BEN. P. CISSELL,   JOHN YOUNG BROWN,
"HARVEY YEAMAN,   JAMES F. CLAY,
"CHARLES EAVES,   MALCOLM YEAMAN,
"GEORGE H. TAYLOR,   GRANT GREEN,
"H. F. TURNER,   P. H. LOCKETT,
"A. J. ANDERSON,   J. C. ATKINSON,
"A. T. DUDLEY,   J. P. BRECKINRIDGE."

The annexed notice of the death of Governor Powell was written by his old friend and school-fellow, the Hon. Samuel B. Churchill, the present Secretary of State of Kentucky, and first appeared in the columns of the *Frankfort Yeoman* on the 9th day of July, 1867:

GOVERNOR L. W. POWELL.

Kentucky has lost one of her brightest jewels. Gov. Lazarus W. Powell is no more, having breathed his last at Henderson at four o'clock on the evening of July the 3d. A wail of sorrow will come up from every county in the State, for he was honored and loved wherever known—and he was well known throughout the length and breadth of the entire Commonwealth. He leaves behind him a name as unsullied as the spotless snow, and Kentucky will engrave it upon the tablets which transmit to posterity the memory of her Clays and Rowans, her Breckinridges and Crittendens, and her illustrious host of heroes and statesmen who have already passed "the slender bounds which separate time from eternity."

We knew Governor POWELL intimately, long, and well. We were school-boys together, and well do we recollect the first day he entered St. Joseph's College, at Bardstown. He came there in 1830, a tall, manly, energetic boy, full of life and pluck, eager after knowledge; and most rapid was his advancement. He came alone, without acquaintance or friend, and unknown to all; but his genial manners, his noble bearing, his bright intellect, and close application to study, soon won for him a host of friends. He not only won the friendship but the perfect confidence and esteem of all, and they felt that, when he went forth to the battle of life, he would not only leave behind him an unsullied name, but that he too, perchance, might leave his foot-prints on the sands of time. Many of those college boys have passed to the shadowy land; but there remains not one, wherever he may be, whose eyes will not be suffused with tears when he reads the sad announcement of his death.

In 1833 he took his degree of Bachelor of Arts, and then commenced the study of the law with the distinguished ROWAN. Judge ROWAN was not only one of the greatest orators, but one of the most thoroughly accomplished gentlemen of his day—the very soul of truth and honor; and, listening to the counsel and instruction which fell from the lips of this wise Gamaliel, Governor POWELL learned those lessons of truth, wisdom, and justice which he never forgot or cast aside throughout his whole brilliant career. Governor POWELL also attended the law lectures at Transylvania University, and was admitted to the bar in 1835.

Governor POWELL commenced the practice of his profession in the county of Henderson, where he was born October the 6th, 1812, and he soon took rank with the first lawyers of the State. He was not permitted, how-

ever, to devote his time entirely to his profession; for, as
early as 1836, he was elected a member of the House of
Representatives, where he gave promise of that future
which he so nobly redeemed in after years. In 1844 he
canvassed a portion of the State as one of the electors
for President POLK, and in 1848 he was the Democratic
candidate for Governor. His opponent was the Hon.
JOHN J. CRITTENDEN, who was the candidate of the Whigs,
and who was one of the most popular and brilliant men
that ever adorned the State. The Whigs at that time
were in the ascendency; but in that heated contest Gov.
POWELL exhibited such energy, eloquence, and talents, as
made him then the acknowledged leader of the Democratic party.

In 1851 Governor POWELL was again the Democratic
candidate, and was triumphantly elected. For twenty
years before this the Whigs had entire control of the
State, and when he came to Frankfort to administer the
government he had much to encounter, both in the way
of social and political prejudice. At that time partisan
feeling ran high; but no man in the whole State could
have been elected Governor who was more fitted for the
difficult position in which he was placed. Dignified and
yet affable, manly and yet courteous, and dispensing a
hospitality alike graceful, profuse, and heartfelt, he banished all political asperities from the social circle, whilst
his administration of public affairs was marked by prudence and energy, purity and firmness, statesmanship and
wisdom.

During his term of office there was no embezzlement
of the public moneys, no fraud, no peculation, no oppression, but four years of uninterrupted confidence and quiet
and happiness among the people. They knew that an
honest man and able statesman was at the helm, and
that the ship of State was moored in a safe harbor. In
Frankfort Governor POWELL will be long remembered,

both as the eminent statesman and the gentleman, who made the Executive Mansion the home of elegance, hospitality, and refinement.

When we had the prospect of a Mormon war, Gov. POWELL was appointed by President BUCHANAN one of the Peace Commissioners to visit Utah, and, in compliance with instructions and the duties of his office, he proceeded to Salt Lake City in the spring of 1858. We met him in St. Louis on his way there, and found that he was filled with the hope that he would be able to give quiet to the country and prevent all unnecessary effusion of blood. That distinguished General, ALBERT SIDNEY JOHNSTON, was in command of the military, and, by the joint efforts of himself and the Commissioners, quiet and order was restored without the firing of a single gun.

Returning from this mission, where he had rendered such signal service to his country, he took his seat in the Senate of the United States on the 4th day of March, 1859, the Hon. JOHN J. CRITTENDEN being his colleague. At this time the political atmosphere looked darkly ominous of coming evils, and, in 1860, in a calamitous hour for the Republic, ABRAHAM LINCOLN was elected President. Most of the Southern States seceded, and many Senators retired from their places in the Senate. Gov. POWELL, however, retained his seat to the conclusion of his term, and his manly voice was constantly raised in behalf of the Constitution and civil liberty. Although threatened with imprisonment and exile, his brave heart was not daunted, and his eloquent denunciations of the usurpations of the Government were read throughout the land. Nobly did he vindicate the privileges of the writ of *habeas corpus*, and many a lonely prisoner, ruthlessly torn from his family and sent without trial or accusation to be immured in the gloom of loathsome bastiles, felt his heart cheered and his hopes revive when he heard how nobly and fearlessly the Kentucky

Senator stood forth in defense of the Constitution and the liberty of free speech and a free press.

His voice will be heard on earth no more, but his noble deeds will be remembered, and his memory will be cherished in the hearts of all true Kentuckians. Passion and prejudice will pass away, and coming generations will enshrine his name among the truest patriots of the land. When the base sycophants of power who are willing to degrade their own race, and "bend the supple hinges of the knee that thrift may follow fawning," have sunk into infamy, then will the name of LAZARUS POWELL shine forth as pure and bright as the stars of Heaven. Oh that he had lived to have seen restored the liberties of his country! How sadly do we miss him, and how much we need his counsel now. Kentucky would love so much to honor him and to show all the world how much she prized and valued and loved him; but, alas! he can receive no more honors, and can do the State no more service. He was one of the most sincere, candid, and upright men we ever knew, and no man ever confided in him in vain. Frank and open in the avowal of his principles, he was always ready to maintain what he believed to be truth, and was in its truest sense an honest man—that noblest work of God.

Let Kentucky, his native State, and the State he so much loved, guard well his name and fame, that, in the great Hereafter, it may shine forth as a beacon light to cheer on her sons who tread the paths of honesty and honor. Such men as LAZARUS W. POWELL are the brightest jewels of a State, and are the gems which glorify God, dignify man, and ennoble history.

PROCEEDINGS OF THE GENERAL ASSEMBLY IN RELATION TO
THE DEATH OF GOVERNOR POWELL.

On the 5th day of March, Mr. I. A. SPALDING, in the
Senate, and Governor BERIAH MAGOFFIN, in the House of
Representatives, reported the following resolutions from
the several committees to whom had been referred that
portion of the Governor's message which relates to the
death of Governor L. W. POWELL:

WHEREAS, An inscrutable Providence has terminated the
career of LAZARUS W. POWELL, in the prime of his manhood and in the maturity of his fame, it is deemed
fitting and proper that the representatives of the people
of his native State should pay a becoming tribute to his
memory and give formal expression to their appreciation
of his virtues. Nature had richly endowed him with all
the nobler characteristics of the people among whom he
was born and had lived, and these characteristics he
illustrated in every relation of life. He was an indulgent yet watchful parent, a generous and exemplary
citizen, a sincere and unfaltering friend, a sagacious and
prudent statesman, a brave and incorruptible patriot,
whose philanthropy embraced all his kind and all his
country; therefore, be it

1. *Resolved by the General Assembly of the Commonwealth
of Kentucky*, That in the death of LAZARUS W. POWELL
the State has lost one of her most cherished sons, the
people one of their most trusted and valued friends, and
the Republic a statesman whose wise counsels and lofty
patriotism were never more needed than in the perils
through which the country is now passing.

2. That we sincerely sympathize with his children and
family in the irreparable loss they have sustained.

3. That, as a mark of respect to the memory of the
deceased, we will wear the usual badge of mourning for
thirty days, and that a copy of the foregoing resolutions
be transmitted to his family.

Said resolutions were twice read and unanimously
adopted.

7

REMARKS OF SENATORS.

Mr. Speaker : The resolutions just read recall to our minds a man whose life was the pride of the people of Kentucky, and whose death fills their hearts with sorrow. In adopting them, we propose not merely to observe a custom—not to offer a cold and formal tribute to departed greatness, nor to tender empty adulations to gilded and soulless glory—but we come, in obedience to the dictates of a generous affection, and as the representatives of a stricken Commonwealth, to render a mournful tribute to to the name and memory of one of her most gifted and beloved sons.

No country has more glorious recollections than Kentucky, and no people cherish them with a deeper reverence than do her children.

The world always appreciates and honors true greatness. In all ages and among all peoples, the richest treasures of language and the best efforts of genius have been lavished in the attempt to honor the names and perpetuate the virtues of the great.

And should the benign genius of our Commonwealth—the nursing mother of us all—summon from her silent sepulchres those of her children who have best illustrated the virtues of true manhood and elevated statesmanship, prominent in their ranks would stand him whose loss we now deplore and whose name we here unite to honor.

Equal to the duties and responsibilities of every station to which he was called, Governor Powell seemed pre-eminently endowed with the virtues appropriate to all the relations of life. The history of such a man is a most useful study. In contemplating it we are impressed not more with the noble objects of his ambition and the splendid success achieved in their pursuit, than with the sublime and beautiful virtues that adorned his course. And we cannot fail to be impressed by its lessons with a higher regard for that truth and justice and patriotism which characterized his life.

LAZARUS W. POWELL was born in Henderson county, in this State, on the 6th day of October, 1812, and grew up to manhood amid the wild and rugged scenes of what was then a backwoods country. On this hardy theater he developed a form naturally good into the full proportions of a perfect manhood, and a disposition naturally frank, sincere, and kind into a perfect model of cordial and generous and manly character. At the age of nineteen he entered St. Joseph's College, at Bardstown, from which he carried, in 1833, the devoted love of professors and students, and the highest honors of the institution. On leaving college he read law with the accomplished, erudite, and chivalrous ROWAN, then in the front rank of a bar which could boast a HARDIN, a WICKLIFFE, and a CHAPEZE. From this great jurist and statesman young POWELL learned to understand, to admire, and to love not only the pure teachings of the law, but the great fundamental principles of Republican liberty as embodied in the doctrines of that noble party to which he so ably, so faithfully, and so successfully devoted his life.

In 1835 he attended the Law Department of Transylvania University, and soon afterwards began the practice of his profession at the county seat of his native county. Henderson county was at that time largely opposed to him in political sentiment, yet such was the influence of his mental and social worth that he was returned to the Legislature from that county in 1836, during that memorable national contest in which Democracy arrayed itself against the most powerful combination (that of Bank and State) which ever sought to rule a people.

In 1844, as Elector, he canvassed the State for POLK.

In 1848 he was the Democratic candidate for Governor against Mr. CRITTENDEN. His contest with that renowned man was marked with energy and ability; and though defeated at the election, his canvass was a most substantial triumph; for he spread broadcast the great truths of Jeffersonian Democracy, and reanimated the minds and hearts of the people with the recollection of the glorious traditions of that party. That policy culminated in the formation of the new Constitution.

In 1851 he again became a candidate for Governor, and gathering inspiration from the spirit which had presided over the Constitutional Convention, he canvassed and carried the State against one of the strongest and most gifted men that Kentucky has ever produced. His administration as Governor is a part of the history of the State. To it we can proudly look as an illustration of his political wisdom and as a monument of his surpassing statesmanship.

After his term expired, he was appointed, with Major BEN. McCULLOCH, to adjust our difficulties with the Mormons, and in this, as in every other public position, he discharged the duties of his office with eminent success.

He was elected Senator in Congress in 1858. His career upon that elevated theater was very marked. It was the most trying time that has ever fallen upon our country. The whole structure of our Government was shaken, and the wildest and bitterest passions of our nature aroused by the terrible civil war then raging. Amid the fierce excitement of this dark hour, Governor POWELL stood erect and firm. Adhering with death-like tenacity to the Constitution of his country, and with no stain on his official garments, he pursued, undismayed and unterrified, that policy which in his honest judgment was best calculated to uphold the liberty and preserve the civilization of his countrymen.

These events are too recent, and the feelings engendered by them still too fresh in our bosoms, to warrant·an attempt at a judgment as to their true merits. We must leave it to time to set these, as all other things, right; and in doing this we commit the conduct of Governor POWELL to that inexorable tribunal, with the fullest confidence that reason will place her seal and sanction on it.

In summing up his character as a public man we are struck with the simplicity of his political creed, and with the beauty of the few plain rules which governed his life.

Politically he was a Democrat, because he believed the doctrines of that party to embody the great truths of republican liberty, and its teachings most nearly to conform to the genius of our people. For the Constitution he cherished a veneration almost religious, deeming its observance the sure and only guarantee of exact justice, undisturbed tranquility, a perpetual Union, and well regulated liberty. He entertained an unwavering confidence in the intelligence and integrity of the people, and it was a rule of his life never to avow before them anything he did not honestly believe, and never to conceal from them anything that he did believe. He never deceived either friend or foe—both always knew where to find him. Always a decided partisan, he was constantly engaged in heated contests with the enemies of his party. Yet a true courage and a generous courtesy so shed their blended influence over all he said and did that his adversaries were disarmed of their hostility, and his friends were drawn and bound more firmly to him. It is a sufficient eulogy of Governor POWELL, and one that should gratify the highest ambition, that he had no enemy to be gratified by his death, whilst the people of his State feel it both as a personal bereavement and an irreparable public loss.

Gentle in his strength, modest in his frankness, unobtrusive in his honesty, conciliatory yet firm in his sincer-

ity, LAZARUS W. POWELL stands forth prominently as one
of the best models of a republican statesman, of whom it
may well be said,

"A rarer spirit never did steer humanity."

Hitherto I have spoken of the public career of this
great man. Our admiration of his character increases
as we view him in the private walks of life. As a friend
he was kind and true.

To the young especially he was a most wise and affectionate friend, ever ready to counsel what was right and
assist in its achievement. It was his delight to take generous and aspiring youth by the hand, and to guide its
footsteps along the pathway of preferment.

To his parents he was a model of filial piety, at once
the pride and comfort of their declining years

For the children left him by the wife of his youth, too
soon taken from him and them, he cherished the most
tender affection, and to them alone, for her sake, he
devoted the love of his manly and magnanimous heart.

As a member of society he was beloved by all. The
social virtues reigned in his heart, and social pleasures
environed his hearthstone.

In his native county, where death overtook him on the
3d day of July, 1867, he so lived that all revered and
loved him; and when it was known that he was stricken
by the destroyer, and was, perhaps, in his last struggle,
the whole community was saddened and hushed as though
the shadow of death had fallen upon every household;
and when his death was announced, the common anguish
was as though the first born of every family had been
taken. And even yet they feel that there is in their community less of truth and justice and goodness and manly
charity than before his sad decease.

Mr. Speaker : It is not my purpose to attempt to deliver an eulogy upon the character of the distinguished deceased to whom the resolutions under consideration refer, to the performance of which I freely acknowledge my inability. Nor shall I attempt to take up his history as a public man, but simply to add my tribute of respect to the memory of Mr. Powell as an humble citizen of the Commonwealth, that stands ready to-day to do honor to the memory of one of her most cherished sons. The sable drapings of this Chamber, sir, reminds us of the fact that another of Kentucky's honored sons has been taken from us by the ruthless hand of death.

> Leaves have their time to fall,
> And flowers to wither at the North Wind's breath,
> And stars to set—but all,
> Thou hast all seasons for thine own, oh Death!

It has been the custom, Mr. Speaker, from time immemorial, amongst all civilized nations, to pay a tribute of respect to the dead, and more especially to those who have been instrumental in conferring benefits upon their fellow-men. This, sir, is the duty that we are called upon to-day to perform—sad, yet pleasant. Death, sir, whether it is visited upon us in youth, in the vigor of manhood, or in the full fruition of years, is, nevertheless, accompanied with an inseparable gloom, which all of our philosophy cannot overcome. The stoicism of the ancients is no part of our inheritance; but, sir, we are here to-day, in the full possession of our natural sympathies, to mourn the loss of departed worth. We come not, sir, for the purpose of investigating the conduct of our departed statesman, and determine whether or not his name is entitled to be enrolled in the archives of the State as one of the good and great. This, sir, has already been done; every page of the history of our State for

the last thirty years bears the impress of his genius. His
life, sir, was dedicated to the service of his country,
not bounded by geographical lines or sectional divisions.
His, sir, was a devotion commensurate and co-extensive
with the vast domain which embraces the sisterhood of
States which form our glorious Republic. Born to the
inheritance of Republican and Democratic principles,
their culture, dissemination, and perpetuation became
the chief object of his noble and useful life. As to the
measure of his success in his laudable work, we have
only to refer to the proud Commonwealth during the
time of his almost unexampled administration of public
affairs for the attestation of the success which attended
his labors as a statesman. Entering the political arena
at a time when his party was in the minority and opposed by the ablest men of the age, such as CRITTENDEN,
DIXON, WOLFE, and MOREHEAD, seconded by the influence
of the great Commoner then in the nation's councils,
whose political opinions were received as oracles, and
under whose influence and guidance the Whigs had had
control in the State for upward of twenty years—surrounded by difficulties of this character, the road to political preferment was uninviting, to say the least of it.
But his, sir, was not the nature to be intimidated by the
obstacles that loomed up before him. Girding himself
for the contest, he entered the list as the champion of
Democracy. Nerved to the conflict by a laudable and
praiseworthy ambition, coupled with a zeal that knew
not defeat, he pressed forward to the goal of success,
and, by his indomitable perseverance, changed the political complexion of the State for the first time in twenty
years. Though strictly partisan in his feelings, he possessed in an unequaled degree that rare but invaluable
power of binding his friends with bonds that could not
be broken, and, at the same time, conciliating his opponents and thereby relieving his contests from the asper-

itics that are usually engendered by political discussions. Kind, affable, and obliging in his manners—to know him was to love him. The aristocrat and the plebeian received the same cordial greeting at his threshold—none was turned away empty. His great heart was ever open to the plea of the poor and the unfortunate. His love and devotion for his own native Kentucky knew no bounds—her destiny was his. In her prosperity he rejoiced; in her adversity he mourned. Hence his solicitude for the State that he loved when the clouds of war were gathering thick and fast around her. Gladly would he have thrust himself into the breach and arrested the impending shock. The ties that had bound us together as one common family were in danger of being torn asunder. He hesitated—not that he loved the nation less, but Kentucky more. If in this there is error, Mr. Speaker, let us kindly cast over it the mantle of charity, and accord to our distinguished statesman the ruling motive of his life, namely, to do right in the sight of his God and his countrymen in all things. It is said, Mr. Speaker, that the good men do, is oft interred with their bones. Let it not be so with our distinguished and beloved countrymen; but let his many and exalted virtues be engraven upon our hearts as they are indelibly in the history of his country; as in life, so in death will his example stand out as a beacon light to encourage the youth of the land to press forward in the path of usefulness and honor.

But, sir, whilst we are here to-day to render this tribute to his memory, let us not forget that our loss is his gain, and that sooner or later we will all have to pass to that bourne from which no traveler returns. The contemplation of these things, sir, should enable us to bear with Christian fortitude the dispensations of an all-wise Providence, who does all things for the best. Let us for the time being lay aside our differences of opinion, and, as one common brotherhood, meet at the shrine of our country and offer this tribute of respect to the memory of one whose fame has become the common inheritance of Kentuckians, and remember that

> "The gloomiest day hath its gleams of light,
> The darkest wave hath bright foam near it,
> And twinkles through cloudiest night
> Some solitary star to cheer it."

REMARKS OF BEN. J. WEBB, OF LOUISVILLE.

Mr. Speaker : The name of Lazarus W. Powell has been familiar to me since we were boys together attending the same school. He was a leader from the time I first knew him up to the day of his death. He led in his classes at school and he led in the sports and pastimes that occupied, for himself and his fellow-students, the hours of recreation. He took the lead in forming for himself a distinctive character, and he took it also in the assertion and defense of distinctive principles. Open, manly, and generous by nature, he used his extraordinary gifts for the support of the weak, to curb license, and to incite emulation. Enemies he had none, for his motives, in whatever he did or said, shone forth transparent with candor and with good will toward all.

At the time of which I speak, from my place among the college juniors (he was two years my senior), I remember well to have been in the habit of looking up to the person of the future Governor of the Commonwealth with a feeling that was somewhat akin to envy, on account, as well of his manly bearing, as of his wonderful influence over the entire body of his fellow-students. Though he was himself a laborious student, and was always well up in his classes, he was no mere book-worm. He gave to both body and mind that relaxation

from toil which was necessary for their healthy development. Thus early in life did LAZARUS W. POWELL give
evidence of his future greatness—of his ability to reach
the goal of a just man's ambition. I left college long
before Mr. POWELL's graduation in 1833, and had, unfortunately, few opportunities afterwards of renewing
the relations of our early days. But never, up to the
day of his death, had I ceased to feel the warmest interest in every thing that concerned him as a man, or that
had reference to his fame as a political leader among
the people. He became identified in my mind as something in which I had a part. I gloried in his successes
and I shared the humiliation of his defeats.

I shall not pretend to follow him in his public career.
His political history, and that of the times in which he
acted, are familiar to all of you. But it has been said
of me, as it has been said of thousands of better men,
that I "must be either practical or nothing." In proof
of this, and at the risk, possibly, of offending against
good taste, I cannot permit this occasion to pass without
attempting to apply, in a practical way, the lessons of
his life for the benefit of those who are seeking a like
path with that trod by the lamented dead, whose memory
we would keep alive in the hearts of his countrymen.
What were the means used by Governor POWELL to ar-
rive at distinction in the councils of the nation? And
how did he succeed in winning the love and confidence
of his fellow-citizens? He was, it is very true, a man
of genius, but there have been geniuses that we all have
known, that received not, as they did not deserve to
receive, either private respect or public confidence.
They lacked the ballast of steady habits, of industry, of
unselfish and patriotic purpose, of unswerving integrity,
of modest candor and fidelity to principle. These were
Governor POWELL's distinguishing characteristics, and it
was through their possession that he became what he

was. Both in public and private life he gave assurance to all that he was simply and wholly a man, earnest in vindicating the right and fearless in condemning the wrong. He was no creature of impulse or passion, but he had regard, in his every public act, for those amenities of social life which forbid the introduction of irritating personalities into political controversy, and which are so characteristic of the true gentleman. He enforced the respect of his political foes as much by his courtesy as by his ability to defend his positions through the medium of unanswerable logic. He did not reach the position to which his talents and his exalted moral attributes enabled him to aspire without labor. He accepted this universal law of progress, and he bent all his energies to the acquirement of that sum of knowledge which is indispensable to success in every profession, and in every undertaking that is worthy of human effort. He cultivated his will, or his moral affections, together with his intellect, for he well knew that man's happiness here on earth is as the measure of his good deeds; that he owes to his neighbor not only justice but sympathy, and not only sympathy, but also practical aid in his troubles and miseries. He studied his country's history and the lives of her patriotic founders, in order that he might labor to subserve the true interests of the former, by founding himself in the principles of the latter. Finally, he lived to illustrate his love of country and the Democratic principles which he had inherited from the fathers of the Republic, on fields where, with the great body of the combatants engaged, reason was thrown to the winds, and where, aided by a few kindred spirits, he was to the last found battling for the right, and urging upon all counsels of moderation, in words whose echoes will only cease to ring in the ears of his countrymen when liberty shall have lost its meaning in their hearts.

The most glorious act in the public life of Governor POWELL was his defense of his colleague in the Senate of

the United States from the charge of constructive treason—a charge which involved expulsion from that body.
It will be remembered that, early in the history of the
late civil war, the Hon. GARRETT DAVIS, in his zeal for the
preservation of the Union by making treason odious, as
the phrase still runs, had his colleague, Governor POWELL,
arraigned at the bar of the Senate on the charge of dis-
loyalty. The charge was not sustained. At a later day,
Senator DAVIS, having arrived at more just conclusions as
to the purposes of the men in power, discarded the heresies of the party with which he had up to that time acted,
and, on account of his change of views, was placed at
the bar of the Senate to answer a charge similar to
that which he had himself previously preferred against
Gov. POWELL. What was our late Governor's action in
the premises? Did he take advantage of his position to
strike at the man who had before caused his own arraign-
ment? Not at all; but with an eye single to principle,
and with a zeal commensurate with the occasion, he
entered the lists beside his former enemy, and manfully
defended him on the floor of the Senate. I call this a
glorious record—one that combines within its scope the
love of truth for its own sake, and superiority to personal
resentment on account of personal injury.

Truly, I know of no example more worthy of the imitation of the rising statesmen of our Commonwealth
than that afforded them in the public life of LAZARUS W.
POWELL. As it is on the basis of public virtue alone that
we can hope to preserve the institutions of our fathers,
so the student of statesmanship that would make himself worthy of the office of guardian over the liberties of the people, should prune his mind of all mere
selfish aspirations, of party and personal spites, and arise
to that height of patriotic devotion which looks beyond
self to the welfare of the country and to the happiness
of the people.

REMARKS OF EX-GOVERNOR BERIAH MAGOFFIN.

Mr. SPEAKER : Wearied and worn down, as I know we all are, by the arduous labors of a three-months' session of the Legislature, I would not say a word, under ordinary circumstances, upon the resolutions just read; but I hope I shall be pardoned by the House for asking its indulgence to drop a flower and a tear upon the grave of my departed friend. Neither my feelings nor my duty will permit me to remain silent. My relations with the late LAZARUS W. POWELL, in every regard, from my boyhood to the end of his life, were such as to forbid that, upon such an occasion as this, I should not bear willing testimony to his great worth while living. I know, sir, that no word of mine can add anything to the fame of the distinguished and departed statesman ; I know that no praise, no eulogy that I could pronounce, will add one leaf to the evergreen laurel which he has twined around his brow by his many and noble services to his country ; I know that no poor tribute that I can now pay to his sacred memory will brighten the halo which now surrounds his consecrated and immortal tomb ; but it is meet for us to show a just appreciation of his great efforts for the good of his country, and to bear witness to the spotless purity of his private and public life. All enlightened people have been prompt to perpetuate the fame of their great and good men. All civilized nations know that their history is the sum of their glorious deeds, and it is well to inspire the ambitious and hopeful living to follow their example, by living just, generous, and grateful to the patriotic and illustrious dead.

Governor Powell's active, laborious, and useful life is now the common property of the State and of the whole country. He has bequeathed to us some of the brightest pages in our history. We should show that we appreciate the noble legacy by imitating his example.

In all the social relations of life none knew him but to love him, few spoke of him but to praise. Kind, courteous, and frank in his winning manners, he was as genial as a bright May morning. His heart, his hand, and his purse were never closed to charities, and always open to his friends. Courteous, prudent, just, generous, brave, and magnanimous, he had the qualities that made him the very soul of honor. Truthfulness, honesty, frankness, and wisdom marked all his dealings with his fellow-men, and were, in fact, the most conspicuous traits in his thoroughly balanced character. In the nearer and more endearing relations of life—as a son, he was dutiful; as a husband, he was indulgent, tender, and affectionate; as a father, playful, kind, and gentle, almost as a loving, doating mother.

I knew him intimately well, for a long time, in all the relations of life, and it did seem to me that all the qualities which make up the highest type of a man were most harmoniously blended in him. As a business man, he was thoroughly honest, just, and prompt. As a lawyer, he had few superiors in the State; and no one was more respected, where he practiced, by the bench, the juries, or the bar. As a Representative in the Legislature, in early life, from the county of Henderson, he was ever vigilant, industrious, and attentive to the interests of his constituents. As a candidate for office and a public speaker, he was always popular with the people and pleasing on the stump. As Governor of Kentucky, no man ever discharged his duties with greater satisfaction to the whole people of the State. Firm in the execution of the laws, his ears were ever open to the tender and touching appeals of mercy; but, sir, it

was not until he was elected to the Senate of the United
States that extraordinary circumstances displayed, in the
highest degree, that power of intellect, patriotism, firmness, and great courage, that endeared him so much to the
people.

Who, let me ask, ever served the people of this State
with greater fidelity, under more trying circumstances?
During the late horrid and never-to-be-forgotten war, in
the darkest days of the bloody conflict, when passion
ruled the hour, and bold men stood aghast—when the
laws were silent, and military necessity was made the
plea for every infraction of the Constitution and for every
outrage which was perpetrated upon the rights of the
States and the people—unseduced by flattery, unmoved
by threats, and unawed by power, he boldly stood up on
the Senate floor, almost alone, and defended with great
ability every right dear to freemen and every principle of
constitutional liberty.   He won from his political opponents, by his honest and manly course, their admiration
and respect, even in that fearful hour.   I wish not to claim
for him more than he deserves; but who, among our great
statesmen, is deserving more of the gratitude of the people?   We have had men of more genius—greater orators,
scholars, and statesmen in Kentucky; but where was
there ever a purer or a nobler patriot, or one who was a
truer representative of the people of his native State?   I
claim not that he was a brilliant man, nor a man of
genius, nor a finished scholar, in the highest sense of the
word, nor a man greatly learned in the sciences, nor a
man of very extraordinary or profound information.   No
one will claim that he was, as an orator, the equal of Mr.
CLAY or Judge ROWAN or Mr. BARRY, of Judge HISE or
Mr. CRITTENDEN.   He had not some of the commanding
traits in the characters of the lamented BOYD, the gallant
CLARKE, or the gifted, dashing, and chivalrous O'HARA,

the remains of the last two of whom now sleep in a foreign land—

"Dante sleeps afar,
Like Scipio buried by the upbraiding shore;"

but whose sacred dust will soon be reclaimed by a grateful people, and brought back to mingle with their native
soil. Unlike any of the persons alluded to in many particulars, he was emphatically an honest man of the
strongest common sense, whose judgment seldom erred
about men or measures. In solid judgment, in unswerving will, in firmness and fixedness of purpose, in devotion
to principle, in understanding the wants and wishes of
his constituents, and in the display of the highest moral
and physical courage in acting for what he considered
to be for their greatest good, their greatest prosperity
and happiness, he was not inferior to the noblest Roman
of them all. He was not less faithful in the discharge of
his duties than any of them.

In my intercourse with public men, there was one
thing most remarkable about the man. From the colli-
sions which necessarily take place among politicians and
statesmen, and others, perhaps, struggling for wealth,
for place, position, and power, great antipathies and
very bitter animosities are almost universally engendered,
and from disappointment or some other cause they speak
with great bitterness of each other, especially after they
pass the meridian of life, and to its close. It was not so
with Governor Powell. He seemed to have no unkind
feeling toward any human being, always speaking charit-
ably and respectfully of his political opponents or friends,
even after they had done him injustice. When any
wrong was acknowledged and atoned for, no man was
more magnanimous, more free to forgive. When sufficient
apologies were offered for injuries, they were remembered
no more. A Kentuckian by birth and education, he shed

8

lustre upon every position, both public and private, he filled. Elected to fill the most exalted positions within our gift, he came up to the full measure of our highest expectations. The fame of some of our great men may be perpetuated in the marble column that towers to the skies, or in brass that dazzles in the sunlight—on the living canvass—in undying painting, story, and song, they may live as they deserve, but none of them will have, or deserve to have, a warmer place in the hearts of all true Kentuckians, or in the affections of his countrymen, than the late LAZARUS W. POWELL. Cut down by the fell Destroyer, who is no respecter of persons, but who, *cum equo pede*, knocks at the door alike of the rich and the poor, the high and the low, and will take no denial, he went down into the grave in the prime of life and the fullness of his usefulness, without a stain upon his name, without a breath of suspicion upon his character. He passed into the unknown future like the sun as it sinks in a clear sky without a shadow on its disc. Honored, trusted, beloved by the people, he died full of honors; but, alas! I fear too soon for the good of his country! He sunk to rest

"By all his country's wishes blest."

And he will be gratefully and affectionately remembered as long as truth, sincerity, friendship, talent, fidelity, generosity, magnanimity, justice, patriotism, and honor are duly appreciated among men. Surely, if the spirits of the just while on earth are made perfect in Heaven, he has his reward.

Mr. SPEAKER : I arise to second the resolutions offered by the Committee, and in doing so desire to make a few remarks upon the character and services of the distinguished statesman who is the subject of them. The State of Kentucky has ever manifested a proper respect and veneration for the memory of her great men. She loves to nurture and encourage the aspirations of genius and talent employed in promoting the welfare and happiness of her people, in defending their rights and advancing their interests. After death, she generously erects over the remains of these suitable monuments, and with maternal tenderness wreathes them with the bright garland of her public approbation. This sentiment has caused the present Legislature to pass resolutions to remove the remains of two distinguished Kentuckians to our State cemetery—one who had died in a foreign State while employed in the service of the country, the other a man of genius and misfortune, whose short but brilliant and checkered career was closed by death in a neighboring State. Resolutions to honor the memory of the late lamented Gov. HELM have been passed by this House, a patriot whose name and fame will ever live green and fresh in the hearts and affections of all true Kentuckians.

But among the names of the public men of our State, that of LAZARUS W. POWELL will ever find a prominent place. Born and reared in our State, where he received his education, he early cultivated and ever retained the generous impulses and honest frankness of a true Kentuckian.

The pursuit of knowledge threw us both together in our youth, and I shall ever cherish a pleasing recollection of the years which I thus spent with him. In those days —from 1829 to 1833—there was no boy in Kentucky who did not talk politics and have his own political opinions. POWELL and myself at that time differed on this subject. I was a Clay Whig, whilst he was even then the most staunch and consistent advocate of Jeffersonian Democracy.

He was bold and fearless in his opinions, and gave evidence of deep thinking upon the great principles of republican liberty, as contained in our mixed form of government. He was a Democrat, not from impulse, but from principle. He had accepted that doctrine from conviction; had made it his political faith; and even as a boy he evinced a resolution to remain faithful to it in good report and in evil report—in the bright day of victory and in the dark hour of defeat. While a student at college he applied himself assiduously to the pursuit of knowledge, and by his progress in science gave evidence of more than ordinary talent. He graduated with honor to himself and the institution in 1833.

On leaving St. Joseph's College he began the study of law in the office of Judge ROWAN, of Bardstown. Bardstown at that time was called the Athens of Kentucky, and certainly it then possessed some of Kentucky's greatest men. BEN. HARDIN was there. In original genius and natural reach of intellect, in perspicuity of thought and power of analysis, in wit, in bitter and withering sarcasm and invective, no man in the State was his superior. CHARLES A. WICKLIFFE, who still lives, almost the only survivor of a race of great men, distinguished at the bar and in the councils of the nation, was also there. Judge ROWAN, the able statesman and profound jurist, the accomplished gentleman and the erudite scholar, who was unequaled in conversational power and natural flow of eloquence, was also there. BEN. CHAPEZE, the peer of these, and a lawyer of distinguished ability, and JOHN HAYS, a prodigy of genius and eloquence, were likewise there.

Many young men of talent and ambition had gathered around these great names.

The lamented Governor HELM was studying there, and there also LAZARUS W. POWELL began the study of the law in 1832.

Governor POWELL was blessed with a warm and ardent nature, and when he resolved upon a thing he concentrated in it his heart and soul. He prosecuted the study of the law assiduously, knowing that labor is the only key to success, the only passport to distinction and honor. In his hours of social relaxation he was always gay and cheerful, and a most excellent companion; yet the attentive observer could easily perceive that his heart was bent on labor and progress, not on pleasure. After having passed through the usual course of study, he was admitted to the bar in 1835.

As a lawyer, Governor POWELL will never be classed among the great jurists of the nation. Nevertheless, during his life-time he held a high position at the bar. Early in life he entered the arena of politics, and it is as a statesman that he especially distinguished himself.

He passed through all the grades of political preferment, and reached the highest office in the gift of the people of Kentucky—that of Governor of his native State. I do not think that any of the many distinguished incumbents who have filled the gubernatorial chair of Kentucky ever left the office with greater popularity than Governor POWELL. In the legislative halls of the nation he stood prominent among the statesmen of the country, who, in whatever light they may have regarded his political views, never failed to esteem and admire the sterling worth and incorruptible honesty of the man.

In 1861, when party spirit was at its height, intensified by sectional hate and fanaticism, when the great principles of State rights and restricted Federal sovereignty, as

laid down in the Constitution, and illustrated by the practice and teaching of the fathers of the Republic, were
involved, and in imminent danger of overthrow, Governor
POWELL, then a Senator in Congress from Kentucky, stood
firm and unshaken to the traditions of the Democratic
faith. He invoked the spirit of peace and compromise
upon the troubled waters of party strife. He urged, with
patriotic ardor, the adoption of measures which would
harmonize sectional interests and the war of sectional
animosity, and save the vital principles of liberty to the
people. He labored long and ardently to compromise
conflicting policies and to avert the impending storm of
war from his country. He early, and then clearly, saw
the aims and purposes of the revolutionary party which
then held in their hands the destiny of the country. He
opposed persistently every attempt they made at usurpation of power, whether urged under the plea of State or
military necessity. He contended that the life of the Government depended upon adhering to the principles and
spirit of the organic law. At that time—the most trying
period of his public life—he was denounced everywhere
as disloyal to the Government; he was abandoned by his
own State, and declared unfit to represent its people in
the councils of the nation. A resolution of expulsion
from the Senate was introduced into that body. POWELL
felt and knew the importance of the occasion—the truth
of the political faith of his life was on trial—and he was
nerved with the energy and strength of the patriot to meet
with defiance the unjust charges.

In a speech—the most elaborate, logical, and eloquent
of his life—he conclusively vindicated the truth and loyalty of his public acts, the consistency and constitution-
ality of his opposition to the war, and he overwhelmed
with defeat his enemies and the enemies of his country's
liberty. This was, perhaps, the most glorious of his life;
it gave him a national reputation, and endeared his name
to the friends of constitutional freedom over all this land.

Consistency is very rarely found in the political lives of the public men of our day and country. Politics and policy are too often confounded. Principle is sacrificed to interest, lasting honor to the vulgar success of the passing hour. In our day, especially, we find few statesmen of stern convictions and unshaken integrity—few men who seem to consider the general weal of the nation rather than the petty interests of party—few men who seem willing to love their country's permanent good, even though that love bring upon them unpopularity for the time, and the odium of party and of faction.

The men who framed our Constitution, and who gave to the country the blessings of free institutions, were not of this character. They were unselfish and self-sacrificing in advancing the public good. The same patriotic devotion, and the same honesty of purpose have distinguished the men who were intrusted with the administration of the Government from the days of Washington down to 1861. These men maintained that instrument as the paramount law of the land, to which every citizen owed obedience and fidelity. Oaths to support the Constitution in these palmy days of the Republic were respected by all classes of officials. This character of statesmen must be again placed in power if the people desire to perpetuate for themselves and their posterity the inheritance of free government, and save the country from tyrants and despots.

Such a man was LAZARUS W. POWELL, and his death was not only a loss to his friends and to his State, but a loss also to the nation.

In person, he was a man of fine appearance, above medium height, and of full habit. His high and ample forehead gave evidence of the noble and exalted ideas which guided him in all his actions. His expressive blue eye told of restless activity, of lofty aspirations, and of a generous, kindly heart. In his personal friendships and

attachments he was warm and sincere. He loved to retire from the eager strife of political life to the genial and
more peaceable enjoyments of social friendship.

As a man, as a statesman, and as a patriot, he was an
honor to his native State, and the people of Kentucky
will ever hold his name in veneration.

REMARKS OF MR. LILLARD, OF OWEN.

I will not trespass upon the time or patience of the
House by any extended remarks on the life, character,
and distinguished services of Gov. POWELL, whose un-
timely death we all mourn.

All that could be said on this melancholy occasion has
been well and eloquently said by the distinguished gentlemen who have preceded me. But, sir, I cannot remain
utterly silent. I feel that I must say something as a slight
tribute of respect to one who in life I loved and whose
memory I hold sacred and dear.

I had been from early manhood an admirer of Governor
POWELL, not alone for his intellectual worth, but for his
virtues, his goodness of disposition, and kindness of heart.

His noble, generous, unselfish nature gained for him
the admiration of all with whom he came in contact.
No man within the State of Kentucky had as strong a
hold on the affections of the people as he, save Kentucky's
illustrious exiled statesman, Mr. BRECKINRIDGE; and when
the unexpected intelligence was heralded throughout the
Commonwealth that LAZARUS POWELL was no more; that
he had passed from this earthly stage on which he had
acted so prominent and useful a part to that "bourn
from whence no traveler returns," every patriot's heart
was filled with gloom and sadness.

He had in every position in life to which he had been
elevated by the voice of his countrymen, whether as leg-

islator in the councils of the State, as Chief Executive of
the Commonwealth, or as her representative in the Senate Chamber of the United States, ably and fearlessly
discharged his duty and faithfully performed the duty
confided to him.

As a lawyer, he had attained a high and eminent position at the bar; as a statesman, he had few equals and no
superiors; as a politician, he was firm, unwavering, and
incorruptible, and as a private citizen, his character was
as pure and spotless as the untrodden snow.

During the Senatorial contest last winter, I, as one of
his friends, had a favorable opportunity of learning the
true nature of the man. We had been balloting unsuc-
cessfully for weeks, and it was evident that we could not
secure votes sufficient to elect him; but some of us were
averse to withdrawing his name, preferring to leave the
responsibility of the election of United States Senator to
the present Legislature.

In this condition of affairs Gov. POWELL urged the
withdrawal of his name, remarking that he was satisfied,
from the formidable opposition waged against him, that
his election could not be secured, and that, owing to the
proposed impeachment of the President of the United
States by Congress, for the discharge of his sworn duty
to protect and defend the Constitution of the country,
he deemed the election of a Senator then a necessity.
His name was of course withdrawn, and the result the
House is familiar with.

Mr. Speaker, Gov. POWELL was ardently attached to
the State of his birth and to the section of country in
which he lived; but his patriotism was bounded by no
contracted limits; it embraced the whole country, from
the lake shore to the Mexican Gulf, from the Pacific to
the waters of the Atlantic.

In every position he assumed he was actuated by
patriotic impulses.

In the early part of 1861, when the dark clouds of civil strife were just beginning to cast their gloomy shadows over the land, his eloquent voice and masterly statesmanship were brought to bear to avert the threatened storm and prevent the carnival of blood which succeeded it; but his warning and advice were unheeded; fanaticism ruled the hour, and the country was plunged into the dark vortex of civil war, which resulted in the destruction of Republican Government and the establishment of a military despotism in eleven States of this Union.

Sir, I indorse every sentiment embodied in these resolutions, and will vote for the appropriation proposed to erect a monument to POWELL; but it requires no marble shaft to perpetuate the memory of such a man—he will live forever in history and in the hearts of Kentuckians, and in the hearts of lovers of Republican Government and civil liberty everywhere.

REMARKS OF MR. ROBERT T. GLASS.

The Representative from Henderson county (Mr. ROBT. T. GLASS) having been called home, the following remarks of his were read from manuscript by the Clerk of the House:

As it is my fortune to represent that constituency by whom the honored dead was so cherished, and from whom is taken not only the statesman whose fame is co-extensive with the country and whose services are a part of its valued history, but also the public-spirited citizen, the beloved friend, the sympathizing neighbor, and generous benefactor—as I represent that bereaved people among whom Governor POWELL was born and lived and gave up his life, it is proper, perhaps, I should say something on this occasion for them and in their name of their sense of the great loss the country and State has sustained in his death, and their appreciation of his many and eminent virtues.

You, gentlemen, have seen one of the pillars from the temple that supports the national arch of the unity of the States rent from its base, and prone headlong on the alien ground; but over *us* it is the roof-tree of our home has fallen. *You* miss the profound student of political his-. tory and the skilled controller of political events, and are appalled that one so able and useful stands dumb in the presence of the great master and teacher, Death. *We* are bowed in sorrow that the patient friend and counselor of our daily lives, by a higher election, has entered into a diviner council than any earthly assembly, leaving us no discipline but the unutterable pathos and instruction of his pure example. It is proper that a constituency so nearly afflicted should seek an expression of its pervading sorrow as dumb but eloquent nature, in unsyllabled measure, strikes deep the common chord of grief, and that I, perhaps, should be the instrument—imperfect and tuneless, it may be—to respond to the touched and trembling keys of a people's lamentation.

If, from the remarks which fall from the lips of speakers to-day, and your knowledge of the universal sorrow which pervades the State, you can judge the magnitude of the common deprivation, let your own full hearts recognize and appreciate *our* peculiar unlanguaged grief.

As the time fixed for the offering of these resolutions drew near, I cheerfully acceded to a delay that gave an opportunity to the once coadjutors of the illustrious dead to bring their worthy and graceful offerings to this social shrine. So delaying, that more honor be done to the memory of him whom in life " all delighted to honor," the earnest call of duties at my home leaves me no other means of expression than this written rendering of a wail of mourning. In the wreath of immortelles now made by loving hands to grace his political fame and perpetuate its memory, let these dark leaves of neighborhood regret and personal sorrow be wrought into a background to bring into more prominent relief the nobility of his life and the virtues of his private character.

LAZARUS W. POWELL was born in Henderson county, Kentucky, and nurtured in the generous traits and impulses which are the birthright of the people of his native State. Adopting the law as his profession, his legal training became the pathway to a position of political eminence in the ranks of a generous Democracy. Trusted and admired by the people of his county, he was, in early life, elected to the State Legislature, and in that wider field made known his talents and worth to the people of the State. Honored for his talents, and respected for his character, a few years later, the discriminating judgment of his party chose him from a noble list of rivals, the Agamemnon, beseiging a political and hitherto invincible Troy of Kentucky, to lead their forces in the gubernatorial contest of 1848. A Hector in all that constitutes genius and chivalry headed the resisting battalions in the person of the brilliant, highhearted CRITTENDEN, called home from clustering honors at Washington to rescue the declining fortunes of his party, wounded deeply in the neglect of Mr. CLAY. In a canvass exceedingly arduous, Mr. POWELL met the accomplished athlete, practiced in the giant arena of the Federal Senate of that day, and everywhere was shown the elastic muscle and steely tendon of this David from the brooks and fields. Comparatively unknown, and jeered at by the opposition press as one dragged from obscurity only to be offered up on the alter of a necessary party organization, he responded to the marching cry of " Lazarus, come forth!" and stood a defiant champion and brave defender of popular rights and State integrity. A new Lazarus had arisen, indeed, around whose advocacy

of the true theory of governmental affairs lived an elder
faith, now for the first time for years renewed and re-
vivified in Democratic sentiment; and beneath him the
seared and unfruitful abstractions of a mistaken creed
broke and shivered into dust. It compelled all his rival's
surpassing eloquence, the power of the prestige of his
unsullied reputation, and the strong sympathies of a past
of unbroken victory, to resist the desperate energy of this
unheralded reformer, tearing to pieces with relentless
hand plausible sophistries and extinct precedents. He
stamped the serpent of prejudice in its native mud, and
throttled the old lion of Federal power in his chosen
cave, until, step by step, forced through the rugged un-
dergrowth of old habit and custom, he brought his adversary back to the common birth-place of a people's
freedom—the true sovereignty of confederated States.
He lost at last, but wrested victory from defeat, for
POWELL, vanquished, stood on a field victorious. The
traces of that mighty struggle remained ineradicable and
potent in their influence upon the political issues of the
next four years. And now, when the prize for which
these intellectual athletes contended again glittered before the eyes of party leaders; when the period for a
second struggle came, who so fit as he to champion
the confident hosts of Democracy? The Democracy of
Kentucky, now no longer divided by the claims of rival
aspirants for political leadership, set its all upon the
vigorous nerve and unflinching courage of this green-
wood and Green River trained rustic, fresh from the
buxom air and healthy embrace of independent popular
life. Again, as before, the noble Whig party, strained to
the utmost by the hardy fight, and warned beforehand
of the pith and marrow of this vigorous rival, chose their
most illustrious victor in many a scarred arena, in the
person of Hon. ARCHIE DIXON. But the struggle was no
longer equal. The Whig party was like a stately man-

hood, healthy and kindly, whose youth had been inaugurated with the robust juices and strong sinews of a nervous life, and still stood erect, a symbol of athletic vigor. Yet it was but a symbol. Age had sapped the secret sources of its strength, robbed its blood of the iron, and bones of healthy lime, and no more was the name of the Great Commoner an ever-renewing wine of life to it, and vain the efforts of its gallant leader to restore to it its pristine strength and spirit. Against this young Orson from the woods, with every nerve and muscle full of life—the embodiment and exponent of that pure Democracy, which, born in the country and nurtured in the hearts of a patriotic yeomanry, sought only the greatest good to the greatest number by a strict conformity to the Constitution and laws, by protection to property and industry, and by its advocacy of the doctrine of State rights as taught by the fathers of the country—the splendid externals of a show of strength were as nothing. None could have fought braver, or as well, or put in play the moral and physical energies, and even the petty nerves and arteries of Whiggery, as vigorously as did Dixon, this mental master of its being; but it fell, and Powell stood over it master of the field, and master of a gallant force in the Whig party—that party that had fallen, alas! to rise no more.

It is not my purpose to touch upon what will be so much better done by others of your number—the political life and services of Gov. Powell. As a Representative in this body, as Governor of the State, as United States Senator, and as Commissioner to pacify the Utah troubles, rising into threatened war in the dim obscurity of the Rocky Mountains, he proved himself courageous, able, and patriotic, knowing no master but duty, and cheerfully obeying its behests.

On all these he left the impressible elements of his character and the enduring marks of his fame, and no wave of popular opinion or prejudice, however constant or violent, can wear them from the face of the rock on which public events are inscribed. Others, by age and association better fitted to interpret these scrolls, may explain and elucidate from them the strong, earnest life of this great-hearted, generous, noble nature.

The gubernatorial victory of 1851 I have tried faintly to depict, and you can realize, for the hard breathings of the desperate conflict have hardly yet ceased, though one of the gallant combatants breathes no more. This victory, with the consequences which followed it, broke the wand of the opposition power in this State, and made Kentucky, in heart and sympathy, a Democratic State, ranked with the true friends of civil order in a just distribution of the powers of government. In some sense, POWELL's victory of 1851 made possible the Legislature of 1867, and compelled and consolidated Kentucky into the position of a besieged citadel, the last stronghold of civil liberty, under a white man's government, on the Western continent. Let me leave the political to other hands, and view this great eventful nature by a nearer observation— this man, as he stood in the perfect plenitude of matured powers, in his daily life. An attribute greater, perhaps, than those that lent commanding fame to his memory, in that it was of the germ from which it sprung, was that quality of kindness, so earnest, simple, and sincere, that attracted friends to him from every quarter and all parties—the great pervasive and reciprocal tie of humanity. None were more true, faithful, and tender in their friendships, more firm and resolute, more amiable and forgiving. Always prompt in response to the cry of suffering, he made the sorrows of others all his own. Want was his mother, in the noblest sense, in that the wants of others commanded him to give, by nature's signet of their common humanity. Benevolence flowed from the deep, rich fountains of his heart, and, like the rivers of a continent,

left untold treasures everywhere—not only in contribu-
tions to public benefactions and institutions to mitigate
the sufferings of mankind, but in that humble charity
wherein the right knows not what the left hand gives.
Humble, did I say? Aye, by the tests of men; but, tried.
in a truer scale, as much higher as his general philanthropy exceeded the narrower meaning of the word and
deed of charity. To the young he was fostering, gentle,
and kind—a pleasant monitor, a priceless, sympathetic
friend. The inexperienced lawyer was cheerfully assisted
in his cases; principles were elucidated, precedents and
decisions searched out, technicalities made plain in
usefulness, and all as simply and naturally done as
by a fellow-student, working steadily on a common
footing in a common class. So in his domestic life:
his house stood with hospitable gates ajar, welcoming
the stranger and the friend, the wayfarer and the distressed. No cloistral quiet there, with grave and irk-
some duties, where life was treated as a great sorrow
to be borne in peace, but a genial, home-like pleasantness, rife with joyous sounds, and echoing with
contagious laughter from its open windows and light-
inviting chambers. Little children loved and came to
him. Their intuitions, wiser than our skill, recognized
his kindly, generous nature, and they climbed about
his knees, roguishly and confidingly, at once companions, playmates, and friends.

In some things this nature was too perfect to err; he
could sympathize with the child over its broken doll, as
well as with a great people borne to the earth with sorrow for its national sins; the young maiden strange with
the new love springing in her innocent heart, and won-
dering over the prize, found in this plain and simple man
the tenderest adviser and friend—a confidant more true
than her old school-mate, to whom she planned a future
in the soft brilliance of their moon-lit chamber, as sweet
and warm and rosy as the coming day itself.

This enlarged charity—for charity as God made the word, and not narrowly as man uses it, is the correct description—was one of the qualities and attributes of power of this pre-eminent man. In it and of it, drawing its sympathies and love, he grew into larger proportions before us, and greater in our hearts. All shared in it, all felt and acknowledged its influence. It is no more possible to resist a kindly nature shining from a noble heart, than for earth to turn ungrateful to the sun, and refuse its plants and flowers to his generous kiss. It softened the asperities of life; plucked thorns of rivalry from the rich roses of success, and toned in a responsive chime the alien feelings of political opponents. It became an impossibility to know the man with his approachableness and familiarity of manner—his love and kindliness—and be able to resist or distrust him. His open nature was but a consequence of his loving and tender sensibilities, and drew to him confidence from quarters unexpected—a striking example of which I will relate.

In the spring of 1864 I went to Washington City to obtain a passport to Virginia, that I might bring to Kentucky, her native State, a lady relative and friend, who was then within the Confederate lines. This I obtained from President Lincoln, with some difficulty, after a personal interview. The lines on both sides were at the time closed and carefully guarded, for Gen. LEE occupied a defiant attitude, and GRANT was about to enter upon his celebrated advance and campaign upon the Rapidan. A close espionage upon all going to or coming from Virginia was maintained, and it was difficult to escape arrest and imprisonment, even when passes legitimately obtained and properly authenticated were in the possession of parties seeking to enter the lines. Gen. BUTLER was then in command at Fortress Monroe, at which point I expected to meet the flag-of-truce boat, and commu-

9

nicate with the Commissioners of Exchange in regard to the object of my mission. It was thought better by my friends in Washington City that letters of introduction to the Commandant at Fortress Monroe should be procured, as he could greatly facilitate my business, and, in case of difficulty or detention by subordinates, would extend to myself and friend that protection and aid which civilians so frequently required during the late war. These letters Gov. POWELL undertook to procure. Taking me into the Senate Chamber just before the opening of the morning session, he introduced me to various Republican Senators, and of the most prominent and influential of these—men whose names, then and now, were and are distinguished in their party—he requested letters of introduction to Gen. BUTLER in my behalf. To each one he undertook to explain who I was and why I desired to obtain the letters; but the same unvarying answer was returned: "*It is enough for us to know, Governor, that he is a friend of yours. We are satisfied you would not recommend any one who was not, in your opinion, honorable, and every way worthy of confidence.*" Thus, at a period when the national existence was thought to be imperiled; when grand armies were marching and preparing for the greatest and most decisive campaign of that sanguinary war, and a necessarily strict surveillance on all who were not known to be in full accord with the Government was maintained—the personal respect and regard entertained for the distinguished gentleman whose memory we seek to honor to-day, induced Senators who differed with him as widely in political views as in sympathies, to trust a friend of his of whose opinions and antecedents they knew nothing nor sought to know at the most vital crisis of the nation's life.

It was a striking mark of confidence in the man, and singular in the occasion and circumstances; but it illus-

trates the power and influence of that extraordinary
quality of kindliness and generosity in his nature, and
I offer it as explanatory not only of his great success in
life, but as a key to that success itself.

We never know how much a single kind word may do;
how much less, then, can we estimate the measure of a
life filled to the brim, as was Governor POWELL's, with
words and deeds of kindness? Thus the amiability of
his character and mind was promotive of harmony and
concord, as, on the other hand, the tendency of some
sharp incisive natures is to intensify differences and
develop prejudice. That these two are constantly at
war, and mingle in general political divisions, often to
the detriment of the public interest, no one will deny.
He sought diligently to promote the one and subdue into
silence and harmlessness the other; and his efforts, in
conjunction with those of other able men of the party
in the State, were successful in bringing into something
of organization the elements of conservatism, which, for
a brief time after the war closed, could find no nucleus
about which they were inclined to gather. But gather
they did at last—Federal and Confederate—blue-coat
and gray—Whig and Democrat—forgetting past differences in a common interest for a common cause and
country, and striking hands across the bloody graves of
comrades and friends, as they pledged to each other
political and personal faith for all time to come. Thus
the canvass of 1865 was inaugurated; thus a Democratic
Legislature—our immediate predecessors—was elected;
thus, and by these elements and agencies, was formed
the great Democratic party which dominates Kentucky
to-day. This and such like actions harmonized with his
life and character. The aim was high and patriotic,
and it was loftily and gloriously achieved; for he sought
to twine the various strands of public sentiment into a
single cable, to hold firmly forever to the rock of the

Constitution his loved native State—that Kentucky in
which is preserved now, as in the ark which arose over
the desolate waters of the deluge, all the good in government and civil liberty left out of the terror of revolution and rebellion.

Courteous, amiable, and polite, he was withal cool, decided, and courageous. He adopted no opinions hastily
and without deliberation; but when fully matured, and
he convinced of their correctness, he adhered to them
with tenacity, and defended them with skill and ability.
When, in the Senate, during an exciting period of the
late war, an apparent majority of the people of the
country, and a large portion of the people of his own
State, were wildly striking at and assailing him for the
entertainment of certain opinions inimical to their peculiar views, and the cry arose, "expel him from the seat
he disgraces," he stood, his head high lifted in the eternal
sunshine of truth and conscious rectitude, unmoved like
Atlas, and as calm 'mid the storm of popular fury, and
smiled as it crashed so threateningly but harmlessly by.
A short time thereafter, and in the kind words and approving smiles of enlightened conservatives all over the
land, he received the reward of his constancy and devotion to principle.

> "Assailed by scandal and the tongue of strife,
> His chiefest answer was a blameless life;
> And he that forged, and he that threw the dart,
> Had each a brother's interest in his heart."

It was this quality of firmness and decision which
peculiarily illustrated his administration as chief executive officer of the State and his career as a Senator in
Congress, and which rendered him so eminent and successful as the leader of his party in the State.

In the character of the man, we may well differ as to
the causes of his elevation. One may compare him to a
mountain whose rocky base is ever lashed by the turbu-

lent waters and blasted by the hurricane, yet upon whose
higher slopes the peasant pastures his peaceful flock, and
everlasting sunshine crowns its head. But Powell's was
not the deep-seated indifference of a cool phlegmatic nature, cautious per force. Another may see in his forecast
and seemingly wonderful political prescience the workings of an intellect lifted into serenity by lofty abilities,
rivaling the star whose placid splendor adorns the riven
earth, yet in its glorious beauty ever lifted above and de-
tached from the world it brightens. But his was none of
this. He was true to human nature by every fibre of his
heart. From it he drew his strength and elevated his
stature; for never were his brains and sympathies an idle
gold. If he wore some of the brilliance of the star, the
radiance was won from elements which belong to earth;
if he was calm amid turbulence, it was not from the hard
impassiveness of a stern and unimpressible nature. He
was to us and our common human nature rather like the
tree, which, first a slender shoot, peers up into the air,
and drawing life and nutriment from its native soil, new
strength enters its stalk, and it bursts into leaves and
branches: so, year by year, growing and strengthening
in root, fibre, and branch, spreading its gnarled and mossy
limbs, and lifting itself higher against the sky it almost
touches, we sit under its shelter and are safe. Every
breath of Heaven stirs its leaves; the imperceptible wan-
dering air moves it; the shock of earth, in its motion, is
acknowledged; yet, steady in its rugged bark and heart
of oak, it defies the whirlwind and the storm, and shakes
off the tears of rain in flashing rainbows of supernal light.
Thus was the lamented dead. So he grew from our human nature; our sympathies in common were the fibres,
our breath of favor the healthful air. He was strong only
as he drew strength in the nourishment afforded by nature,
and in giving back his love in return, as the healthful sap
follows the beckon of spring and fall. It was his humani-

ty which, like earth to the oak, gave impulse, strength, and success; the firmer and stronger he grew the more gently, and, as the leaves to the winds of heaven, he yielded to the sympathies and love of his fellow-men.

Under the green shadow we have rested for the last time, and now the fallen oak needs but these tender mosses to grow over it, watered by our tears, and becoming greener year by year over the grave of the statesman, patriot, and gentleman—Lazarus W. Powell.

MONUMENT TO GOV. L. W. POWELL.

On the 6th of March, 1868, ex-Gov. Beriah Magoffin, from a Select Committee, reported to the House of Representatives the following bill, which was passed unanimously; and being reported to the Senate on the same day, it was also passed by that body without a dissenting vote, and approved by the Governor on the 9th of the same month:

An Act to erect a Monument over the Grave of the late Governor Lazarus W. Powell.

§ 1. *Be it enacted by the General Assembly of the Commonwealth of Kentucky*, That the Acting Governor of this Commonwealth, John W. Stevenson, be, and the same is hereby, authorized to contract for the erection of a monument over or near the grave of the late Gov. Lazarus W. Powell; and, before contracting for said monument, he shall advertise for proposals and plans for the same.

§ 2. That when said monument shall have been erected according to contract, and the same certified to the Auditor of Public Accounts, it shall be his duty to issue his warrant on the Treasurer for an amount not exceeding fifteen hundred dollars, which amount is hereby appropriated, to be paid out of any money in the Treasury not otherwise appropriated.

§ 3. This act shall take effect from its passage.

Yours truly,
John L. Ashm

BIOGRAPHICAL SKETCH

OF THE

HON. JOHN L. HELM,

LATE

GOVERNOR OF KENTUCKY.

PUBLISHED BY DIRECTION OF THE GENERAL ASSEMBLY OF KENTUCKY.

FRANKFORT, KY.:
PRINTED AT THE KENTUCKY YEOMAN OFFICE.
S. I. M. MAJOR, PUBLIC PRINTER.
1868.

IN THE SENATE OF KENTUCKY,

MARCH 6, 1868.

Mr. ALEXANDER moved the following resolution, viz :

Resolved, That a Committee of two of the Senate be appointed by the Chair, to act in conjunction with a similar Committee of the House, to prepare Biographical Sketches of the Hon. L. W. POWELL and the Hon. JOHN L. HELM, and that the Public Printer be directed to print three thousand eight hundred copies of each Biography for the use of the Senate, together with the speeches delivered on the passage of the resolutions in regard to their death in the Senate and the House, the same to be published in pamphlet form, accompanied with lithographic portraits of the deceased, and that they be mailed to the members of both Houses, postage paid.   .

Which was twice read and adopted. Senators JOSEPH M. ALEXANDER, of the county of Fleming, and BEN. J. WEBB, of the City of Louisville, were appointed, in pursuance of the resolution, to perform the duty assigned thereunder.

On the same day Mr. McKENZIE presented the above resolution in the House of Representatives, where it was unanimously adopted, and the following named gentlemen were appointed to perform the duty indicated by the resolution, viz: Messrs. J. A. McKENZIE, of Christian county ; S. I. M. MAJOR, of Franklin county ; and R. M. SPALDING, of Marion county.

INTRODUCTION.

IT is a well-established fact, that success has rarely resulted from the efforts of even able and experienced writers, when they have attempted to bring before their readers personations of individual character and habit. Few have been the really readable biographies that have appeared in our language, and of these, immeasurably the best was written and compiled by one whose literary reputation has no other foundation for its support. Writers of biography are apt to have too little regard for details. They write in the style of the historian, and appear to contemn every circumstance in the lives of those whose characters they would depict which has not a direct connection with certain grand purposes in the pursuit of which their years were passed.

The great Lexicographer and Essayist, Dr. SAMUEL JOHNSON, though he possessed a mind immeasurably superior to that of his biographer, could not have written a book of the kind that would have held its place in the world of letters as has his own Life by JAMES BOSWELL. As the inferior mental organism of BOSWELL had no capacity for learned display, so the superior one of Dr. JOHNSON had none for that which was merely *postprandial*. The latter's ponderous intellect would have held in contempt the club-conversations and table-talk which, in the former's work, are found so charming to the great mass of readers.

Just as the aggregate of human miseries is made up, for the most part, of little cares and annoyances, so true human happiness has much affinity with little things.

There is a certain charm about the conversations—the trivial incidents of every-day life—of men who have filled high places in the State, or in the world of science, which

is appreciable by everybody. But these, as connected
with great numbers of eminent men, have all been lost
for want of a chronicler. Hence it is, that biographers
are so often obliged to assume in style the dead level of
compact history, which is altogether unsuited to such
writings; and hence, too, their works are little read and
less appreciated.

In justice to one of the most useful—as he was certainly one of the most esteemed—men of our day, we have
sought diligently to remedy, in the present instance, this
usual defect of all modern biography, but with results,
we cannot but acknowledge, by no means commensurate
with our wishes.

Governor Helm's was a mind of no common order; and
dying, as he did, in the zenith of his fame, it is not to be
wondered at that his fellow-citizens should desire to preserve the record of his life. We, who have been commissioned to perform this duty, may well fear that the result
of our labors will be found very imperfect by those who
had the honor of the late Governor's intimate acquaintance. They will believe us, however, when we state that
we have given to our work such attention as was in our
power and such ability as we could command.

It is due to the members of Governor Helm's family to
state that they have furnished us with almost the entire
details of his private life contained in the following pages.
We are indebted, likewise, to the Hon. Charles Wintersmith, of Elizabethtown, for much valuable information
that has either been embodied in the text of our work or
in the copious notes which will be found appended.

JOS. M. ALEXANDER,
BEN. J. WEBB,
Senate Committee.
J. A. McKENZIE,
S. I. M. MAJOR,
R. M. SPALDING,
House Committee.

JOHN L. HELM.

"VITA ENIM MORTUORUM IN MEMORIAM VIVORUM EST POSITA."—*Cicero.*

The above sentiment of the great exponent of ancient Roman law is peculiarly applicable among a people whose liberties and liberal institutions are the fruits of the blood and labors of a truly virtuous ancestry : " The life of the dead is placed in the memory of the living." In other words, a virtuous people will always seek to perpetuate the memory of its virtuous dead. It is only by doing this that progress is at all possible, whether in social elevation or government, in science or morals. Example is the best of teachers. For the ninety years of our existence as a nation, we are indebted for the liberties we have enjoyed, more than to any other cause, to the fact that we have kept constantly before our eyes the examples of virtue, of patriotism, of courage and endurance, left to us by WASHINGTON and the Fathers of the Republic.

The biographies of the eminent men who have illustrated the periods in which they lived, make up a large portion of the history of the world. They are the landmarks of past centuries. The positions in which the individuals they commemorate were placed, whether in the confidences reposed in them, the persecutions to which they were subjected, the uprisings against their misrule, or the patient submissions to their prowess, are facts from which we may infer much of the character of the people among whom their lives were cast. But their memories stand as living and grouped monuments, whose shafts point to their cotemporaries and after generations the way to fame and eminence, and incite to emulation when good, or to avoidance when bad.

It is meet and appropriate that each State and Government should, in some form, preserve the records of such

as have "done the State some service," or have advanced
the general interests of their race. The neglect, in this
particular, which has heretofore characterized the State
of Kentucky, certainly does her no credit, but is a stain
on her otherwise bright escutcheon. Her record is one of
which her people need not be ashamed, but of which, in
many things, they may entertain a just sense of pride.
This record may be greatly attributable to what was formerly called *Kentucky stump speaking*, which was nothing
else than a free interchange of opinions among the people.
In its widest acceptation, the distinction between large
employers and dependent employes has never obtained
in Kentucky; but every man has considered himself a freeman, and the equal of any other, legally, socially, and
politically, whether he lived in a cabin or a stately mansion—whether he cultivated a few acres or was the lord
over a vast domain—whether he labored in the workshop,
was engaged in commerce, or was eminent in professional
life. Amongst us, however, public opinion has ever been
led by men of mark, and the actions and characteristics
of such, their modes of thought and life, claim such illus-
trations of them as will convey a proper idea of what
they were and are, and the means by which they attained
their eminent positions over others who had before ranked
as their equals. The only nobility they claimed, or could
claim, was private worth or merit, and the only distinction that has been paid them was a just homage to their
virtues.

In seeking to keep alive in the hearts of the people the
benefits conferred upon their State and the country by
two of their eminent departed citizens, the General Assembly has acted wisely and well. Thousands of our
youth, the future hope of the Republic, who are to become
in due time the custodians of the priceless liberties which
we trust to bequeath them, as we ourselves inherited them
from our fathers, will read the records of their lives, and

be thereby stimulated to walk in their footsteps and become, as they were, men worthy to be intrusted with
powers over the rights and the interests of a free people.
Some may be disposed to doubt if it would not have been
better to await the development of a more assured public
sentiment in regard to the value of their services to the
State and the country before publishing their lives. We
do not think so. Ours is a progressive people—progressive especially in material ideas and their solution—and,
like all such, we are too much given to thoughts of self
to bear in mind and transmit to our children, in the form
of oral traditions, the life-records of those among our cotemporaries who have deserved well of their country. A
good and a great man dies, and after the first outburst of
our genuine lamentation and somewhat showy grief, our
thoughts are diverted into other channels, and, after a few
short years, unless it be prevented by the very means that
have been adopted with reference to the lamented dead
whose biographies we have been commissioned to write,
he is no more remembered by even those amongst whom
he lived and labored, than the man that fills the smallest
point in the history of the nation. If our children should
happen to hear his name mentioned, it will only be in
connection with the office he once filled, and the whole
example of his life is lost. The services that an individual
may have rendered to his country, or to society, are pro-
portionally valuable as they are remembered or lost sight
of after his career is closed; and as it is only by the aid of
the press that it is possible for us, under the circumstances
in which we are placed, to extend beyond our own brief
spans of existence the memory of such services, so do we
confer a real benefit upon our children when we seek to
preserve for them the examples of virtue, patriotism, courage, and the like, which have been set before us by the
good and the great of our own day and generation.

The family from which the late Governor HELM descended was one among the most respected and influen-

tial of those that originally settled the Old Dominion
Colony.   His grandfather, THOMAS HELM, was born in
Prince William county, Virginia, where he continued to
reside up to the year 1780.   In February of the year
named, he joined a colony of emigrants, consisting of
his own family and those of WILLIAM POPE, HENRY FLOYD,
and BENJAMIN POPE, who had determined to seek their
fortunes in the yet unexplored wilderness of Kentucky.
The emigrants reached the Falls of the Ohio, now Louisville, in March, 1780, in the vicinity of which the POPE
families finally settled, and where their numerous descendants are still to be found, highly respected citizens
of the community of which they form a part. Mr. FLOYD,
with his family, first settled near Bardstown, in Nelson
county; but a few years later he removed to the lower
part of the State, into the district now known as Union
county.   Mr. HELM remained at the Falls for about one
year, his family suffering greatly, during the summer and
fall after his arrival, from the bilious diseases so common
to the first settlers of the place.   Having lost four of his
children by death, he determined to seek for a home in a
more healthy locality.   Mounting his horse, he set his
face inland, with the determination not to return until
he had selected a permanent abiding place for his family.
On the third day of his search, he reached the foot of the
hill in the vicinity of the present village of Elizabethtown,
which commands the site upon which he afterwards lived
and died, as well as that of the cemetery where he now
rests, surrounded by his descendants to the fifth generation.*

---

* A singular circumstance is related in connection with the selection made
by Mr. HELM of his future place of residence. Before leaving Virginia, but
while deliberating on the subject of a removal, he had dreamed of just such
a spot as that upon which his eye rested when he ascended the hill spoken
of in the text. The very spring at which he had slaked his thirst, rushing
out of its rocky bed, strong, clear, and sparkling, was as the visionary foun-

THOMAS HELM was just the kind of man to make his way in a new country. Daring, active, and possessing habits and tastes that were well suited to the life of a pioneer, he was soon the occupant of a strongly-built *Fort*, which he had erected for the protection of his family against the then frequent predatory excursions of roving bands of Indians. This Fort was situated in the small valley which intersects the hills traversing the farm now known as the " Helm Place." Mrs. HELM, *née* Miss JENNY POPE, a near relative of the gentlemen of that name that had accompanied her husband to Kentucky, was a remarkable contrast to the head of the family. While her husband's ordinary weight was considerably over two hundred pounds, her own was little over eighty. Small as she was in stature, her courage was equal to the situation in which she found herself placed, as was abundantly proved on several occasions when hostile rifles, in the hands of Indian marauders, were directed against the stronghold which contained her household gods.*

JENNY POPE HELM is still remembered by several of her surviving grand-children and others of the older members of the settlement, as she appeared during the last years of her life, an infant in size beside the almost gigantic proportions of her husband—quick of movement, erect as in her youth, always busy and always good-tempered.

tain that had appeared to him in his dream. The coincidence startled him greatly; and, though anything but a superstitious man, he accepted the omen as a happy one, and concluded to search no further.

* On a certain occasion, one of her sons, in company with a party from an adjoining settlement, had been dispatched to the Bullitt Licks, near Shepherdsville, for a supply of salt. The party was attacked by Indians, and her son killed. The body was recovered by one of his companions, who bound it on his horse and brought it to the Fort. The mother was on the watch for her returning boy; and seeing the horseman approaching with his strange-looking burden slung across the shoulders of his beast, she hastened to the gate in order to open it for his entrance. Who can paint the horror of the moment, when just as the heavy gate swung back upon its hinges, the mangled remains of her son, the bands breaking which had held them in their place, fell from the horse prone at her feet.

Almost to the end of her days she was able to undergo
fatigue that would now send to her sofa or to her bed
many a woman of our own times of half her years.
When she was eighty years old she thought nothing of
springing from the ground to her horse's back without
assistance.* Though both had come of comparatively
wealthy families, neither did THOMAS HELM nor his wife
ever regret the hardships they encountered in the backwoods. Gradually the Indians were driven from the
State, and a comfortable log house was built beside the
old Fort, which served them for a residence for the remainder of their days, and where, surrounded by dutiful
sons and daughters, they lived contented and happy, and
died mourned by the entire community. ·

Gov. HELM's maternal grand-parents were JOHN LARUE
and MARY BROOKS, who had emigrated from the Valley of
the Shenandoah, Virginia, in the year 1784.† Mrs. LARUE

---

* When a boy of ten years, the late Governor HELM was a great favorite
with his grand-parents. He often spoke of his grandmother's brisk ways,
as she pattered about the house in her high-heeled shoes and short skirts.
His grandfather HELM was the oracle of the whole neighborhood on all
matters connected with the revolutionary era and the Indian troubles in
Kentucky. It was at the knees of his venerable progenitor that Governor
HELM drank in the history of his country, and learned to appreciate the
sacrifices made by the patriot-band that achieved our liberties.

† JOHN LARUE settled on a knoll in the vicinity of a creek then unnamed,
near the present town of Hodgenville. We mention this circumstance in
order to notice a tradition that has come down to the present inhabitants of
the vicinage, in relation to the name by which the creek is now known. A
company of pioneers had agreed to meet on the knoll near LARUE's house on
a certain day, for the purpose of giving a name and designation to the
stream. One of the pioneers, named LYNN, failed to make his appearance.
The last one that arrived, looking around, exclaimed, "Here we are on the
knoll, but *no* LYNN." Knowing LYNN's character for punctuality, the remark seemed to rivet the attention of all present and to create disquiet in
their minds, lest their absent friend had been waylaid and killed, and they,
too, and their families, might be the unwarned victims of a lurking and merci-
less foe. They instantly agreed to call the stream *Nolynn;* and it still rolls
its beautiful and limped waters, by that cognomen, on by the Dismal Rock to
Green River, into which stream it empties at the foot of the Indian Hill, one
of the grandest curiosities in Kentucky.

In connection with the name of JOHN LARUE we append an extract from

was not only a highly cultivated woman, but she was considered the beauty of the settlements. It were impossible to doubt this, since she was thrice married, and survived all her husbands. They settled in what is now Larue county, adjoining that of Hardin. Mrs. LARUE, finding that the entire settlement contained not a single physician, obtained the consent of her husband to apply herself to the study of medicine. With such text-books as were within her reach, she set to work, and soon became so noted for skill in the curative art that her services were in requisition far beyond the line within which she had designed to practice. Often, at the risk of danger from the prowling savages, she was known to ride for miles through the forests to reach the bedside of the sick, who had learned to depend upon her skill with as great faith as if she had carried a regular diploma pinned to her bonnet. Her first husband rather encouraged her charitable work; but her second husband, a Mr. ENLOW, fearing the danger to which she was constantly exposed in her too

a letter addressed to one of the Committee, from an old and highly influential citizen of Hardin county:

"HELM'S maternal grandfather came from the Shenandoah Valley, near Battletown—now called Berryville—at the foot of the Blue Ridge mountains. I have visited the spot, and it was then as lovely a portion of God's earth as eyes ever beheld. Since that day, alas! it has been swept of its beauties by fire and the desolating tread of a brutalized soldiery. There is a fact connected with the wanton destruction of property in this part of Virginia which I cannot forbear mentioning. The Valley of the Shenandoah had been the home of the LARUES ever since the settlement of the country, and many members of the family continue to reside there to this day. The late Mr. LINCOLN'S father lived close by those of them that had emigrated to Kentucky and settled on Nolynn. He was poor, and, at the time of Mr. LINCOLN'S birth, his family was almost subsisted by the charity of the LARUE family. When the order was given to render desolate the Shenandoah Valley, it was an ukase against the near relatives of those who had given Mr. LINCOLN bread in his impoverished infancy. The LARUE family, though none of its members ever attained any marked eminence, was made up of industrious, quiet, unobtrusive people, who were not only excellent citizens, but also pious Christians."

lengthened journeys, and dreading the effects of the often inclement weather upon her health, absolutely forbade her any longer to practice her art.* Her daughter, RE-BECCA LARUE, the eldest of thirteen children, was a babe in arms when her parents came to Kentucky, having been born in Frederick county, Virginia. . She afterwards be-came the wife of GEORGE HELM and the mother of the late Governor JOHN L. HELM. . It was in compliment to her, too, that the present county of Larue owes the name by which it is known.†

---

* A short time after she had ceased, in obedience to her husband's com-mands, to respond to the calls of her numerous patients, a woman living several miles away, and who was thought to be in great danger of death, sent her an urgent request to come to her assistance. The woman was very poor and helpless; and for this reason, she begged of her husband to be permitted to go. He told her no; he had made up his mind that she must give up all thought of resuming an avocation so unsuited to her sex. It was but a short time before the messenger returned, bringing with him still more urgent appeals from the suffering woman not to permit her to die unaided. With tears in her eyes, Mrs. ENLOW fell on her knees before her husband, and prayed that she might be permitted, for that one time, to go to the assistance of her stricken friend. This happened in the fore part of the night. Her husband, melted by her entreaties, agreed that, should the woman survive till morning, she might then go to her. Through the long hours of the night Mrs. ENLOW closed not her eyes, but patiently awaited for the dawn. With the earliest gleam of returning day, her watchful ear distinguished the distant galloping of a horse. It was the returning mes-senger, and her heart bounded with joy when she thought of the possibility that she might yet reach her patient in time to save the poor woman's life, and to prevent her little ones from becoming orphans. She sprang from her bed, and in answer to her husband's deprecatory words and looks, exclaim-ed: "You promised that I might go, and you must stand by your word." Bounding on her horse, she soon reached the bed-side of the suffering woman, to whom she administered in such wise as to give her immediate relief, and contribute to her ultimate recovery.

† This happened in this wise: When the new county was formed, the late Governor was a member of the Legislature, and out of compliment to him, it was proposed to call it HELM county. There were a few negative votes given against the resolution that was offered to this effect. These dissenting voices touched the pride of the Representative from Hardin, and rising to his feet, he declared he would not accept a compliment that was not unani-mously rendered. He suggested, at the same time, that the new county should be called after the maiden name of his mother. He thought this

GEORGE HELM, the father of the late Governor JOHN L. HELM, was born in Prince William county, Virginia, in the year 1774, and was, consequently, six years of age when his father removed to Kentucky. Having taken an active part in redeeming from the wilderness the fruitful farm upon which his father lived and died, he remained an agriculturist all his life, superintending and directing, up to the year 1820, all the farming operations on the place. In 1801 he was united in marriage with REBECCA LARUE, who bore to him nine children—four boys and five girls, only four of whom still survive.* No man was more respected than he in Hardin county, and none had warmer personal friends. At one time or other he filled almost every office, civil and legislative, in the gift of his fellow-citizens.

In 1821 GEORGE HELM, becoming embarrassed in his business operations, undertook a journey to Texas, with the expectation of entering into business in that then

particularly appropriate, as the family of the LARUES, whose progenitors had been its first settlers, were numerous in the county. A resolution to this effect was afterwards unanimously carried.

* ELIZA HELM, the late Governor's eldest sister, at the age of seventeen, married her counsin, WARREN LARUE, Esq., and has ever since lived in Elizabethtown, where she is beloved and honored by every one. Wherever sickness and poverty have their abode, there oftenest may be seen "Mamma Eliza," as she is called by high and low, brisk, helpful, and overflowing with pity toward all that are sick and suffering. WM. D. HELM is a highly respected physician residing in Bowling Green, Kentucky. THOS. P. HELM died young. LUCRETIA HELM married STEPHEN YEAMAN, Esq., and her second son, GEORGE H. YEAMAN, is now Minister from the United States to Denmark. She has also a son who is a highly respected Baptist Minister in New York City. LOUISA HELM married Mr. ISAIAH MILLER, a well-to-do farmer of Hardin county. She died many years ago. MARY JANE HELM married the Hon. PATRICK TOMPKINS, of Vicksburg, Miss., who was at one time a member of Congress. Both herself and her husband are long since dead. SQUIRE L. HELM and MALVINA HELM, who were quite young when their father died, were reared up and educated by the late Governor with his own children. The latter died in her girlhood, and the former is now a much esteemed Christian Minister, connected with the Baptist Church in Kentucky, and now acting in the capacity of "State Evangelist."

wild dependency of the Mexican Government. There he died in 1822.

JOHN LARUE HELM, late Governor of Kentucky, was born on the 4th day of July, 1802, at the old HELM homestead, near the summit of Muldrough's Mountain, one and a quarter miles north of the village of Elizabethtown. Amid the bold, wild scenery of the mountain's northern face, and in the beautiful prairie which courses its southern slope, rich with its waving grasses, wild strawberries, and hazel shrubs, he spent his childhood and youth. The country at the time was sparsely peopled. The valley in which his paternal ancestry resided was distant eleven miles from the residence of his maternal grand-parents, and between the two localities was one vast prairie, with but a single house, situated on a small stream, to relieve the monotony of the panorama. The country, only a few years before, extended from the Rolling Fork of Salt River on the north to Green River on the south, and then embraced a territory which is now divided into three counties and parts of others, and which then contained scarcely as many hundred inhabitants as it now does thousands. The war-whoop of the red man had then scarcely ceased its echoes through the forests, and herds of wild animals and flocks of wild birds wandered and flew over woodland and prairie fearlessly and almost undisturbed.

Such were the scenes and times in which the subject of our memoir was born and reared, only changed as time progressed by the continued flow of immigration and the labor of the strong arms which were opening the country to cultivation. He lived with his father and grandfather up to the age of sixteen, and, for about eight years of the time, attended various schools in the neighborhood. He had for his master during the latter years of his school life the afterwards celebrated Democratic politi-

cian and editor, DUFF GREEN,* under whose instructions
he made rapid advances in his studies. Another one of
his masters was a certain DOMINE RATHBONE, whose memory is still preserved in the annals of Nolynn Valley.
He was a ripe scholar, but singularly odd in appearance
and manner. Like Goldsmith's Village Schoolmaster, he
impressed every one with the idea that what *he* did not
know was not worth learning.

> "Amazed, the gazing rustics ranged around,
> And still they gazed, and still the wonder grew,
> That one small head could carry all he knew.
> But past is all his fame; the very spot
> Where many a time he triumphed, is forgot."

With a mind that was naturally bright, and with habits
of industry that were remarkable in one of his years, the
boy's advancement in knowledge was swift and easy.

---

* An anecdote illustrative of the Governor's character thus early in life is
related in connection with his school days under Mr. GREEN. On a certain
occasion, when about thirteen years of age, he refused obedience to a command of the master which he deemed tyrannical and unjust. For this his
teacher determined to punish him. At the time referred to, discipline in the
school-room was preserved only by one method—the use of the rod. The
boy was decidedly averse to this method in his case, because he thought
the punishment was both degrading and undeserved. After having received
a single blow, he bounded to the door with the hope of escaping from the
room. As is usual on such occasions, however, the teacher had his toadies
among the larger boys, and these prevented his exit. Finding he had no
power of resistance, he submitted to what he esteemed a degradation. With
lips firmly set and eyes boldly bent on the face of his tormentor, he received
without flinching or murmuring, many strokes of the rod, until the marks
of blood appeared in blotches through his garments. His sisters and others
of the school-girls beginning to cry, the teacher was forced to desist without
having conquered his obstinate pupil. Years after he had reached manhood,
HELM remembered and resented in his heart the insult, as he called it, which
he had been forced to submit to. But he was himself gray-haired when he
next met DUFF GREEN, who was then an old man. When the latter recognized his former pupil, who had then become a man of distinction in his
native State, the tears rushed to his eyes, and grasping his hands with a
warmth of affection that was indicative of the pride he took in his former
pupil's advancement in life, all resentment vanished from HELM's mind, and
the two remained fast friends up to the late Governor's death. DUFF GREEN
long since retired from the turmoil of partisan politics, and now resides in
Baltimore, Maryland, beloved and respected by all who know him.

2

The fact that he had been born on the anniversary day of his country's independence appears to have influenced his entire life. Imperceptibly to himself, he was led thereby to study the history of his country, and make himself familiar with the lives of all those eminent men who had taken part in the events which preceded and immediately followed the formation of the Government. Certain it is, before he had attained the age of sixteen, he had accumulated a sum of knowledge in regard to the past history of the country, and the character of its institutions, which is rarely acquired by men of mature years. Unwittingly, he was fitting himself for the patriotic duties that devolved upon him in after life. His school life ended when he had barely attained the age of fourteen years. About this time his father suffered a series of severe pecuniary losses, which made it necessary for him to withdraw his son from school, in order that he might avail himself of his services on the farm. He remained in this position till the year 1818, when a situation of more pecuniary value was offered him in the office of the Circuit Court Clerk of Hardin county.* His duties as Deputy Clerk of the Court were of a character to incline him to the law as a profession, and doubtless his preliminary legal studies were prosecuted while he was still an inmate of Mr. HAYCRAFT's office. It was not

---

* SAMUEL HAYCRAFT, Clerk of the Hardin Circuit Court, was, and still is, a remarkable character. He was, at the time referred to in the text, not only an excellent clerk, exact and industrious, but he was looked upon as the most interesting conversationalist in the county. His peculiar fondness for anecdote, of which his head was a perfect store-house, rendered the sessions of the Hardin courts singularly attractive to the members of the bar throughout the district. They would come from the neighboring counties, not merely for the transaction of business, but in order to refresh themselves, as it were, at the ceaseless fountain of HAYCRAFT's wit. All admitted that much of the pleasure of the hour was attributable to the great good humor of the Circuit Court Clerk, and the constantly varying little histories of men and things with which he was wont to beguile their leisure moments. He yet lives, in a good old age, with all his fondness for jest and humor unabated, and none is held in truer veneration throughout the community.

till the year 1821, however, that he was regularly entered
as a student of law in the office of the late BEN. TODIN,
Esq.,* a lawyer of high standing and ability, then practicing in the courts of Hardin and the neighboring counties. Never did student more earnestly devote himself to
the pursuit of knowledge, from the moment he made up
·his mind upon the question of a future profession to that
in which a license was issued to him to practice law in
the courts of the Commonwealth, than did the subject of
this brief memoir. He was at his books before others
had arisen from their beds, and long after these had
retired he was to be found "burning the midnight oil,"
and storing his mind with the wisdom of the past.

Young HELM had scarcely reached the age of twenty,
when death deprived him of his father, and he was not
only thrown by that event upon his own resources for the
means of subsistence and further necessary tuition, but he
suddenly found himself burdened with the care of a helpless mother and her large family of small children, who
had been left without any provision whatever for their
support. No word of complaint or of repining was heard
from his lips; but he resolutely set himself to work to repair, for himself and the loved ones dependent on him,
the family's broken fortunes. The close observer of men
and manners will recognize, in the position so early forced
upon young HELM, a truly fortuitous circumstance. There
is nothing so incentive to exertion as the feeling that
there are those dependent upon one's care who have none

---

* BEN. TOBIN was an excellent lawyer and a shrewd practitioner. He
possessed a power of satire that was almost unequaled. No one that
deserved it, whether acting in the capacity of litigant or attorney, in
opposition to his clients, was ever permitted to go out of the court-house
without having received at his hands such a torrent of uncomplimentary
invectives as almost to drive him mad. Withal, he was clever, honest, and
faithful, and his cynicism was, perhaps, in a great degree attributable to the
fact that he lived and died a bachelor. He has been dead for over thirty
years, and his remains are interred in the village cemetery, no one knows
exactly where.

other to look to for the necessaries and consolations of
life. It is always pleasant to contemplate a scene of unselfish family devotion. The members of this bereaved
family found their hearts more closely drawn together in
their affliction; and mutually striving to lessen each other's
burthens, they lived on in the hope of a happier future,
which came at length, principally through the unflagging
devotion, energy, and judicious management of the elder
son. Young HELM's thorough manliness of character was
further exemplified by his assumption, a few years later,
of the entire indebtedness of his father's estate, which he
paid off out of the first fruits of his legal practice.

Mr. HELM was admitted to the bar in July, 1823, and he
soon acquired a lucrative practice. The bar of the neighborhood was then one of the first in Kentucky, being
composed of such men as BEN. HARDIN, BEN. CHAPEZE,
CHARLES A. WICKLIFFE, JOHN ROWAN, RICHARD A. BUCKNER,
SAMUEL BRENTS, JOS. ALLEN, JOHN CAHOUN, A. H. CHURCHILL,
BEN. TOBIN, and numerous others, who were all eminent
men in their profession, and some of whom held then,
or have since held, high positions under the State and
Federal Governments.

His steady habits, together with a certain energy of
character which prompted him to give immediate attention to whatever matters of business were intrusted to
his direction, soon enabled him to add materially to the
comforts of his mother and her helpless family of children.
His business office was slimly furnished, to be sure, the
entire catalogue of its contents being a couple of chairs
for the use of his clients, and another, to one arm of which
he had ingeniously fitted a sort of writing-desk, for his
own accommodation. A more uncomfortable article than
the latter never was contrived; but so enamoured did
HELM become of it—most likely from the associations connected with it in his mind—that for years he would use
no other. The net results of his first year's practice sum-
med up just twelve hundred dollars.

Few of our eminent men have exerted a greater influence in the political party contests of the State than did
JOHN L. HELM. He was eminently a man of decision and
energy. Impulsive, straightforward, and always bold in
giving utterance to his opinions, for nearly forty years of
his life he was regarded by his political associates as an
element of unmistakable party strength. He was never
an advocate of the policy of mere defense. He had
learned in the school of experience that he that would not
fight at a disadvantage, must not be content to parry the
blows that are struck at him. He left to others all
" womanish uplifting of the palms" in deprecatory and
futile resistance, and boldly dashed to the attack of his
adversaries with a momentum of fiery energy that was at
times resistless.

Governor HELM's first essay in the field of political controversy owed its origin to the excited contest in Kentucky
in the year 1825, between what were termed the " Old
Court" and the " New Court" parties of that day. He
was then only twenty-three years old. The annexed ex-
planation of the question at issue between the two political organizations of the time we take from the published
writings of that eminent jurist, the Hon. GEORGE ROBERT-
SON :

" Shortly after the close of the last war with England,
the Legislature of Kentucky initiated what has since
been called 'the Relief System,' by extending the right
to replevy judgments from three to twelve months. To
minister still more relief to debtors, 'The Bank of the
Commonwealth' was chartered by a statute passed on the
29th of November, 1820, and without any other capital
than the net proceeds of the sales, as they might accrue,
of some vacant lands, and for the debts or notes of which
bank the State was not to be responsible beyond the said
capital, which was scarcely more than nominal. It was
foreseen, and by the debtor class desired, that the notes

issued by that bank would soon become depreciated; and, in a short time, the depreciation fell to two dollars in paper of said bank for one dollar in gold or silver. To effectuate the relief intended by the charter, the Legislature, on the 25th of December, passed an act providing that, if a judgment creditor would indorse on his execution that he would take the paper of said bank at par in satisfaction of his judgment, the debtor should be entitled to a replevin of only three months; but that, if such indorsement should not be made, the debtor might replevy for *two years;* and, by an act of 1821, the *ca. sa.* for debt was abolished, and the right to subject choses in action and equities to the satisfaction of judgments was substituted. These extensions of replevin and this abrogation of the *ca. sa.* were, in terms, made applicable to all debts whenever or wherever contracted, and were, consequently, expressly retroactive in their operation, embracing contracts made in Kentucky before the date of the enactment as well as such as should be made afterwards. To the retrospective aspect many conservative men objected as inconsistent with that provision in the National Constitution which prohibits any State enactment '*impairing the obligation of contracts,*' and also with that of the Constitution of Kentucky which forbids any legislative act '*impairing contracts.*' A majority of the people of Kentucky desiring legislative relief, either because they were in debt or sympathized with those who were, endeavored to uphold the whole relief system, while a firm and scrupulous minority denounced it as unconstitutional and void. That collision produced universal excitement, which controlled the local elections. The question was brought before the Court of Appeals of Kentucky, and, at its fall term in 1823, that tribunal unanimously decided, in an opinion delivered on the 8th of October, 1823, by Chief Justice Boyle, in the case of Blair vs. Williams, and in opinions *seriatim* by the whole

Court on the 11th of the same month, in the case of
Lapsley vs. Brashear, &c., that, so far as the Legislature
had attempted to make the extension of replevin retroactive, its acts were interdicted by both the Constitution
of the State and of the Union. As was foreseen, those
decisions produced very great exasperation and consequent denunciation of the Court. The Judges were
charged with arrogating supremacy over the popular
will; their authority to declare void any act of the
Legislature was denied, and they were denounced by
the organs and stump orators of the dominant Relief
party as usurpers and self-made kings. No popular
controversy, waged without bloodshed, was ever more
absorbing or acrimonious than that which raged like a
hurricane over Kentucky for about three years succeed-
ing the promulgation of those judicial decisions."

Mr. HELM, who was then full of life and energy, and
hopeful of a future that would compensate him for the
labors and struggles he had hitherto undergone in preparing himself for the active duties of his profession, entered
the lists with the opponents of the proposed change in the
Supreme Judiciary Department of the Commonwealth,
and did eminent service in the interests of his party and
the cause of right and justice. He not only addressed
his fellow-citizens of his own county in their primary
meetings, but he canvassed the adjoining counties, everywhere stirring up the people to a sense of the dangerous
doctrine that had been broached by the party that had
been in power, and effectually silencing, wherever his
voice could reach, the formidable opposition that had
lately arrayed itself against the promulgations of the
organic law. Not content with his oral efforts, he had
recourse to his pen, and in a forcible and well-digested
address, in pamphlet form, scattered his thoughts from
one end of the State to the other. The "Old Court"
party succeeded in returning a sufficient number of mem-

bers to the Legislature to defeat its antagonists, and at
the session of 1825–6 the vexed question was settled in
its favor.

In the latter part of the year 1824, the organization of
the new county of Meade took place, and as there happened to be no attorney residing within its limits, Mr.
HELM was commissioned by the Governor to discharge
the duties of County Attorney. The duties of this office
he fulfilled with a degree of efficiency and fidelity that
made his name known throughout that county and his
own, and caused him to take immediate rank with his
elders at the bar.

In 1826 he was the candidate of the " Old Court Party "
for the office of Representative from his county in the
State Legislature. From the time that the question at
issue between the Old Court and the New Court Parties
had been an absorbing one in the State, a large majority
of the voters of Hardin county had been attached to the
latter. The study which he had bestowed upon the subject during the previous year gave him a great advantage over his competitor in this canvass, and he secured
his election without difficulty. In the session of the
Legislature which followed, he made his influence felt
in putting to rest a question which had excited most
bitter antagonisms all over the State.

In 1830, at Bardstown, Kentucky, JOHN L. HELM was
united in marriage with LUCINDA B. HARDIN, the eldest
daughter of the Hon. BEN. HARDIN, of that place. The
courtship between the two was a long one. He had met
her accidentally seven years before, and from the first
had perseveringly laid siege to her heart. It is not for us
to inquire why she remained so long obdurate. It suffices
to know that she relented at last, and that a better and a
truer wife than she afterwards proved never gave cheer
and comfort to a fond husband's heart.

Absorbed during the greater part of his life by professional and official duties, Governor HELM intrusted to

his wife the entire control of their children and all domestic affairs. He soon learned to depend upon her judgment; and whatever she said or did in connection with
the education and training of their children was considered by him the best that could be said or done under
the circumstances. The winter after his marriage, Mr.
HELM removed from the country, in the Nolynn neighborhood, where he had been residing with his mother, into
Elizabethtown. On the second day of June, 1831, his
first child was born at Bardstown, Kentucky, whither
Mrs. HELM had gone in order to be with her own mother
during her confinement. This child was a son, to whom
was given the name of his maternal grandfather, BEN.
HARDIN.*

Mr. HELM was, for a second time, returned to the Lower
House of the Legislature in 1828; and only a few days
before the date of his marriage, he was elected to the
same office for the session of 1830–31. At that day there

* Mrs. HELM bore to her husband twelve children, viz: BEN. HARDIN HELM,
educated at West Point, afterwards a lawyer of high standing, practicing at
the Louisville bar, and finally a Brigadier General in the Confederate service,
who fell at the battle of Chickamauga; GEORGE HELM studied law, and commenced the practice at Memphis, Tennessee, where he died in 1858; LIZZIE
BARBOUR HELM, the oldest daughter, married to the Hon. H. W. BRUCE,
formerly a member from Kentucky to the Confederate States Congress, and
now Circuit Judge of the Ninth Judicial District; REBECCA JANE HELM died
in 1859; SARAH HARDIN HELM, now dead, was the wife of Major THOMAS
HAYS, an officer of high standing in the Confederate States service; LUCINDA
BARBOUR HELM, EMILY PALMER HELM, MARY HELM, JOHN L. HELM (born, as
was his father, on the fourth of July), JAMES PENDLETON HELM, and THOMAS
PRESTON POPE HELM, are all unmarried, and reside with their mother at the
old Helm Place. One child died in its infancy.

Never was mother more devotedly loved—more thoroughly confided in
by her children—than was and is Mrs. Governor HELM. Inheriting, in a
high degree, the intellectual gifts of her distinguished father, and possessing
with these a true woman's affection for her children, she has ruled her
household with a sway that was neither too harsh nor too indulgent, but in
which was judiciously blended the forces of a mind that was prompt to
distinguish every peculiarity of disposition in her children, and of a heart
whose strong affection for them, made perceptible to their understandings,
proved their greatest incentive to walk uprightly in her sight.

were few aspirants after official position, in any portion of the State, that were more intelligent canvassers among the people than was JOHN L. HELM. From early boyhood, he had been noted for his physical strength and his great powers of endurance. In the severe exercises of jumping, wrestling, and racing, there was not his match to be found in the whole county. He was a good hunter, too, and seldom found himself surpassed as a marksman. These were all appreciable accomplishments in a community for the most part composed of unpretending farmers, few amongst whom were more than superficially educated, and none at all inclined to exclusiveness on account of any thing they possessed beyond their fellows.

Shortly after his marriage, Mr. HELM removed from the country, in the Nolynn neighborhood, where he had been residing with his mother, into Elizabethtown, the county town of Hardin. He remained in the town, however, but a single year, when, having succeeded in redeeming from his uncle, BENJAMIN HELM, his father's inheritance, he took up his abode upon his ancestral acres at Helm Place, then called Helm Station, where he continued to reside for the remainder of his life.*

Mr. HELM continued to represent the people of Hardin county in the State Legislature, during each consecutive session of that body, up to the year 1838. He was elected Speaker of the House in 1835, and again in 1836. In the spring of 1838, at the earnest solicitations of his fellow-citizens of the county, he announced himself, in the interests of the Whig party, a candidate for the office of Representative from the District to the Federal Congress. He had two competitors in the race, one of whom, Mr.

---

* For more than eight years the late Governor occupied the house, opposite to the old Fort, in which his grandfather and father had resided. Immediately after removing to the place in 1832, he laid the foundations of a commodious residence; but it was only after an interval of eight years that it was ready for occupancy. Here he afterwards lived, and here his death took place in 1867.

HUFF, was from his own county, and the other, the late Hon. WILLIS GREEN,* was a noted politician from the county of Breckinridge. The district was largely Whig in political sentiment, as was shown by the slim vote given to Mr. HUFF, the Democratic candidate, at the August election. The interest in the race was confined to the friends of the Whig competitors, Messrs. HELM and GREEN, and a more warmly prosecuted canvass never engaged the attention of the voters of the district. Of all the public men of Kentucky at the time, there was not one that was more practiced in the ways and means of securing a political triumph than WILLIS GREEN. In natural mental gifts he was not the equal of HELM, but he was his superior in that knowledge which can be made effective in a canvass among the people. HELM was beaten in the race by a trifling majority, and he never afterwards aspired to any office that was national in its character.

In 1839 Mr. HELM was returned, for the ninth time, to the House of Representatives of Kentucky, where he was again elected Speaker. A better presiding officer never sat in the Speaker's chair. Together with a thorough knowledge of the rules governing the daily proceedings of the House, he possessed a clear understanding of what was due to the dignity of a deliberative assembly met together for grave objects, as well as a suavity of manner which went far toward rendering the sessions both pleasant and orderly. It must not be supposed that, because of his position of Chairman, he took no part in the many interesting questions which were, from time to time, brought up for consideration. On all matters of peculiar

---

* The Hon. WILLIS GREEN was a Kentuckian by birth and a lawyer of distinction. He resided for many years in Shelby county, where he married a Miss ALLAN. When first elected to Congress, in which body he served for six years (from 1839 to 1845), he lived in Breckinridge county. He went to Texas for the benefit of his health in 1858, where he died about the commencement of the late civil war.

interest, whether they referred to the State at large or only to his own constituency, he was in the habit of vacating the chair in order to present, from the floor of the House, the results of his own experience, observation, and study, before the people's representatives.

Governor HELM cannot be said to have been a finished orator; but few men had greater power than he to arrest and fix the attention of his hearers. His voice was full, rounded, and sonorous. He had a sufficient command of language to express his thoughts with clearness and perspicuity; and though his address was not precisely courtly, it was both easy and natural. He was more of a logician than a declaimer; and yet, at times, when he became impassioned in debate, he could be truly eloquent.

When speaking before a deliberative body, such as the Kentucky State Senate or the House of Representatives, he was always careful to preserve the proprieties of the occasion most scrupulously. He appeared to feel that there was due to the body whom he addressed that full measure of courtesy in demeanor and language which not even great provocation should be permitted to lessen or destroy. It was not so when he mounted the "stump" to address his fellow-citizens in the many canvasses in which he took part. He never waited for the attack, but, with all the energies of a mind fully convinced that his political antagonists deserved no quarter at his hands, he seized every opportunity to crush and destroy their prospects before the people. At one time he would submit their political faith to the test of his extraordinary reasoning powers; at another, he would ridicule their pretensions and satirize their principles; and, at still another, he would let fall on their luckless heads, pitilessly and remorselessly, the vials of his wrathful invective.

Governor HELM truly loved his country, and he as truly hated her enemies. He had firm faith in the wisdom that had conceived the organic law, and he seemed to feel toward all tamperers with the Constitution a measure of repugnance that was illimitable. Ardent and impulsive by nature, it may well be conceived that his language, when speaking of those whose policy he condemned as subversive of the best interests of the country, was often more characterized by severity than prudence. He was of a class of men that prefer to suffer on account of their open advocacy of preconceived ideas, rather than to earn a position of mere sufferance from their fellows, together with self-condemnation, through a system of discreet silence.

With an interval of two years, Mr. HELM continued to represent the people of Hardin county in the Lower House of the Legislature up to the year 1844, when he was returned to the State Senate from the district. He held this position until he was elected Lieutenant Governor on the ticket headed by the Hon. JOHN J. CRITTENDEN, in 1848.

As early as the year 1830, and at almost every meeting of the Legislature from that time up to the year 1848, the question of calling a Convention to form a new Constitution for the State had been brought before the people's representatives and fully discussed. The old State Constitution, though it had long been regarded as defective in some minor particulars, was acknowledged on all hands to be, in other and more important respects, a monument of the wisdom of its framers. A large number of the most respected and highly influential of the public men of Kentucky were opposed to the idea of tampering with an instrument under which the people of the State had reaped so full a measure of prosperity and happiness. Others were urgent in their endeavors to have a Convention held in order that the minor defects to which we have referred might be eliminated from the organic law. The contest between the two parties thus formed in the Commonwealth culminated in the passage

of a bill in the session of the Legislature of 1847–8, by
which the whole matter was directly referred to the people. Governor HELM was a member at the time from
Hardin county in the House of Representatives, and his
vote was recorded in favor of the passage of the bill.

Immediately preceding the election of August, 1848,
when the question of holding a Convention was to be
tested by the popular vote, Mr. HELM published an address to his constituents explanatory of the vote he had
given, in which he laid before them an entirely candid
synopsis of the arguments adduced during the debate in
the Legislature, both by the advocates of the bill and
those who opposed its passage. He thought the people
were entirely capable of deciding for themselves whether
any necessity existed for holding a Convention. He knew
that there were defects in the Constitution; but as to
how far a Convention would succeed in weeding the instrument of these acknowledged defects, and whether
their agents might not introduce into the organic law
provisions that were absolutely evil or of doubtful propriety, would depend entirely upon the wisdom and integrity of those selected to carry out the contemplated
reform. For himself, he thought the old Constitution
defective in these particulars:

First. It was defective in securing uniform and equal
representation in the Legislative Department of the Government.

Second. It was defective in its definitions in regard to
succession in cases where the administrative officers of
the government died in office, resigned their offices, or
were removed from them for cause.

Third. It was defective in its provisions in regard to
the appointment of county justices and sheriffs.

Fourth. In requiring yearly elections of members of the
Legislature and yearly sessions of the General Assembly
of the State, it imposed a public expense for which the
people received no adequate compensation.

Fifth. That provision of the Constitution which regulated the tenure of office of the Circuit Court and the
Appellate Court Judges was calculated to gradually foist
upon the State an incompetent Judiciary.

The late Governor's notions on the subject of the judiciary will be found of practical value, even at the present
time. He tells us that there were in 1848 three distinct
parties in the State, each holding views adverse to the
others on the subject of the Judiciary, viz: One for a
Judiciary holding office during good behavior; one during good behavior for a limited term of years, and one
for an elective Judiciary.* He thought at the time the
Government was founded, the "tenure of good behavior" provision had been adopted on account of its having
worked well in the administration of law in Great Britain;
but that no necessity exists here, where the sovereignty is
with the people, for any such provision. He continued as
follows:

"It seems to be feared that those who favored the
passage of the Convention bill were for an elective
Judiciary. I can say, for one, I am in the most unqual-
ified and uncompromising terms opposed to it. Nor did

---

* The Judiciary Department of a Government ought to be its chief bulwark against disorder and dissolution. Its entire independence is a necessary ingredient of its efficiency. Place over it a higher authority in the
Government, and you at once shackle its freedom, and place it under the
heel of despots. Make it subservient to the popular will in the field of party
strife, and you cannot avert the danger of its becoming prostituted to purposes foreign to the design of its creation. To the writer, it has always
appeared one of the saddest evidences of our failure to appreciate the high
destiny foretold for the nation, when he beholds a would-be Justice perched
upon the stump, descanting on political issues, and soliciting the votes of
his hearers on the grounds of his political orthodoxy, and not for reasons
that have any affinity with the high office which is the object of his aspirations. The grand idea of the sacred character of the Judge's office, which
has been so familiar to us all since the formation of the Government, is fast
losing its hold on our minds, through the belittling effects of the law as it
stands, by which the Judiciary is leveled to a standard not one whit above
that of a partisan scramble after position.

I hear one single gentleman who voted for the bill express such as his sentiments. There are many reasons why the Judiciary should not be elective, and why there should exist a difference between their mode of appointment and the other Departments of the Government. It is the province of the Legislative and the Executive Departments to act upon such subjects as bear alike upon the whole community. But it is the province of the Judiciary to decide upon individual right; and to expound the laws which determine the life, liberty, and property of the citizen. To place a Judge in the political arena, where he may contract prejudices and partialities, you make him more or less subservient to the wealthy and influential citizens, to the prejudice of the poor, the unknown, and the indigent. The scales should be poised with a steady and even hand, and Justice administered blind to its objects. An elective Judiciary would certainly be at war with what time and experience have proved to be political wisdom.

"I am for an independent Judiciary; but not so independent as to be placed beyond just responsibility. I think experience has clearly demonstrated that the tenure of good behavior is equal to a term for life. I am for good behavior for a limited term of years—say seven or ten—when the Judge should come back to the appointing power, that he might have an opportunity of inquiring whether all is well, antecedent to a reappointment. I am inclined to believe it would have a happy effect upon the officers of the Judicial Department, if you would fix a day to which they would look forward as a day of trial and examination: that they might say to themselves on that day, the manner in which I have discharged my public duty is to be brought in view; I must rely upon the qualifications of my head and heart for my reappointment."

The popular vote was largely in favor of holding a Convention, and in August, 1849, an election was held, in pursuance of an act of the General Assembly, approved January 13th, 1849, for delegates to the same. The Convention met in October of the same year, and continued its sittings, from day to day, until it had finished its work. By a provision of the new Constitution itself, that instrument was to be submitted to the people for their approval at the general election to be held in May, 1850, before being declared the organic law of the State. Many eminent men throughout the Commonwealth were greatly dissatisfied with the action of the Convention. Among the most prominent of these was Governor HELM, who was then Lieutenant Governor of the State, and the presiding officer of the Senate. At an early day of the session of the General Assembly of the Commonwealth in 1850, a bill was offered in the Senate, by Mr. GEORGE W. TRIPLETT, to postpone the vote on the new Constitution until the August election of 1850. One of the most masterly speeches ever delivered by Governor HELM was made on this occasion in favor of the bill, and in condemnation of the new Constitution. The great importance of the questions debated, which we consider fully as important now as they were then, induces us to quote freely from this speech. Addressing the Senate, Mr. HELM is reported to have said:

"Mr. CHAIRMAN: I address the Senate to discharge a duty which I owe to myself and feel that I owe to my country. I am aware that I place myself in an attitude to become the subject of assault, if not bitter vituperation. We live in a community too prone to censure the acts of public men.

"I propose to review the instrument submitted to become the Constitution of the State upon the ratification of the people. I wish to put the machinery to work, and invite attention to its practical operations.

3

"No man in Kentucky has written more and spoken more than I have, with a view to press upon the country the importance of organic reform. I presided at every assemblage held in Frankfort, having for its object the organization of a party for reform. I drafted the greater part of the manifesto of the party. In the advocacy of those principles we entered the field and won the two important battles, without which, victory would not have crowned our efforts. Under its auspices there seems to have been embodied a force of public opinion threatening to sweep down all that stands in its way. Were I to look to myself alone, and consult the probable results of a single day, selfish policy would dictate a quiet submission to the things that are. Every personal motive would prompt such a course. In addition to my own position, I stand connected by a tie of relationship to one whom public opinion regarded as the master-spirit of the Convention—one whom I have loved as a father, and to gratify whose wishes has ever been my anxious desire.* But I have a public duty to perform, and I have determined to perform it, and abide the consequences. It is said I have planned my own destruction. Sir, if that storm of public opinion with which gentlemen threaten me was now placed before me in its most frightful form, with a full consciousness of its desolating blast, I would look it in its very face, and speak what I thought. He who shall shiver as a reed in the wind, at a crisis full of importance to the State, is a faithless public sentinel. I was for reform, and not for revolution. I was for amending the Constitution, and not for obliterating every vital principle which it contained. I was not without my fears that, by a combination of political results, the people might be driven to

---

* Reference is here made to the Hon. BEN. HARDIN, Governor HELM's father-in-law. The course taken by Mr. HELM on this occasion caused an estrangement between the two, which was only healed when Mr. HARDIN lay on his death-bed

extremes. I had hoped public opinion had determined
upon two modes of escape : one, to leave the way open
and easy, should experience teach us that we were wrong;
the other, that the work of the Convention would be submitted to the people for their ratification. In the latter, I
thought it was implied that time would be allowed to
read, to hear discussed, and calmly consider the change,
and act with a deliberation commensurate with the importance of the occasion ; that, as we had begun by proclaiming the question as above party, so we would consider the instrument independent of and above party, and
by its intrinsic merits as an organic law pronounce judgment for or against it. I had supposed submission had
for its purpose something more than an idle ceremony.

" I approve much that is in this instrument, and I heartily condemn much. I am fully aware of the difficulty of
forming any human instrument perfect. Nor do I feel
disposed to be carried away by captious objections. Investigation is the handmaid of truth. I struck boldly at
the old Constitution, and for my boldness received the
Herculean blows of some of the most distinguished actors
in the formation of the present Constitution. Standing,
as I do, identified with the present state of things, I will
be bold to call the attention of the people to such portions of the new as I think wrong, relying that the evil
and the good will be weighed by them, and to their decision I will bow. If I had signed that instrument, I
would do what I now propose to do. If my work could
not bear the test of investigation by comparison with that
which I sought to amend, no dogged stubbornness or pride
of authorship could induce me to fasten upon the people
a form of government which would not promote their welfare. If we meet ·in the field of fair argument and free
discussion, by which the defects of the instrument are
made known to the people, and knowing them they adopt,
there will be none to censure.

"The crude and undigested form of this Constitution must be perceived by all. It is freely admitted by its authors and friends. I state a fact with no view to reflection, but as a substantive fact well worth the consideration of the people in deciding this great question, and in justification of myself in calling attention to its errors.

*   *   *   *   *   *   *   *   *   *   *

"'SECTION 36. No act of the General Assembly shall authorize any debt to be contracted on behalf of the Commonwealth, except for the purposes mentioned in the thirty-fifth section of this article, unless provision be made therein to lay and collect an annual tax sufficient to pay the interest stipulated, and to discharge the debt within thirty years; nor shall such act take effect until it shall have been submitted to the people at a general election, and shall have received a majority of all the votes cast for and against it: *Provided*, That the General Assembly may contract debts without submission to the people, by borrowing money to pay any part of the public debt of the State, and without making provision in the act authorizing the same for a tax to discharge the debt so contracted, or the interest thereon.'

"If it was intended to grant a power to be exercised, it should have been done without such restrictions as would render it wholly inoperative. The section purports to be a grant of power to borrow money, doubtless with reference to internal improvement; but the power cannot be exercised without the bill which authorizes the loan couples with it a provision for the yearly payment of the interest and principal of the sum borrowed in thirty years. The two things are to be inseparably connected—they must start together and run their course together—one power cannot be exercised without the other. It would be a perversion of the spirit of the Constitution to repeal or supersede the taxing part of the law, even by the application of other funds, or even to appropriate the proceeds of the investment to relieve the people. Because the sum to be collected would be determined by the bill, and must of necessity be equal to the interest and the payment of such portion of the principal as would, by a yearly application, extinguish the principal in thirty years. If the loan could not be made with such terms of payment, then you would be engaged in raising, by yearly installments, an amount sufficient to pay the principal at the end of thirty years. A proposition so ridiculous would hardly be carried into execution.

' "I was for limiting the power of any one Legislature to create a debt. Thus, if any one Legislature went to its limit, the people through their representatives could control the action of the next. If it was thought proper to consult the public will at the ballot-box, would it not have been sufficient to express in the bill the amount and objects of the appropriation? Submit it to the people and leave them to determine their own mode of payment. Is it right for an organic law to attempt to regulate the policy of the State for forty or fifty years to come?

" I am aware that public improvements by the force of public opinion had received a quietus for the present. That is right. Much of the public money had not a wise direction, and it was right to suspend until time would allow a wise revision. I am free to confess I have been a participant in the good and the evil which flow from it. To improve a country with a view to the development of its wealth and resources has challenged the consideration and approval of the wise men of every age, and is now the settled policy of all civilized communities. Kentucky has wealth in the bowels of her mountains— her coal, her minerals, and her salines. Her vast forests stand ready to bow subservient to the mechanic and laborer. I have stood here upon the floor of this Capitol,

and seen, with a self-sacrificing love of country, the
Representatives of the mountains voting to improve the
centre of the State by such works as pointed to their
country, giving promise that there was a bright future
for them. But now that the centre have most that they
want, the doors are closed against the prospect of the
mountains. Rivers half improved—the natural navigation locked up—burthens imposed by an incomplete mode
of transportation—in other sections roads half finished—
one hour in the mud, the next on a patched turnpike,
paying full toll for half a load. So stands the face of
the country. Not one dollar of the proceeds arising
from the money paid by those engaged in the transportation of the productions of the soil is allowed by this
Constitution to be appropriated to ease their burthens,
or facilitate the means of transportation by completing
the road. All this is done to relieve those who may live
after us in the next five and twenty years. We bear
these burthens the better to relieve and provide for our
children and grandchildren. Will the community stand
it? Can the arm of industry be thus paralyzed? The
community will be driven to seek relief in some form.
That form will be by grants to private incorporations to
construct railroads, and probably followed by ceding to
companies the navigation of your rivers upon the bonus
of completion. Thus will the people, driven to this extreme, be compelled to cede away the sovereign power
until the combined influence of corporations will be
enabled to control the policy of the State, and the people made to pay the tribute. Trade and commerce must
and will go on—it cannot be arrested. One of two
results is inevitable—the State will be compelled to cede
to individuals the interest she has to secure the completion of her works, or she will be compelled to grant
incorporations to aid in the carrying trade, which will
supersede her own works costing five millions, and leave

them in a dilapidated state, unworthy of use. By such means, too, the resources of the Sinking Fund may be wasted away.

"But what do we behold around us? Our sister States vicing with each other in a race of improvement leading their citizens on to wealth and greatness. By bars of iron, laid by the strong arm of sovereign power, they seek to bind our happy Union together. To facilitate social intercourse, and by a commerce promising reciprocal advantages, they seek to supply the wants of each other by an exchange of commodities peculiar to our variegated soil and climate. In this great march to glory, and the consummation of freedom, where stands Kentucky? She who, by her geographical position, and no less by the soul-stirring chivalry of her citizens, stands as the heart of the Confederacy, and, by her noble pulsations, should throw the vital fluid to the extremities, is suddenly converted into an iceburg, coldly defying penetration."

His remarks touching the Judiciary System of the State will be found most pertinent:

"It is due to candor to say, that the organization of the Judiciary System under this Constitution constitutes, with me, an insurmountable objection. To destroy the independence of the Judiciary is to sap the foundation of civil liberty. To maintain the independence of that Department of Government has been the subject of inquiry and the anxious desire of civilized nations. For the want of such a department in Governments, history is filled with scenes of individual oppression. Read the history of those Governments where such a department was unknown, and the heart sickens in the very comtemplation of the scenes of oppression falling upon the weak and the powerless. Man's war upon man constitutes one of the most prominent features in the history of the world. We are taught by divine authority that man is as prone to

evil as the sparks are to fly upward. By the wisdom of
the Lord's prayer we are taught that man should not be
led into temptation. Man is a compound of good and
evil; he has frailties, he has passions, and he has prejudices; he loves, admires, and hates; he has affections,
and, by individual associations, he acquires partialities.
It is the instinct of our nature to love those who manifest
love for us. He who refuses to return favor for favor is
regarded as a bad neighbor. If there is any one general
principle which more closely connects itself with the
operations of our Government than another, it is that of
returning favors for the bestowal of the right of suffrage.
The passions of men sleep in their bosoms, until aroused
into action by some exciting cause, and then waste their
fury upon some living object. I appeal to the experience
and judgments of men, if there is any one thing in life
better calculated to make men hate and love each other
than the exciting scenes of a popular canvass. An independent judge is one who presides with a perfect consciousness that he whose cause he is about to try has no
power to punish or to reward—that he can neither give
or take away his power. Free to think and free to act,
he poises the scale of justice, blind to those whose rights
throw the balancing beam. To effect this great purpose,
our fathers wisely conceived the plan of a division of
powers into separate departments, that they should operate as mutual checks and balances. Founded in confidence and jealousy, our Government is wisely arranged
to learn and to execute the public will, and to guard
against its errors, and shield the persons of individuals
from oppression. Is not this structure of Government
founded upon the very belief of the absolute necessity to
guard man against man? This very Constitution proclaims that absolute arbitrary power over the lives, liberty,
and property of freemen, exists nowhere in a republic—
not even in the largest majority. Where is the sovereign

power here? Is it not in the people? How is it exercised? By the declared voice of a majority. Are we
blind to the fact that that majority is the result of the
action of certain prominent men or produced by some
exciting cause which, for the time, dethrones reason, and
lets angry passion control the storm? Has man in this
day stripped himself of selfish motives? It is then the
majority who gives to the judge his power. It is the
majority, under the principle of re-electing judges, that
can again give or take away, and may regulate the salary
of a coming term. Do we not attempt to deceive ourselves, when we are betrayed into an argument that men,
when canvassing for popular favor for judgeships, will
be better and purer men than when canvassing for other
offices? Man is man, and his nature the same. Do we
not break the force of a representative government when
we bestow upon an officer an office by popular suffrage,
and at the same time tell him he is independent of the
public will? Can it be possible that men are so blinded
by momentary infatuation as to reject the lessons of
experience of ages? Are we prepared to wipe away the
landmarks of our revolutionary fathers, and at once pre-
cipitate ourselves upon a field of untried experiment? It
seems to be understood as a fact, which should startle the
community, that a majority of this Convention of wise
men, combining those opposed to the election and re-
election of judges, entertained the opinion that the principle was wrong, but yielded their own opinions and
executed those of their constituents. The wise men
thought it wrong, but thought it right to execute a
wrong to satisfy the public opinion.

" The Constitution bears upon its face intrinsic evidence of a distrust of the correctness of the principle.
The Appellate Judges, whose duty it is to decide causes
from every part of the State, are elected by four districts,
so that there may be a majority on the bench that three

fourths of the people had not voted for. The restriction
as to age and practice, the separation of the judicial
from the other elections, and the desire by some to have
them elected by ballot, are all evidence that there rested in the minds of the framers of the Constitution a
well-founded apprehension. They have sought to guard
against the mal-influences of their own system through
the means of those contrivances. If they should fail,
then all the evil consequences follow.

"My very humble political history commenced at the
close of that storm of party which aimed to strike down
the Judiciary in Kentucky. Impressions were then made
upon my mind which I cannot clear myself of. My imagination, in spite of me, will be haunted by the belief
that by some great revulsion in trade, when the people
shall be made to feel a pressure, a storm can be raised
by the popular declaimer which will sweep all before it;
and he who holds his office by virtue of the popular
will, must and will yield to its influence. All powers
will be amalgamated and directed by the popular will.
There will be no power left with the firmness to resist
the storm until a calm will restore reason and preserve
private right.

"Pecuniary storms may not be the only ones disturbing
the popular elements. Other rights may sooner or later
be involved, and those who now seek to compromise conflicting interests or prejudices may be made to feel the
importance of an independent Judiciary.

"I cannot elaborate this subject. I must be permitted
to avail myself of the opinions of gentlemen who, by
their positions as members of the Convention, have some
hold upon the public confidence.

"Wedded, as I have been, to reform—painful as it is to
me to turn away from my old friends—I am bound by
every consideration which ought to regulate the conduct
of a statesman and a gentleman to withhold my assent.

I entered the field a firm opponent of an elective Judiciary. I feel that I was pledged before the country and my honor involved in that pledge. I thought then it was wrong—I think so now, and am still more firmly convinced, that by the shortness of the term and the re-eligibility of the Judges, every vestige of the independence of the Judiciary will sooner or later be swept away—that the Judiciary is doomed to become a part and parcel of the political machinery of the day—made to serve the purposes of party men—a reward to the faithful—a machine in the hands of the wealth and power of the country to grind to dust the feeble, the powerless, and the poor man. I can see nothing in this Constitution which promises good to counterbalance the evil to flow from such a Judiciary. What price can be put upon, or what exchange can be made in the nature of compromise, for the surrender of the great principle of an impartial administration of justice? With such opinions—and that I have them, I call Heaven to witness—where would be my honor—where my own self-respect—if to serve myself I surrender them? Let honors and profit pass away, I must preserve my honor."

Governor HELM appears to have had a clear perception of the evils that have since grown out of that provision of the new Constitution by which so many minor officers in the Commonwealth were declared *elective*. The following is a graphic picture of what takes place at every election for State, city, and county officers:

"Every officer in the State is to be elected, State and county, except the Secretary of State. Let each man look over the list, and he will find it will amount to quite, if not over, four thousand in the State. If there should be an average of three competitors for each office, it will bring into the field an array of twelve thousand seekers for office. Let each man tax his mind for a moment, to sum up all the consequences growing out of this immense

body of men moving for office. May not the people be
brought to the point of exclaiming, in the language of the
Declaration of Independence, 'there has been sent hither
a swarm of officers, to harass us and eat out our substance!'* In the great multiplicity of officers, counting
deaths, resignations, and removals, will not some portion
of the people be at all times engaged in elections? What
a tax upon the labor of the country! I take it for granted
that county and district vacancies will be filled by a re-
election, since the convention provided no mode for filling
vacancies, even for a day, beyond *pro tem.* appointments,
except in the last year of a Circuit Judge. Four elected
Judges of the Court of Appeals are not permitted to fill
the remnant of a term of even six months of a Clerk of
the Court of Appeals. A writ of election must go forth,
and one hundred and fifty thousand men 'called into the

---

* The statements of these paragraphs will be viewed as almost prophetic.
The swarms of office-seekers with which the whole land is cursed is one of
the saddest evidences of the decline of our people from the high patriotic
standard of the fathers. Politics—especially local politics—has got to be a
trade, in which sharpness and cunning are much more regarded than probity
and competency. Men who are too lazy to work, and whose incompetency
in the management of their own private affairs is proverbial among their
acquaintance, strangely enough imagine themselves fitted, in all particulars,
to discharge the duties of any office that is within the gift of the people.

> " Look after your Till, was the rule 'till of late,
> But now, 'tis—look after the Till of the State."

It has long been conceded that the two great prerequisites to success in an
election before the people, now a-days. so far, at least, as the remunerative
offices are concerned, are money and assurance. The office no longer seeks
the man, but crowds of men are seeking after the offices. The very system
which Governor Helm feared for the integrity of the franchise has long controlled all our elections. Political sharpers and wire-pullers make calls for
primary conventions, and these conventions are most generally so *hocussed* in
their hands as to be made mere machines to work out their wills. Or, two
sets of such schemers, the one not one whit more to be trusted than the
other, make a fight, in these primary conventions, over the nominations, and
whether the one clique succeeds or the other, the candidates are foisted on
the people as the veritable choice of *the party*, though not one in ten that
belong to it know anything about their fitness for the places to which they
aspire, and though nine out of ten of them would prefer other men and
men that are better known.

field to elect a clerk for six months. Carrying out the same principle, the Legislature must establish the same rule in regard to Treasurer, Auditor, Register, Attorney General, President of the Board of Internal Improvement, and Superintendent of Public Instruction. Is there not danger to be apprehended that the frequency with which the people may be called to the polls, and the scenes attending elections—too familiar to all—may at last disgust the people themselves, and render them indifferent to the exercise of the elective franchise? Will not the business and substantial men of the country retreat from it, and give up the elections entirely to those who seek for office for sake of employment? Imagine an unlettered man pressing to the polls to make choice among some fifty or sixty candidates for the various offices, with some friend of an aspirant at his elbow to tell over a long list of names.

"Will not this result in fixing as the permanent order of things a system of caucusing? By that system, the Government will be thrown into the hands of, and controlled by, the active and vigilant office-seekers. The mass of the people will have little else to do than go to the polls and register the edicts of a caucus. The great question as to who shall be President is to absorb all others. The parties will be driven, by concentrated action, to present their candidates, and we will come to the polls and vote the partisan ticket by its name. The motto will be, '*to the victors belong the spoils.*' Thus is there to be a perpetual struggle for power and the emoluments of office. The policy of the State will be lost sight of, and each man's qualification will be tested by his opinions upon some national question. Can there be imagined a more irresponsible and corrupting mode of managing a government than that of a system of caucusing? It has a tendency to destroy freedom of thought, freedom of action, and freedom of speech. To

my mind, the very freedom of our institutions depend
upon breaking the force of any state of things which
has a tendency to stifle that open and manly mode of
talking, thinking, and acting, without the dread of punishment or hope of reward, which has hitherto marked
the course of our people. I was for extending the power
to elect officers to that point at which the mass of the
people, by personal intercourse, had an opportunity of
knowing the fitness and qualifications for the office
sought by the candidate. But is it not surprising, when
we recur to the provisions of this Constitution, that its
most distinctive features are its crimination and the reduction of the powers of those officers who have been
elected? The Governor is stripped of his power, and
against that officer the heaviest battery of this Convention has been played. The Legislature is stripped of
almost every power worth reserving. The interval between its sessions is doubled, and it is not permitted to
judge for itself as to the time necessary to the completion of its business. Is it not a strange state of public
opinion to cry out, in one voice, extend the right of
suffrage, for in that our liberty consists, and in the next
moment demand that elective officers be stripped of their
powers because they have been faithless to their trust?
But what man has complained that the laws have not
been faithfully expounded? Yet the Judges, against whom
the least of all complaints have been made, are to be
made elective, whilst we are stripping those heretofore
elective of all their powers.

Section eight of the new Constitution requires that
every voter shall have been a resident of his precinct for
sixty days next preceding an election. Though he may
have been born and raised in the county, he is not permitted to vote at all, should he have removed into another
precinct (in cities, frequently, only across the street), and
there resided for a term less than sixty days. On this
provision Gov. Helm thus spoke:

"I hold it to be the duty of the law-maker to afford to the citizen who has a clear and indisputable right to vote, every facility consistent with the purity of elections to cast his vote. No honest and well-known citizen should have his rights restricted or denied him, because his business or condition shall require a change of residence, in order that a dishonest man may be caught in an attempt to transcend his right. The true principle is, catch the offender if you can, but do not make the punishment of the innocent the means of detecting the wrong-doer. By geographical boundaries and ideal lines subject to changes, you embarrass the citizen in the free exercise of his most invaluable right by imposing penalties for voting on the wrong side of a precinct line. There should be at least one place in a county which a freeman could approach as the alter of his liberty, and feel a consciousness that he does not make himself a criminal by the exercise of a right purchased by the blood of his fathers. That place should be the court-house. Under the provisions of this Constitution, a man may have been born in, and never lived out of the county until he shall have children, and grand and great-grand-children; yet he cannot vote at the court-house, if his residence be within the boundary of a country precinct. He has been taxed to make it; he does not engage in broils with his neighbors, and therefore does not use it in that way; and yet he is denied its use for the sacred purpose of casting his vote. You can't restrain men in their business pursuits; they must and will go where their business calls them. If a man be born and raised within a county, change his residence from one precinct to another, in the months of June or July, he forfeits his right of suffrage. Will not this operate peculiarly hard upon those whose condition in life force them to become tenants, or laborers by the day or by the month? The tenant may be made to shelter at the will of his landlord; the laborer finishes his labor in a crop in the months of June or July, yet he cannot seek for employment in another precinct, unless at the sacrifice of his right to vote. Does not this result in an advantage to those who have fixed homes? The young man who labors for his living, the country's surest support in a call to arms, restrained from seeking profitable employment when he shall have finished one contract. He who shall be called from home upon indispensable business, and interrupted by unavoidable delay, approaches one place of voting where he is known to all, yet as he lives within the boundaries of another precinct, he is turned away and loses his right. I can imagine an old revolutionary soldier, a pioneer of the West, who had bared his bosom to the stealthy savage, approach the polls in a county where he had resided from his earliest settlement, and he is turned away because he lives at home, or with some child in another precinct. I venture to predict that in the various elections, regular and irregular, to fill vacancies, there will be thousands disfranchised who have an indispensable right to vote. Is it right to punish the innocent as a means of detecting the rogue? Heretofore a known citizen had the right to cast his vote whereever he had a known residence, if for a day only. Have our popular elections been hitherto conducted with so many marked evidences of fraud as to make this change necessary? The restriction is an admission of the fact on the part of the members of the Convention, and yet the popular essence of the instrument is its willingness to submit everything to the ballot-box, where, in their estimation, so much fraud has been perpetrated. A most remarkable contradiction. Flattery of virtue and intelligence on the one hand, and an imputation of fraud and corruption on the other. Has not enough been done by the Constitution in limiting the elections to a single day, that the balance might have been left to statutory provisions?"

The Gubernatorial canvass of 1848 was characterized by a greater display of individual exertion on the part of both the Whig and the Democratic candidates than had been witnessed in any previous election for many years. The late Governor POWELL headed the Democratic ticket, and his great personal popularity rendered him an opponent that was by no means to be despised, even when confronted by such a man as JOHN J. CRITTENDEN. Mr. HELM, who had been placed on the ticket with Mr. CRITTENDEN for the second office in the gift of the people, made a thorough canvass of the State. It was the first time that he had had occasion to address his fellow-citizens outside of his own Congressional district, and, immediately after receiving his nomination, he addressed himself to the business before him with the determination of a man who knew what he had to encounter in order to succeed in the canvass. In every quarter of the State his voice was heard in defense of the principles and policy of his party and in reprobation of those of his Democratic competitors. The race was a close one, but the Whig candidates were elected and took their seats.

Mr. HELM continued to fulfill the duties of Lieutenant Governor and President of the Senate till July 31, 1850. When Mr. CRITTENDEN, having accepted from President FILLMORE the position of Attorney General of the United States, resigned his office, the former was installed as Governor of the Commonwealth in the place of that eminent statesman. It is needless for us to speak of Gov. HELM's administration of State affairs. Here, as in every position filled by him in his long public career, he proved himself the faithful agent of the people and the watchful guardian over their interests. From his only message to the General Assembly, delivered November 7th, 1850, which he had occasion to present, we give below such extracts as we think are illustrative of his character, as well as certain passages on topics that have not

4

yet lost their interest with the general public.   The message begins :

"Gentlemen of the Senate and House of Representatives :

" Since the adjournment of the last General Assembly,
the duties of the Chief Magistracy of this Commonwealth
have devolved upon me, in consequence of the resignation of Governor Cʀɪᴛᴛᴇɴᴅᴇɴ.   Governor Cʀɪᴛᴛᴇɴᴅᴇɴ could
not well be spared by Kentucky at this period, and the
people are only reconciled to his departure by the fact
that he has accepted a post at Washington which, though
its duties required a resignation of the office confided to
him by the people of Kentucky, extended the sphere of
his action and his usefulness.   Kentucky gave him up
that he might, on another theatre than that which she
had assigned him, devote himself to his country and the
promotion of his country's welfare.

" The present is an important period in the history of
our beloved State.   In the month of June last, the new
Constitution was proclaimed as the paramount law of
the land.   On that day, the organic law—the Constitution under which for fifty years Kentucky had kept her
onward march—the Constitution which for half a century had secured to her people all the rights of freemen,
was done away, and a new instrument proclaimed in its
stead.   May we not have reason to congratulate ourselves as a people, if fifty years hence we shall find
ourselves as prosperous, as happy, and as contented as
we now are?   The changes in Government made by the
new Constitution are many—some of these changes are
radical—yet they were made without bloodshed, without
strife, and without disturbing the peaceful current of
public and private business.   How different the scenes
from those which, in days past and even now, mark
changes in government in the Old World.   A handful of
men assembled in the Representative Chamber, by a single dash of the pen, change the whole structure of the

Government. No scenes of disorder or of violence attend the proclaiming of the new system. All is calm and quiet. The proclamation is made—the handful of men adjourn and depart for their homes. Their authority is gone—they have finished their labors, and their power has ceased. The new order of things begins, and the people move on peacefully and quietly as before. Such a spectacle challenges the admiration of the world. It teaches a lesson invaluable to the cause of freedom.

"Differ as we may as to the propriety of many of the changes in the form of Government, it is our duty, and should be our pleasure, to acquiesce in them, and so direct legislation as fairly and fully to test their wisdom. Any factious opposition to the Constitution now would, it seems to me, be unwise if not unpatriotic. The people, through their chosen representatives, have ordained it as the law of the land. The people, by a direct vote at the polls, by a majority almost unparalleled in our history, declared in its favor, and is it not now the duty of every good citizen to give to it a steady support, that the changes it proclaims may be fairly tried? This, in my judgment, we owe to the people, to the country, and to ourselves.

"I tender you my cordial congratulations upon the general good health and prosperity of our people.

"I may also congratulate you on the financial affairs of the State. The revenue is abundant to meet the ordinary demands upon the Treasury, and will furnish a handsome surplus to be applied in payment of the public debt."

*   *   *   *   *   *   *   *   *   *   *

"The surplus in the Treasury is under the control of the General Assembly, and may, from time to time, be profitably and wisely used in aid of the Sinking Fund, by judicious appropriations to unfinished public improvements. Whether there will be an increase in the valua-

tion of the property of the State, and an increase from
that cause of the surplus in the Sinking Fund, will depend mainly upon the selection of faithful and competent Assessors. I am inclined, however, to think the
surplus will not probably exceed $100,000, nor will it fall
short of $50,000. If, however, nothing shall be derived
from the revenue—and the probabilities are there will
be no surplus from the revenue for a few years—then we
may safely set down the annual surplus in the Sinking
Fund at from $65,000 to $75,000.

" I cannot in candor restrain the expression of my fears
that the election of the Assessors of taxable property will
not prove to be a successful and valuable change, and
that it may result in consequences tending to embarrass
and confuse our system of finance. Allow me, therefore,
respectfully to suggest that their duties be plainly prescribed and enforced by the infliction of adequate penalties. I have long entertained the opinion that the
employment of a number of persons in the same county
to assess the value of property could not fail to multiply
the chances of unequal taxation. With a view to guard
against such a result, I suggest for your consideration
the propriety of providing by law for the appointment
in each county of a board of equalization, consisting of
two or more persons; the duty of such board to be to
meet after the return of the commissioners' books at the
county town, and to carefully examine the valuation of
property, and to equalize the same by increasing or de-
creasing the value as assessed by the Assessors. Such
a system has been adopted by other States, and has been
attended with success, not only in guarding the public
interest, but in giving satisfaction to the people. Such a
supervisory power could not fail to render the Assessors
more vigilant and uniform in the discharge of their
duties, and guard the citizen against the partiality or

prejudice which may he engendered by a heated election
or other improper cause."

* * * * * * * * . * * *

"Fifteen years have passed away since the laying of
the statutory foundation of common schools. During
the greater part of that time nothing was accomplished,
either from the jealousy of parties or unbecoming timidity on the part of the representatives of the people.
The genious of orators was employed in amusing the
children and their parents by naratives of what had been
and what had not been done for them; yet, while they
amused and entertained, they left the children uninstruct-
ed. At length a resolution was taken to submit the great
question to the people, and most nobly did they rebuke
the timidity of their former representatives, and fully
vindicate the truth that bills drawn upon them for the
noble purpose of educating the youth of the country will
not be dishonored.

"Since that time, I am happy to say, the Common
School System is rapidly and steadily extending itself
throughout the Commonwealth. The people in every
part of the State are becoming more and more interested
in this great scheme, and there remains no doubt of our
ability to accomplish everything that the most sanguine
friends of the cause have every proposed. In this, however, as in every great and beneficent undertaking, we
must not forget that the results to be attained bear a
constant proportion to the wisdom, the energy, and the
steadfastness with which the object is pursued. The
general education of the people is an object of the very
highest importance in all possible conditions of human
society, and is absolutely vital in free States. It has
been from the foundation of this Commonwealth the
subject of many and highly favorable legislative enact-
ments, and of many and most honorable exertions, both
general and local. Now, more than ever, we must con-

sider it as one of the settled and most important questions of the public policy of Kentucky, to bring the
blessings of education within the reach of all her youth.
I have to assure the General Assembly that no part of
my public duty will be more grateful to me than a hearty
concurrence in all that may be judged needful in carrying to the highest perfection a system of public education
which will be worthy of the State, and answerable to
the high career which she proposes to herself. This is a
platform upon which, for a glorious and common object,
all men, all parties, and all interests, may cordially unite."

*   *   *   *   *   *   *   *   *   *   *

" The change in the mode of selecting the public officers, and in the tenure of office, under the new form of
government, will make it your duty, in my judgment, to
readjust the tariff of salaries and fees paid to the several
officers. This task, I am very well aware, is a delicate
one, and will be attended with no little difficulty. But,
delicate and difficult as the task is, I do not entertain a
doubt that you will agree with me in opinion that the
success of the experiment of popular elections depends
greatly upon its manly and fearless performance. You
must inspire confidence in the new system by inviting men
of good judgment, sound principles, and practical business
habits, to fill the various offices of the Government.
Yours is a highly responsible, and, to the mere politician, by no means an enviable position. The framers
of the Constitution have given the people a Government eminently popular. To you is confided the difficult,
and certainly not less responsible, duty of putting the
Government into successful operation. The services of
men who are honest, competent, and faithful, can be secured only by offering good salaries. If the fees and
salaries be fixed at a low rate, the standard of merit and
worth in an officer will be correspondingly low. A man
who is found willing to work for the State at a merely

nominal salary will most frequently be found to be worth less than his pay, little as that pay may be. For good work we must be willing to pay a good price. I wish it understood, however, that I do not advise an extravagant or wasteful expenditure of the public treasure. There should be economy in all the departments of the Government. The burthens of the people should not be unnecessarily increased. Men differ, however, very widely in their views of public as well as private economy. Some measure the standard of economy by the sums actually paid out. I do not so view it. In the employment of public agents, true economy consists in procuring for the least price the services of men who are qualified to perform the duties of their respective stations with promptitude, with skill, and with fidelity. The services of such men are well worth the largest sum the most liberal would be willing to pay.

"In the consideration of this subject, allow me, with earnestness and deep solicitude, to call your especial attention to the compensation of judicial officers. There is no principle, in the change from the old to the new form of government, in which the triumph of the new is so deeply implicated as in the success of the judicial system.

"It would be an idle task, if not indeed an insult to your judgment, for me to consume your time in an elaborate essay upon the importance of an independent Judiciary. Freemen—intelligent freemen—understand the importance of having a Judiciary free and independent. They know it is essential to the preservation of the rights of a free people. It is essential to the preservation of the Constitution—the people's charter. It is necessary to the protection of the weak against the oppressions of the strong. It is necessary to hold in check the bad passions of the mob. No nation can be free if it have a dependent Judiciary. There is but one way to secure an independent Judiciary. You must offer such inducements as

will invite to the bench the best men of the State—men
of known legal ability and of unquestioned integrity—men
who will not fear to look danger in the face—men who
will not hesitate to shield the innocent and. punish the
guilty—who will interpose between the mob and its victim.   You must secure men who will represent truly the
majesty of the law; then, and not till then, will you have
secured a firm, faithful, and independent Judiciary.

"I am aware that there prevails in the minds of many
of the people a prejudice against the payment of what
are called 'high salaries.' What are high salaries? Certainly the people of Kentucky have no reason to complain
that their public treasure has been squandered in the payment of exorbitant salaries to their public servants, at
least not to their Judiciary. It is a fact, known to us all,
that the salaries heretofore paid, even with the limited
amount of labor to be performed, have failed, to some
extent, to command the services of the ablest and best
lawyers. The reason is too obvious for comment.

"In consequence of the reduction of the number of
districts, the physical and mental labor to be performed
by the judge will be increased probably one third, and
his personal expenses will be in like manner increased.
If when, heretofore, the labor was less, the place obtained
without a struggle, and the tenure was for good behavior,
the salary offered failed to command, generally, the best
men, is it probable it will do it now? I am sure you will
answer it will not. Will a lawyer in good business, with
many and valuable fees half earned, with a practice
confined to a small circuit, allowing him time for repose
and improvement to enjoy some of the comforts of domestic life, and to aid by personal superintendence an econ-
omical administration of his private affairs; will such a
man consent to receive a judgeship? to receive less pay,
perform more labor, and to submit to the very many
deprivations which he must necessarily undergo; to in-

volve himself first in a doubtful contest in which he will be subjected to all the unpleasant incidents which we know attend a popular election, and at the end of six years run the risk of being superseded and brought back to the bar to renew his practice? Your own good sense will furnish a prompt answer to the question. The increased labor, mental and physical, will render it necessary that men who attain judicial stations should be sound lawyers when they enter upon the discharge of their duties, for they will have but little time afterwards to read and acquire a scientific knowledge of the law. They must be good lawyers when they go upon the bench or they never will be good judges afterwards.

"I deny that it is either just or proper to make the allowance to a public officer barely sufficient to meet his necessary yearly expenditures. Men should employ the vigor of manhood in acquiring the means of support in advanced age. They must guard against penury and want when they shall be no longer able to labor. Wise men plant the tree in the days of their youth, that shall shelter and protect them on their road to the grave. If you do not provide a salary sufficient to justify the employment of the whole time of a judge, he will, if a man possessing the proper amount of energy to make him a useful public officer, prompted not less by interest than by the instinct of his nature, look to other means to supply the wants of his family. Thus he may be part judge and part farmer, trader, merchant, or something else, until at length he will become an incomplete part of anything. But it is said much is due to the honor of the station. True, it is agreeable to a large majority of men to be placed by the confidence of their fellow-citizens in positions from which they derive distinction and honor. But the lives of our public men too well attest that men cannot *live* on honor. I submit, whether by making your offices places of honor alone, you will not

confer them upon that class of men who have wealth to
live independent of office, and thus rather create distinc-
tions than produce equality in society. To my mind the
true policy is to give a full, fair, liberal, and just equiva-
lent for the services of a capable man, whether rich or
poor, that the offices may be objects of fair competition
among the meritorious, and let honor follow a faithful
and enlightened discharge of the duties of the station.

"You cannot be blind to the fact, that, in this glorious
country of ours, there are vast fields everywhere opening
to the enterprising and energetic men of thought, which
promise most bountiful returns for labor. If we would
appropriate to our State the services of men who are
invited to those fields of promise, we must pay them, and
that liberally. The State should not ask the labor of her
citizens for a less sum than that labor will command from
others. A parsimonious allowance to the public officers
will cause the offices to be looked to with indifference by
the really meritorious and worthy, and ultimately the
Government must fall into the hands of those who will
rely more on the chances of peculation than the compensation allowed by law."

*   *   *   *   .*   *   *   *   *   *   *

"The question of internal improvement I regard as
settled for the present, so far as the participation of the
State in any new scheme is concerned. The constitutional provision on the subject makes it altogether unnecessary to enter into an argument upon the policy of
expenditures by the Legislature in new schemes of public improvement; but I cannot, consistently with what
I conceive to be my duty, fail to recommend and urge
you to employ all the means at your command and under
your proper control towards the completion of the great
lines of improvement that are now in an unfinished condition, and in which the State has an interest. It is certainly an unwise policy to permit these improvements,

upon which very large sums have been expended, to remain unfinished and go to decay and ruin for the want of the inconsiderable sums necessary to complete them; and I feel satisfied that many of the lines yet unfinished, and which now pay no return into the Treasury, would, if finished, very soon yield a handsome dividend, not only on the sum necessary to complete them, but on the whole amount of the State's interest in them. If the General Assembly has not the power to appropriate money in aid of these unfinished lines, that body, in my judgment, should not hesitate to offer the most liberal inducements to individuals and companies to take hold of and finish them. I beg to refer you to the report of the able and enlightened President of the Board of Internal Improvement for a statement of the condition of the public works."

* * * * * * * * * * *

"I submit for your consideration the propriety of ordering a minute geological reconnoissance of the State, especially of those regions which are supposed to abound in minerals. The importance and usefulness of such a measure cannot be estimated by conjecture. The discoveries that may follow a careful and extended survey by competent geologists may lead to results of much greater importance than would be supposed upon a superficial view of the subject. It is a well-established principle in domestic economy that nothing should be purchased abroad that can be produced or manufactured at home. This principle applies even more forcibly to the management of the affairs of a nation. Immense sums, we know, are annually withdrawn from circulation in Kentucky to be expended in other States in the purchase of coal, iron, salt, and of many manufactured articles necessary to the household, the field, and the work-shop. It is confidently believed that we have hidden beneath the surface of the earth within the limits of our State the means adequate not only to the production of all those articles needed for our own use, but that we may become large exporters. Develop the mineral wealth of the State, and you will open to the people new branches of industry; you will diversify labor; you will invite large investments of capital, and you will make the regions, which are now considered poor, by far the most wealthy and prosperous in the State. Manufacturing establishments will spring up all around you. They will afford a good home market for your agricultural products, and the aggregate wealth of the State will be greatly increased.

"Kentucky must not close her eyes to the future. Her sister States, with fewer natural advantages than she possesses, are far ahead of her in the struggle for wealth and greatness. They work while we are idle. Difficulties that seem to appall our people are apparently unnoticed by them in their onward march. Nature has not slighted us. She has given us a soil unequaled—a position, geographically, that will enable us, if we will but avail ourselves of it, to rival the most favored and prosperous of our sisters."

*   *   *   *   *   *   *   *   *   *   *

"Since the adjournment of the last General Assembly, the nation has been called to mourn the loss of a great and good man—ZACHARY TAYLOR, Chief Magistrate of the United States. Though we deeply and sincerely lament his death, we have great reason to congratulate ourselves that his mantle has fallen upon a man worthy to wear it. MILLARD FILLMORE, the President of the United States, has exhibited, in his administration of the affairs of the General Government, a liberality, a fairness, and a fidelity to the Constitution that have won for him a widely-extended and an honorable fame. His manly and patriotic devotion to the Union entitle him to the gratitude of every true lover of his country. With such a man at the head

of affairs, we may feel well satisfied that all the powers
of the Executive will be honestly, faithfully, and firmly
directed to the execution of the laws and the preservation of the Constitution.

" The clouds which for some months past blackened the
political horizon and threatened the safety of the Union
have been dispelled, and the skies are again bright and
full of promise and of hope. In the passage of the compromise measures by the last Congress, the friends of the
Union achieved a triumph that carried joy and gladness
to the fireside of every habitation in Kentucky, and
caused a thrill of pleasure in every patriotic heart in
the Union. The plotters of the nation's ruin have been
defeated and put to shame, and the friends of liberty
everywhere rejoice.

" The people of Kentucky learned with honest pride
that their Representatives played a conspicuous and
noble part in the settlement of the questions which
menaced the Union. Fired by an honest zeal and patriotic devotion to the nation, they forgot or disregarded
all mere party differences and party divisions, and united
as one man in the support and vindication of the Constitution. As, in times past, when danger threatened the
Union, when disunionists and factionists and fanatics
united in an attempt to sever the bands that bind this
glorious confederacy together, our own great statesman
was found foremost in the ranks of the defenders of the
Constitution. In the council and in the cabinet—whereever there was found a Representative of Kentucky—
there was also found a true, loyal, steadfast, and un-
yielding friend of the Constitution and the Union. The
promise given by my immediate predecessor, in his annual communication to the last General Assembly, that
' Kentucky will stand by and abide by the Union to the
last,' has been thus far nobly kept. It will never be
broken.

"Kentucky owes a debt of gratitude—a debt she will ever be ready to pay—to those distinguished statesmen of the North and the South, of both the great political parties, who, disregarding all sectional and party divisions, boldly and patriotically stepped forth in the defense of the Constitution, and rescued it from the hands of its enemies and despoilers. They have preserved the Union —and they have won for themselves a place in the hearts of their countrymen.

"May we not hope that their labors will be crowned with complete success, and that the spirit of disorder and misrule, now broken, will be banished forever. The judgment of the sound and reflecting portion of the people of all sections condemns, I am sure, the dangerous radical doctrines of both extremes of the Union. The people are not agitators; the people are not factionists. Will they not fix the seal of their disapprobation upon those, who, for selfish purposes, would fan the flame of discord in the nation, and renew again the fearful fire that threatened to consume us? Kentucky, I am sure, will stand by the Constitution and the laws. May she not ask—nay, has she not a right to demand of her sisters in the confederacy—partners in the great national compact—that they, too, will be true to the Constitution and its compromises? It is gratifying to observe with what unanimity the people of the South are declaring in support of the great measures of peace passed by the last Congress. Every breeze brings us the glad tidings that the friends of the compromise representing that quarter in Congress are hailed with pride by their constituents. It was feared that the angry feeling there engendered would not soon subside. But we have reason to hope it is gone—the conviction that the Constitution has been vindicated and that the Union is safe, has filled the hearts of the people with joy. We turn with unfeigned sorrow and regret to the accounts that reach us from some of our sister States in the northern portion of the confederacy. There we hear loud murmurings at the passage of one of the compromise measures—the fugitive slave bill. There the friends of that measure are openly denounced and contemned; even more, armed resistance to its execution is gravely threatened. I cannot believe that any respectable portion of the people of the North participate in this feeling. It cannot be that they are willing again to stir up the spirit of discord. Who is there to guarantee that our noble old ship will be able again to weather so dire and dreadful a storm as that from which she has just escaped? No man who loves his country or values properly her institutions will aid in bringing about again the fearful crisis we have just passed. An armed or forcible resistance to the execution of the fugitive slave law is treason, and those who counsel, aid, or assist in that unholy work, are traitors to the Constitution and enemies to the best interests of the nation.

" It should ever be borne in mind that the General Government is one of limited powers, and was never designed to interfere with the domestic institutions of any of the local sovereignties, directly or indirectly. The power to declare what should or what should not be property was never intended to be delegated to it; but its protecting shield was extended over whatever had been recognized as such by any of the States. I cannot but be deeply and profoundly impressed with the importance of maintaining with inviolable sanctity the great doctrine that a Government which is the Federal representative of all the States should, in its legislation, abstain from hostile action against the property of any State or section. It has no right to throw its moral influence against the tenure of property, recognized as such by any of the States. It prostitutes its powers and the purposes of its organization by assuming an attitude of hostility to the

existence of any particular property in any State or section.   It wisely conformed itself, in its original organization, to the domestic institutions then existing.   The Government was made with a reference to the institution of
domestic slavery.   Any, the slightest interference with it,
was cautiously avoided.   The surest and most certain
mode of perpetuating that Government peaceably and in
harmony must be by administering it in the spirit in which
it was made.   As the common Government of each and
all the States, it is bound not to discriminate between the
domestic institutions of one State or section and another.
Strict non-intervention by the General Government, with
the protection guaranteed by the Constitution, is the only
true and safe doctrine.   It is the doctrine upon which the
great compromise questions were settled.   Those questions
could not have been settled upon any other principle.   It
is the only doctrine compatible with the great fundamental
principle of our political system, that a people have a
right to establish whatever government they think proper
for themselves."

With the inauguration of Governor POWELL, which
took place on the 5th day of September, 1851, ended
Governor HELM's term of office.   Returning to his home
in Hardin county, he applied himself to the duties of
his profession, almost wholly, up to the year 1854.   It was
during the latter year that he appeared as counsel for
the prisoner, the late MATTHEW F. WARD, in one of the
most noted murder trials that ever took place in the
State.   It would be altogether out of place in this sketch
to give even a synopsis of the masterly argument made
by Governor HELM on the occasion referred to.   A few
paragraphs from the speech, however, are so characteristic of the man that we cannot forbear inserting them.
Addressing the jury, Governor HELM is reported to have
said :

"I have often addressed you in the jury-box and from the rostrum; on the stump and in the muster-field You are all aware that in the discussion of any subject in which I feel a deep interest, my manner is usually excited and earnest; but on this occasion I speak under great disadvantage, having been confined to my bed by illness almost constantly for the last two months; and only hoping that I may be sustained, and that you may bear with me until I can discharge the solemn duty I owe to my client.

"I feel perhaps more deeply interested in this case than I ever have felt in any other in which I have been engaged. I feel thus from the nature of the ties that bind me to the family of this defendant. Many years ago, when I first entered the political field, I met his father in the councils of the State; and again and again have I associated with other members of the family there. And, as in the beginning of my humble political career, these men took me by the hand and gave me their aid and support, I have ever felt grateful to them; and now that an event has unfortunately occurred by which I hope to be enabled to do something, so far as my poor ability goes, to cancel the debt, you cannot wonder that my deepest sympathies are enlisted.

"The gentleman who preceded me has alluded to outside influences—to the fact that this prisoner was driven from his own home to seek justice here. It is true that, from the moment the event occurred for which he is now on trial, distorted and prejudiced accounts of it were given to the public; and, accompanied by articles of the most inflammatory character, were spread upon the wings of the wind by the newspaper press. Therefore this excited feeling was caused, and therefore the prisoner asked only what the law gives—that he might be tried in an unbiased and unprejudiced community.

5

"Complaints have been made that this defendant has been living in luxury and splendor in jail here, while others have suffered from having their absolute wants neglected. That others have suffered, there is no doubt. But after the accused was removed to this place, I visited him in jail, and found him suffering from a severe attack of neuralgia and inflammatory rheumatism—the same disease that had recently confined me to my bed, and, notwithstanding all precautions, had racked my limbs with a thrill of pain at every blast that swept over the hills. I went, hoping at least to keep this man alive until he could throw back the foul charges that have been heaped upon him, show their falsity, and vindicate his conduct, as he humbly hopes he can, in the eyes of this jury and the people of this country. I visited him, and I had a partition and a stove put up in his cell, that his disease might not be aggravated by the inclemency of the weather; and for these precautions his own money paid, so that no wrong has been done the State.

"Is it a part of your wish that men should be punished to the death before they are tried? Even if this accused was provided with the simple necessities of life, if that mother wished to go and lay her tender hand on his aching head, if that wife would seek his lonely cell, and soothe and cheer him by the light of her presence and her love, was it wrong? Who, with a heart not glutted with blood, could object to it?

"I know that the prisoner has much to contend with outside of this prosecution; but, gentlemen, yours is a proud position. You are placed by the law a firm shield before him, to protect him from all unjust and improper attacks. With no aim but to learn the truth and to do justice, I feel confident that you will stand like a rock in the midst of the ocean, unmoved by the fury of the wild waves that dash madly against it only to be broken in pieces. We only ask that you will perform your duty, and that justice may be done, though the heavens fall.

"But the gentleman tells you you have no right to retain a single particle of mercy. This is the first time in my life I have heard such a sentiment gravely announced by a man acquainted with the books.

"'To err is human—to forgive, divine.'

"He has alluded to the first murderer. But did not GOD in mercy hear even *his* prayer, and place a mark upon his forehead that none might slay him? And when a woman was arraigned on a high charge before the SAVIOUR of the world, when none was so guiltless that he might cast the first stone at her, then there was mercy from on high, and He sent her away with the kind injunction to go and sin no more." *

The excellent condition of the State Treasury at the present time is, in a great measure, the result of Governor HELM's admirable financial abilities and forethought. On the 12th day of January, 1834, he moved the following resolution in the House of Representatives, which was twice read and adopted:

"*Resolved*, That a committee of thirteen be appointed, whose duty it shall be to take into consideration the resources and means of this Commonwealth, and to devise, if practicable, some plan by which a specific fund can be raised for the purpose of carrying on a comprehensive system of internal improvements and establishing a sys-

---

* The writer was well acquainted with the late MATTHEW F. WARD. In a moment of passion, he shot to death one of the most amiable and popular citizens of Louisville. The killing was wholly unjustifiable, and that he so considered it to the last day of his life, none that knew him can doubt. He lived afterwards a quiet and unassuming life, and bore on his features the impress of a mind that was constantly burdened with the sense of his sin. His whole existence, after his legal acquittal, appeared to those, who had the best opportunities to witness and to judge, one continuous act of repentance. He removed to Arkansas shortly after his trial, and was killed during the war, while standing in his own door, by some roving guerrillas.

tem of common schools, and that they report to this
House."

The committee appointed under this resolution, of
which Mr. HELM was named chairman, not only originated the present Common School System of Kentucky,
but laid the foundations of the Sinking Fund laws, by
which certain resources of the State were set apart for
the extinction of both principal and interest of the State
debt.   Under the new Constitution these specific resources
were further added to, and any expenditure of money due
to the Sinking Fund was absolutely forbidden, except for
the purposes named.

During his entire public life, Governor HELM was the
consistent advocate of a liberal system of public improvements.   To effect this object, not even Mr. CLAY, the
father of the system, was disposed to go further, or labored more perseveringly.   It was not his idea that the State
should place in jeopardy her resources or her credit by
taking on herself the prosecution of complicated and cost-
ly works of internal improvement.   But he thought that
the credit of the State might well be extended to all private enterprises that had for their object the opening up
of the resources of the country.   He considered that full
reimbursement would follow these outlays of the public
money from the increased taxable value of all lands con-
tiguous to such improvements.

But not only was the late Governor an advocate of
public improvements at the expense of the State; he
labored with great efficiency, also, in his own county, to
induce his fellow-citizens to form connections with their
neighbors through the construction of turnpike roads and
substantial bridges over the various streams intersecting
the county.   The turnpike highway between Louisville
and Nashville, which passes through Hardin county, was
a favorite scheme of his long before its construction was
decided on, and to no one man is greater credit due for

its ultimate completion. As early as 1836, from his place on the floor of the House of Representatives, he sketched out the course of the railroad, which was afterwards built, connecting the commercial metropolis of Kentucky with Nashville, Tennessee. He was a liberal subscriber to the original stock of this road, and through his influence with the capitalists of the county and State, contributed large-ly to the subsequent success of the gigantic undertaking.

In 1854 he was elected President of the Louisville and Nashville Railroad Company. The affairs of this or-ganization were at the time in a wretched condition, its funds exhausted, and its credit impaired. Many citizens of Hardin and Hart counties had refused to pay their assessments towards the building of the road, and a large portion of the work, as a consequence, had to be suspended. Those who had originally subscribed stock were beginning to fear that their investments were about to be swallowed up in the insolvency of the com-pany. It was under these discouraging circumstances that Governor HELM took charge of the road. Such an impulse did he give to the undertaking, by his energetic yet careful management of the affairs of the company, that confidence was soon restored, the suspended ,portions of the work again put under contract, and the bonds of the company, which had before ruled in the market at a mere trifle of their cost, were bought up by prudent cap-italists as a safe and remunerative investment.

The first locomotive that crossed the Rolling Fork into his native county, bore, with its other burdens, the presi-dent of the road. He was a proud man that day. He realized the importance of the work which had so long engaged his thoughts and his labors. He had lived to serve the material interests of his own people—to see his own beloved county wedded to the beautiful Ohio, fifty miles away, and his heart dilated with a sense of pleas-ure that it had never before experienced, as his life-long friends and neighbors, from the positions they had taken up beside the track all along its course, waved to him their congratulations as he was swiftly borne on his way to the station at Elizabethtown.

Governor HELM retained the position of President of the Louisville and Nashville Railroad Company until 1860. At the date named, in consequence of a divergence of views between himself and the majority of the Board of Directors, in regard to the proper policy to be pursued in the affairs of the company, he thought proper to resign his office.*

Previously to his acceptance of the Presidency of the Louisville and Nashville Railroad Company, President FILLMORE had appointed Governor HELM Commissioner of Claims in California. The Senate, however, declined to ratify his nomination.

In the great struggle that took place in Kentucky, and throughout the United States, in 1855, between the Democratic party and the short-lived organization known as the American, or *Know-Nothing* party, Mr. HELM acted with the latter, though he expressed his opposition to certain of its proscriptive features.†

---

* The arduous labors which Governor HELM imposed on himself while President of the Louisville and Nashville Railroad Company came near costing him his life on one occasion. In 1857, after months of incessant toil, he found himself prostrated on a bed of sickness at Nashville, whither he had gone to attend the interests of the road. It was long before he was again able to perform the duties of his office. He had scarcely recovered from his illness when he received the news of the death, in Memphis, Tennessee, of a favorite son, GEORGE HELM, who was at the time a young man of great promise. He continued, to be sure, to fulfill every duty of his office with the decision and promptitude which characterized all his acts; but the spirit and buoyancy of life seemed to have left him. It is the opinion of his immediate family that the disease, of which he afterwards died, was contracted and aggravated by his unceasing labors in the service of the railroad company.

† Large numbers of the leaders of the old Whig party of the country, after the death of HENRY CLAY, DANIEL WEBSTER, and others, who had been its apostles when the organization was able to compete with the Democratic

During the brief period that intervened between his retiracy from the office of President of the Louisville and Nashville Railroad Company and the commencement of active hostilities in the late civil war, Gov. HELM applied himself with earnestness to the practice of his profession and to the cultivation and improvement of his farm. But the conflict was close at hand which was to involve irretrievably his own material interests and prospects, and those of thousands of others all over the land, and which was to bring upon him and them a weight of personal affliction of which they could have had at the time but little conception. He and they were yet to learn the heart-pangs of the bereaved—to experience a woe similar to that which was proclaimed in Rama: "Rachel bewailing her children, and would not be comforted, because they are not."

Governor HELM never favored secession. While he fully recognized and condemned, with a patriot's indignation, the shamefully unjust policy, as it affected the interests of the South, of the majority that was supposed to represent Northern sentiment in the Congress of the United States, he appeared to entertain, at the same time, an abiding faith in the people's regard for the Constitution to correct every evil under which his own section was suffering,

party in an equal contest before the people, found themselves, in 1854, so reduced in numbers and influence as to feel justified in resorting to a species of party trickery in order to prevent the Democrats from obtaining control of the Government and absorbing all its patronage. They attempted, in direct conflict with the letter and spirit of the organic law, and in opposition to the genius of Republican Government, to organize a party based on the proscription of individual citizens on account of their peculiar views of religious faith. Stultified men never committed a greater blunder than this. But they went further, and fixed on the country a system of political engineering, by means of secret organizations, which has ever since obtained in the land, and which, in the opinion of many, more than anything else, led to the late deplorable civil war. Governor HELM voted with this party, as did thousands of others—not because of any respect he had for its proscriptive features, but because of his then innate aversion toward the Democratic opposition.

without any resort, on the part of its citizens, to a measure so sweeping in its character and so problematical in
its consequences. Alas! neither did Governor HELM, nor
the prudent statesmen that thought as he did, have any
power to arrest the storm that had long been brooding
over the country. In an evil hour ten States severed their
connection with the rest of the Union, and the red flame
of war was lighted from the Potomac and the Ohio to the
Gulf—from the borders of Kansas, in the North, to the
Rio Grande, in the South.

Every one will remember the general indignation that
was felt throughout the State on the announcement of
the fact that President LINCOLN had issued his proclamation calling for seventy-five thousand volunteers to operate against the South. On the question of the policy
of this measure the people of the State were then almost
a unit. They regarded the act as an assumption of
power on the part of the President that was not warranted by the Constitution. They looked upon it as indicative of a coalition between the President and the
anti-slavery party of the North, having for its object the
enforced extinction of the institution of slavery. When
this latter presumption was denied by the President and
solemnly declared false by Congress, a large party was
formed in Kentucky pledged to the prosecution of the
war till such time as the Southern States, through the
voice of their populations, should agree to lay down their
arms and submit to the requirements of the Constitution.
Fully as great, if not a still greater, number of the people of the State, who could not be brought to assume
an attitude of hostility to those who were naturally their
friends and neighbors, and whose institutions and interests were identical with their own, though few among
them had any sympathy with the movement in its incep-
tion, determined either to remain neutral in the conflict
or to unite their fortunes with the weaker party.

Governor HELM acted as chairman of the famous meeting held in Louisville on the 8th of January, 1861, in
which the neutral policy of Kentucky was declared the
sentiment of men of all parties in the State. Appended
to the resolutions passed at that meeting will be found
the names of men who afterwards were loudest in their
denunciation of the act in which they themselves took
part. Governor HELM, at the meeting referred to, and
on all proper occasions afterwards, was open in his condemnation of the war; but he was equally open in declaring the act of secession one of great danger and of
doubtful propriety. He stood aloof from the conflict
from first to last, though often sorely tried by the interference in his private affairs of the Government officials
by whom he was surrounded. His son and son-in-law
had made choice to cast their lot with the people of the
South in resistance of the purposes of the Government;
and he did not feel that he would be justified in opposing
their election. This fact was sufficient to affix to his
name, with the so-called Union party of Kentucky and
with the military authorities that were then preparing to
invade the State, the title of *rebel*. At length the news
reached him that ex-Governor MOREHEAD had been arrested, and that warrants were out commanding his own
arrest. Knowing that he had been guilty of no act to
warrant interference with his liberty, he was at first disposed to await further developments; but having again
been cautioned to avoid the emissaries of the Government, with a sorrowful heart he bade his family farewell
and repaired to Bowling Green. By the intervention of
the Hon. WARNER UNDERWOOD, who stood in high favor
with the invaders of his State, Governor HELM, after a
brief absence, was permitted to return to his home. By
agreement, he was to report on his arrival to General
SHERMAN, then commanding in Kentucky. On doing so,
he was required to take an oath to support the Constitu-

tion of the United States. This he had done many times before, and he had no difficulty in doing it again. For a while after having performed this ceremony, he remained unmolested. When Gen. MITCHELL's troops, by express order to that effect, were encamped on his farm, Governor HELM was treated with becoming courtesy by the officer in command, because, as he said, of his former acquaintance with his father-in-law, the Hon. BEN. HARDIN.

From this time till the close of the war he enjoyed little peace. Rude soldiers were permitted to enter his house and to frighten his children; the growing and matured crops on his farm were consumed, destroyed, and wasted without compensation of any kind; his house was ransacked from cellar to garret, and what was seen and coveted, abstracted; he was himself repeatedly insulted and threatened, without the shadow of justification; his negro servants were tampered with and induced to abandon their places; in a word, nothing was left undone, by both officers and men, that they thought calculated to injure him in his means, and to degrade him as a man.

Finding it impossible to preserve the fruits of his toil from the rapacity of the soldiery by whom he was surrounded, he made the attempt to raise a crop of tobacco, on the supposition that this could not be eaten before it was cured, and trusting to be able to secure at least a portion of the crop for his own needs; but just at the time when the labor of his negro servants was most required to prevent the ruin of the plants, in what is called by tobacco-raisers *the worming season*, every able-bodied servant on the place was taken into the service of the Government for the purpose of building fortifications; and thus all his expectations of a crop were brought to nought. The courts were all closed, and he had nothing to hope for in the way of legal practice. He had no recourse but to borrow money for the support of his family, and thus, in a few short years, he found himself reduced from affluence to poverty, with the prospect before him, since too sadly realized, of leaving his family destitute when he should himself be called away from life.

Under all these heavy trials Governor HELM retained his patience. He endeavored to encourage the desponding hearts of his wife and daughters, on whose account alone he seemed to care for the reverses he had sustained. Sometimes, however, he appeared to give way to utter despair. On one occasion, when he was visited by a squad of soldiers that had been ordered to search his house, he met the officer in command at the door, and solemnly protested against the indignity to which he was being subjected. He exhibited before his eyes that clause of the Constitution of their common country which denounced as illegal the very act in which he was engaged. All useless this, as he might have known from the first. What was the Constitution when brought into contact with *military necessity?* This latter was then *the* potent power in the State, and overrid not only constitutions and laws, but a proper regard for the proprieties and decencies of civilized social life also. Governor HELM should have known that the Constitution that had proved unequal to the protection of his rights of property in the corn raised on his own farm; the mules and horses paid for by his own money, and any other property to which he had a legal title in accordance with the laws of the country, would be equally powerless to prevent the ingress of the agents of the Government to his own house. The officer "had to obey orders," and the Governor had to submit to military necessity, and there was the end of the matter.

A few days prior to Gen. BRAGG's entry into Kentucky, in September, 1862, Governor HELM was arrested by Col.

Knox, who was then in command of the forces stationed
at Elizabethtown. He was met by that officer on the
high road when returning to his home from his farm,
where he had been laboring all day, and this doughty
official, leveling his pistol at his breast, declared him his
prisoner. In company with several other citizens of the
county, who had been arrested at the same time, he was
placed under guard and kept for several days in camp,
without proper protection against the heat of the day or
the chill of the night, and the entire band was afterwards
dispatched to Louisville. While the prisoners were being
taken from the cars to the military prison, Governor J. F.
Robinson, then the Chief Magistrate of the State, a man
that stood high in the confidence of the military authorities, and a personal friend of Governor Helm, accidentally saw the cavalcade as it marched through the streets,
and was much surprised and distressed to behold in it the
dignified form of one he had so long known and so greatly
respected. Hastening to the office of Gen. Boyle, who
was then commanding the District, Governor Robinson
protested against the indignity to which his old friend
was being subjected, and earnestly besought his immediate release. Gen. Boyle assured him that he had issued
no order for Governor Helm's arrest, and expressing great
surprise at the circumstance, he at once handed to Governor Robinson an order addressed to the officer in charge
of the prison for the enlargement of the Governor, with
the permission that he might return to his home.

In the meantime, Bragg's army had reached Elizabethtown, and a strict surveillance being kept up by its own
outposts and those of General Nelson, the commander of
the forces left for the protection of Louisville, it was with
difficulty that Governor Helm was enabled to reach his
own home. On the evening of his return, the members
of his family were gathered together, painfully brooding
over their miseries, and fearing for the husband and

father a long imprisonment, when they were aroused by the glad shouts of certain of their servants that had up to the time remained faithful, "Massa John's come! Here's Massa John!" We shall not attempt to describe the meeting with his family that followed. There was little about it that was demonstrative, but there were gladsome faces and thankful hearts that night under the roof-tree of the Helm mansion.

In September, 1862, took place the bloody battle of Chickamauga, in which the life of the Governor's oldest son, Gen. BEN. HARDIN HELM, was sacrificed in defense of Southern independence.* This was the crowning sorrow of Governor HELM's life. In vain he summoned to his aid the fortitude, often mistaken for the stoicism, of his character. Not even the mother of his boy, that had nursed him at her bosom, felt a greater pang in the sorrowful intelligence of his fall. So deeply at times did he appear to feel the blow that had been struck him in the death of this favorite son, that his family were fearful for the stability of his reason. The so-called *results of the war*—which, in his case, meant the seizure of his

---

* BEN. HARDIN HELM, oldest son of Gov. HELM, was born June 2d, 1831. He graduated at West Point when about twenty years old, and entered the United States military service as 2d Lieutenant of Cavalry. He was first stationed at Carlisle Barracks, Pennsylvania. Thence he was sent out on frontier service in Western Texas, where he was seized with a very severe illness in 1852, which caused him to come home. While at home, his father persuaded him to resign his position in the army and study law. After finishing his course of studies at the Law Schools of Louisville and Cambridge, he commenced the practice with his father at Elizabethtown. He was a fine lawyer, and won rapidly popular approbation. In 1855 he was elected to the Legislature, and the next year Commonwealth's Attorney. In 1858 he moved to Louisville, where he practiced law until the commencement of the war, when he entered the Confederate service as Colonel of the 1st Kentucky Cavalry. He was soon promoted to the rank of Brigadier General. He was a popular, skillful, brave officer; won a high reputation as a soldier; had his horse shot under him, and was badly wounded at Baton Rouge, and was finally killed at the head of his command—the 1st Kentucky Brigade of Infantry—on the 20th day of September, 1862, on the bloody field of Chickamauga. He left a widow and three children.

property without compensation and the manumission of
his slaves, valued five years before at forty thousand
dollars—had reduced him to absolute poverty, and he
could not get rid of the conviction—alas! since too sadly
realized—that the labors of his entire life had turned out
fruitless, and that his family would be left unprovided for
at his death.

In 1865 Governor HELM was again returned to the
State Senate from the Tenth Senatorial District, and
served in that body on the Committee on Federal Relations. On the 20th of January, 1866, he moved the following resolution, viz:

"*Resolved*, That the joint committee appointed to take
into consideration the altered condition of the colored
people of this Commonwealth inquire into the expe-
diency of repealing laws requiring that slaves shall be
listed for taxation; and into the propriety of levying a
poll tax on all able-bodied negroes over eighteen years
of age and under sixty-five, to create a fund to erect
houses of correction, and to purchase farms and erect
houses to be used in taking care of old and infirm
negroes, and looking ultimately to the creation of a fund
for the education of children of color."

From the day the war ended to the present time, it has
been a marked feature of legislation in what were lately
slave States, wherever their white populations have been
permitted to exercise uncontrolled authority, to so alter
and amend their statutes as to secure to the blacks every
available means, consistent with the peace of society, of
bettering their condition. Governor HELM's motive in
offering the above resolution was clearly of this character. As much as he desired that the body of newly-
created freedmen should not become an impediment to
the prosperity of the State, much more even was he
solicitous that the means should be afforded them to
raise themselves in the scale of humanity and human

progress, and to thus become useful and contented members of the social fabric of which they were likely to
remain for ages so large an element.'

On the 24th of January, 1866, Mr. HELM presented to
the Senate an able protest against the action of the
United States Congress in declaring the complete abrogation of the institution of slavery in all the States.
The protest, which originated in the Committee on Federal Relations, goes on to say :

" The people of Kentucky, through the General Assembly, protest against the constitutional amendments
referred to, both because of the manner in which they
were proposed by Congress to the States and the manner
of their ratification. They protest against the legal
effect as claimed for them in Kentucky.

" The people of Kentucky insist that the people of the
States originally possessed all the sovereign power; that
in the adoption of the Constitution of the United States,
for the purposes of a General Government, they surren-
dered certain powers which were specified in the Constitution, and such other powers as were necessary to carry
into effect the granted powers—the States then having
all sovereign power reserved to themselves respectively—
that is, each individual State, to itself or the people, all
powers not delegated to Congress.

" It is insisted that the States hold these powers which
they reserved as individual States, in their original capacity and character as peoples of separate and distinct communities. They are held as all power was originally held
by them, subject alone to their individual will; they are
not within the scope of the amending power in the Constitution. They are in no manner made subject to the
will of the General Government. The powers of the
General Government cannot be increased by a transfer of
the reserved powers of the States, except by the consent
of each individual State.

"The State of Kentucky, in the exercise of the highest attribute of sovereignty under the reserved powers to the States, formed for the local government of the people a Constitution, by the provisions of which the right of masters in slaves is secured.

"Slavery existed before the formation of the General Government, and was never subject to its control. The proposed amendments are objected to because of the time and the circumstances under which they were proposed by Congress to the States. It was in the midst of a civil war, when eleven of the fifteen States on whom it was especially designed to operate were not represented on the floor of Congress; its passage did not express the will of the people of the whole nation.

"They are objected to because of the manner of their ratification. The Southern States lately in rebellion are counted in the number necessary to make the ratification complete.

"Without inquiring into the fact whether the plan of the President for the restoration of those States to their political relations with the General Government is right or wrong, it is sufficient that it is known that the ratification, claimed to be the acts of those States, was when the Governments of those States were provisional only; they had no other authority than the military authority of the President. The ratification was under the dictation of the President, when he held the lives and fortunes of a vast number of the best citizens of those States in his hands. They had been conquered, and many of the conquering army was in their presence. Martial law was declared to be in force. Their Conventions and Legislatures were elected under a proscribed right of suffrage. They were powerless, and laid prostrate at the feet of power. In that condition the act was insisted on as indispensable to a restoration of the civil and political rights of the citizens of those States under the Constitution.

"It is insisted that the fact of a restoration must have been completed at the time of their respective ratifications. It is not pretended that such was the fact. The restoration should have been so far complete that the citizens of those States should have been recognized as citizens of the United States, and, as such, admitted to representation on the floor of Congress.

"If these things were not necessary, and the relations of those States were restored on ceasing their resistance to federal authority, then they were not possessed of, and did not act under, regular State governments, such as are contemplated by the Constitution of the United States. The Constitution, in its reference to States, must be understood to be, States acting under such regularly formed and organized governments as existed at the time of its formation. The people of Kentucky insist that the assemblies which assumed to ratify the amendments on the part of the States of Tennessee, Arkansas, and Louisiana, were not the regular State Legislatures of those States. The so-called State of Western Virginia was not a member of the Union according to the forms of the Constitution. That the acts of States in rebellion, having no recognized rights under the government, shall be made to destroy the rights to property of citizens in a loyal and adhering State, is anomalous in the history of governments. Such position cannot be sustained on principle, or justified by reason or common justice. The people of Kentucky regard these acts revolutionary and dangerous encroachments upon the reserved powers of the States, and protest against them.

"They protest against the second clause, because its language confers upon Congress a broad and unlimited, and what is claimed to be an intended, power to legislate for the protection of a particular class of persons within the States. Besides being an innovation on the time-
6

honored principle, that each State has the exclusive right
to legislate over their own domestic affairs, they feel
assured, under it, a system of legislation may and probably will be indulged which will *make the negro a more
disturbing element in our political system than ever before*, and
will ultimately terminate in the destruction of his race.

"They deem this a fit occasion to make this, their
solemn protest against the Freedman's Bureau into this
State. It was done without authority of law. In its
operations it is offensive to the people. It combines judicial with military authority, a combination forbidden by
the letter and spirit of the Constitution. The same officer
who passes his judgment executes it at the door of a
prison or at the point of the bayonet. They deny that a
judicial officer may be appointed otherwise than by the
President, with the advice and consent of the Senate.
The introduction of this swarm of Federal officials without authority of law they regard as an exercise of arbitrary and despotic power. Its effects will be to oppress
the people and to defeat the enactment or the enforcement of wise and just laws for the protection and government of persons of color, over whom the Bureau has
assumed jurisdiction. It will defeat contracts for labor,
and ultimately destroy those whom it professes to protect.

"While thus protesting, the people of Kentucky recognize as an existing fact that those who have been held to
service, many of whom are now in our midst, have been
placed beyond the control of their masters by the action
of the Government. For that reason they do, and will
insist, that the masters of such persons are entitled to a
just and adequate compensation, and in their behalf the
Legislature now assert claim against the Government of
the United States. But the mere loss of property sinks to
insignificance when compared with the enormity of the
manner in which it was done—with the palpable viola-

tion of the Constitution and the solemn pledges of the party in power to the effect that the institution should remain unharmed.

"It is a palpable violation of a great fundamental principle enunciated by their chief—'the right of each State to order and control its own domestic institutions according to its own judgment *exclusively*, is essential to the balance of power on which the perfection and endurance of our political fabric depends.'

"The people of Kentucky now, as ever, unalterably attached to the principles of the Constitution, do further solemnly protest against the many and palpable violations of the letter and spirit of the Constitution which, in the last four years, have been committed by those in power and their subordinates.

"The continued denial to them of the privilege of the writ of *habeas corpus;* the suppression of the liberty of speech and of the press; the arrest and imprisonment of citizens without due process of law, and upon charges unknown to law; the trial and punishment by military commissions of citizens not connected with the military or naval service; the taking of private property for public use without just compensation; the denial of the right of the citizens to canvass for and hold office when qualified by law; and the employment of Federal soldiers to control the freedom of elections in the States—these are acts of tyrannical usurpation to which uncontrollable force has compelled their submission, but for which their duty to themselves and to their posterity requires them to set their seal of condemnation."

Though there is still lying before us a mass of other published evidences of the late Governor's powerful abilities as a speaker and writer other than those given in the foregoing pages, we propose to close our report of his official declarations with the above protest. He was present in his place in the State Senate during the entire adjourned session of that body, which assembled at Frankfort on the 3d. day of January, 1867, and which closed its sittings on the 11th day of March following.

The most important act with which his name stands connected during the session referred to, was his report from the Committee on Federal Relations, presented on the 29th of January, 1867, favoring the call of a Convention " to be held at an early day, in the city of Louisville, for the purpose of taking into consideration such measures as will promote the public welfare, maintain inviolable the Constitution of our fathers, the enforcement of constitutional law, and to bring to bear the whole power and influence of the National Democracy to the support of the President (Johnson) in his efforts to restore the Union, now dissevered by the unconstitutional and revolutionary acts of Congress."

We come now to the last and crowning labor of Gov. HELM's life : the canvass he made for Governor immediately preceding his last sickness and death. The Democratic State Convention which met at Frankfort on the 22d day of February, 1867, for the purpose of nominating suitable candidates for Governor, Lieutenant Governor, Treasurer, Auditor, and other State offices, fixed its choice on JOHN L. HELM for Governor and JOHN W. STEVENSON*

---

* JOHN W. STEVENSON, of all the eminent politicians of Kentucky, undoubtedly stands first at the present day, as well in position as in influence. He was born in Richmond, Virginia, and graduated at the University of Virginia. Having prepared himself for the profession of the Law, he settled in Covington, Kentucky, in 1841, where he soon took high rank in the practice of the law. He served in the Kentucky State Legislature in 1845, 1846, and 1847, and was elected a member of the State Constitutional Convention in 1849, in which he took a leading part. He was a member of the Democratic National Conventions of 1848, 1852, and 1856. He was twice Senatorial Elector, and was one of three Commissioners appointed to revise the Civil and Criminal Code of Kentucky. He was elected from the Covington District a Representative to the Thirty-fifth Congress, and was a member of the Committee on Elections. He was elected also to the Thirty-sixth Congress, in which he served on the same committee. He was the nominee of the Kentucky State Democratic Convention of 1867, for the office of Lieu-

for Lieutenant Governor. At the time referred to there were three distinct political organizations in Kentucky, viz : First, the Old Democratic party, which numbered in its ranks fully two thirds of the voters of the State ; second, the Union Conservative, or Third party, which was made up of timid Democrats, afraid to co-operate with the majority, lest, because of the latter's coalition with what was known as the "rebel element" of the State—a term given to those citizens that had taken an active part in the late civil war in favor of the South—evils should result to the State through the unfriendly legislation of the dominant party in Congress; and third, the out-and-out Radical party, scarcely numbering one in ten of the entire population, and closely affiliated in sentiment with the Congressional majority in respect to Southern reconstruction. Judge WILLIAM B. KINCAID* was the candidate for Governor of the Third party men, and Col. SIDNEY BARNES† accepted a like position on the Radical ticket.

tenant Governor, on the ticket with Governor HELM, and, in the canvass which followed, did eminent service to his party by addressing his fellow-citizens in different parts of the State. On the death of Governor HELM he became acting Governor. He was the candidate of the Democracy in the State election of the present year (1868) for the office of Governor, securing his election by the unprecedented majority of nearly ninety thousand votes. Governor STEVENSON is a ripe scholar, a lawyer of rare abilities, and is generally regarded as the most able and finished public speaker in the State.

* WILLIAM B. KINCAID is a native of Woodford county, Kentucky. He is a fine lawyer, wealthy, and of high social position. He resides on his farm, near the city of Lexington, and practices in the courts of Woodford and the adjoining counties. We should judge his age to be from fifty-five to sixty years. For a brief period he sat on the bench of the Lexington Judicial District, having accepted the office from the late Governor OWSLEY to fill out the unexpired term of a former incumbent.

† Col. SIDNEY BARNES is a lawyer of distinction, practicing in the Courts of the Ninth Kentucky Congressional District. He is a native of Estill county, where he was born about the year 1821. He has never held any civil office under either the Federal Government or that of the State. He is now, however (October, 1868), a candidate for Congress in the District, in opposition to G. M. ADAMS, the present Representative. Col. BARNES commanded the Eighth Regiment of Kentucky Infantry in the late civil war.

Governor HELM, on accepting the nomination of his party friends assembled in Convention, deemed it a duty he owed to them and to the principles and policy by which he and they professed to be governed, to make a thorough canvass of the State. His immediate family, and others who had reason to fear that his physical strength was unequal to so laborious a work, in vain endeavored to dissuade him from the undertaking. He was not to be moved, declaring that he "would go, though he were sure that it would kill him," as he "believed it to be imperatively necessary, under existing circumstances, that Kentucky should present a solid Democratic front in the approaching election." At another time, addressing one of his friends, he said: "Great trouble is brewing for Kentucky in the future, and I intend doing all in my power to prepare the people for it, that it may not take them by surprise and overwhelm them when it comes." To his brother, Rev. SQUIRE HELM, who added his entreaties to those of his wife and children, imploring him to remain at home and to leave the prosecution of the canvass to younger men and to those more fitted to bear the labor it imposed, he answered: "I feel it to be my religious and patriotic duty to serve my country in any capacity I may be considered useful, though I should shorten my life in the effort."

In due time he started out on his canvass, and prosecuted it with a degree of energy that would have been in the highest degree praiseworthy, had he not, at the same time, been exhausting his vital powers and further aggravating, from day to day, a malady from which he had been long suffering; and which was eventually to deprive himself of life and the country of one of its most useful public servants. The end of the canvass found him completely prostrated in health, and he returned to his home only to seek the aid of his physician, with the hope of recuperating his seriously shattered physical constitu-

The history of the events that followed the election of Governor HELM, up to the day of his death, occupying in their recurrence just thirty-three days, can best be related by one who was with him from the beginning of his sickness to the closing scene of his life.

Among the late Governor's children; there is one that has long suffered from a distressing spinal affection. MARY HELM has for many years lived in a little world of her own, that extended only to the limits of " Helm Place," and that was peopled by the beings she most loved on earth—father and mother, brothers and sisters. Kind neighbors, to be sure, the young and the old, the happy of heart and the seriously inclined, would often pass hours by her bedside, with a half purpose, apparently, to amuse their bed-ridden friend, and another to learn of her how to suffer and still be patient and happy. MARY HELM's neatly written diary lies before us, and from it we take the loving daughter's pathetic account of her father's last days:

" During the whole of the mountain canvass my father's health grew worse from day to day. When he at last returned to his home, after the election was over, he greatly complained of a sense of weariness. He thought a few days of rest and quiet would restore him to his wonted health. The days passed, but the weariness continued, and he was heard to say, ' I greatly fear I have broken myself down.'

" When the election returns were coming in and he saw the majorities rising with every mail that came to hand, and every flash of the telegraph, his gratification was greater than I had ever known it to be on any similar occasion. He appreciated with honest pride the honor that had been conferred upon him by the people; and he appeared, also, to keenly feel the responsibility he had assumed. He loved Kentucky better than his life, and he seemed to be filled with sad forebodings for the future of his beloved State. During the few days that he was her Governor, he expressed with intense feeling his determination, 'come weal or woe,' to guard her liberties and her rights, and to resist any invasion of either, no matter from what quarter it might come.

"His health did not improve; yet no one, save my mother, seemed to fear that anything serious ailed him, and when she gave expression to her apprehensions, we were all very much surprised and distressed. But seeing him still occupying himself in the affairs of the farm, sometimes engaged in writing, and occasionally even walking over the place, we would not be convinced that his disease was fast sapping the foundations of his life. He took interest in conversing with his friends, was often cheerful, and, on one occasion, rode into town for the purpose of attending to some legal business. The consequences of this act showed its imprudence. The heat of the crowded court-house and the fatigue he underwent in endeavoring to settle the business in hand, were too much for his strength. He was seized with a violent attack of vertigo, and reaching his home with difficulty, he laid down upon that bed from which he was destined never more to rise. The family physician, Dr. Slaughter, being sent for, he found the case so alarming as to induce him to call to his assistance other medical men, among whom were Dr. J. L. Helm, of Louisville, and the Governor's brother, Dr. Wm. D. Helm, of Bowling Green.

"The physicians treated my father for an affection of the brain, though he was undoubtedly suffering as well from other ailments. In a few days he appeared to be much restored, so much so, indeed, as to announce his determination to go to Frankfort to be inaugurated. He appealed to his physicians to do all they could to give him strength to bear the fatigue of this journey, as he 'must be there.' His physicians shook their heads, and his family and friends remonstrated with him against

such a proceeding; but he was immovable in his determination to make the effort, cost what it might. His
strong will had borne him through many difficulties,
and I really thought it would be equal to the task he
contemplated in this instance. He might have made
the attempt, had it not been for my mother, who, with
prudent firmness, took the matter into her own hands.
Without consulting my father, she addressed a letter to
Col. SAMUEL B. CHURCHILL* (having been apprised of her
husband's intention to make him his Secretary of State),
informing him fully of her husband's condition, and requesting him, if the thing was legal and possible, to so
arrange as to have the inauguration take place at Helm
Place. In a few days she received Colonel CHURCHILL's
answer, and was glad to learn that the plan she had
proposed was both legal and possible; that every ar-
rangement should be made to carry it into effect, and
that the Hon. THOS. E. BRAMLETTE,† the retiring Governor, would be present at the inauguration.

---

*Col. CHURCHILL is a native of Louisville, Kentucky, where he was born
in 1813. He was educated at St. Joseph's College, Bardstown. He adopted
the profession of the law, and, shortly after obtaining his license to practice,
removed to St. Louis, Mo., where he acquired an extended legal practice,
and was a noted Democratic politician. He served for several terms in the
Missouri State Legislature, and was Postmaster in St. Louis for a number
of years. When the war broke out he was regarded as a "Southern sym-
pathizer," and suffered much in consequence, being several times imprisoned,
and finally ordered to leave the State. Through the intervention of friends
in this State, Col. CHURCHILL was permitted to remove with his family to
Kentucky, and has since resided in Frankfort. He was appointed Secretary
of State by Governor HELM, and he still retains the same position under his
successor.

†The Hon. THOMAS E. BRAMLETTE was born in 1817 at Elliott's Cross
Roads, Clinton county, Kentucky. His father was the late Hon. A. S.
BRAMLETTE, who represented his county in the Legislature for many years,
and was also returned twice from his district to the State Senate. Governor
BRAMLETTE is by profession a lawyer, and has acquired much distinction
at the bar. When only twenty-four years of age, he was elected to the
Lower House of the General Assembly. In 1848 he received from Gov-
ernor CRITTENDEN the appointment of Commonwealth's Attorney for his

" Well pleased at the success of her scheme, my mother laid the whole matter before her husband, who, having in the meantime become fully conscious of his inability to . take the journey to Frankfort, answered her : ' You have done wisely and well, my love.' I think he was now gradually growing worse every day. His sufferings were apparently becoming more and more intense, and if aroused to talk at all, the only subjects that seemed to interest him were the political situation of parties and the condition of the country. His thoughts seemed to be constantly running on matters of State. One day some one very imprudently read to him an account of a recent outrage perpetrated on a Southern community by Federal officials. He became violently excited, and his voice, suddenly raised to its healthful compass, rung out in denunciation of the act, and of those whose reckless disregard for constitutional law had made such an act possible. He was much worse after this occurrence, and all reference to political subjects was from this time interdicted in the sick-room.

" The 3d of September, the day fixed for the inauguration, came at length. Preparations had been made in the

Judicial District. In the Presidential contest of 1853, between Franklin Pierce and Gen. Winfield Scott, he served as District Elector on the Whig ticket. He was afterwards nominated for Congress by the Whig party of the district, but was beaten in the race by a trifling majority, by the Hon. James Chrisman. In 1856 he was elected Judge of his Judicial District, which office he held up to the beginning of the late civil war, when he resigned it in order to raise a regiment under the authority of the United States Government. He commanded the regiment so raised—the Third Kentucky Infantry—up to July, 1862, when he retired from the army. In the spring of 1863, Mr. Lincoln proffered him the position of United States Attorney for the district, which he accepted and held until he received the nomination of the Union party of Kentucky for the office of Governor of the State. He made the race in 1863, against the Hon. Charles A. Wickliffe, the Democratic candidate, and was elected. He filled the office of Governor till the end of the term, September, 1867, with much fidelity and greatly to the satisfaction of all parties. On retiring from the office, he removed to Louisville, where he is now engaged in an extensive legal practice.

town for a grand display. Special trains brought in large numbers of friends and political admirers, from Louisville, Frankfort, and other cities and towns of the State; crowds flocked into the town from Hardin and the surrounding counties, all anxious to witness the inaugural ceremonies. At 11 o'clock a procession was formed in the town, and, preceded by a band of musicians, took up its march toward Helm Place. Before they had gone half the distance, they were met by one of the physicians, who begged them to desist. Absolute quiet was necessary, and the music and shouting would be apt to excite his patient to such a degree as to render him physically unable to undergo the fatigue of the ceremony in which he had necessarily to take a part. Only those officers of State whose presence was necessary were permitted to enter the sick-room.

"That inauguration of a dying man was the saddest, as well as the most impressive, scene I ever witnessed. Propped up in his bed, his features worn and haggard from disease, and his hands lying in weakness beside him, it was a scene to make one's heart ache—and ache mine did, as I gazed through my tears on my father's pallid face. But the old spirit shone out of his eyes, and the strong will, for a time, overcame the weakness that had resulted from disease. He spoke to his friends as they approached his bedside, and expressed to each and all the pleasure he felt in their presence. To Governor BRAMLETTE, especially, he expressed his grateful sense of the kindness he had shown in coming so far. On one side of the bed stood Gov. BRAMLETTE, Judge WINTERSMITH, and Col. CHURCHILL, while on the other stood my mother and the attending physicians. Grouped around were the members of his family, with his two sons-in-law, Judge H. W. BRUCE and Major T. H. HAYS, together with a few intimate friends, among whom were Judge ALVIN DUVALL, the Hon. JOHN RODMAN, and Major FAYETTE HEWITT.

"While Judge WINTERSMITH was administering to him the oath of office, every one listened in breathless silence, and seemed to be duly impressed with the solemnity of the occasion. He became very faint, and it was only after a stimulent had been given him that he had strength to sign his name. After this, he handed to Col. CHURCHILL his commission as Secretary of State. Judge DUVALL stepped forward and asked: 'Do you authorize Colonel CHURCHILL to sign appointments?' He answered, in a distinct manner, 'I authorize *Sam.* CHURCHILL'—placing a strong emphasis on the Christian name, and showing his consciousness of the fact that *Colonel* had no significance in a legal document. He was totally unable to sign the appointments of Col. WOLFORD* and Maj. HEWITT, though they had both been prepared, and were ready for his signature. Seeing that nothing further could be done, all left the room, and proceeded to Elizabethtown, where the Inaugural Address was read.

"It was apparent to us all, long before nightfall of the 3d, that his disease wore a more alarming aspect, and that he was sinking fast. The physicians declared, if a

---

*Colonel FRANK WOLFORD is a Kentuckian by birth, having been born, if we mistake not, in the county of Casey, in 1818. He served with distinction in the war with Mexico. In the late civil strife he proffered his services to the Federal Government, and raised a regiment of troops, which was afterwards known as the First Kentucky, or "Wolford's Cavalry." He proved himself a gallant and a meritorious officer, saw hard service, and was several times wounded in battle. In 1864 he was dismissed the service on the alleged grounds of having expressed, in a public speech, "disloyal sentiments." Colonel WOLFORD thought the war should be carried on for the precise objects stated in the famous resolution of Congress, solemnly declared after the first great battle of the war—to bring back the old Union of the States, under the Constitution, and not for purposes of vengeance, or to insure the success of any political party, or the ascendency of one section over the other. During the war he was arrested by orders of the Government, and was for some time confined in the Newport, Kentucky, Military Prison. He served in the State Legislature during the sessions of 1865 and 1866. After the death of Governor HELM that gentleman's successor commissioned him Adjutant General of the State, a position which he still holds.

change for the better did not occur within the next twen-
four-hours, it was impossible that he should live. Oh,
how terrible was the anxiety with which we watched beside him, waiting and hoping for that 'change for the
better,' which never came! Kind and faithful friends—
God's blessing rest upon them for it—united with his
family in doing all they could to assuage his sufferings,
which had now grown so grievous that he drew his breath
laboringly, groaning pitifully with each aspiration. It
was all in vain. Hourly he grew worse, until, on Thursday morning, he had lost even the power of speech. On
Thursday night his brother, Rev. SQUIRE HELM, reached
his bedside. He was immediately recognized, though my
father was unable to utter his name. It was sufficiently
evident to all of us, from the manner in which he followed
him with his eyes, that he was greatly pleased to have
this brother, whom he had himself raised from early childhood, and for whom he had felt at once a father's and a
brother's love, near him in his last moments. For many
years he had been in the habit of talking freely with him
on the subject of religion, and no one knew better than
he the sincerity of my dear father's faith in the Saviour
of the world.

"On Friday morning we ceased even to hope. They
told us that the texture of the brain was broken, and we
knew the end to be near. They said he might die that
day, or he might live until the next. He had been speech-
less now for twenty-four hours, and none may know the
anguish of heart with which we looked upon him, lying
prostrate on his bed, and unable even to move, gasping
out feeble moans between his parted lips, yet knowing
that he was still conscious, by the earnest, almost beseech-
ing look, with which his eyes followed us as we moved
silently around his bed. Oh, yes; he still recognized the
faces of those he loved—still had us in his eye and in his
heart.

"That morning, at 9 o'clock, we were all gathered together in his room—wife and children, brothers and sister, relatives and friends, and some of the old family servants. We all kneeled around his bed, while his brother read and prayed. He seemed interested, checked his deep groanings, and listened intently to the passages that were read from God's Holy Word and to the touching prayer that was offered in his behalf to the Throne of Grace. When the prayer was finished, he fixed his eyes upon his brother with a longing meaning. In answer to this, the latter asked: 'Brother John, are you willing to die?' No answer came, and we could not tell whether it was because he could not speak or because he was unwilling to do so. I think, myself, that he was examining his own heart; for, when Uncle Helm again addressed him, 'Brother John, are you willing to trust in God?' he moved his lips, and after a moment's effort to speak, answered distinctly, 'Yes.' Oh, how that little word thrilled our hearts! It was the first time he had spoken for a whole day, and in hushed silence we listened as his brother again asked: 'Brother John, is your trust in Christ?' and again the answer came, clearer and louder than before, 'Yes!' This was heard distinctly all over the room, and we rejoiced to know that it was from his heart of hearts that he made his confession of faith in Christ the Redeemer. Yet this was no death-bed confession. All his life he had been an humble believer in God and His Christ. To those dearest to him he had before professed that faith, and it was only because of his humility that he had not professed it publicly.

"His daughters came and each pressed a kiss upon his poor pallid lips. Then came our mother, and bending over him, said in heart-touching, broken accents: 'Kiss me—do *you* kiss *me*, my husband, once more.' With an effort he pressed his lips to hers. It was the last kiss he ever gave her. Turning away, she saw their oldest living son, John L. Helm, sitting bowed in grief, in a far corner of the room. She called to him to come and bid his father good-bye. Sobbing, he answered: 'Ma, I cannot, cannot do it.' She then spoke to the youngest, a boy of sixteen, who came and knelt beside his bed. Much agitated, his father placed his trembling hand upon his head, and fervently exclaimed: 'God bless my son Tommie.' Hearing this, John also threw himself on his knees beside his brother, and as he did so, his father's hand was lifted to his head. Gazing upon the face of this son, upon whom he had expected to lean as the staff of his old age, and to whose care he had left his soon-to-be widowed mother, his heart seemed to be stirred within him to its lowest depths, and again his voice was lifted up in prayer: 'God bless this, my son.' The second living son taking his brother's place, again the self-same scene was enacted, and the self-same prayer evoked upon his head. Once only, afterwards, did he open his lips to speak, and then he enunciated the single word *Ma!* showing that his mind, reverting to the days of his own childhood, was losing its hold on the things that had occupied and interested him since he had set out on the serious business of life.

"All through the rest of the day and night he lay in a kind of stupor, but toward the morning of Saturday, having slept a little, he awoke apparently better. Hope again visited our hearts, and a dispatch was sent to Dr. Foree, of Louisville, begging his immediate attendance. About nine o'clock we again gathered about his bed for prayer, and again my father ceased to groan and listened, with apparently deeper interest than before, to the earnest supplications made to God in his behalf. He had entirely lost the power of speech; but oh, if you could have seen his face as his brother spoke of the love of God for sinners, and of His rich mercy through Christ Jesus, who had said, ' He that cometh to me, I will in no wise cast out,' you would have thought it that of one already glorified. All sensation of pain appeared to have left him—a sweet smile played around his lips, and from his eyes shone out a holy, happy, peaceful light, that was indicative of a spirit at rest in God—of a heart possessed of 'that peace which passeth all understanding.' I will never forget that expression, for never before had I seen it on mortal face. My heart stood still within me. Looking around, I saw that every eye in the room, as had been my own, was fixed with breathless interest upon the face that lay so calm and peaceful before us. An indescribable look of awe pervaded the features of all save his own. Upon these seemed to rest a halo as of the glory of the blessed. I know not how long this scene lasted, for I took no note of time. I only know that after a while they said he slept.

"All day Saturday we thought him slightly better; but with the evening came Dr. FOREE, and the result of the consultation of physicians which followed blasted all our hopes: 'It was impossible that he should recover.' As the Sabbath dawn approached, he was observed to be fast sinking. The lamp of his life had almost gone out, and hour after hour we stood and watched its flickering flame. All through that Sabbath morning we watched and waited, with aching hearts, as the struggle went on. For many hours he had been wrestling with Death, and now that mighty conqueror would be put off no longer. The pulse grew feebler, the moanings fainter, and as the sun marked the hour of noon, the summons came. With a quiver of his mortal frame, the spirit departed and ascended to the God who gave it. I saw his beloved features once again when he lay in his coffin. The smile that I had noted the day before was still there, and it was a joy to us all to observe it, speaking to our hearts as it did of the happy passage he had made into that life which is eternal."

To the above touching account of Governor HELM's last illness and death we have little need to add any-thing. The house of mourning was visited by hundreds while his coffined body lay waiting for the solemn con-signment of "dust to dust."· Among these visitors were many farmers from the county, with their wives and children, who had known him all their lives. With faces bathed in tears, they would lead their sons, mostly farmer boys, to the coffin, and bid them look upon the face of one who had once been himself a farmer boy, and who died the Governor of the Commonwealth. It was, a double lesson that they seemed anxious to inculcate upon the minds of their children. They wished to show them, in the first place, that the end-all of their existence here on earth would find them, no matter what stations they should occupy in life, reduced to the condition of him whose remains lay before them. They desired, in the second place, to teach them that the only success in the affairs of life that was worthy of a good man's ambition, was that which is the guerdon of a life of virtue and of talents wisely directed.

The funeral took place on the 11th. The morning train from Louisville had brought a large number of friends of the lamented dead. Crowds came in from the country to witness the last funeral rites over the remains of their fellow-citizen, who had in his life-time shown himself to be so sincerely their friend, and the consistent advocate of their interests. They came to show their respect for the man, and to do honor to the office to which the people had so recently elevated him. Most of the State officials who had come to his inauguration were present at his funeral. The scene in and about Elizabethtown was mournfully impressive and deeply respectful to the deceased. Upon every face was depicted the sincerest grief. The court-house and many other buildings, public and private, were draped in black, and, at several points,

7

the avenues through which the procession was expected to pass were crossed by festoons of crape. The church bells tolled their measured knell, as if speaking from their mid-air steeples to a sorrowing world. The members of Morrison Lodge, No. 76, of the Masonic Fraternity, to which the late Governor had been attached, headed by a band playing a funeral dirge, and followed by a large concourse of citizens and strangers, formed in procession and slowly marched from the town to Helm Place.

A march of a mile and a quarter brought the procession to the family mansion of the deceased Governor. So immense was the concourse that comparatively few could gain admission to the house. The State officials, the clergy, the pall-bearers, and some others, gathered with the bereft family around the form of the Governor, now "hearsed in death," and after many last fond looks upon his placid, memorable features, the funeral service of the Methodist Episcopal Church was begun. This service was brief and simple, but indelibly affecting. It consisted in the reading of the 19th Psalm, the 15th Chapter of Paul to the Corinthians, and the offering of a singularly appropriate and eloquent prayer—all by the Rev. A. L. ALDERSON, of the Methodist Episcopal Church, South.

After the exercises at the residence, the procession was reorganized. The corpse was taken in charge by the Masonic pall-bearers, and by them conveyed in the prescribed order of march to the family burying-ground, on a commanding eminence distant from the house about one thousand yards. When the rites of the church were concluded at the grave, the honors of Masonry, in all their imposing solemnity, were conferred by Worshipful Master FAYETTE HEWITT, Rev. E. B. SMITH, Masonic Chaplain, and the brethren in attendance. And thus closed the final tributes of love and respect to the memory of Kentucky's fallen chief.

Our task is nearly finished. It remains for us but to give, in a condensed form, from the mass of evidence that is before us—letters from his friends, eulogiums delivered on the occasion of his death, and newspaper criticisms of his public life—our own estimate of Gov. HELM's character as a man and as a public servant. We shall neither begin nor end by saying that he was faultless. He was human, and it is human to err. He had been taught self-reliance from his youth, and this continued to be a leading characteristic with him to the end of his life. He had, doubtless, too little regard for the advice of others, and often gave offense by exhibiting more confidence in his own judgment than in that of those from whose greater experience he might have benefited.

He was reserved in his manners, and, by those who did not know him intimately, was often mistaken for a proud and haughty man. In truth, there was no one that was less so. He held that man to be his social inferior only who was willing to lower himself by the commission of acts degrading to humanity. His habit of thinking and acting for himself on all occasions gave to his manner of speaking a certain air of egotism that was foreign to his real character.

Governor HELM was seen to best advantage in his own home. Here, surrounded by wife and children, and basking, as it were, in the sun-light of their love, his manners lost all their stiffness, and he entered into all their little plans for amusement with the readiness and simplicity of a child. His affection for his wife and children was beautiful to behold. To gratify either—whether it was in the purchase of a keepsake, or to walk a mile to gather a nosegay for his wife or his invalid daughter, or to do any little service to please either one of his children—he would willingly put himself to trouble, and he valued not the cost. A friend writes:

"It would have done you good to see Gov. HELM in the midst of his family. His very presence appeared to give joy to all around him; and to see his household happy was his own greatest delight.   On all such occasions, whether the time was spent in instructive discourse, having for its object the welfare of his children, or in relating anecdotes and incidents connected with the settlement of the country and the personal histories of the early pioneers, or drawn from his own recollections of the past, he seemed to feel as if he was enjoying himself to the fullest bent of nature.   He was not of the class of parents of whom their children are always shy, and sometimes afraid.   His daily intercourse with them had in it that pleasant familiarity which emboldened them to give him their fullest confidence, and to depend upon his judgment in all matters of moment to themselves."

The uniform confidence placed in Governor Helm by the people of Hardin county, during his entire public life, is, perhaps, the most extraordinary feature of his whole history.   He was eleven times elected to serve the people of Hardin in the Lower House of the General Assembly of Kentucky, and on six of these occasions he was elected by his fellow-members to preside over their deliberations. Three times he was returned by his Senatorial District to the Upper House of the General Assembly.   When he ran for Congress against Willis Green, and was defeated, Hardin county was still true to him.   She was equally true to him in his contests for the offices of Lieutenant Governor in 1848, and Governor in 1867.   We can draw from this remarkable fact but one conclusion : his fellow-citizens regarded him as possessing talents of a high order, and they knew him to be both faithful and honest.

From what has been written, it will be seen that Gov. Helm's public career was a long one.   He served the State and the people faithfully; and yet he died impoverished, except in good name.   He was not of the class of officials, of whom we have heard something in these latter days of the Republic, who are in the habit of using their positions for purposes of self-aggrandizement. He never touched a dollar of the people's money for which he had not rendered honest service. In these days of official misrule and of official neglect of public interests, we hold it to be a high compliment to his memory to say of him, as we do, that in every position of trust held by him throughout his public life, he labored earnestly and perseveringly, not for himself or for selfish purposes, but for those, and the interests of those, whom he represented. His immediate family may well consider that, though he served not himself in serving his State and the nation, and though, on leaving the world, he left to them none of its riches, he was still able to bequeath them as honorable a name as was ever yet written on the scrolls of his country's history.

Our task is ended. "Governor HELM is in his grave! Calmly he slumbers beneath the soil of his beloved native county. Embowered in the peaceful shade of his own forest trees, through whose evergreen boughs the gentle autumn winds chant their low, sad requiem, the hero lies in the embrace of that profound sleep that knows no waking. A bereaved family, friends, community, State, and nation, grieve that one of earth's best and purest and brightest spirits has winged its flight from their presence forever."*

* GEORGE D. PRENTICE.

APPENDIX.

STATE OF KENTUCKY, }
HARDIN COURT OF COMMON PLEAS. }

The above Court being in session at the court-house in Elizabethtown, on Monday, 9th of September, 1867, the following proceedings were had in said Court:

The death of our lamented fellow-citizen, His Excellency, JOHN L. HELM, Governor of the State, at his residence in this county, at half-past 12 o'clock on yesterday, the 8th of September, 1867, was announced in Court by Col. W. B. READ, a member of the bar.

On his motion, a committee of three members of the bar was appointed by the Court to draft resolutions suitable to the occasion, to-wit: W. B. READ, M. H. COFER, and TIM. G. NEEDHAM, Esqs.

The committee reported the following preamble and resolutions, which were unanimously adopted by the bar, officers, and the jury of the Court, to-wit:

WHEREAS, The Court and members of this bar have learned of the death of His Excellency JOHN L. HELM, and believing that God in His inscrutable providence does all things well, and as a mark of our high appreciation of his inestimable worth as a citizen, friend, lawyer, and statesman—

1. *Resolved*, That in him we recognized all the high qualities which served to adorn the citizen, lawyer, and statesman; and in his death humanity has lost a friend, the profession a superior light, and the State a noble Chief Magistrate.

2. That we sympathize with his sorely bereaved family in the loss of a kind husband and father; and, as a token

of our respect and esteem, we will attend his funeral in a body, and wear for thirty days the usual badge of mourning.

3. That the foregoing preamble and resolutions be spread upon the order books of the Court, and the clerk is requested to furnish a copy of the same to his family.

4. That a copy be furnished the Louisville papers for publication, and others in the State are requested to copy.

His Honor CHAS. G. WINTERSMITH, Judge of the Court, from the bench pronounced an address and eulogy upon the lamented dead.

The greater portion of the honorable gentleman's address referred to matters that have already been adverted to in the foregoing pages. The residue of the address is appended :

"Before entering upon the records of this Court the resolutions presented and adopted with perfect unanimity by the bar, officers, and jury of the Court, all neighbors and associates of our departed friend, I hope I may be indulged in giving utterance to the feelings and sentiments which inspire my bosom at this moment.

"The death of His Excellency, JOHN LARUE HELM, Governor of Kentucky, is no ordinary event. He was no ordinary man. As a friend and relative, I have known him from my earliest childhood. His mother and my mother were cousins and loving friends; when children, they emigrated together from the Shenandoah Valley of Virginia, and their parents settled on Nolynn, within one mile of each other. Upon its banks they were reared in a close intimacy, which existed during life. Their children maintained the same intimacy. The county of Larue was named in honor of his maternal grandfather, JOHN LARUE, and its county seat was named in honor of my maternal grandfather, ROBERT HODGEN, they having resided in Virginia and Kentucky in close proximity for many years, and were bound to each other in the ties of a most cordial and intimate friendship.   .

"Having known Gov. Helm so long and so well, I feel that I may well bear testimony to his great private and public worth.

*   *   *   *   *   *   *   *   *   *   *

"In 1867 he was called to the Chief Magistracy of the State, in which elevated position, on his sick bed, he was installed on Tuesday, September 3, 1867, and now, within one short week, we mourn the announcement that *he is no more*, but is removed to another sphere; and we have good reason to hope and believe his removal has been from gloom to a happy-resting place in the bosom of his Heavenly Father. We bow with humble, though sad submission, to the great fiat which none can gainsay or disobey.

"I regard him as a martyr to the zeal, energy, industry, and anxiety which he felt it was an imperative duty he should exercise in undertaking a canvass for what he believed the right, at the call of his fellow-citizens, beyond his physical power. As a result, while the laurel encircles his brow, the cypress is wreathed over the casket which incloses his inanimate form. He began his political life an unequivocal, true, and ardent devotee of constitutional liberty and government, administered in the protection of citizen and State rights, and in the advancement of general public good. He made these the polar star of his manhood. In his maturer years— in his old age—when he believed in the honesty of his heart, and thought that he had good reason to believe, that mighty efforts, with prospect of success, were being made for their destruction, in one grand effort to avert the dire calamity, he has yielded up his life a sacrifice upon the altar of his country. ·

"Associated with Governor Helm from the time of my admission to the bar, I have ever found him prompt and zealous in his client's cause—bold and fearless in the defense of right, and a very powerful and effective advocate.

" As a man, in all the relations of life he commanded the admiration of all who knew him personally or by reputation.

" In his domestic relations, he was exemplary, kind, affectionate, generous, and faithful to all his marital and parental obligations.

" In social intercourse, he was courteous and conciliatory.

" In his friendships, he was true and loyal.

" As a neighbor, he was accommodating, social, hospitable, and charitable.

" As a citizen, he was quiet, peaceful, avoiding all private and public piques and quarrels, pursuing the paths of peace, and always with a heart full of public spirit.

" Pertinacious in maintaining his own opinions, he freely yielded to all others the same right unquestioned; and all his argumentations with his fellow-men were characterized by fairness, mildness, and candor. In his dealings he was honest and upright. His tongue was never heard in aspersion of other men. He was a man of high moral character, eschewing even all the smallest vices to which so many men are addicted—never profane, never using stimulating and intoxicating beverages, never engaging in play for money. In short, as a practical moralist, he was a model man.

" Such a man was JOHN LARUE HELM; and now he descends to the tomb, with honors thick upon him, amidst the deep and sad regrets of a vast multitude of friends and admirers, with a record of public services which will be an enduring monument to his frame, and a reputation and character so spotless that it will ever be a source of comfort, consolation, and pride to his family, his friends, his State, and his country.

"'Sic iter ad astra.'

"May we who survive him be able to feel, 'when life's last lingering sun goes feebly down and death comes to our door,' that naught but good can be said of us.

"With no ordinary feelings of satisfaction, though mournful, do I realize the power to order that the resolutions passed and presented be spread upon the records of this Court, and therefore I order it to be done."

TRIBUTE BY MORRISON LODGE.

WHEREAS, It has pleased the Supreme Grand Master to summons from our midst our much esteemed brother, JOHN L. HELM, whose virtues have long been the pride of his Lodge, and whose shining example of uprightness and integrity has been a jewel in the Temple of Universal Masonry; be it

1. *Resolved*, That while the coffin, the spade, and the melancholy grave, remind us that our brother has gone from the portals of our Lodge forever, we will treasure up in our hearts the recollection of his many manly virtues, and of his noble nature, and strive to imitate his worthy example of high morality and unselfish generosity.

2. That in the death of him we mourn to-day this Lodge has lost a true and noble member, whose high morality and dignified and lofty character made him one of the shining lights of the Order; his family has lost a kind and devoted husband and father; this community one it has ever delighted to honor, and who never proved untrue to the trust reposed in him; the State has lost a Chief Magistrate whose long experience in her affairs, and unbending in-

tegrity and lofty patriotism in every place of public trust, gave the highest guarantee of a prosperous and just administration; the nation has lost a patriot and a statesman who had few superiors in intellect, and few equals in integrity of purpose.

3. That we tender to his stricken family the most sincere sympathy in this dark hour of their sorrow and affliction. Though he is gone from them and us, he will live long in the recollection of those who knew him, and who will delight to honor his name and his memory.

4. That a copy of these resolutions be furnished the family of our deceased brother, and also to the press of the State for publication.

ABSTRACT FROM GOVERNOR HELM'S WILL, WRITTEN AND
SIGNED NOVEMBER 15, 1865.

"Assuming it as probable that the Government of the United States will, by force and fraud, against and in contempt of right and justice, of law and the Constitutions, State and National, and all law, civil or moral, deprive my representatives of their labor [that of his slaves], I place those who have and may remain on my place, at the disposal of my wife and son, JOHN HELM. I request that such as remain faithful and obedient shall remain in the service of the family on such terms as may be agreed upon. I regard this act of the Government, looking to it in all its bearings and consequences, the greatest crime of this or any other age.

" In view of all the consequences which, in my honest judgment, would flow from it, I was fixed and unalterable in my opposition to the late unhappy and desolating war; and now, in the performance of this solemn act, I thank God, in the sincerity of my heart, that he gave that direction to my mind. No man that lived and breathed was more devotedly attached to the union of the States, as formed by the compact—the Constitution, as made by our fathers—than I was. I hold that it was formed by the free and unconstrained will of the people, and depended for its perpetuity on the virtue and intelligence of the people, the fraternal affection of the sections, and the promotion of their mutual welfare. I was for peaceful adjustment, and against war, believing as I did, and now do, that war would be, and now believe is, practical dissolution, unauthorized by the Constitution, and against the spirit and genius of our form of government. The South was conquered; but, in my firm conviction, the North will sooner or later learn that it is the whipped party.

"The race of intellectual giants has passed off the stage. The moral tone of the people is gone. Corruption and vice will rule the hour and the day. The masses of the people have lost confidence in the rulers of the Government. They place no reliance in their justice and honor. This is a melancholy picture; but my mind is made up that the future of this Government will have a downward tendency, and ultimately, and at no very distant day, will result in disintegration or a centralized despotism.

"This is an unseemly place to introduce my political opinions. I do it to solemnly impress my family with my opinions, and in the firm hope that they will stand by the form of Government as it came from the hands of our Revolutionary fathers, and oppose modern reforms. I believe the Abolitionists, as a political party, capable of any crime—possessing no redeeming quality."

"The annexed tribute to Kentucky's Martyr Chief," says the editor of the Louisville Journal, from whose columns we extract it, " is from a hand well worthy to bind a funeral wreath upon the brow of the noble dead:

"OUR MARTYR.

"The bitter blast was blowing,
The waves rose mountain high,
When our gallant Captain took the deck,
Resolved to do or die.
He held his post by the main mast,
He flung his flag to the breeze,
And his ringing voice was heard by all
Above the surging seas.

"That voice gave strength and courage
To every man of the crew;
They manned the ropes, they furled the sails,
As his trumpet bade them do.
And the ship was brought to harbor,
And safe at anchor swung,
Before the eyes of the multitude,
'Mid the cheers of old and young.

"Laden with sacred treasures,
More dear to every heart
Than gold or gems, was the Argosy,
Our Captain brought to port.
And the people held high revel,
And the board of state was spread.
And they bade the ship's commander then
Come forth and take the head!

"But the seat they placed was empty,
And the wine was poured in vain,
He had given his life to save their ship
(That life without a stain).
He dies the death of the martyr,
As he lived the life of the brave.
And the hand that wreathed his civic crown,
Consigned him to the grave.

"We shall have other Captains,
And our good ship long shall ride
Beyond the reach of the bitter blast,
Or the ebb of the envious tide;
But let it ne'er be forgotten,
Whatever betide our realm,
That the leader that gave his life for us,
Was our bulwark and our 'Helm.'
"BEECHMORE, Sept. 10, 1867.'"

THE INAUGURAL CEREMONIES.

Owing to Governor Helm's illness, as has already been seen, the ceremonies of his inauguration took place at Elizabethtown, Kentucky, on the 3d day of September, 1867. From Governor Thos. E. Bramlette's Valedictory Address, made on the occasion, we extract the following passages:

"Fellow-Citizens: By appointment of the Constitution of 'the Commonwealth of Kentucky,' this day terminates my official relations with the people of my native State, and inaugurates the administration of my much-esteemed friend and successor, His Excellency, John L. Helm, who has been chosen, in accordance with the Constitution and laws, by the legal voters of Kentucky, Governor for the ensuing four years.

"Deeply do I sympathize with his family and the citizens of Kentucky in the anxiety for his restored health, and regret that his recent illness prevents this day's ceremonies taking place, according to custom, at the capital of the State; but, at the same time, we would indulge the hope of his speedy restoration to health and vigor, and an early entrance upon the active duties of his office.

"Retiring from the weighty cares and labors of office, to resume the more pleasant position and pursuits of a private citizen, it is a source of sincere congratulation that I leave the affairs of our State in the hands of one, who brings into the active service of the State an enlarged and enlightened experience in public affairs, and an earnest devotion to the best interests and welfare of the citizens. Could I impart to him a portion of the delight which I experience upon being relieved from public cares, it would cheer him in many a weary hour of labor and care. But this may not be; for he who accepts the honors of office, must pay the accustomed tribute which a censorious public exacts. He must watch and labor for the public good, and bear with patient silence the abuse of the malevolent, the misconstruction of the careless, the misunderstanding of the ignorant, the misrepresentations of the partisan, and the slanders of the disappointed and unworthy. From all this I this day most gladly retire, and leave my friend, Governor HELM, to meet the occasion for the ensuing four years.

*   *   *   *   *   *   *   *   *   *   *

"We are all embarked on the same vessel—the gallant 'Old Kentucky'—and are convoying the 'Constitution' through dangerous and stormy seas. It is freighted with the treasure of all our hopes and liberties. We must 'sink or swim' together. A common fate, for weal or woe, unites us in a common destiny. We should therefore stand together in harmonious action until, with all our treasure, we are safely moored in the harber of constitutional security. If we then choose, we can renew our 'ancient disputes,' and have a regular political 'set-to.' But now is not a time for jars and discords, and I invoke all to stand by your Governor elect; give him a brave and earnest helping hand; strengthen his arm to uphold the rights and liberties of our people; and the God of our fathers will aid you to defend and maintain the right.

"Fellow-citizens, I now take my leave of you as your Chief Executive, to resume the place and pursuits of a private citizen, invoking upon the people of my loved native State the bounteous blessings and beneficent protection of *Him* who led our fathers safely through the dark days of the Revolution, up to the light of Liberty's day, and inspired them to construct for themselves and their posterity the noblest and freest government that ever sheltered the rights of man. Fellow-citizens, I now retire, and yield the government of the State into the hands of your Governor elect, His Excellency, JOHN L. HELM."

The Inaugural Address of the incoming Governor was read by his Secretary of State, the Hon. SAMUEL B. CHURCHILL, and is as follows:

INAUGURAL ADDRESS OF GOVERNOR JOHN L. HELM.

Profoundly grateful to the people of Kentucky for the high honor they have conferred upon me, in electing me by such an immense majority to the Gubernatorial office, I avail myself of this fitting opportunity to return my most heartfelt acknowledgments to the people of my native State for this renewed evidence of their respect and confidence.

In accepting this great trust I feel no less the honor conferred than the duties imposed, and though I well know that both are great, yet humbly invoking the blessing, guidance, and protection of our Heavenly Father, and firmly trusting in the manhood, self-respect, and patriotism of Kentuckians, I accept the post which has been assigned me, with the firm resolution, to the utmost of my ability, to defend and maintain both the Constitution of our own State and the Constitution of the United States.

I am well aware that some pestilent and evil-minded men in the State, who believe that the country is ruined if they are not perpetually in power and office, have attempted to malign and traduce the Democracy and people of Kentucky, hoping thereby to excite unjust prejudicies against us among our brethren of the Northern, Middle, and Western States; and I therefore feel it incumbent upon me, so far as I can do so in a brief inaugural, to be candid and explicit in the avowal of our aims and objects.

The Democratic Convention which met in Frankfort on the 22d of February, and whose nominee I was, among other things made the following plain and emphatic declarations:

" 1. WHEREAS, In all republics, after the convulsions of revolution, when the storm of passion has subsided and reason has been allowed again to give utterance to the words of immutable truth and justice, it has been deemed proper to pause and assert the true principles of government: Now, therefore, the Democracy of Kentucky, in Convention assembled, do solemnly declare that this Convention doth unequivocally express a firm resolution to maintain and defend the Constitution of the United States and the Constitution of this State against every aggression, either foreign or domestic, and that the people of this State will support the Government of the United States in all measures warranted and sanctioned by the Constitution of the United States.

"2. We most solemnly declare a warm attachment to the Union of the States, under and pursuant to the Constitution, by the adoption of which the Union was effected, and we know of no better or more effectual way of maintaining and perpetuating the Union than by upholding and defending the Constitution, which is the bond of union, by a faithful observance of the principles upon which the Union is based, and by the cultivation of a feeling of friendship and justice toward the citizens of our sister States."

*   *   *   *   *   *   *   *   *   *   *

" 22. In conclusion, we declare to the people of our own beloved Commonwealth, as well as to the people of the whole Union, that we have met, not to foment discord, but to heal dissensions, and to endeavor; to the utmost of our power, to bring back our Government to its ancient purity, and to try to make it such as it was in the days of WASHINGTON, JEFFERSON, and JACKSON. We wish to maintain and save both the Constitution and the Union as they came to us from the hands of our patriot fathers, to preserve the rights and liberties of our citizens, to maintain all the safeguards of the Constitution intact and inviolate,

8   .

and to rescue the Government from the vandal grasp of that Radical Congress whose governing principle of action is rule or ruin. The Democratic party is not sectional, but is co-extensive with the Union itself, and its mission is not to destroy, but to restore concord and fraternity, and to resist all encroachments, from whatever quarter they may come, upon the Constitution and the liberties of the people. This is the great work we propose, and to accomplish these noble and patriotic purposes we invite the co-operation of every patriot throughout our vast domains."

These enunciations of our political faith are clear, truthful, and patriotic; and I here most solemnly proclaim, in the presence of my fellow-citizens, who know me so well, and whom I have known so long, that it is my fondest wish, most ardent hope, and earnest prayer, that all the States may be restored to their equal rights under the Constitution, and that the Union may be as lasting as time itself. Thanks to God, the tread of hostile armies is no longer heard, the roar of cannon and the peals of musketry are hushed, and peace—blessed, glorious peace—sheds her benignant and effulgent beams throughout the entire length and breadth of the Republic.

Now, my countrymen, is the proper time to calm the troubled waters, to heal all wounds and dissensions, to restore concord and fraternity, and nobly to redeem the pledges which we voluntarily and frankly made at the commencement of our late and unhappy civil war.

As early as 1861, Congress adopted, almost unanimously, the celebrated Crittenden resolutions, in which they proclaimed to the world, "That this war is not waged on our part in any spirit of oppression, nor for any purpose of conquest and subjugation, nor for the purpose of overthrowing or interfering with the established institutions of the States, but to defend and maintain the supremacy of the Constitution, and to preserve the Union with all the

dignity, equality, and rights of the several States unim-
paired; and that so soon as these objects are accomplished, the war ought to cease."

Fortunately for us all, the war is now over, the authority
of the Federal Government is everywhere fully restored,
and it is full time that the faith of the nation, so solemnly
plighted, should be redeemed. Let us forget the bitterness of the past, let us forgive its errors, remembering
that to err is human, to forgive divine; and then, when
we no longer keep the heel of military despotism upon
the people of ten sister States, we may cry out against
the oppression of England against Ireland, of Russia
against Poland, of Austria against Hungary; but the
world will think that we may well be silent until then.

The people of Kentucky have just cause to complain
of the action of Congress in excluding from their seats
the Representatives from the State, who were duly elected
in accordance with all the forms and requirements of law,
and who had all the qualifications prescribed by the Federal Constitution.

.Nothing can be more explicit than the Constitution upon
this subject; for, under article first, section second, we
find the following: "The House of Representatives shall
be composed of members chosen every second year by
the people of the several States; and the electors of each
State shall have the qualifications requisite for electors of
the most numerous branch of the State Legislature." 2d.
"No person shall be Representative who shall not have
attained to the age of twenty-five years, and been seven
years a citizen of the United States, and who shall not,
when elected, be an inhabitant of the State in which he
shall be chosen."

These are the sole and entire qualifications which are
required by the Constitution, and Congress has no constitutional power to add to or subtract from them. This is
the fundamental law, and it is admitted by both friend

and foe that our Representatives were all elected by the
duly qualified voters of the State, and that all of them
had the constitutional qualifications above enumerated.
Knowing that these things are fully susceptible of proof,
and cannot be successfully contradicted or refuted, the
foes of constitutional liberty point us to another article of
the Constitution, which says: "Each House shall be the
judge of elections, returns, and qualifications of its own
members;" and under this clause claim that Congress is
omnipotent upon the subject, and can deprive a free people of representation. Nothing can be more absurd, or
at war with common sense and reason. This clause in
the Constitution is as plain as those first cited, and is
based on justice—for it was both necessary and proper
that Congress should see that all its members were elected
by the voters prescribed by the Constitution, and that they
possessed the qualifications required by it. This is the
beginning and end of the constitutional discretion and
power of Congress upon this subject; and if Massachusetts or any other State sees proper to send Turks or Mormons, Chinese or Arabs, to Congress, and they are elected
by the qualified voters, and are twenty-five years old, and
citizens of the State from which they are chosen, and
have been seven years citizens of the United States, they
would undoubtedly be entitled to their seats. Kentucky
fully accords to every State the right to choose its own
Representatives in conformity with the Constitution, whatever may be their political opinions, and she claims the
same right for herself.

Let any other construction of the Constitution prevail,
and let it be understood that the mere caprice, whim, and
political prejudices of Congress are supreme upon this
subject, and it may not be long before Representatives
may be denied their seats because they chance to be Pro-
testants, Catholics, or Democrats; and when elections are
about to take place, the people will have no alternative

left them but to send committees to Congress to ask of
that body for whom they will graciously permit them to
cast their votes.

At the last session of Congress our Representatives were
present and ready to take the oaths of office, as prescribed
by that body, but, as yet, they have not been admitted to
their seats. I sincerely trust, however, that the mists of
passion and prejudice will soon pass away, and that Kentucky will not much longer be denied those sacred rights
which are guaranteed her by the Constitution itself.

The vast majority of the people of Kentucky are loyal
to the Constitution, and desire, above all things, the restoration of the Union, with equal rights to all the States.
We wish to see no single star erased or obscured, but
rather that all of them be blended in one harmonious and
glorious galaxy.

In England, during the reign of George the Third, the
people of Middlesex county thrice elected the celebrated
JOHN WILKES to the House of Commons, and he was thrice
denied his seat by Parliament; but all England was indignant at this foul affront upon the rights of the nation,
and the minions of the King were compelled to submit to
the decisions of the ballot, and JOHN WILKES was at last
admitted to his seat. I am unwilling to believe that the
people of this country love liberty less than the people of
England, and I feel an unwavering confidence that the
people will yet firmly stand by our glorious Constitution,
and demand that its provisions shall be respected and
obeyed. Let us uphold and maintain it, for it is the sheet-
anchor of civil liberty, and, if it shall go down, anarchy
and confusion will stalk through the land, and unbridled
license will produce universal distrust and misery.

In times of high excitement, when our judgments are
clouded by passion, and reason has been dethroned by
frenzy, we madly leap over all legal barriers to attain our
ends; but sage experience always shows that all such

acts are productive of nothing but folly, regret, and crime. In our own country some have been denied even the right of trial by jury, though it was as clear as the noon-day sun that they were entitled to such trial by the Constitution; and, under the sentence of mere Military Commissions, unauthorized by law, have been immured in prisons, or led to public execution, and died upon the scaffold by the hands of the hangman.

Many persons may now believe that some of those who were thus unlawfully punished were innocent of the offenses charged; but the dead cannot be brought back to life, and neither unavailing regrets, nor bitter remorse and tears, or even judicial decisions afterward rendered, can recall those who have passed the slender bounds which separate time from eternity. These acts, with all their attendant horrors, have passed into history, and cannot now be amended; but they remain a perpetual warning unto us, that there can be safety for none, unless the Federal Constitution shall be held the supreme law of the land. There can be no higher law than this.

The negroes everywhere throughout the United States have been emancipated, and, whether wisely or unwisely, it is needless now to say. It is an accomplished fact—a fixed, inexorable fact—and as such we should receive it. It becomes us, also, to see that the negroes are protected to the fullest extent, in both their persons and their property. We should treat them humanely and kindly, and do all we can to better their condition, and make them useful citizens of the State; and in my first message to the Legislature I will make some recommendations upon the subject. They must understand, however, that white men will rule Kentucky. We are not yet sunk so low as to consent to be governed by negroes.

I know that there are a few renegade whites among us, whose appetites so lust after place and power that they would be willing to see the white in subjection to the negro, if they could fill their pockets with filthy lucre, or gratify their unhallowed ambition thereby; but, thanks to God, they are few in numbers, and will decline into insignificance when their diabolical and disgraceful plans are fully disclosed. In Kentucky even the majority of the Radicals declare their opposition to negro suffrage, and my Radical competitor, Colonel BARNES, in our recent canvass, repeatedly denounced it. Had he advocated such an odious measure, the vote cast for him would have been insignificant, even when compared with the small vote which he received. The white is the superior race, as universal history and science acclaim, and will never accept the position of inferiority or negro equality. Such a thought is revolting to the white race. Other States should have the right to act as they please upon this subject. Kentucky fully accords them that right, but she claims the same privilege for herself, and will never consent that any but white men shall represent her interests or her honor.

To my friends of the so-called Third party I have a word to say. For their late standard-bearer, Judge KINKEAD, I have the highest respect and regard, and I believe that a large majority of their rank and file are honest and patriotic men; but I must say, in all candor, that there are a few selfish, ambitious, and designing men belonging to that organization, who, through it, are attempting to bring dishonor, disgrace, and ruin upon the State. I am satisfied that nine tenths of what are called Third party men fully agree with the Democracy in principle, and there is no good reason why there should be any estrangement between us. You are for the restoration of the Constitution and the Union, and so are we; but to give full force and effect to your efforts in behalf of these things you must become a part and a portion of that great, energetic, and living party, whose principles are one and the same from the frozen lakes of the North

·to the Gulf of Mexico, and from the bleak shores of the
Atlantic to the golden sands of the Pacific coast. Come
to us; we extend to you the greetings of friendship and
brotherly love, and, in this crisis of our country's danger,
let us join hands, and work together for our country's
good.

It is the province of the Democratic party now not
only to guard the Constitution, but to warn the people of
the dangers of a central despotism. That great apostle
of liberty, THOMAS JEFFERSON, who so well understood the
workings of our Government, in a letter which he wrote
to GIDEON GRANGER on August 13th, 1800, uses the following forcible language : " And I do verily believe, that if
the principle were to prevail of a common law being in
force in the United States (which principle possesses the
General Government at once of all the powers of the
State Governments, and reduces us to a single, consolidated Government), it would become the most corrupt
Government on earth." These were the principles of
the illustrious Sage of Monticello, the great author of the
Declaration of Independence, and are the vital principles
of the Democratic party of to-day. No party deserves
the confidence of the people whose principles are not
based upon truth, justice, and the Constitution. These
are the great landmarks to which statesmen should look;
and, if the people will firmly and steadfastly adhere to
them, our Government will stand through countless ages
a monument to the wisdom of our revolutionary sires.

I return my most heartfelt thanks to my honored predecessor for the kindly manner in which he has spoken of
me personally, and for the many noble sentiments to
which he has this day given utterance and expression.
Called from the tented field to guide the ship of State,
he has stood at the helm with resolute firmness, and,
though he encountered a rough and stormy sea, which
threatened to engulf us all, he leaves the good old ship

Kentucky, for the present, at least, moored in tranquil waters. I well know the difficulties and dangers which surrounded him, and I know, also, that his prudence, his courage, and his wisdom have averted many an impending blow from the people of the State. A man of generous impulses and high accomplishments, he leaves behind him at the Capital a host of friends, and in his retirement will meet everywhere a cordial welcome from a people whom he has so faithfully and efficiently served.

Fellow-citizens, with my present term of office my political life will close forever. I have no further political aspirations or desires, and feel that I have been often honored more than I deserved. My heart is full of love, affection, and gratitude for the people of my native State, and it will be the earnest and constant endeavor of my administration to promote their happiness and prosperity. I earnestly entreat all my fellow-citizens to forget all past asperities, to cease useless contention and wrangling, and to unite in one common effort to maintain the honor and integrity of our good old Commonwealth. There are no secessionists among us now. We are all for the Union and the Constitution, and let not the true men of the country give comfort to their enemies by foolishly fighting over the dead issues of the past. Kentuckians, be true to your own honor, to your own manhood, and to your own race; fear not, falter not, but maintain the right, and the storm and the cloud will pass away, and a restored Constitution and Union will be the rich fruits of your labors, and universal peace and prosperity will fill the land, whose people will then be united by the golden and indissoluble links of confidence, affection, and love.

PROCEEDINGS OF THE GENERAL ASSEMBLY IN RELATION TO
· THE DEATH OF GOVERNOR HELM.

On Thursday, the 20th February, 1868, Mr. A. H. FIELD,
a member of the Senate, and Dr. G. L. McAFEE, a member
of the House of Representatives, reported the following
ing resolutions to the General Assembly of Kentucky,
referring to the death of Governor HELM :

The Hon. JOHN LARUE HELM, late Governor of this State,
and one of the most distinguished of its native-born citizens having departed this life, it is eminently proper that
the representatives of the people should pay a tribute to
his memory ; therefore,

1. *Be it resolved by the General Assembly of the Commonwealth of Kentucky,* That the people of the State deeply
feel and deplore the bereavement which, under Divine
Providence, has been visited upon us in the death of Hon.
JOHN L. HELM, which occurred at his home in Hardin
county, on the 8th day of September, 1867, shortly after
his inauguration as Governor of the State.

2. That in the various offices of public trust that he has
filled in the State—as a Representative in the popular
branch of this Legislature, and for a number of years
its presiding officer, as Senator, Lieutenant Governor,
and Governor—he so bore himself as to reflect back the
honors conferred upon him by the State.

3. That while Kentucky pays this tribute to his public
service, she would be unmindful of the justice due to the
memory of the *man* if she did not bear public testimony
to his private worth. In all the varied relations of life he
was a model of human excellence—generous, gentle, and
kind ; a man who cherished no revengeful hates ; pleased
in forgiving rather than in persecuting. As a father, kind
and indulgent ; as a husband, devoted and affectionate ;
as a companion and friend, true to the strictest requirements of the social circle. Viewed as the statesman, the

lawyer, the husband, the father, the companion, and friend, he lived a life of distinction and usefulness, and died without a stain upon his glorious escutcheon.

4. That these resolutions be spread upon the journals of the respective Houses, and a copy thereof be forwarded to his family.

5. That the public buildings be draped in mourning, and that the members wear the usual badge of mourning for thirty days.

REMARKS BY HON. A. H. FIELD, OF BULLITT.

MR. SPEAKER: Arising for the purpose of asking the passage of the resolutions just reported, my heart again turns to the sad event that causes this action upon our part to-day, and again the wounds that the hand of time had partly healed are reopened, the tears start again, and memory turns with sadness to the day upon which the remains of our deceased Governor, JOHN L. HELM, were consigned to the tomb.

Glad would I have been, sir, had this solemn duty devolved upon one more able to do his memory justice than I, more conversant and familiar with his life; but as his friend, Mr. Speaker, my heart prompts me to offer at his grave its tribute of deep respect and veneration; not to pluck from the realms of fancy flowers with which to decorate his tomb, but to bring from the depths of a heart devoted to his memory the sacred myrtle, and lay its wreath by the side of the flowers placed by the hands of affection o'er his grave.

But a few months since, Mr. Speaker, he occupied the seat upon this floor from which I have just arisen, representing the same people; and while I feel that the State has lost much in his death, I feel that we, his immediate constituents, have lost more. She knew him as her faithful and devoted public servant; we knew him in addition as a kind, devoted husband, an affectionate father, a cherished friend. She can with pride point to his many public acts, and miss him in her councils; we, too, look with pride upon his public record, that will ever live as a monument to his fame; but we look upon him, in addition, as the husband, the father, and friend, and while she misses him in her councils, we not only miss him there, but in all the relations that render life noble and attractive.

He was born on the 4th day of July, 1802, in the county of Hardin, a day, of all others, of which the American people are justly proud, and, in the language of one who knew and loved him well, "He ever remembered with burning enthusiasm the ever memorable day of his nativity as being the birthday of the nation of which he was a citizen."

He was the eldest son of GEORGE B. HELM, a native of Virginia, and one among the first settlers of the State of Kentucky. His mother, REBECCA LARUE, was also a native of Virginia. Coming from the Shenandoah Valley, they settled in the forests of Kentucky, in Hardin county, and amid its wilds and dangers they commenced to rear for themselves a home, and that reared by them became his home, and on it he resided and died.

While a mere boy his father died, leaving a large family and an encumbered estate. Being the eldest, the care of that family devolved upon him, a charge that he undertook and nobly discharged. The whole estate left by the father being sold, failed to pay its liabilities by about three thousand dollars. This debt was assumed by the son; when of age, he gave his notes for it, and paid them out of the first money realized from his own resources—an example worthy of imitation: a son left without resources; the care of a widowed mother and helpless family dependent upon him; the ties of nature first responded to, the ties of honor next.

At the early age of sixteen years he commenced writing in the Clerk's office of the Hardin Circuit Court, and at twenty-one years of age he was licensed to practice law. Coming to the bar in competition with such minds as BEN. HARDIN, JOHN ROWAN, BEN. CHAPEZE, GOV. WICKLIFFE, WM. R. GRIGSBY, and others, whose names form a legal galaxy not surpassed by the world, he gained eminence and a commanding position at the bar, which position he ever retained, and he was one of its brightest ornaments.

The first official position ever held by him was that of County Attorney for Meade county. There being no resident lawyer of that county, he was appointed, though residing in Hardin.

The absorbing topic of that time was the Old and New Court party. He promptly espoused the principles and doctrines of the Old Court party, and in a pamphlet published by him he defended their position with decided and marked ability. The year following the publication he was elected to the Legislature, barely eligible, on the Old Court question, when his county had been heretofore very strongly, and by a large majority, opposed to his political position.

His first election to the Kentucky Legislature was in 1826. From that period until 1844 he served eleven years, six years of the time as its presiding officer. In his capacity as a legislator he served his State and constituency with distinguished ability. Of fine commanding appearance, a wise and honest legislator, with fine legal attainments, a skillful and able debater, a well-versed parliamentarian, doing nothing as a legislator which was not fully sactioned and approved by his conscience, he soon established for himself a legislative position which few in our State have ever equaled—none surpassed. As the presiding officer of that body he was courteous, calm, self-possessed—actuated alone by a desire to discharge fully and impartially the duties incumbent upon him in that position.

He was then elected to the Kentucky Senate, and upon the expiration of his term of four years in that body, he was elected Lieutenant Governor on the Whig ticket, with the lamented CRITTENDEN, and upon CRITTENDEN'S appointment to the office of Attorney General in Mr. FILL-MORE's Cabinet, and consequent resignation of his office as Governor of the State, he became the acting Governor. The duties of that position were discharged by him with the same zeal and ability which had ever characterized him. Well versed in the needs and requirements of the State, no one knowing better its situation, he was in a position to, and did, render the State efficient service.

Deeply devoted to the principles of the Whig party, he for thirty years gallantly and triumphantly bore its banner; but when the sun of that party set; when the ashes of Kentucky's gallant son—the lamented CLAY—were gathered to his fathers; when the Northern wing of it became untrue to its ancient political faith and principles; when it became untrue to itself and the nation, he, like thousands of others, great, good, and gallant men, came to the breast of their old political opponent, the Democratic party, satisfied that she, above all others, was true to the Government of our fathers.

Upon the expiration of his term of office as acting Governor, he retired to private life, devoting his attention to his farm and profession, laying aside the cares and responsibilities of public life, and returning to the sweet retreat of home, to the bosom of his family, and the society of his true, tried, and cherished friends.

He was not long permitted to enjoy the society of family and friends. The Louisville and Nashville Railroad, then in process of construction, meeting with diffi-

culties, apparently insurmountable, its friends elected him
its President; and when he first took charge of it, its most
sanguine friends had ceased to hope for its completion,
and had almost abandoned it as a failure. Giving up all
other pursuits, he brought the whole energies of his mind
to bear upon the work, made a success out of it, and
he was still its President when the first train ran through
from Louisville to Nashville.

Deeply interested in the internal improvements and
development of the State, he next took interest in, and
assisted by every means in his power, the construction of
the Memphis Branch Railroad.

In 1865 his people again called him from his retirement,
and elected him to the Kentucky Senate; and in August,
1867, when his term was but half expired, he was elected
Governor of the State. Of his career in the Senate, from
1865 to 1867, there are those of you here who served with
him, and can better bear testimony to it than myself; but
you who served with him will bear me witness that the
same honest and conscientious course that he made his
standard in early life was his motto then.

When he secured the nomination for Governor he was
in his sixty-fifth year. Feeling it his duty to answer the
call made upon him by his people—firmly believing in
the political precepts enunciated in the platform of the
party that nominated him—he entered upon a vigorous
and active canvass, from which most of us in the prime
of life would shrink, and his voice was heard from the
valleys and the mountains, in defense of principles whose
triumph he conscientiously believed were necessary to the
salvation of our country. When warned of his failing
health, and that his strength would be insufficient to bear
him through the canvass, his response was, " 'Tis duty; I
must obey." In that canvass, discharging, as he honestly
felt, a sacred and solemn duty devolved upon him by his
party and his friends, his strength failed him, and the

seeds of the disease which so soon thereafter terminated so fatally were developed, and he fell a martyr, discharging his conscientious and whole duty, and the rejoicings over his election were soon hushed in the funeral dirge.

He was elected on the 7th of August, inaugurated on the 2d of September, and died on the 8th; the robe of State replaced by the robe of death; the laurel by the myrtle wreath.

> "Leaves have *their* time to fall,
> And flowers to wither at the North Wind's breath,
> And stars to set. But thou hast all—
> All seasons for thine own, oh Death."

He was buried on the 10th of September in the family burying-ground, his remains being followed to the grave by a bereaved and stricken family, and by a deeply sorrowing community, and the wail of his native State was his requiem.

But he has gone. He sleeps beneath the sod, near his loved home! No polished shaft pointing heavenward marks his resting-place; but in the archives of his State he has left a bright and noble record that will live forever; and as long as Kentucky is true to her ancient renown, she will ever point with pride to the pages of her history on which is written the name of JOHN L. HELM.

REMARKS OF MR. BOYD WINCHESTER, OF JEFFERSON.

MR. SPEAKER: I should do injustice to those whom I represent if I failed at this time to ask the indulgence of the Senate for a brief moment to mingle my humble voice with those who, with an ability that I shall neither attempt nor hope to equal, have sought to do justice to the worth and memory of the eminent deceased, and at the same time appropriately to minister to the sympathies and

sorrows of a stricken people. Death, sir, is the common
lot of all mankind. The first step which man makes in
life, is likewise the first toward the grave; from the
moment his eyes open to the light, the sentence of death
is pronounced against him, and as though it were a crime
to live, it is sufficient that he lives to make him deserving
of death. In the midst of life we are in death—not a
moment but may be our last—no brilliant action but may
terminate in the eternal shades of the grave; and Herod
is struck in the midst of the applause of his people—no
day set apart for the solemn display of wordly magnifi-
cence, but may conclude with a funeral pomp; and
Jezebel was precipitated, the very day she has chosen to
show herself in her greatest pride and ostentation, from
the windows of her palace; no festival but may be the
feast of death, and Belshazzar expired in the midst of a
sumptuous banquet; no repose but may conduct to an
everlasting sleep, and Holifernes, in the heart of his army,
and conqueror of many kingdoms and provinces, fell under the stroke of a simple Jewish woman. In a word,
imagine ourselves in any stage or station of life, and with
difficulty we can number those who have been surprised
in a similar situation. Speaking to us with a solemn
emphasis of warning and instruction that every care,
every movement, every desire of life, should center in
establishing a permanent and unchangeable fortune, an
eternal happiness which fadeth not away.

But, sir, sad as are these inexorable laws of man's mor-
tality, it is nevertheless a consoling, a beautiful truth, that
our *great* and *good* men do not *wholly* die. All that they
achieve worthy of remembrance survives them. They
enjoy what Milton calls that " after life in the breast of
others." They live in their recorded actions—they live
in their bright examples—they live in the respect and
gratitude of mankind—they live in that wonderful and
peculiar influence, by which one single commanding

9

thought or noble deed makes its author an active and powerful agent in the events of life long after his mortal portion shall have crumbled in the tomb. Therefore, as they retreat into the shade of time the more radiant their memory becomes with glory to the eyes of posterity; for great and good men are like mountains: their images seem to grow in proportion as they recede from our view, and stand out alone on the confines of the horizon. It is fortunate, therefore, sir, when the life of a great man may be thrown fully open to the world and challenge its closest scrutiny, with a proud consciousness on the part of the friendly critic that there is no blot to be canceled, no glaring fault which a love of truth forbids him to deny— "Nothing to extenuate or aught to be set down in malice."

In Governor HELM's life is illustrated this fortunate condition. In his life can be found no instance of a mean or equivocal action; none of a departure from the self-imposed restraints of a refined and lofty sense of honor. He trod the difficult and devious paths to political preferment long and successfully, and yet he kept his robes unsoiled by the vile mire which often pollutes those ways. Devoted to his friends, upright, guileless, tender, and blameless in his domestic affections, richly illustrating that beautiful definition of a gentleman, as one whose aims are generous, whose truth is constant and elevated in degree, whose want of means makes him simple, and who can look the world honestly in the face with an equal manly sympathy.

I shall not trespass upon the Senate by any attempt to sketch the character or narrate the services of Governor HELM's long and useful life. His distinguished services as a statesman are inseparably connected with the history of our Commonwealth. For nearly half a century a prominent actor in all the stirring and eventful scenes of our political history—fashioning and moulding many of the most important measures of public policy by his bold and sagacious mind, and arousing others by his unconquerable energy.

As a Senator in this body he exhibited a wisdom and a patriotism, an elevation and originality of thought, a sagacity of observation, a vigor of reasoning, a productive facility, a pungency of repartee, and elaborateness and profundity of discourse, a grandeur and breadth of political views, which have made a deep and lasting impression upon the grateful hearts of his countrymen, and will be cherished and freshly remembered when these walls that surround us, so often the witnesses of his triumphs, shall themselves have fallen like all the works of man, into decay and desolation.

Governor HELM's physical and mental organization eminently qualified him to exercise a great and controling influence among his fellow-men. His person muscular, tall and commanding, his temperament ardent, fearless, and full of hope, his countenance manly and genial, a voice flexibly sonorous and of silvery distinctness, a manner original and expressive—these personal advantages, with his precise and positive statement of the question, his clear narration of the facts, his ample and vigorous phraseology, resembling the spoken phraseology of Cicero, the solemn slowness with which he unrolled the folds of his discourse, the power and adroitness of his logic, the high dignity of his bearing, enabled Gov. HELM to command wherever he appeared the attention, respect, and confidence of his auditors. Thoughts, feelings, emotions, came from the ready mold of his genius radiant and glowing, and communicated their own warmth to every heart which received them. Frankness and directness as a public man, a genius for statesmanship of the highest order, extraordinary capacity for public usefuless, a judgment never misled by imagination, but exact and cogent, an intellect fruitful of resources, prompt in expedients, active and comprehensive in organization, persevering in means, developed in Governor HELM the three great and principal qualities of the statesman— ardor and vivacity of conception, decision of command, force and persistence of will.

Governor HELM was possessed of a talent essentially parliamentary and polemic. · He said just what he meant to say, and, like an expert navigator, he steered his words and ideas through the shoals which might beset him, not only without going to wreck, but without ever running aground. A perspicuity of exposition, a remarkable sureness of judgment, a profound knowledge of details, a clear and vigorous argumentation, a sustained skill, a pointed promptness of reply, a simpleness of dialectics which at once convinced and enraptured his audience. Governor HELM was a man of iron, one of those men of the Napoleonic order, who march to the accomplishment of their purposes with erect and resolute brow, without fear of obstacles or doubt of victory; who sacrifice their days, their nights, their fortunes, their health, their existtence to duty; who never flag, who live and die of the energy of their will.

Governor HELM was also possessed of a deep sense of moral and religious obligation, and a love of truth, constant, enduring, and unflinching, which naturally gave rise to a sincerity of thought, expression, and conduct which was always open, manly, and straightforward. No one could stand before him without knowing that he stood in a majestic presence and without admiring those lineaments of greatness with which his Creator had enstamped, in a manner not to be mistaken, his outward form. His was the appearance described by the great dramatist:

> "The combination and the form, indeed,
> Where every God did seem to set his seal,
> To give the world assurance of a man."

Architect of his own fortune, ripe in years and honors, rich in the affections of his countrymen, he had been

elevated by an unprecedented majority to the highest
position in the gift of his State, a place which was perhaps the chief object of his aspiration ; and yet, as if to
show that even the most successful of men must sooner
or later feel the emptiness of earthly objects, that much
prized honor was to him the dead sea fruit, which turns
to ashes on the lips.   Alas ! in his death Kentucky has
suffered what will be to her a grievous loss.   His high
honor; his chivalrous sense of public integrity; his elevated and ardent patriotism, without stain and reproach;
his warm devotion to the best interests of the State he
loved so well, are qualities much too rare to be lost
without the deepest regret.   But as for him, whose memory we to-day revere, and upon whose grave we would
lay this simple testimonial to a character rich in every
great and manly virtue, we dare have no regrets.   With
the seal of truth and probity upon his brow, with all the
endearments with which affection can beguile the descent
to the grave clustering around his footsteps, he has entered the portals of the glorious life eternal ; he has gone
to the high reward of a life full of eminent services and
exhausting labors for a people who honored and loved
him with surpassing tenderness.   Human societies are
born, live, and die upon the earth.

But they do not contain the entire man.   There remains
to him the noblest part of himself—those lofty faculties by
which he soars to God, to a future life, to unknown blisses
in an invisible world.   This is the true grandeur of man,
the consolation and charm of weakness and misfortune,
the sacred refuge against the tyrannies of this world.
Looking to the distinguished, useful, and spotless life of
Governor HELM, we can but recollect that Cicero, in
mourning over the death of Hortensius, did not hesitate
to pronounce his end not unfortunate, " for he died full of
honors, and revered by all for his great virtues, and at a
moment happy for his fame, though unfortunate for his
country."

REMARKS OF HON. R. T. BAKER, OF CAMPBELL.

Mr. Speaker: At whatever cost of criticism it may subject me, I cannot permit the resolutions under consideration to pass without something more than a single vote from me. It is a time-honored custom for deliberative bodies, by resolutions, to commemorate the life and public services of their deceased friends, and next to the Christian's hope of salvation is the dying consolation to feel that they will not be forgotten when in the grave. It is not my purpose to attempt to give a history of the life and public services of John L. Helm. That has been committed to abler hands than mine. His successor in office and the distinguished Senator (Field), who has just taken his seat, has left nothing to be said on that branch of the subject. But, sir, his public life has not all been given, and perhaps there is no man living that knew more of him in that long and stormy political contest through which we have just passed, and which terminated with his death, than myself, for we canvassed most of the State together, and as a companion he had few equals and no superiors. There was a short period of time, when, lashed by contending passions, we both transcended the limits of parliamentary discussion, and for a time became alienated, and during that period we were both wretched and miserable. But at the Estill Springs, that Eden of the mountains of Kentucky, where we addressed the largest audience that it was my fortune ever to have met, we made mutual concessions, and parted on the public stand in peace. But we met again, and for the last time on earth. It was upon the summit of one of those lofty peaks that overlook that serpentine stream, the Kentucky river, wending its silent way through the mountain defiles to the great father of waters, where we met, and where we parted for the last time on earth. We sat down beneath the shade of a tall oak of the forest, alone, far from home,

wearied, tired, and careworn. We talked about home
and its sacred rest; that our labors were almost o'er; and
no man that ever lived spoke in more touching terms of
domestic life, and with fonder hopes for the future of his
family, than he. No plaudits of the multitude were there
heard. The long storm of passion was hushed. Far out
from home and habitation, where the sound of the church
bell was never heard, we parted for the last time on earth.
I have seen Governor JOHN L. HELM and his now stricken
widow presiding in the Gubernatorial Mansion, and with
their unbounded hospitality make glad every heart that
entered his domicile. I have seen him as the presiding
officer in both branches of this Capitol. I have seen him
in the Senate Chamber, when the full tide of inspiration
was upon him, hold the Senate and the vast audience
that his name always drew, spell-bound by his magic
power. I have seen him before the masses move them to
tears by his appeals, and by the next breath, by the magic
power of his eloquence, elicit rounds of applause; but I
never saw him in the full majesty of all his greatness until that hour when we parted.

Standing upon that mountain brow, in the deep-tangled
wild-wood, when all was hushed to silence, his manly
form erect, his face radiant with the emotions of his generous heart, his eagle eye suffused, his rich mellow voice
tinged with emotion, when he took me by the hand and
said: "I feel that I have done my duty to my party, and I
want to say to you that you have done your duty to yours.
God bless you—farewell!"

That, to me, was the last of JOHN L. HELM on earth;
but the parting scene, and the solitude of the place, his
manly form, are all now before me, and will abide with
me through all coming time. His presence is no longer
in our hall, and we miss him; but there is a lonely habitation, far away in Hardin county, where, when the
shades of darkness gather around that desolated home,

there is a vacant place the world can never find. He was blest with all of earthly honors, and severed as many ties as any man that ever died; but he retained his mental vigor undimmed to the last, and his inaugural was his farewell address. But the pale horse and his rider came, and

> "He sank to his rest like the sun 'neath the billow,
> And calm as the zephyr that kisses the wave,
> Leaving the wild eye of friendship to weep o'er his pillow,
> And virtue to light him beyond the dark grave."

The announcement of his death on the lightning's wing reached as many habitations and touched as many hearts with sorrow and sadness as any man that ever died. His name has taken its place in the galaxy of Kentucky's illustrious dead, and will live as long as these resolutions will sleep in the archives of the State.

I have thus paddled my frail bark across the turbid stream that in life once divided us, to bring this, my peace-offering, and, with a sad heart, lay it upon the altar of his memory. To the name of JOHN L. HELM, peace on earth, and trusting in the mercies of a kind Providence, peace hereafter.

REMARKS OF DR. G. L. M'AFEE, OF HARDIN.

MR. SPEAKER: I arise not to deliver an eulogy upon the character of our lamented Governor; neither do I design making a speech upon the occasion, but simply a few remarks.

Coming as I do from the county so often and ably represented as my constituents have been by one whose voice was heard in this hall nearly half a century ago, and the sound of whose footsteps have scarcely died away upon its outer threshold, my heart prompts me in behalf of my constituents to offer my humble tribute of respect to his memory.

To say that he was virtuous, good, great, and noble in character, gentlemanly in bearing, possessing genius and talents of the highest order, would be but commonplace, and fall far short of conveying to the minds of his friends an adequate idea of his many virtues and high character. The deep emotions of the great heart of the people can feel, more than I can find words to describe, the moral worth and character of such a man as that of the lamented HELM.

Born in an early day, when the facilities for acquiring a liberal education were not as great as they are at the present time—consequently not receiving the advantages of a collegiate education—he was thrown upon his own resources, and much depending upon his individual exertions and perseverance, he set out upon the rugged path of life to carve for himself a character and a name. It was the fortune of this able man to illustrate by his exertions, the noble tendencies of our once free and Republican form of Government, and to teach the rising generation the important lesson that each one may and must be the architect of his own fortune, and that there is no station or position in life to which the humblest may not aspire.

Outstripping many of his companions then on the highway to fortune—some of whom turned aside into paths of idleness and dissipation, others becoming weary and discouraged, yielded up the palm to their more energetic and persevering competitor, and have long since sunk into obscurity ; whilst he, by dint of toil and perseverance, reached a high place in the temple of fame, and has engraven his name upon the tablets of the hearts of his countrymen, and written it in living letters upon the bright page of history, which the finger of time can never efface.

Nurtured in the school of adversity, he acquired a vigor of constitution, an independence of thought, speech, and action, which gave him through life a force of character which enabled him to command the respect of all.

To know him was to love and admire. Many differed with him in political views in days that are passed and gone. Yet they had unbounded confidence in his honor, honesty, and patriotism, and believed that he would do nothing intentionally which would not promote the interest and happiness of his constituents, and redound to the welfare and prosperity of the country. Consequently, when he asked position at the hands of the people, they gave him their warm and hearty support, as is well attested by the many high positions of honor and trust he so ably and faithfully filled. Eleven years a member of this House, six of which (if I mistake not) he filled the high and responsible position which your honor now occupies.

Believing, as he honestly did, that the interest and happiness of his country in a great measure depended upon the success of the principles he espoused, he exerted every energy of body and mind to stay the cloud of fanaticism which was gathering thick and fast over the land, and to roll back the waves of *despotism* which were threatening to sweep over us, and engulf us in one common ruin with our sister States of the South. How well he succeeded, let the voice of a grateful people testify. With a majority over both of his honorable competitors, unprecedented by any heretofore given, he returned to the bosom of his family exhausted in mind, his physical powers prostrated, there to enjoy but for a short time the unfading laurels he had so nobly won.

In one short week from the time he was inaugurated Chief Magistrate of this Commonwealth he was summoned to the land of spirits; death, the great leveler of all, has laid him low, at a time when we most needed his cool deliberation, his wise counsel, and mature and sound judgment, to guide and direct the ship of State to a peaceful mooring. He gave his life a sacrifice upon his country's altar, and died a martyr to the principles he espoused.

"*Dulce est pro patria mori.*" He has left a whole people to mourn his loss with a sorrow deep as the love they bore him.

Mr. Speaker, our loss has indeed been great, but it is nothing when compared with that of the bereaved widow. When the twilight of evening draws the mantle of darkness over the face of nature, a gloom of sadness and sorrow gathers around her heart and hangs like a pall. The chastening rod of the Almighty has fallen heavily upon her. One son, in the prime of life and vigor of manhood, fell a prey to disease in a distant city, and now sleeps beneath the silent sod of his nativity. When Kentucky's sons shall tread the soil of the sunny South, and turn aside to linger awhile upon the blood-stained field of Chickamauga, in their wanderings and meditations, their eyes shall chance to fall upon the last resting place of the gallant, brave, and warm-hearted General HARDIN HELM, who gave his life for his country's cause, what deep emotions of patriotic pride will swell their hearts, and tears of sadness suffuse their eyes, to think that there sleeps the son, in every respect worthy of his illustrious sire.

> "How sleep the brave who sink to rest,
> By all their country's wishes blessed.
> When spring, with dewy fingers cold,
> Returns to deck their hallowed mold,
> She then shall dress a sweeter sod
> Than fancy's feet have ever trod."

Deprived of the advice and counsel of the partner of her joys and her sorrows, and those she dearly loved, may she bow in meekness and humiliation to the will of Him who has promised to be a father to the fatherless, and a husband to the widow.

REMARKS OF JUDGE E. C. PHISTER, OF MASON.

MR. SPEAKER : This is a sad occasion in the history of Kentucky. The elected Governor of the Commonwealth has fallen. Elevated to his position by a manifestation of popular confidence never before witnessed in the State, he was prostrated by a fatal disease immediately after; and, before he entered the Executive Mansion, he was swept into the grave by the great reaper—Death.

This calamity reminds us impressively how vain is earthly ambition, how uncertain are human expectations; and that there is no sure reliance in time of trouble but Heaven.

In our beautifully arranged system of Government we have no interregnums. By operation of law, on the death of the Governor, there was advanced to the position a statesman of enlarged views, mature thought, great wisdom and firmness, and true virtue, who will preside over the destinies of the State wisely and well. Still the loss of Governor HELM, at any time a misfortune, is at this period a great calamity.

We have recently lost the noble, generous, and true-hearted POWELL ; the great statesman HISE ; and soon after the Governor was taken from our midst. We needed his great industry, activity, and energy—his patriotism, courage, sagacity, and practical wisdom.

In the presence of such a calamity, language is inadequate to express the sense of our loss, and eulogy would be powerless to do honor to the virtues of the deceased. He was true in all the relations of life, and faithful to every trust. He possessed in an eminent degree all the domestic affections and virtues. He was a good husband, kind father, and devoted friend. He was a lawyer of great ability, a statesman of foresight and wisdom, whose name is identified with many measures of policy for the benefit of his native State.

But, if I were called upon to give the prominent characteristics of our fallen Governor, I would say that two were remarkable. Their manifestation was ever observable. These were, his sound practical wisdom, his common sense, better adapted to achieve great results than the learning of the schools, and his State pride—his devotion to Kentucky. He was never promoted to Federal positions; but he was honored by his State with many places of responsibility, and he was proud of her greatness and glory.

As he was devoted to Kentucky, she was fond and proud of him. But, alas! her pride is bowed and her trust in her chosen son no longer availeth. Let us join with his sad friends and sorrowing family in dropping a tear over his new-made grave and pay a tribute of affection to his memory.

Let us wreathe his name with the evergreens and flowers of affection, and enroll it upon the scroll of those who honored their State, and whom she delighted to honor—among those of the immortals who were not born to die.

Let us treasure his memory in perpetual remembrance, and transmit it to posterity as an inspiration to truth and virtue and honor in all time.

REMARKS OF HON. W. B. READ, OF LARUE.

Mr. READ, of Larue, said that he did not know that the resolution now under consideration was in existence until a few moments ago, and felt that he was unprepared to do the occasion and subject justice, and that, on the other hand, he would feel that he had not done his duty, were he to say nothing on this mournful and sad occasion.

He further said: Sir, 1 have known the distinguished dead from my earliest recollection. I had the honor of being born in the same county that he was born in—the county of Hardin. What few remarks I shall make, shall be addressed to the life and character of that noble man.

Governor HELM was born on that notable day, the Sabbath of our independence, in the year A. D. 1802, and died in September, 1867, at the ripe age of 65 years. He was born upon the same farm upon which he died. He descended from a long line of noble and patriotic ancestry on both sides. His parents were not blessed with an over abundance of this world's goods, and he being bereft of his father while he was yet very young, and being the oldest child, and upon whom depended, to a very great degree, the support of his mother and his brothers and sisters, his means of obtaining an education were very limited; he only received a common English education.

At about the age of seventeen or eighteen he entered and wrote in the clerk's office of SAMUEL HAYCRAFT, who was then Clerk of the Hardin Circuit Court. He remained there some time, and then studied law, and commenced the practice of the profession of his choice at the age of twenty-two; and by his industry and hard study he soon took a high position in his profession as a lawyer and an advocate. As an advocate, he had no superior. He was affable, courteous, and kind to the young men of the legal profession, and none knew him but to love and admire him. He was possessed with a commendable ambition, and at the age of twenty-four he was elected by the voters of his native county to a seat on this floor, and was re-elected, first and last, a member of this House for eleven terms, and was Speaker of this body six years of that time. He presided with such dignity and impartiality as to challenge the admiration and respect of all. He was elected twice as a member of the Senate, the last term of which he resigned to make the race for Governor.

He was elected Lieutenant Governor in the year 1848, on the ticket with the late lamented CRITTENDEN, during which term Governor CRITTENDEN resigned, and the administration of the affairs of the State fell upon Gov. HELM for the balance of the term. The history of his administration is well known to you all. He was elected, as you all know full well, last August to the Chief Magistracy of this proud Commonwealth, and died in one week after his inauguration, His history is an eventful one, and is well known to many of you. He left a lovely and devoted family, and I greatly sympathize with them in their sad bereavement.

No one knew him but to love and admire him, and his memory is indelibly written upon the hearts of the people, and the State to-day stands draped in weeds of mourning because of the death of her honored and beloved son.

Sir, Governor HELM was a good as well as a great man. He was the noblest work of God—an honest man, true to his friends, and lenient to his enemies. He was a good neighbor, a kind husband and father.

He was a statesman and patriot of the first order, and it seemed through all his life that his chief object was to promote the interest of his State and people. He never held a Federal office in his life. He ran one race for Congress many years ago, and was defeated by a small majority by the Hon. WILLIS GREEN. Although he and I always differed in politics until within the last few years, yet our relations and intercourse in life were of the most amicable nature.

Yes, I repeat, Governor HELM was a great and good man. He was held in the estimation of the people of his State as ALEXANDER the Great and WASHINGTON were and are held by the civilized world. ALEXANDER is claimed as the world's warrior, and WASHINGTON is held and claimed as the world's patriot and statesman; and any prefixes attached to their names would but detract from their greatness. The name of ALEXANDER and WASHINGTON is enough; they need nothing more; the mention of their names alone sends a thrill through the hearts of all the civilized nations of the earth. So it is with Gov. HELM in Kentucky. The title Governor is not needed to give potency to his name,; it detracts from, rather than to increase, the estimate placed upon him. Then let the name HELM be a synonym of all that is good and great throughout this proud Commonwealth. He has been gathered to his fathers, and it is to be hoped that our loss is his eternal gain. Peace be to his ashes.

www.ingramcontent.com/pod-product-compliance
Lightning Source LLC
Chambersburg PA
CBHW060605030726
47498CB00005B/1551